CROÍ DÀN –
HEART OF DESTINY

CROÍ DÀN –
HEART
OF
DESTINY

DÀN CYCLE THREE

JAMES RAQUEPAU

BOOK COVER ART © 2024 BY NADIIA KOLPAK & JAMES RAQUEPAU

ILLUSTRATIONS © 2025 BY NADIIA KOLPAK & JAMES RAQUEPAU

LYRICS © 2024 BY CLAIRE ODLUM, PRISCILLA FIUMARA, & JAMES RAQUEPAU

ISBN

979-8-9919723-4-5 *IngramSpark Paperback*

979-8-9919723-3-8 *Other eBooks*

979-8-2953545-9-5 *AudioBook*

Brought to you by:

Destiny Cycle Publishers

Gaels Rule!

www.destinycycle.com

Croí Dàn: Heart of Destiny – Dàn Cycle Three

Dedication & Author's Note

For my family – Cynthia, Jereme, and Gwyn
Thanks for supporting my dream!

Dear Reader – Please note that I occasionally use some Gaelic words.
If you would like to learn more about this language, I have included
a section in the back matter titled *Guide to Gaelic Language*.

There are also sections in the back matter that list
Central Characters & Places & Terms (with pronunciations),
provide a summary of *Mythology & Legends*, and
offer an overview of *Gaelic Druids & Sigils*.

I point these sections out, as some readers suggested they would
have used this information had they been aware of it.

TABLE OF CONTENTS

MAP OF EASTERN ERIN

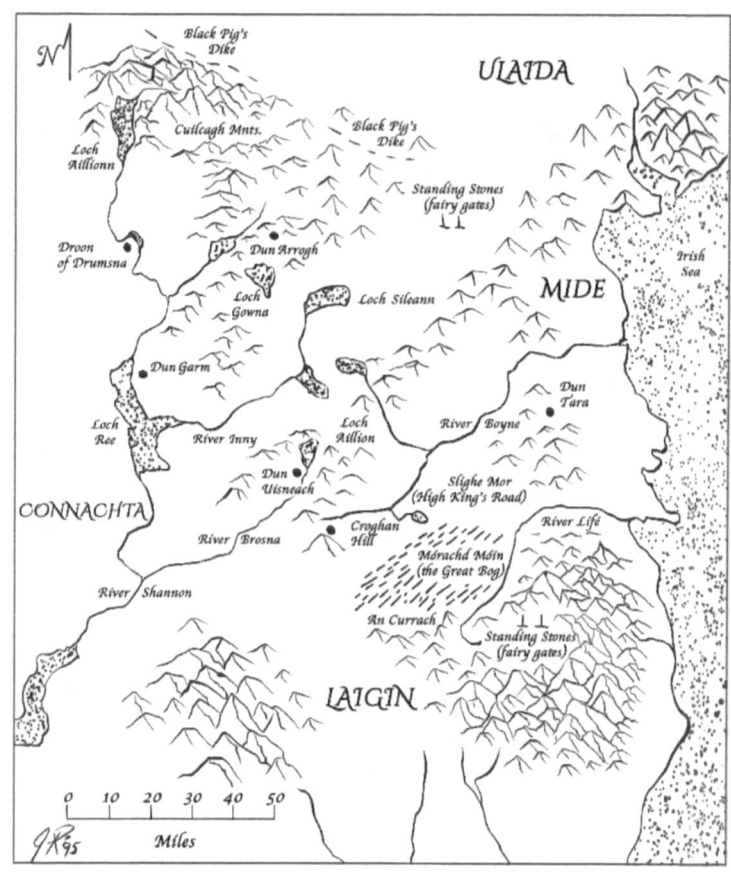

Map of the Irish Sea

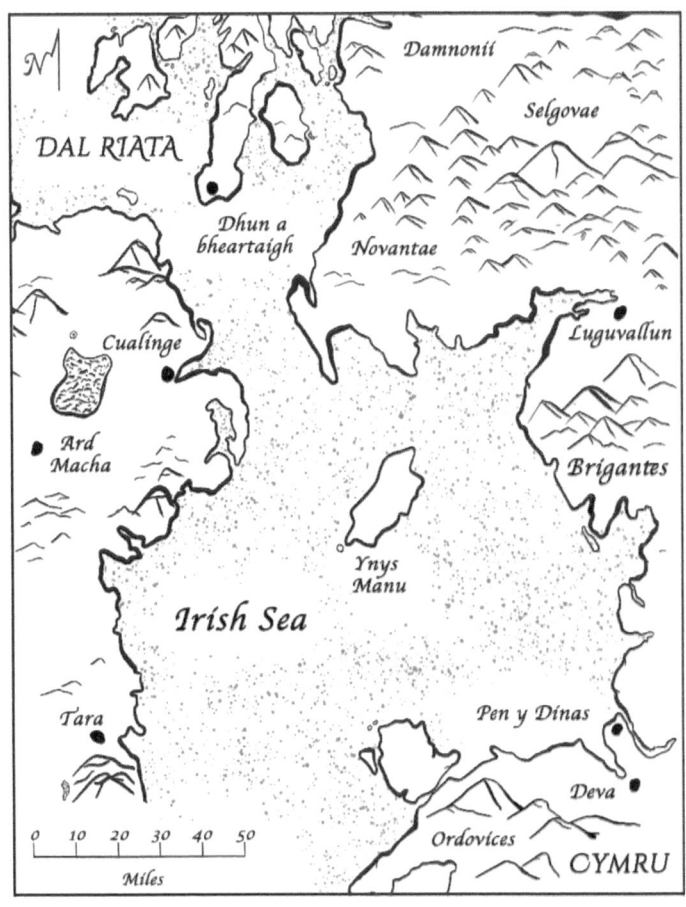

MAP OF SOUTHERN PRETANNIA

Brigantes

North Sea

Mona

Parisii

Gangani

Deceangli

Ordovices

Coritani

Coritani

Irish Sea

Dubunni

Din Aur
Iceni

The Fens

Rhyd Ecen

Tranovantes

Demeta

Caer Didi

Din Dubnos

Silures

Caer Went

Dubunni

Catuvellauni

Camulodunu

Severn Estuary

Lughdun

Durotriges

Belgae

Atrebates

Cantiaci
Dubrac

Isca

Dumnonii

Mai Din

Din Albion

Gesoricaon

0 10 20 30 40 50

Miles

LOOSE THREADS

Breanna

Breanna Ban Morna let her long blades flash in toward Eoin, who deflected the first one and swirled just out of range of the other before attempting a riposte. His sword swung wide of her as she spun outside of his reach, her flaming red hair flowing behind her. They clashed several more times, with no successful touches. When Eoin tried another backslash, she cast the word *shield* into the *void* so he could not see her counter in the space they shared and deftly rolled beneath his sword.

The grassy meadow cradled her shoulders briefly as she regained her footing, letting a haft flick out to catch the back of Eoin's knee. When he tumbled to the ground, Breanna was quickly on top of him, straddling his hips, her ancient long blades crossed over his exposed neck.

Eoin puffed out a breath, protesting, "No fair! You cut me out of our joint space in the *void*!"

"Then get better at using it! You rely on sharing too much."

"Aye, I should," he rejoined with a grin. "Though if I have to lose this bout to you, I prefer it end with you on top of me over any other."

Breanna blushed, realizing their respective positions. "Och, you oaf, I should draw a little blood for that comment—to show the others I beat you again! I'm sure you'd rail at me if I ended up on top of a Connachta or Ulaidian raider like this, ready to slit his throat."

"Aye, I might do just that," Eoin replied. "Seeing my wom— Champion bestriding anyone else would be troubling."

Breanna caught his slip of the tongue. Now and then, she would think she and Eoin might be able to build a life together, but then he would start on one of his diatribes about what a woman should and shouldn't be. She hissed, "You only get that way when I show you up after we have fought off a Connachta raiding party, especially when I take out more warriors than you. I hear the rumors, you know, that many other clans fear me in battle. I was born to be a warrior. We both know it!"

Bristling with sheathed dirks, she rose above Eoin, nicked his neck with a long blade, and angrily spun away from him, only to come face to face with Ulicia. She gruffly demanded, "What do you want?"

The Healer Druid ignored her tone, save for a raised eyebrow. "Bre, it's your mother. She's taken a turn for the worse."

"No," she murmured and turned to speed toward Dun Arrogh.

Later, after the sun had set, Breanna sank to the rushes on the packed earthen ground, her heart heavy as she held her mother's frail hand in hers, a hand that had carried her throughout her childhood. Their wattle-and-daub hut felt empty. Tomorrow, she realized it would be even more so. Her sisters, Olra and Ronat, had spent time with their mother earlier, so they were alone. Everyone in Dun Arrogh knew Morna wouldn't last the night, that on the eve of Samhain, they would be burying another Clan Dálaigh matriarch.

She gazed at the fire as her mother stroked her lustrous, red hair. When Breanna looked up, she saw her mother smiling faintly, her eyes glistening with tears. Morna whispered, "You remind me so much of my younger self, though that white streak in your hair is a mystery."

Breanna brushed her fingers over the white shock, her frown deepening. "I always wondered about it, but it's not important now."

Morna added more intently, "Bre, I sense a fresh scent about you that speaks of blooming youth, one destined to burn brightly."

Breanna's skepticism flickered to life as she looked up to catch her mother's gaze. "I don't know how that could be. Sometimes, I feel lost, like a leaf tumbling in a fall breeze. And now, Ulicia says you'll be gone by morning, and I don't know what course my life will take, save I want to be a warrior."

Morna sighed. "Just yesterday, you were a tiny bundle in my arms, your father beaming with pride beside me. So many cycles lost—but our Druid Healer has it right. I'm fading. I don't have the will to send you away, but it's probably best you let me go peacefully into the night so I can find Nevan once more."

Breanna offered, her voice quivering, "I wish your *anam* peace during your journey to find him, Mum."

She had lost her father to a sparring match gone wrong just after she was born. No memory of him survived her childhood, save for tales that others told her of his bravery with his long blades. They had been her grandmother's before that—the same blades passed down to her.

"Thank you, my lovely daughter. While I realize Kyras is busy with his forge, he and Lissa will look after you. If only you and Eoin could find a workable arrangement, I would go more peacefully."

At their previous Beltane Festival, Breanna had turned down Eoin's suggestion that they join as mates, and Morna knew why. Breanna looked away. "Mother, find solace in Ronat and Orla making good matches with their mates. I must find my destiny somehow and somewhere in our land."

Morna wheezed, drawing Breanna's eyes back to her mother. "I never puzzled out where you got your green eyes from. I remember them as blue when you were little, and no one on either my father's or your father's side has those glowing red flecks. It's like they were a gift from the Mother Goddess herself."

Breanna shrugged, unsure of what to say. "Much of my life feels like a mystery, save for being a warrior. Our Druids can only shake their heads over my strange ways of sensing things I shouldn't be able to, especially in duels or battles. Perhaps our ancient gods hold the key to my fate. I'd certainly like to know what Dagda and Danu had in mind for me when they cast my lot."

"Few of us know such things, Bre, but you must find a way to move forward," Morna advised. "You'll soon have to accept the man who loves you. It is time to start a new life."

"A man who loves me," Breanna echoed, dropping her gaze to the rush-covered floor as if it held the answers she sought. Then she looked up and added bitterly, "A man like Eoin Mac Cairbre, who wants me as his mate, expecting me to abandon my dreams so I can stand beside him! I bested him again in our match today, and he made light of my victory."

"Bre, I tolerated your passion for battle—even when you insisted on winning a gold Celtic Knot this past summer. Much like your father did, and before him, your grandmother, all wielding those ancient long blades with pride."

Morna grumbled, "Maybe I shouldn't have. Yet you must understand that men can feel threatened by a woman who battles as fiercely as you. That said, Eoin, our next Dun Chief, is certainly invested in you."

"A woman has every right to fight as fiercely as any man—"

"We've had this discussion before." Morna raised a hand, her voice faltering as a cough seized her. "Now, it's time to let me die in peace. Leave me with a kiss, my sweetest child."

Breanna leaned down, pressing her lips to her mother's forehead, a mix of sorrow and love swelling within her. After a lingering hug, she rose and picked up her long blades. Next to them lay a new spear, a bow, and a quiver full of arrows. She grumbled to herself, as she couldn't recall how she'd acquired those weapons. Then Breanna slid her blades into their harness and shrugged the supple leather construct onto her shoulders.

Looking at her mother one last time, she found her asleep and stepped out of their small hut, her refuge throughout the cycles. A thick fog clung to her memories, obscuring the vibrant moments of her past and leaving only vague impressions. It was a life woven with the struggles of her kin, the whispers of ancient spirits, and the enchantments that shaped their fate. She asked the night sky, "Why do I feel so unmoored? By the stars, what's happened to me?"

Breanna stood amongst the huts, looking across Dun Arrogh's yard to the central hall. Smoke rose from two round vents at each end, one for the ovens and one for the fireplace. She wondered why her life seemed jumbled as she took in the gloomy firelight from various torches.

Breanna caught sight of her sisters, who stood in the hall's doorway. They had been chatting with their Druid Healer when they looked her way, their expressions dour as always. Prepared to abandon the dun for a time, she turned away and abruptly ran into her cousin Toal.

He hesitated, momentarily holding her arms, then said, "Sorry to hear how badly your mother is ailing, Bre. Our family will miss her. If I can do anything for you, you will let me know, right?"

When Toal's earnest gaze told her he needed acknowledgment, Breanna pulled him into a hug, something she rarely did. He stiffened for a moment and then hugged her back.

"I will. You've always been my favorite of our clan. Thanks for those words." Untangling herself from him, she added, "I need some fresh air. I'll see you in the morning."

Breanna Ban Morna, the fierce and feared warrior of the Clan Dálaigh, headed away from the huts and walked to the gates alone. The familiar weight of her well-worn oak hafts pressed against each shoulder as if they were an extension of her body, a legacy passed down through generations, each warrior forging a bond with the long blades, always kept as sharp as she could make them.

When she reached the gates, she stopped. Thick clouds blanketed the chilly black night, an apt sign of the weight she felt upon her. The layer hid what would have been a nearly full moon, the body in the sky that Mother Goddess claimed dominion over.

She lifted a hand to her neck, took a deep breath, and pulled her heart-shaped ruby pendant from her tunic. It felt familiar, as if holding secrets of another time. She could not remember who had given it to her, but every time she closed her hand around it, the gem seemed like something she had always worn, almost as if it had known her and could talk to her. Yet, that could not be—jewels couldn't speak. Could they?

Their Druids claimed the barrier between the living and the dead was at its thinnest during the Harvest Festival, and few would spend the night beneath the sky with the many spirits of the Tuatha Dé Dannan walking the land. Breanna held her head high, for while there were truths in those tales, she was unafraid. Though the source of her certainty eluded her, an unshakeable instinct told her such spectral creatures could not and would not touch her.

Strangely, that was another of her many memories that seemed blurred. Breanna shook her head, hoping to clear the cobwebs, unable to fathom why nothing made sense. Why did it feel like she had lived a different life?

As the evening deepened, a couple walked through the gates, arriving late for the ancient festival called Samhain. All living nearby, in both settlements, or those living alone, were welcome to the communal gathering at Dun Arrogh. This pair was likely the last to arrive for this evening. She recognized them as being part of Calla's clan, who frequently visited their cook's family. Yet, the promise of more revelers would come with the dawn. The two mates nodded respectfully at her, which she returned in kind before her gaze drifted back to the enveloping shadows, a hint of unease flickering within her.

A voice Breanna recognized broke the silence, pulling her from her tangled thoughts. Eoin, her staunch friend—and would-be lover if she ever accepted him—offered quietly, "Ulicia says your mother's *anam* will seek her next destiny by morning. I'm truly sorry, Bre. Her absence will echo in our hearts. And I am sorry for my ill-timed words after our match this afternoon."

"It's okay," she replied, her voice barely above a whisper, unwilling to meet his eyes. She wished to be alone, yet she lacked the strength to send him away. The thought of solitude sent a chill through her bones, a reminder of the soon-awaited emptiness.

Turning that concern aside, Breanna wondered why she could battle as she did, understanding that not only could she seize the *void*—what their Druids called the *urghabháil an neamhní*—but her abilities were unmatched. Only Eoin came close to being her equal in blade skills from time to time. Their Fáidh, Beatha, insisted their gods had touched her at birth.

Yet Breanna's memories seemed full of holes. She looked down at her fine boots, sleek dirks strapped to each of them, not remembering when she'd bought them or where the money to do so would have come from. There were dirks sheathed to her vambraces and two more on her waistbelt positioned to each side. She also wore simple yet flexible boiled-leather pauldrons to protect her shoulders. Then, there were the expertly crafted spear and bow with a full quiver and gloves back in her hut.

With a shake of her head, she asked, "Eoin, I know this will sound strange, but I feel like a hedgehog. Where did all of this fine weaponry come from?"

Eoin looked at her quizzically. "You don't remember? It was a great moment in your life and a prodigious honor for Dun Arrogh."

She looked up at him with pleading eyes. "No."

"At the Dun Uisneach summer games, you were declared the Annual *Comórtas* Champion," he stated.

"That doesn't seem right."

"Then Faolán and Falyn, the dun's joint *Ceann-cinnidh* and *Ceann-feadhna*, showered you with praise and gifts of new weapons, armor, boots, tunics, leggings, and that fine otter skin cloak. It has been six generations since a wielder of long blades bested one with a sword, and longer still since it was a woman named *Comórtas* Champion. You did both, and everyone started comparing you to former legends like Macha and Maeve. You quickly bested Bradaigh and claimed your grandmother's golden armring."

"Hmm," Breanna said. "That's not how I remember the moment. It was a tie."

"No, Bre, it was not a tie," Eoin countered. "It was not even close. Rather, it was an exhibition of a warrior with complete command of the *void*. Somehow, later that day, you showed us your path to reach the place between the realms and wield the *void* as you do. Certainly not as well as you, but much better than before."

"Us?"

"Me, Fergal, Toal, and someone else, a warrior about your age named Braoin, who hails from the south end of Loch Síleann," Eoin informed her, his gaze concerned.

Breanna commented, "I remember Braoin and his twin swords. He moves swiftly and is certainly much easier to get along with than that brawny Bradaigh."

"When we returned to Dun Arrogh, we started teaching our younger warriors about your way. Yet now I am concerned that something is very awry with you. We need to seek out Beatha."

"Aye," she agreed. Then Breanna stiffened. "Yet the Seeress has always meddled in my life. I'm not sure I truly trust her. My mother once mentioned Beatha cast a *geas* over me before I was born, but I can't remember why she created such a compulsion. Then she left us to her bumbling apprentice, Aodhfin."

"What are you talking about?" Eoin asked. "Beatha and Ulicia have shared the same hut for cycles. While Aodhfin is still, indeed, a bumbling fool, I'm very concerned about you, Bre."

When she added nothing else, Eoin sighed. "What will you do now?"

Breanna knew what that question meant. Could she accept his proposal to join hands and dance around the Beltane Tree with him in the coming spring? Yet, how could his mother, Aife, a Princess of the Blood, accept a half-breed like her into their clan? *What? Half-breed? Who was a half-breed?* Unsure where that thought came from, she shook her head.

Breanna finally answered, "I don't know. Rumors have it that the *Ard-Rì* is seeking *fían* leaders to assist him in monitoring the followers of the One God. I was thinking about going to Tara and seeing if I could fight my way to the leadership of a band of nine. Then I can roam the countryside, enforcing his laws. Or maybe the High King will take me abroad, and I can help him trade with and raid other lands. He is said to like such adventures."

Eoin shrugged. "While others might question those dreams, I can understand them. You always wanted to be a warrior first—not a Chief's mate. I suppose there's nothing I can do to change that. Today's match proved that yet again."

Breanna nodded, surprised he had acknowledged her desire. She knew how others saw her, for they had often mentioned the way her graceful steps around her opponents seemed choreographed to some strange music that only she heard. Her flaming red hair, with a white slash at her left temple, flowed behind her with each swift step. The calm and icy demeanor with which she fought made it seem like their gods had cast her destiny.

Yet her Chief—no, her Prince—wistfully added, "A lonely life, but being a *fían-ceannard?* That's beneath you, my love. We could be like Faolán and Falyn, joint *Ceann-cinnidh* and *Ceann-feadhna*, joint leaders, here at Dun Arrogh. You saw what they had together at the games. She is his *Taoiseach.* I want something like that with you."

"You could join me," Breanna suggested, turning her eyes on him. "We can renew our ties to Dun Uisneach on the way, yet still strive for more."

Eoin sighed. "Everyone's expecting me to be *Ceann-cinnidh* once my father dies."

"That won't be for cycles, and he's not so old and still fearsome. Maybe just for a season?" Breanna suggested hopefully. Doing such a tour would be a dream come true. "While you're better than Fergal, you could use more—well, seasoning. Since I am your Champion, your father will know that no single combat challenge would put you at risk from becoming the next Chief of Dun Arrogh."

"Fergal would not be happy."

"Och, well, he is often unhappy with his life." Breanna shrugged. "Anyway, it was but a thought. It might have been fun battling together while the seasons cycle from autumn to winter to spring, showing the world we are the best warriors in our land."

"Aye," Eoin answered with a smile, his eyes shining. "That would be glorious, wouldn't it? Yet, what about Breanna's Band? They would want to join us. It would be a great experience for them, but my father wouldn't let all of them go with us."

"Breanna's Band? You mean your Red Branch?"

"What are you talking about, Bre?"

"We created our own Red Branch—because the younger ones needed training in our warrior ways. To fight off, um, invaders. Only yesterday, I bested Fergal to earn the right to be your Champion."

Eoin frowned and shook his head. "Nay, once you won the *Comórtas* this past summer, Fergal resigned. He declared that your way with the *void* made you his superior, and that's when we all started calling Dun Arrogh's warriors Breanna's Band."

"What?" she demanded. "How can that be?"

"It just is," came his answer. "Fergal and Toal can confirm it. We must talk with Beatha in the morning."

Breanna was silent for a time, wondering what was making her feel like she genuinely had no right to be his Champion due to her tainted blood, but tainted by what?

Eoin broke into her thoughts, saying, "For tonight, sleep in my clan's roundhouse so you can let your mother pass on in peace."

Breanna could only nod as Eoin wrapped her in his strong arms. "Please take the lead with Beatha," she requested. "I don't fully trust her, and I don't know why. In the meantime, seize the *sight* with me."

As they did so, she felt the land around them, and all was at peace like she had not felt in a long time, as if she and the land could be one. Yet, to the east, something was off. Something was not right—something near Tara.

What could be wrong in her land? Wait! What? When did Erin become her land? That notion made her shudder.

 Danu

The Mother Goddess stood in the same grove where she had first met Breanna Ban Morna via the Druid Beatha. It was when *Croí Dàn* proclaimed her Erin's Hero, on a night surrounding her with nary a light to see by. With a blanket of clouds overhead, despite a full moon, she had bounded into the clearing where Beatha had started a fire and met a warrior who made Erin whole. Now, using the *sight*, Danu watched the meeting between Dagda's brilliant young warrior and Eoin Mac Cairbre play out for another moment before she pulled her attention from *Lia Dàn* and placed it in a pouch on her belt.

Even though she knew Breanna had fragments of memories from her life as the Norvegr Destroyer, Danu was pleased with what she had wrought. When the *Cycle of Time* was about to sweep away Breanna's *anam*, at that precise moment between life and death, Danu accomplished what was needed, what her conscience demanded. Thanks to All-Father's help. Without him, she might have failed to save Erin's Hero, especially now that she knew about his bond with her. Together, she and Dagda could do more. Yet it was early in Breanna's return to her land.

The effort needed to make Breanna whole by working through the young warrior's dreams would not be easy.

Standing supportively beside her, Lugh commented, "As I watched you work within the newly woven pattern that now makes up Erin's Hero, pulling a thread of time here and there as if weaving a tapestry, I have to say it was magnificent. It was as if the *Cycle of Time* sang to you."

"Thank you, but it was not all me. Without Dagda and *Croí Dàn*, Breanna would likely not be here. We all spun her *anam* away from the *Cycle of Time*. If it had seized her, we would not have won."

"Are you sure you should have left the Heart of Destiny with her?" Lugh queried. "She was mine at one time."

"Jealous, some?" Danu chided. In the Stone of Destiny, she knew Lugh had seen that their land was no longer threatened by Norvegrs, at least not as long as the magic of Erin's Veil stood in place.

The Sun God protested, "Our Heart is—inexperienced."

Danu sighed. "As I said, *Croí Dàn* was not ready to come home to me. As Dagda often reminds me, I agreed for her to have a piece of me so she could be sentient. I can no longer dictate her path and must let her decide on how to chart her way with her Hero. She's grown significantly since choosing Breanna and casting the vision her Hero held while wielding the *Triple Dàns*. Not to mention helping create Erin's Veil. It's all tied together and will collapse if my Heart's chosen one passes back into the *Cycle of Time*. It is why they need to be together."

Lugh cocked his head. "Still, what Breanna has done is locked inside her—a part of her *anam*. Her *geas* may no longer be an influence, but the warrior part of her that dealt with the Dreadlord very much is. She is going to need, well, a tutor to learn about the magic she bears. Maybe it would have been better to let her go."

"Dagda would not have allowed it," Danu answered. "As for a tutor, All-Father will take on that role. You already know we did not take lightly the decision to pull her through that life to this one. *Maorgairme* compelled me when Breanna used it with her last breath. Because of her sacrifice for her land, I might have done it regardless. We certainly need her to rise once again to defend our Gaels. Few in Erin have such courage or such heart."

"Then she deserves to know what she has done and why she is so driven," Lugh said firmly. "You and Dagda pulled all impacted by the Dreadlord's presence into a new timeline envisioned by Breanna, one without the Norvegrs, but the *Triple Dàns* didn't completely rewrite time. That will be a challenge for anyone with memories that don't quite fit, as they haven't truly lived those lives."

"Aye, it will likely be an issue. Yet it's not like we knew exactly what Breanna's wielding of the *Triple Dàns* would bring about. Even Badb Catha didn't know and declined to wield it. Breanna's troubles now, though, might be due to her being the one who cast the vision."

Lugh was critical. "Likely best not to have used that magic."

"Water under the bridge, Lugh, but when Breanna pieces enough together and calls on me, I will answer," Danu insisted. "Yet it must be of her accord. That said, given his bond with her, Dagda will be a better choice to help her with any concerns she may have. I don't think he'd have it any other way, especially since he gave her a piece of himself as I did with my Heart."

"What of Eoin and the others in her band? Those warriors will likely need a sign from us to ensure they know that the Breanna they once supported needs their help again."

"Not Eoin, for he is also Dagda's, but do what you will for the others," she commanded. "All-Father will see to Breanna's mate."

Cróí Dàn interjected cautiously, *"Mother? I can feel it when you're nearby, in this realm. I have to thank both you and Dagda for saving my Hero. Yet I'm unsure why you are here?"*

"Daughter," Danu offered warmly. *"There has been no opportunity to say this, but well done. You've grown, and I'm proud of you. Breanna will need your help to settle into her new timeline, which I'm sure you'll manage perfectly. As to why I'm here, that also involves you. Your Hero must claim her land as she did in her previous life if she is to have any chance of changing the Gaels' ruling class. While not her primary goal, I expect she will want this outcome. When she asserts herself as your Hero, I will lead my wolf pack to support her, as Badb will lead her crows and raptors, Manannán his creatures of the sea and waterways, Étaín her wild horses, and Lugh, his deer herd. We did not do that in the before-time as we should have."*

"Thank you, Mother. Breanna needs to be Erin's Hero once more!"

Toal

Toal rose when dawn was barely touching the eastern sky. He slipped on his tunic, leggings, and boots. Since his parents were still asleep, he crept to the door as quietly as possible, donning his cloak and snatching up his bow and a quiver of arrows. His first stop was the nearly dark bathhouse, where he fed the peat-banked fire the wood needed to warm the water for others on this festival morning. He filled the empty buckets and set them on the hearth to warm.

With the water in the tubs still chilly, he skipped a full bath and just used a wet cloth to wipe himself down. After slipping off his cloak and tunic, Toal set about the task as the bathhouse started to warm. When he raised his arm to clean his neck and face, he saw a woad Druidic sigil drawn on his forearm. A glance at his other arm revealed another one there as well.

"What in the world?" he questioned. "Where did these come from?"

With a closer look, Toal saw that they were similar but not a perfect match. His mother was a true Tuatha believer and would think they were a sign from the gods. But why now? He would have to ask Beatha, their Fáidh, what they meant. The Seer would likely know more about them than anyone else. Given it was Samhain, he might have to wait for her to finish his aunt's casting ceremony this evening and the Harvest Festival rituals to get an answer. Left wondering about them, he finished wiping himself clean and put his tunic, leggings, and cloak back on.

His next stop was the main hall, with each chimney belching smoke at either end of the structure. That meant Calla had her ovens baking fresh soda bread. The smell of it wafted over him as he entered. "Calla, you're a wonder!"

"Och, Toal, you say that every morning!" she rejoined. "But I'm glad you're here. With yesterday's hunt a failure, I need you to head out early with your bow and take down a buck, or it will be a thin and fishy Samhain celebration dinner."

Toal left his cloak on, as the hall was still chilly, and approached the serving table. He filled a bowl with hot porridge, added a few strips of dried boar, and two chunks of warm buttered soda bread. Sitting at a table near the rear cooking hearth, where it was warmer, he answered, "Aye, I can undertake a hunt, but it would help to have Cilla join me. Your daughter is getting quite good with that bow I brought her from this past summer's *Comórtas*. Dun Uisneach has a fine woodwright, and she makes good use of his craftsmanship."

A dark head of braided hair popped out of the kitchen, and Cilla asked, "Mum, can I go on the hunt with Toal?"

Calla shook her head as if to say no, yet surprisingly agreed after considering the request. "You can, but eat something before you go."

Cilla smiled brightly. "Aye, I will, and thanks, Mum!"

When she sat next to Toal with her bowl and bread, he looked up from examining the new sigils on his forearms with a grin. She was a cycle older than he, with light brown eyes; they briefly met his darker brown ones before she looked down at his bare arms.

"Och! Where in the world did you get those?"

"Um, I'm not sure," he stated. "I found them this morning."

"You found them? Woad-inked Druidic sigils don't just appear," Cilla hissed. "Och, they're very intricate! I wonder what they mean."

Toal said defensively, "I know that sigils do not just appear, Cilla. Only Beatha will know what they mean, but with it being Samhain, I'll have to wait to find out about them, not to mention that Morna's *anam Cycle* ritual will be this evening."

Feeling self-conscious, he pulled down the sleeves of his tunic.

"Maybe they're a sign from the gods," Cilla added before filling her mouth.

Toal smiled at her. "You sound like my mother."

Cilla only shrugged. A moment later, they finished the morning meal. Then she fetched her bow and quiver, and they headed out. Once in the woods, Toal took her hand, saying, "Join me in the *void* the way Breanna taught us."

She did, and paused to seek that place; he could feel Cilla with him in the *void* space they shared as the forest around them teemed with life. Toal led her toward the grove where they often practiced, stopping at the edge of the woods. He saw three bucks and two fat and very pregnant does grazing on grass and fall flowers on the far side. He whispered, "Nock."

"It's too far," Cilla protested in a hushed tone. "I can't shoot anything at such a distance. It's impossible."

"Trust me, it's not, and you can," he countered, feeling the sigils on his arms tingle. He pushed up his sleeves and found them glowing. It was surprising, but he had no time to contemplate the significance of his sigils coming alive with Druidic magic; the hunt mattered more. "We will try for the two younger bucks. I'll take the left, and you take the right. Now, seize the *void* with me again."

With that, he raised his bow, seeing the trajectory the arrow needed to find its target in his mind, a hundred and fifty-seven yards away. Toal looked to Cilla, whispering, "Five degrees higher and a little more draw. See its flight path in the *void* with me. Release on one."

She nodded and adjusted her aim as the two bucks turned their sides to them. Toal counted, "Three, two, one!"

Each arrow flew true, and both were heart shots, dropping the bucks within three bounds as the other three deer scattered.

Jumping up and down a few times, Cilla squealed, "We did it!"

"Aye, we did." Toal smiled a little smugly. "Told you we could."

She pulled him close and kissed his cheek. "That was amazing. How could you see the arc like that?"

"I'm not sure, but I think it might be these sigils," he responded, wondering why he wasn't unnerved by his feat. "Ulicia has a similar sigil on her hand for healing, as she often touches Earth to heal. Yet our Druids will figure it out. Now, you must fetch Fergal and have him bring the cart while I bleed out these two beasts. Otherwise, we'll never get them to the dun in one piece, and I expect you would prefer your deerskin intact as I do."

"Aye, I would indeed," Cilla said. "Mum will be thrilled!"

As she ran for their dun, Toal made his way to their kills. He had to drag the hind legs of one around to higher ground so the blood would flow better before slitting its throat. He moved to the next one and did the same. A nearby angry snort had him whipping his head up. His bow felt like it jumped into his hand, and he had an arrow nocked instantly, staring down a good-sized boar only twenty-five yards away.

The creature pawed the ground and charged as Toal aimed. His only chance to drop the boar would be a shot in the eye. Seizing the *void* as his sigils glowed, he did just that. The beast covered five more yards before crashing dead at his feet. Toal's heart thundered as he blew out a shaky breath. "What a morning! And what can these sigils do? Or can't do? I have to talk with Beatha!"

⤞⧆ Beatha ⧆⤝

It was early when Beatha rose with Ulicia in their shared hut. That evening, the two Druids would send Morna's *anam* safely off to the *Cycle of Time* so she could be spun into her next life. With Samhain upon them, preparing for their fall rituals would make for a busy day as they added Morna's casting upon them.

The pair emerged into a misty morning, with Beatha telling the Healer, "There was a significant event yesterday in the *Cycle*. Possibly, it is in the future or a past that never was. The *sight* is chaotic, and our gods are strangely silent. Or maybe tired, as if they worked great magic."

"That is unlike you, sister," Ulicia commented. "Our gods always speak clearly to you. Only the High King's Fáidh has a connection to them anywhere as close as yours."

"Aye," Beatha agreed, frowning. "Something significant is in the air."

Then, Eoin and Breanna approached the two Druids, and he asked, "May we have a word with you both?"

Ulicia answered, "Of course, our Chief's son. You are a Prince of the Blood. The *Aos Dána* place only our gods above our leaders."

Eoin bowed at the Healer's homage. "Enough formality, you know I don't abide it unless required. My Champion is having problems with her memory. It started last night."

"Curious," Beatha stated as she looked at Ulicia. "I felt a disturbance with or in the *Cycle* last night, and the *sight* is still disturbed. And now this. Breanna, what memories are missing?"

"Everything is not as it was, not how I remember it."

"How so, Bre?" she inquired.

"Everything around or just after the *Comórtas* Championship last summer is not how we each remember things," Eoin said.

"I don't truly know, but it feels like everything is different," Breanna answered. Her eyes begged for clarity. "It is like I have someone else's memories jumbled up with mine. There are things I don't remember as Eoin does, and I now have these weapons. I do not know how I came by them, such as my dirks, bow, and spear. And this cloak and these leather pauldrons. Eoin said they were a gift from the leaders of Dun Uisneach, but when? And now I have an ache in my chest, and I found this ruby pendant around my neck last night. It's something I feel I have known before, yet I know not how."

Breanna pulled her tunic down to reveal her breastbone, where a pink six-inch scar between her breasts was evident. Above it lay a heart-shaped gem. Below it, dissecting her scar, was a complex sigil.

Beatha sucked in a sharp breath, questioning mentally, "*Ćroí Dán?*"

"*Aye, it is me, Dagda's Seer. And Breanna is indeed my Hero, Erin's Hero. She has made a great sacrifice for her people and her land. You do not recall it because she wielded the magic of the Triple Dàns.*"

Breanna looked startled, questioning, "*Mo Chroí?*"

"Yes, my Hero. *You are still mine, and I am yours. Forever.*"

Eoin had to steady Breanna as she sagged into him, and then he heard the Heart of Destiny add, "*And you, as well, Eoin Mac Cairbre, Cosantóir to Erin's Hero. Breanna's actions also impacted your timeline. You have a significant role in helping her become whole once more, to bring Erin's Hero back to her land and people.*"

Eoin nodded. "How can a mythical legend such as *Croí Dàn* speak to me as if she were inside my mind?"

"*Because I'm not corporeal and have no voice to speak with!*"

Ulicia questioned, "Sister, is that the Heart of Destiny I heard?"

"Aye, it is," Beatha confirmed. "A mystery, to be sure."

Croí Dàn commanded, "*Beatha, while I know Morna has just passed, you must take Breanna to Dun Uisneach and meet with the Druid Bláth. The dun's Master Bard will help fill in the gaps until Dagda seeks out his new daughter.*"

Having heard that exchange, Breanna croaked a question out loud. "Dadga's daughter? How is that so?"

"*It just is,*" the Heart of Destiny replied, with a tone that suggested a stated fact. "*You ate a piece of him in your other life.*"

Beatha let the *sight* take her and then sighed at the vision.

Ulicia asked, "She's now truly one of the Tuatha?"

Croí Dàn answered smugly, "*Aye, like me, she has a piece of a Tuatha God in her. Mine came from Danu, and hers was from Dagda. My Hero, I know this is a lot to internalize. Go to Bláth. While a Master Bard who wields Air as her Element, she also has a fair bit of Seeress skill and might be able to help Beatha guide you to the Cycle of Time. Only through that magic can you see who you were and what you did to save your land and people."*

Eoin told Breanna, "We can leave tomorrow, as I know you'll want to see your mother's *anam* off tonight. You'll also join us, Ulicia and Beatha, in going to Dun Uisneach?"

"Aye," Beatha answered. "Given that we will have worked the Samhain rituals in the early morning, we can leave afterward. There is much to unravel."

Croí Dàn said, *"Beatha, I am bringing your Healer into our mind-speak. Ulicia, you must begin the healing process, my Hero requires."*

Ulicia turned to Breanna. "If I'm to help heal you, I need to feel your *anam* to see if we can determine what is not right. As it reaches into Erin's roots, we need an old tree to see what the *Cycle* tells us. Then we must decipher the sigil between your breasts."

Eoin pulled down his tunic. "It looks like mine."

Beatha and Ulicia looked at each other in surprise; the former was certain their gods were actively at work.

Breanna protested, "What about my mother?"

"My apprentice will help prepare her body with your sisters, and we will see her *anam* off this evening," Ulicia tried to console her. "I know this is not the best time for a daughter to lose her mother, but we need to help you now."

With that, the Druid Healer led them out of Dun Arrogh and through the woods to a mighty black oak. "Breanna, lie your back against this trunk, place your hands on the earth, and seize the *void*. Then request it awake and ask for its insight, ask for its wisdom and healing, and demand it to join you with your land."

"Ask a tree?" Breanna questioned as she sat at the base of the oak. Ignoring her protest, the Fáidh and Ollamh placed a hand on the tree and the other on each of her temples, murmuring an ancient chant. Then Beatha nodded to her sister and felt the

Healer Druid pulling on her Elemental Earth power to awaken the old black oak.

 Breanna

Croí Dàn commanded, *"Seize the void, my Hero!"*

As Breanna opened herself to that place between her realm and that of the Tuatha, she allowed the massive tree at her back to seep into her body and soul, drawing the power of Erin's Earth into her. She felt the ancient oak sigh, speaking in her mind with a rumbly voice, something Breanna sensed had not been used for eons, as no one had awoken him since the Tuatha walked the land.

"Daughter of our gods, Hero of our land, you need to heal, not in your body but in your spirit and soul. You sacrificed more than you know, and greater magics have torn you apart. Yet your faith in your land has won you a boon. Take some of my power and energy, pull your land into you, and be all that we need you to be."

Through the *void*, Breanna connected with the massive tree, sensing that Ulicia was helping to solidify the bond. Then, that first link spread to other trees and plants, small creatures and larger ones, those living in rivers and the nearby seas, those on small windswept islands, and those on her mountains and plains. Breanna was one with her land, and they were one with her. And whoever she had been, Erin's Hero was once more joined with those across the Emerald Isle, its creatures, and her people. And she would protect Erin at any cost, for Breanna now understood that was her role.

Simultaneously, Breanna knew that her land would protect and defend her, just as a *ceannaire pacáiste*—like the Silver Huntress—protects its wolf pack, and that power seeped deep into her bones and soul. With the mighty black oak cradling her, she drifted through Erin, soaking up its unique and rich energy, welcoming its recognition, and feeling it heal her.

She sensed it was not a new experience—more of a reconnection, an acknowledgment—as if she had done this before, and the land of Erin had already received her. She knew she had previously claimed her land and taken responsibility for it as Erin's Hero. Yet, now, her purpose was more profound because their Tuatha gods and goddesses consecrated the bond between Breanna and Erin by marking her as one of them. Somehow, she knew she could command her land, its creatures, and people to support her. And that she would do the same for them.

The mighty black oak insisted, *"Take your land!"*

Breanna felt *Croí Dàn* in her mind, somehow knowing she would cast her command as the tree demanded. The Heart of Destiny sent out Breanna's call, *"As Erin's Hero, I claim the Emerald Isle and all its living things are mine!"*

Croí Dàn seized on that decree with her magic and let Breanna's claim flow throughout Erin. Her land and its creatures answered with acceptance. A nearby pack led by a giant silver wolf surged out of the woods and into the glen that hosted the mighty oak, all howling before bowing in submission. A large brown bear roared with her cubs in tow as they submitted to her at the edge of the deeper forest. Then, a small band of red foxes emerged on the opposite side of the glen, yipping their approval.

Next, a murder of crows, led by a sizeable Carrion Crow, flew to her oak tree, their caws proclaiming Erin's Hero by name, and falcons, hawks, owls, and eagles circled in the sky, screeching. A massive white stag, the legendary Cernunnos, emerged from the tree line with his deer herd and lowered his head, as did the Goddess Étaín, who led her wild horses into the far side of the meadow. Across Breanna's land, creatures responded to that claim, along with Manannán's creatures of the sea and waterways. Even common animals, like cattle, goats, pigs, and sheep, appeared from Dun Arrogh. Even the great wyrm of Erin, *Caoránach*, gave her a nudge.

For those people who heard that call, Breanna was a Tuatha goddess living amongst them. The claim from Erin's Hero offered them a promise, one that carried protection. It had been eons since one of the *Tuatha Dé Danann* walked amongst them, one who would reconnect them with their gods. As *Ćroí Dàn* let that notion wash through the Emerald Isle, Breanna sighed as her shredded soul fell back into place, and she felt one with her Emerald Isle.

⟶⟡ Ćroí Dàn ⟡⟵

The Heart of Destiny wanted to demand that every Gael be sworn to Erin's Hero. And for those who did not, she should banish them!

Then, the Silver Wolf looked at her and said quietly, *"Daughter, you broadcast too much. In the before-time, Breanna admonished you about making such demands. Go slowly. Your Hero needs time to settle into her redrawn life threads. Her people must accept that their Tuatha gods walk amongst them again. That will take time and likely some struggles.*

"She is yours, yet you must give her peace and time to assimilate her new reality, as she will bear a heavy weight. The time will come when she will fight larger battles abroad to ensure our future—our fate, and that of her Gaels, will be in her hands. As our time is in them as well."

"Thank you, Mother. She is so different from my other heroes; she is more one with her people. Or maybe one of her people."

"Och, she certainly is that. And you will be her guide! Yet you need to learn restraint, my daughter. Might does not make right!"

⊶⊷ Breanna ⊶⊷

The next thing Breanna knew, it was nearing sundown, and their Druids were lifting her to her feet. She felt for *Mo Chroí* and noted that her chest no longer hurt. Looking beneath her tunic, she found the odd pink scar had vanished, leaving her sigil unmarred; she hazily remembered that her original Norvegr father had flung his sword at her as she wielded the *Triple Dàns* against him.

Ulicia said solemnly, "Now we know who you need to be, and the challenge before us is how to make you whole. You were broken into pieces when our gods pulled you through time to us. Our efforts were just the first step toward making you truly Erin's Hero again."

Beatha added, "More is in play with our gods than we know. Both yours and Eoin's sigil reflect each Element – Earth, Air, Fire, Water, and Aether. Dagda's marks as the sigil creator are clear. The pattern implies the Gaels will not be ruled. I don't know what that means."

"I remember Dagda gave me a golden apple, but any more than that is still lost to me," Breanna said. "Something about destiny."

Seeing the Druids cast puzzled looks at the mention of All-Father's name, Breanna wondered why having Dagda involved in her dilemma would be a concern. Yet, silence reigned as they returned to Dun Arrogh to send her mother's *anam* to the otherworld, where Morna would hopefully find Nevan in a coming *Cycle of Time*, and they would find a better life. Eoin held Breanna, lending his strength through his muscles, bones, and spirit.

Her experience with the black oak and her land had been deeply fulfilling, comforting her mind with its tangled memories, but also perplexing. The expectations and responsibilities were vast. Yet, she knew she could manage it with Eoin and her band to support her. She had to let her troubles go. For this evening, she could only hope her mother's *anam* found the one who had been her true father, and they sought their true love in their next lives as Erin's *Cycle* would see fit.

Then she found Toal standing in her path with his apprentice-friend Cilla and Fergal at his side, stating, "I've heard whispers you're not well."

"From where?" Breanna asked.

"The *void*," he answered. "It called to me. I felt your claim."

Beatha told him, "Your cousin is better, but she has much to process and more to remember. We must prepare to send Morna's *anam* off to the *Cycle*. If it's not important—"

Toal pulled his sleeves up. "Hmm, I'm not sure if these sigils are related to her problem, but I think so. They appeared overnight. This morning, Cilla and I went hunting. Using the sigils, we simultaneously took down two bucks with our bows—heart shots at a hundred and fifty-seven yards, exactly with wind carry. These told me so in the *void* space I shared with Cilla.

"Then, as I went about bleeding the two bucks, a boar came out of nowhere and charged me, and my only option to prevent him from goring me was to put an arrow through his eye—at fifteen yards and closing—or I'd likely be dead. I used the *void* and these sigils again, and I'm alive. What are they?"

When no answer came, Toal added, "That tree line is one hundred ninety-four yards away. With my bow, the arc needed to nail a buck is sixty-eight degrees, with a likely kill percentage of seventy-two percent if I had a target. The sigils told me this."

Beatha moved in to inspect the woad designs, saying after a moment, "These symbols call on the Air and Aether Elements, reference accuracy, and this is Lugh's mark. He cast them, I'm sure."

Fergal stepped next to Breanna. "I noticed similar Drudic woad sigils on my forearms this morning while helping Toal and Cilla recover their kills. When it came time to get beasts onto the cart, I easily lifted them as if they didn't weigh what they should have."

The Seer said, "They call on Earth and Aether, indicating strength in life, and the casting also includes Lugh's mark."

Breanna was wide-eyed. "How can this be?"

"Like Eoin, these two must be a critical part of the *before-time* for Breanna," Beatha answered.

When no one responded, Cilla said nervously, "At least our Samhain celebration will have freshly cooked meat. My mum is hard at work. I should go help her."

Toal smiled at the lassie as she left, then turned to Breanna. "I'm here for you, Bre, no matter what. We will honor Morna's casting back into the *Cycle* tonight as part of our clan."

"I know that deeply, Toal. So, I welcome you all to attend my mother's farewell. Please, be at my side."

"Aye, that I will, cousin! Your mum will be missed."

Fergal echoed that sentiment. "Indeed, Breanna, I also will bear witness beside you."

Later, after Calla had treated all to an evening meal of roasted boar and venison to honor the memory of Clan Dálaigh's matriarch, Breanna was surprised to see the entire dun gathered to cast her mother's *anam* into the *Cycle of Time*. Morna's body lay on a bed of pine boughs next to a blazing bonfire in the center of the yard. Chief Cairbre and his mate, Aife, stood beside her, along with Eoin, each lending their support to Orla, Ronat, and Breanna over their loss.

While mournful notes flowed from their Bard's flute and two lads carried the beat on bodhrans, Beatha led the chant:

"In the hush between heartbeat and sky, your *anam* slips the bonds of flesh and sails the misted path to the stars, delivered into Danu's moonlit arms. May the winds bear you gently, the sparks light your way, the waters remember your name, and the earth cradle your rest. We unbind you, unlacing the cords of time, and open the veil to the ever-turning *Cycle of Time*. As the *Cycle* spins you out, be whole once more."

Breanna's Uncle Kyras and Fergal lifted the bows that cradled Morna's body, carrying her off so she could be buried next to her mate Nevan. With tears streaming down her cheeks, she felt Eoin's muscled arms wrap around her, supporting her like the rock he'd always been for her. It was as if a chapter in her life had closed in the blink of an eye.

⸺⸙ Fergal ⸙⸺

The following morning, Fergal was finishing hitching two hill ponies to one of Dun Arrogh's two chariots when Eoin strode toward him, carrying four packs: one for Breanna, one each for Beatha and Ulicia, and one for himself.

At Eoin's side was his Champion, leading another hill pony, her countenance energetic. Fergal was surprised to see that Breanna planned to ride to Dun Uisneach, as she was usually not fond of horses. He shrugged, thinking it might be humorous to watch her try to mount the little beast when Eoin interrupted his thoughts. "Fergal, I've spoken with my father, and he has agreed to have you act as his second while I tend to the demands of our Druids and escort Beatha and Ulicia to Dun Uisneach with Breanna."

Fergal bowed slightly. "I'm honored by your trust in me."

Eoin smiled. "Keep practicing with the *void* in different ways, such as having contests with Toal's archers. It will keep you sharp and allow you to teach the younger ones our ways of fighting, using more than just a sword. Hand-to-hand matches would also be good to see how they can handle Breanna's *void* path in close quarters."

"As you command, my Prince. All of our warriors are improving. That said, you can count on me to implement your suggestions. I daresay your father was skeptical, but since Bre won the Annual *Comórtas* Championship last summer, he's come to embrace your way."

"Not my way, cousin. Breanna discovered the lost warrior art of seizing the *void* during battle. It will make our clans an unparalleled force in Erin, especially with the Heart of Destiny supporting her."

A voice spoke in their minds, *"I am the Heart of Destiny, and my name is pronounced Kree Dawn. I can confirm that there was a sect of Druids known as Laoch. Those Warrior Druids faded as Gaels lost faith in their gods. You, my Prince, will resurrect the sect in the coming Cycle of Time. Very few are still living, all in Dál Riata and Galicia."*

At hearing the strange woman, Fergal looked up in surprise while he worked to ready their mounts. "How did I hear a lady speaking in my mind?"

"Because you were a sworn Warrior of Destiny during the beforetime," Croí Dàn answered. *"Sworn to my Hero, Erin's Hero."*

Eoin added, "Cousin, it's why we travel to Dun Uisneach."

Fergal thought back to the night before, when, after they sent off Morna's *anam*, Breanna mentioned that magic from their gods' realm was the cause of her jumbled thoughts. Yet, he strangely believed that hearing the Heart of Destiny speaking to him was fitting. *When did that happen?*

Fergal noted that Beatha and Ulicia emerged from the small hut they shared, and they marched toward the chariot, with Aife joining them, her expression stern.

Eoin broke into his thoughts. "While we don't know what the Druids will find or where that will lead us, I'd like Breanna's Band ready to march to Tara upon the next full moon. All must have won at least their Celtic Knot silver armring to join you with a bow or sword. If I don't return by then, I'll meet you in Tara with those who earned that right. Any questions?"

"Toal and I will have at least six, maybe seven, ready by that time, my Prince," Fergal answered. "Yet, will your father be happy about that?"

"I've already spoken to him about this possibility. Kyras will be his second if I don't return, and you must depart."

⸻⸱⚮ Breanna ⚮⸱⸻

Breanna listened to the exchange, approving of her Chief's handling of Fergal.

"Wait, he's not my Chief yet! His father is alive! He was killed—"

"My Hero, stop!" Ćroí Dàn demanded. *"You changed that. Yes, his father died like yours did. Like you, he was pulled into this timeline. It would help if you accepted that you have changed everything in our land. We will get this all sorted out with All-Father soon. Dagda will want to help his daughter, as I know he has plans for you, Eoin, and me."*

What was she thinking? Of course, Eoin's father was alive. They had discussed him the first night her memories failed her. Then Breanna grumbled, *"But why was my birth father pulled into this time only to die soon after I was born?"*

Her Heart answered, *"I do not know, but I do know my mother and your new father nearly lost you. It was a close moment. You would have left me. I'm not sure I could have gone on without you."*

Breanna wondered how her Heart loved her so much that she would not want to live without her. How she ended up as Dagda's daughter suddenly seemed to matter little in comparison. As she threw herself on her hill pony, Breanna realized she somehow had more experience than she remembered with riding.

She felt *Mo Chroí* smile inside her mind. *"You have a horse friend in Dun Uisneach who will be happy to see you!"*

Breanna raised an eyebrow, but Beatha interrupted her discussion with her Heart as she stepped onto the chariot with Ulicia, saying, "Thank you for fetching our bags for this trip, Eoin. Shall we be going?"

Ulicia nodded in return and joined her.

Yet Aife marched up to her son, her expression cool. "So, you'll be leaving us on this errand, and it won't be a short one."

"Aye, Mother," Eoin said with deference. "I've arranged things appropriately with Father. Our Chief knows it is an urgent thing—we must address with the Druids at Dun Uisneach."

Aife looked about, clearly unhappy. "Remember, our clan holds much sway in Mide and Ulaida. Use it or call on it if needed. Our Dál nAraidi Clan is not far from Tara."

Eoin enfolded her in his big arms. "Mother, I know you trust me to do the right thing for our land. I must do this—as the Tuatha Gods are back, and my love is at the heart of it."

Aife nodded. "I know. It's just hard to let you go."

"I understand, but you won't lose me again," he added.

She looked unsure of what he meant, but Toal and Cilla raced to Breanna's side, each with a quiver full of arrows, and the moment was lost.

"We made these for you," Toal exclaimed. "Well, my father helped with the tips. They are better for hunting game than enemy warriors, fighting arrowheads, that you now have."

Breanna grinned for the first time that morning, slipping off her pony to hug the lad and lass. "That was thoughtful of you two. Nonetheless, I expect you to help Fergal train our band while I'm gone. Everyone must master the bow as you two have. Well, not that good, but enough to earn a silver armring for the skill, and don't neglect the sword. Can you do that for me? I'll need them and you, and they must be ready by the next full moon. Understood?"

"Aye," Toal said. "Cilla is now my second. We will make it so."

As Breanna flung herself back on her pony, Eoin snapped his reins to get the hill ponies pulling the chariot moving. "Bre, what was that about?"

Riding beside him, she answered, "Something tells me that pair has a role to play in Breanna's Band, as does Fergal if I heard your discussion with him correctly."

Eoin nodded, but Breanna pulled ahead of the chariot before he could add more. While she remembered it being a challenge to stay on top of such beasts, she was genuinely enjoying the ride. Yet she found the journey south to Dun Uisneach on her hill pony somewhat dull. The creature had little spunk in her. It did leave time to contemplate the holes in her memories over the last day or so, some of which the mighty black oak had helped fill. When she'd heard Eoin mention Breanna's Band earlier, it seemed right this time, as if she had previously led such a group of warriors.

"You did, my Hero," Croí Dàn injected. *"And it was glorious!"*

Breanna had to shake her head while maintaining her pace ahead of Eoin and his cart with the two Druids. She knew the Heart of Destiny had also spoken in their minds yesterday while the oak commanded her attention. And now she was back. Her bond with her Heart was familiar, not something strange or concerning. It was like they were sisters.

"More like cousins, My Hero, as Danu and Dadga are not a couple," Ćroí Dàn corrected. *"If Badb Catha had given me a piece of herself instead of Danu, we'd be sisters, as The Mórrigan and The Dagda are on-again, off-again mates."*

Breanna chuckled. *"Aren't you a chatty one today?"*

"Och! I am just thrilled to have you back."

Breanna rejoined wryly, *"Hmm, at least one of us is happy. I'm still getting used to this mind-speak ability you have."*

That seemed to quiet her Heart down, but she couldn't be upset with her delighted *cousin* over the distracting conversation as the hills rolled up and down as they traveled south. They followed the long ridges that flowed out of the base of the Cuilcagh Mountains. She let a smirk slip to her lips, as she had learned something about her gods that few knew. That All-Father and the Dark Goddess were a thing, even if it sounded like it was a rocky relationship. Breanna still didn't understand how she could be Dagda's daughter, but she let it go and seized the *void* to see what animals or people were nearby.

The sun burst from behind the clouds, and Breanna felt the length and breadth of her land rush through her, its streams and rivers teeming with fish, its hills and valleys filled with wildlife, its plains rich with fields of grains and domesticated animals, and its coasts and lochs and rivers rolling in sealife. She had felt some of this when linked to the oak tree, but it was not as clean and fresh as it is now. It was as if someone had cleansed her mind and her land. There was a peace about what she felt, like a breath released, a sigh of relief. All was well on the Emerald Isle of Erin.

As Breanna was about to release the *void*, there was a note of discord again to the east, where sprawling Dun Tara lay. She reined in her pony in a circle to ride next to the chariot once more. "Beatha, when I seize the *void*, I can feel it in the health of our land, from shore to shore in all directions. It is as if our gods are pleased about something. Except in the east, where I know Dun Tara sits. What is that sourness?"

The Fáidh scowled. "It could only be one thing. More One God followers arrived at Dun Tara, as they did at Laigin's Dun Feare some cycles back. Some are just traders, but others are more zealous about their beliefs. While they are conflicted about this notion of their trinity, it is, in reality, initially based on Yahwism, a pantheon of gods that drifted toward monolatry, where people believe in a single god.

"Strangely, while Rome was subsuming the lands across the Sea of Erin, their leaders began elevating themselves as deities. Then they veered even more toward the notion of their One God, with their emperors fulfilling both political and theological roles. It ensured their control over every aspect of their subjects' lives.

"That resulted in the transformation of Yahweh God into the One God concept established in Rome. They now desire to cast out all Gaelic and Celtic gods, save their own."

Breanna didn't know how she understood it, yet she did, and looked east again. She whispered fiercely, "Eoin, we're going to Dun Tara after visiting Dun Uisneach. I have something to address."

"Aye, my love," he agreed. "I suspected that would be the case."

Breanna flinched at the words *my love*, which Eoin had used several times now. She was unsure how to respond. She had felt his love when he'd wrapped his arms around her last night during her mother's casting ritual, and she had to admit she had been infatuated with him while growing up, especially when they battled, with her using a child's set of wooden long blades and him his wooden sword. Then she wondered why her mother had allowed her to pursue a warrior's path so young, only to fight it recently. Something was missing.

Pulling her mind into the present, she thought about her Heart's comments about Dagda being her father and how that could be. What did it mean to have a god give a piece of themselves to another?

"Mo Chroí, when you said Dagda was my father, I remember he gave me an apple. That is how he gave me a piece of himself, right?"

"Yes, my Hero," she answered. *"It is the only way we Tuatha Dé Danann can procreate, as the great magics wielded during the Fomorian war rendered them infertile. They must give away a part of themselves and their power."*

"Is that what Danu did with you?"

"Yes, that is how I became a Tuatha goddess. Badb created the magical construct that enables me to wield the magic of the Heart of Destiny and claim Erin's Hero, and Danu cast me into this gem with a piece of herself to make me sentient so I could make each choice."

Breanna was silent for a time, thinking about how her *cousin* had been created, and then asked, *"When did Danu give you a piece of herself to make you sentient? Perhaps it would be better to ask it this way. When were you born?"*

Croí Dàn hesitated. *"Lugh was the first to bear me—we fought against the Fomorians and the Fir Bolg. Those were terrible battles."*

"I asked when."

"It was before the Sons of Mil came here and fought us over Erin when the great magic war raged between Fomorians and Tuatha."

"Again, tell me when that was."

Her Heart's voice was small. *"I guess two thousand cycles."*

"And you've chosen only six heroes in that time?"

Croí Dàn whispered, *"Yes."*

A wave of sadness washed over Breanna. *"Oh, Mo Chroí, how did you survive the loneliness?"*

"Barely. Yet, now I have you!"

Tears stung Breanna's eyes as she couldn't imagine such isolation, and she wondered how Danu could be such a cruel mother. *"I will discuss this with Dagda."*

"Och, don't do that, my Hero."

Breanna said stiffly, *"You requested I call you 'Mo Chroí,' I requested you address me as cousin. I will discuss this with my father and your mother."*

Croí Dàn went silent at that declaration.

"I am Erin's Hero, Mo Chroí, and I need to understand my new relatives better—they are our clan, if I can use that term."

"Aye, but they are not who you think they are. Time—eternal life—has hardened their hearts."

Breanna heard a word of caution but let the subject drop.

After the four travelers—or five with *Croí Dàn*—passed Loch Gowna, the terrain became more manageable as they rode south and into the plains east of Loch Ree. Along the way, the wolf pack she'd met when she merged with the mighty black oak would skirt along the treeline as if following her. A large silver wolf led the pack, howling from time to time.

Shortly after midday, they stopped for lunch atop a hill that afforded them a view of the large loch to the west, with mountains rising to the north. They'd nearly finished their meal when they spied six warriors bearing Connachta colors riding along the shoreline.

"Raiders!" Breanna hissed.

"Aye," Eoin said grimly. "String your bow and nock."

"Och, they've seen us," Beatha added as Breanna took up her bow and the quiver with her man-killer tips, not Toal's hunting arrows. As the warriors thundered toward them, swords held high, she stuck five arrows in the ground beside her and nocked the last. When the lead warrior was a hundred yards out, she seized the *void* and targeted his shoulder. As the arrow flew, the rider tried to veer away but chose the wrong direction, and it pierced his heart. He flew back, crashing to the ground, dead.

Breanna grimaced at that and nocked again as the other raiders veered around their fallen and kept coming. Seeking another shoulder shot, her arrow flew true toward the new lead warrior, punching into his upper shoulder and out of his back, with its impact flinging him off his mount. The other four still charged uphill toward them, and she loosed her third arrow. Another rider went down. At thirty yards away, the remaining trio reined in their mounts as Breanna nocked again.

Eoin, sword in hand, commanded, "Keep your distance, you Connachta scum. This land is not yours. Ride off, and you'll live."

"Still three against two!" one yelled back.

Breanna released her arrow, taking him in the shoulder that held his sword. When his weapon dropped from his hand, she nocked once more. "I think your man needs to learn how to count," she said. "How about the two of you? If you think I'll hesitate to take you down, bring it. Otherwise, one of you fetches my arrows while I hold the other hostage. Then you can leave, and be sure to take the dead one with you; I don't want his head as a trophy. For your failed attack, you've forfeited three mounts to me. I'll make them a gift for the leaders of Dun Uisneach."

One raider turned his mount, saying, "Fiachra, I'll get the warrior's arrows. Don't do anything stupid, like get yourself or us killed. She's likely as good with those blades as her bow."

"Didn't even get to cross swords with them," Fiachra grumbled.

The last warrior wounded ground out, "Count yourself lucky—he is a Prince of the Blood, and they both wear the gold!"

After gathering the arrows, the raiders dejectedly rode away, each doubled up on a mount with the wounded or dead. Breanna shook her head. "Fools. Yet, now I have a present for those at Dun Uisneach!"

"I'm glad you have that bow," Eoin commented.

Breanna sighed. "It appears I know how to use it."

The Druids agreed as Eoin tied the new horses to the chariot. "Still, if the first one hadn't veered into my shot, he'd still be alive. I'd rather not kill any of my Gaels unless I have to."

Later, as sunset neared, they came upon a ford along the River Inny. Eoin claimed Guestright at the small settlement on the river's edge. As a place that seemed familiar to her, there was just enough light for Breanna to go for a walk along the river's edge. Seeing no game to hunt, she seized the *void* and, with a lightning-quick jab, speared a good-sized trout so the four of them would not be as much of a burden on the settlement's residents. When her net was filled with fish, she decided it would be enough to feed all of them.

The same large silver wolf sat on the far side of the river, appraising her in the moment. *Croí Dàn* said, *"Mother, you honor us!"*

The Silver Huntress nodded and was gone.

Breanna asked, *"Mother? As in yours? And honor us?"*

"Yes, it was Danu, my mother," her Heart answered. *"As to why she was here, I'm not sure. Maybe you called her with your claim."*

"Why would our Mother Goddess bow to me?"

"Our land accepted you as Erin's Hero, so must she acknowledge you, but not as Mother Goddess. Her wolf must accept you as her ceannaire pacáiste, the leader of all packs and all clans in this land. Of everything alive. It's part of my magical construct as I choose my Hero."

Breanna tried to digest that thought as she returned to the settlement after her sizable trout catch. The evening meal was pleasant, with their hosts appreciating their efforts.

They rose in the morning and helped the elderly settlers as a gesture of appreciation for sheltering them, with Eoin chopping wood and Breanna spearing more trout for breakfast. With thanks from their hosts, they crossed the ford and followed the trail along the River Inny's bank east. By midday, they headed south again, stopping briefly at another settlement to water their hill ponies. The day was bright and sunny, making their travel easy. They reached the High King's road in the early afternoon and turned east toward Dun Uisneach. After passing a few more settlements that looked like the hillforts of long ago, the massive hillfort came into view. It was perched below the peak of Uisneach Hill, and the High King Road rose to meet it.

A chariot, followed by nine warriors—called a *fian* by the Gaels—rolled through the open gates and turned toward them. A grizzly older man named Corbmac, whom Breanna and Eoin had met the previous summer at the *Comórtas*, a contest she had won. He held the reins, a big smile on his face. He raised a hand to halt his men. "Breanna Ban Morna, as I live and breathe, it is a pleasure to see you again! Your dance with your blades this past summer is well remembered at Dun Uisneach, and I'm sure Faolán and Falyn will be thrilled to see you as well."

As Eoin pulled the chariot with their Druids to a halt and Breanna dismounted, Beatha cleared her throat. "We seek Bláth, as there appears to be an unexplained disturbance in the *void* and *sight* that somehow has affected Breanna. Is she here?"

Corbmc answered, "Hmm, no, but she is due to return by sundown with Maoilir. They spent Samhain at Dun Tara, my—Bre."

Seeing his quizzical look, Breanna shrugged. "We can wait. I'm unsure if you remember Beatha, but she is our Seeress. With her is Ulicia, our Healer."

Corbmac tipped his head. "Aye, I've met these two Druids long ago. Their special skills are renowned in our province. I take it you have traveled here safely?"

"No," Eoin answered dourly. "Connachta mounted raiders on the east side of Loch Ree foolishly decided to challenge us—well, to challenge Bre. Their mistake was in underestimating her skill with her bow. Six on two seemed good odds for them, but that quickly became two on two, with Bre ordering them to retrieve her spent arrows and forfeit three horses before they could leave alive."

Corbmac said, "I'm not surprised. Connachta's king knows he can flaunt the province's border, given who his father is. I'll inform my Chief, but our Horsemaster will surely appreciate the gift!

"Now, to you, Breanna. What news do you bring?"

Breanna raised an eyebrow. "I see you bear sigils on your forearms that you did not have last summer. Beatha can tell you what they mean, as they are similar to others we've seen. She says they are gifts from our gods."

"Hmmm," Corbmac grumbled. "They appeared in the middle of a recent night. Later that day, we all felt Erin's Hero claim her land. You wouldn't know anything about that, would you?"

Breanna dropped her gaze. "Aye, I might."

Corbmac nodded stoically, giving way as his *fian* warriors eagerly gathered around Breanna to greet her. She knew they had become fond of her during the summer games. Few of the warriors who earned the status of gold armrings bothered to talk with lowly spearmen, let alone share secrets such as seizing the *void* with them. Breanna returned the greeting to each one, grasping their forearms as if she remembered them all, some pulling her into hugs.

When they finished, she stood again before Corbmac and drew him into a warm embrace. The old warrior suggested after a moment, "Please follow me, my—Bre, and we will get you all settled."

The old warrior stepped back onto his chariot, turning back toward the dun, and his *fian* thumped spears on their shields in unison, taking up the chant, "Bre! Bre! Bre!" as the four of them followed the warriors through the gates.

"Cousin, I don't understand why they honor me."

Croí Dàn answered with a mental shrug, *"Because they know you as Erin's Hero, at least in their hearts, they do, if not yet in their minds. Some may even have a memory echo of you from the before-time as they fought at your side."*

As they trotted, rolled, or rode into the courtyard, many living in Dun Uisneach stopped long enough to hail them. The four of them neared the stables, and as Breanna dismounted, the sound of a horse kicking its stall door reached her. Then the rope holding it closed gave way, and a horse bolted into the yard toward those from Dun Arrogh. Breanna stood her ground as the mare came to a halt and reared with a loud whinny.

"My Hero, you are back!"

Croí Dàn laughed. *"Eimar certainly remembers you."*

Breanna questioned dubiously, *"Horses can talk?"*

The mare snorted. *"Only the smart ones like me!"*

"Mo Chroí, these are some strange times," Breanna stated.

"Cousin, you don't know the half of it! Eimar was your mare during your last quest in the before-time. You two hit it off very well."

Eimar wickered her approval as a chagrinned stableboy approached his charge, ready to lead the mare back to her stable. Breanna held up a hand to forestall him. "It's okay, lad, leave her with me—we need some time to catch up. I'd appreciate it if you could fetch an apple for Eimar here."

Her horse wickered again and nodded her head as if to say yes. Breanna had to chuckle over the notion.

Fergus, the Dun Uisneach Master Smith, strode out of the shed that housed his forge, bellowing, "Breanna and Eoin! You've returned!"

Breanna could not contain her big grin as Eoin took the muscled man's arm and said, "Aye, Gus, we've some matters to discuss with your Master Filídh. Let me introduce Beatha, our Fáidh, and Ulicia, our Ollamh, at Dun Arrogh."

"Good to meet you, Beatha and Ulicia," Fergus said, taking each one's hand and kissing their knuckles. "It's a pleasure to welcome you to Dun Uisneach."

Breanna saw the Fáidh and Ollamh roll their eyes at the smith's action and grinned over their discomfiture. Then Fergus turned back to Eoin, saying, "I found a barter note in my ledger that says I owe you thirty gold coins for some weapons—both swords and knives—that you sold me. I noted them as battle spoils."

Eoin shook his head. "That can't be right."

"It's right here," Fergus countered, pointing at his ledger. "It notes I would keep half the barter amount we agreed to until you returned. This is your mark, is it not?"

Breanna and Eoin looked at the entry and saw his initials, *EMC*. "Those are your marks," Breanna said.

Croí Dàn chided, *"Eoin, leave it be. It was a trade made in the before-time when you helped my Hero save our people and our land. Dagda will clarify everything soon. But protesting will not deter the hard-headed Fergus here."*

Breanna heard the exchange as Eoin took *Croí Dàn's* advice and conceded, "That's my mark."

"Well, that's good," Fergus confirmed, letting out a great sigh. "You had me concerned there, as I found a stack of thirty gold coins I'd set aside for that trade. I could not have made that big of a mistake!"

As the stableboy returned with the requested apple, Breanna was pleased to see there was something Eoin had not remembered as well. Then Eimar nudged her shoulder, and she held the fruit in her palm for the mount to munch on. Once her horse finished its snack, Breanna threw herself onto Eimar's back and trotted around the courtyard. *"Eimar, we will have a proper ride tomorrow!"*

A moment later, Faolán and Falyn strode from the main hall. Breanna commanded her mount to stop by Eoin, their Druids, and the stableboy, adding to the latter, "You can take her back to the stables now, along with our hill ponies and these Connachta forfeit warhorses. I'll try to stop by and see her later."

Breanna turned to find the Chieftess closing in with wide open arms that quickly wrapped around her, while the Chief took Eoin's arm in his own. Falyn gushed, "Bre, I'm so happy to see you, our *Comórtas* Champion! What brings you and Eoin here so soon after Samhain?"

Faolán turned to her and gave her a fatherly hug. "This is a surprise. And these are my children, Dáithí, Oisín, and Teagan. I think you met them at the *Comórtas*."

"Aye, we did, but only briefly," Eoin responded. "And I believe you know the Druids of Dun Arrogh. They have a matter to discuss with Bláth. There was a disturbance in both the *sight* and the *void* the day before Samhain. It affected Breanna's memories. The same is true for me, as all is not as it was."

Beatha said, "There's more to it than that. Bre, show them the gem."

When Breanna pulled the ruby from her tunic, Falyn cried, "The Heart of Destiny! We felt Erin's Hero claim her land and people two days back, but didn't know who it could be. Yet, here you are, one of our very own."

Beatha answered, "It is a deeper matter. Something happened recently in space between the Tuatha realm and ours; thus, the *sight* and the *void* are now in turmoil. It was disconcerting to feel that special space in such turmoil. With Breanna's claim of her land, we hoped it would settle, but it is still hard to hold on for long."

"By the stars!" Falyn stated. "This is momentous. Yet why has *Cróí Dàn* called her to be Erin's Hero?"

"Maybe we should move this discussion inside," the Seeress suggested. "There's more that we need to tell you in private."

"It sounds like we'll need ale and lots of it before we dine this evening! Keegan, let's move this conversation to our personal meeting room."

"I'd prefer mead," Breanna countered.

The Seneschal nodded, indicating that he would make it so, as Falyn laughed. "A young lady after my own heart!"

With the children off to their law lessons with the Druid Tadg, the group settled into their seats with mugs in hand. Beatha looked to Breanna, who took Corbmac's hand and nodded, and the Seeress continued with, "It appears this is not the first time our *Cróí Dàn* has claimed Breanna Ban Morna as Erin's Hero."

"Not the first time? What does that mean?" Falyn asked.

"We do not remember Breanna's original claim as she completed a quest laid upon her by our gods. She saved Erin's people and land from whatever fate lay behind us during that alternative time. Yet, whatever her task, it produced a conundrum that disturbed the connection between the Tuatha realm and our own."

With a quiet voice, *Cróí Dàn* said to Breanna and Beatha, *"May I provide the details on your quest?"*

"*Yes, and please include everyone here,*" Breanna answered. "*Let me introduce you first.*"

Then, looking at those around her, she confirmed, "I only have scattered memories of what we are calling the *before-time*. As one of the *Dáns*, only my *Heart* can provide the details. In her form, she must speak in your mind, though she can hear your spoken words through me."

Ćroí Dàn, using her mind-speak, said, "*My Hero's quest was to obtain and wield the magic of the Triple Dáns and remove Norvegr invaders who settled just northwest of here, an act that rewrote Erin's timeline in this part of Mide. During that period, my Hero was a half-breed. As Danu foretold, only warriors who bore the blood of both sides, like Breanna, could remove the roughly eighteen cycles of the brutal Norvegr's presence. Through my Hero's vision of her land without her tainted blood, she invoked the magic of the Blades, Stone, and Heart, something even Badb Catha dared not do.*"

Falyn asked, "Wait, wouldn't that have ended, Bre, too? If she removed all traces of the Norvegr's blood, she could not have been born."

"*Aye, that is true, and she did so knowingly. Having lost everything, Erin's Hero chose her land and sacrificed herself. In the final moment, All-Father blessed her due to her love for her land and Eoin. Danu and Dagda saved her after she wielded the magic of the Triple Dáns and pulled her anam away from the Cycle of Time and back to us.*

"*Like the Mother Goddess gave a part of herself to me, All-Father gave a part of himself to Breanna. He has a plan for her, and we must support that plan, whatever it is.*"

The room was silent. Then Corbmac stood. "I propose a salute to Breanna for giving up her life to save our land. I do not remember that time, but our Heart has spoken to my bones. To Breanna!"

With that, they rose around her, in unison, saying, "To Breanna!"

She was unsure how she felt about that declaration, but when Breanna looked up, an elvish-looking woman stood in the doorway, whom she knew was Dun Uisneach's bard, Bláth.

"That was quite enlightening," the woman commented.

Falyn asked, "My Bard, where is our Seer, Maoilir?"

"The High King's Seer requested that he remain at Dun Tara to help sort out the claim of Erin's Hero in our land. Our King is, shall I say, unnerved by the claim Erin's Hero has made. But I believe a mug of mead is in order, as I've ridden hard this day."

Keegan filled a mug for her and left to ensure his servers set up a high table with appropriate trenchers. A short while later, Faolán led them from the private room to the main hall. As they entered, a collective murmur ran through those seated at the long tables, while the four from Dun Arrogh moved to the high table with the heads of Dun Uisneach.

The serving staff scurried about pouring ale and mead while the kitchen staff hastened to deliver the first course. Keegan arranged the seating at the high table, putting Breanna between Faolán and Falyn. Eoin sat to the right side of the Chief, Beatha to the Chieftess's left, with Ulicia beside Eoin. At the mid-table, Breanna took in their host's children, whom she had met in the yard earlier; the eldest, Dáithí, seemed to be a bright lad; next came Oisín, and last was Teagan. They appeared to sparkle with a bloom of youth.

Bláth

Bláth diverted herself to the mid-table, whispering to Dáithí, "The guests who arrived this afternoon are the key to a puzzle. Listen closely, and you'll likely learn some legends of old."

She stepped up and took her seat next to Eoin. It took Bláth only a moment to cast her less-used Druidic Seeress powers to look deeply into the disturbed path of the life threads around Breanna. Using the *sight* to reach into the *Cycle of Time*, Blath demanded it yield to her will, seeing what others missed, digging deep despite the agony it caused to hold the roiled *sight*. Bláth would not be denied the truth. Somehow, she sensed that Breanna was her friend in some *before-time* that *Ćroí Dàn* had mentioned. She would push through it regardless of the cost and the pain her effort inflicted.

Then she heard a song she and Dagda had jointly composed about how Erin's Hero would rise to battle the Norvegrs with her band. Breanna had faced her one-time father and made him no more. Amidst a brutal battle, she'd sent him into the abyss of time regardless of what it meant for her fate.

Grimacing at what she beheld in the *Cycle*, she shook herself and stood. Bláth commanded, "Rise, Breanna Ban Morna, rise as Erin's Hero, chosen by the Heart of Destiny twice, and be welcome to Dun Uisneach!"

The *fians* gathered at the lower tables also rose, chanting, "Bre! Bre! Bre!" repeatedly. Soon, others from Dun Uisneach stood, and Breanna rose and bowed to them all. Amongst them was Corbmac, who had not sought the high table as *fian-ceannard* of Dun Uisneach. He stood proudly, and his smile could not have been brighter as Breanna waved to him.

Bláth turned to Breanna and sank to one knee. "My friend, my Hero, welcome back to your land. Thank you for saving us. When I touched the *Cycle of Time*, I saw how you were reborn to us. You fought for us. Danu and Dagda fought for us, and they fought for you. We will fight with you. Forever!"

The *fians* once more chanted, "Bre! Bre! Bre!", beating their fists on their chests or rapping the butt of their dirks on the tables.

Outside of Dun Uisneach, a pack of wolves howled.

───✦◈ **Breanna** ◈✦───

With her jumbled memories, she felt it was an unearned gesture and asked, *"Mo Chroí, how did Bláth see what happened?"*

"The Bard used the sight to breach the troubled connection to the Tuatha realm. She remembers some of you from that time—something I can confirm, as I was with you. She's still missing many memories, but not all of them. It is clear that she is as much a Seeress as a Bard."

The evening meal was more than Breanna expected; it was more like a feast than a spontaneous meal. As the evening wound down and the mead went to her head, Breanna had to shake herself to stay awake.

Seeing this, Faolán and Falyn rose together, and the *Taoiseach* said, "Eoin and Breanna, I think it is time our Master Bard guides you to one of our noble abodes. They are behind the bathhouse. Sleep well. I expect tomorrow will be busy, but there is no need to rise early. Our servers can bring you breakfast if you like. It sounds like you've both had some troubled days recently."

"Happy to escort you," Bláth chimed in.

Eoin raised an eyebrow but only nodded his assent.

Faolán added, "Keegan, please see Beatha and Ulicia to a similar abode."

The Seneschal held out his arms for the old Fáidh and Ollamh to take, and they tottered off with him.

Bláth led Breanna and Eoin through the baths and out a door to a series of small but comfortable huts. "Feel free to use the private baths tonight or in the morning," she said. "Or both. Call for a page if you want to eat here when you rise."

Breanna responded, "Thank you, Bláth. *Croí Dàn* tells me you are a true friend."

"I couldn't see all when I reached through the *sight* to see what you two did for us, but enough," the Master Bard answered, "Most importantly, I took note of your love for each other. Please, do not lose that bond to this moment of madness. Everything should be clear soon."

With that, she turned away, leaving Breanna and Eoin alone. "That was a lot to take in," Eoin said. "I don't know about you, but I'd like a bath before we sleep."

"Together?" Bre squealed.

"Aye, my love, aye. To both bathing and sleeping."

Croí Dàn told the pair, *"I will give you some time alone, but know this. You previously worked through these issues that blocked your love for each other. Dagda made the space in you to love him and still be Erin's Hero of our land."*

Later, after their bath together, where Eoin washed Breanna's scarlet hair with that strange white streak, they put on their night clothes and lay in bed together, watching the embers glowing in their hearth. Breanna whispered, "I'm not sure how, but this feels right."

"Aye, my love, it does," Eoin answered. "But now is not the time for questions. You're still unsettled. I suggest we get some sleep and see what the morning brings. Just holding each other is enough for now."

Morning came and went, yet Eoin and Breanna did not rise. It felt decadent not to have chores to attend to, but finally, Eoin said, "I suppose we should make an appearance in the hall."

Breanna stretched like a cat. "But Bláth said we could have breakfast here. I like that idea. Please, make that happen for me."

Eoin shook his head at her expression. "How could I deny such a request?"

He opened the door to their abode to find a page waiting for them. The lad said, "My Prince, how may I serve you?"

Breanna was surprised that a servant was waiting for them as Eoin answered, "Er, my, ah—Hero requires breakfast, as do I. If you'd be so kind."

"Of course, my Prince. It will be delivered shortly."

Eoin tended to the fire, and in a short time, there was a knock on the door. As Eoin greeted the young man, Breanna sat up with her blanket tucked in around her. The server placed a tray of food at the foot of their bed and promptly left them.

"I could get used to this," Breanna said, rubbing her hands together. "I am starved!"

"Hmm, me too," Eoin added with a raised eyebrow. "We had quite a trying past couple of days."

Breanna mumbled in agreement, her mouth full. Yet she was soon lost in her breakfast of gooey sicín eggs, fresh fried boar, porridge with bilberries sweetened with honey, and buttered soda bread. The tea that accompanied the meal had a hint of thyme and mint. Finally finished, she said, "I think I need a ride with Eimar, and then we should spar. *Croí Dán*, let Corbmac and his men know I'll need them in the yard later."

"I have put out the call."

Breanna tried to reach for the *sight* but frowned when nothing she sought came. *"What about the other two white-haired warriors I vaguely recall? The ones who joined me in the before-time?"*

"My Hero, I expect you'll find your then half-brothers soon."

"Hmm," Breanna muttered, wondering how it had come to be that she had half-brothers. "Eoin, please ride with me. Eimar needs some exercise."

"Of course, my love."

After breakfast, the pair took a quick dip in the baths before donning their tunics, leggings, and leathers. Then, they headed to the stables.

Eimar said with a note of loss, *"I hoped to see you last night."*

Beanna sighed. *"Eimar, much has happened. I needed some space, time, and sleep."*

"With your lover. That is good. He fits well with you. I honor him as well because he honors you."

"Aye, he does," Breanna agreed with a bit of a blush. *"That's why we are riding together this morning."*

Eimar whickered her approval.

Eoin took the reins of his mount. "This stallion seems familiar. It is as if I have ridden him before."

The beast was feisty, and Breanna grinned when Eoin used a heavy hand to rein him in. "Looks like you learned to manage a mount better in the *before-time* as well."

Eoin grinned at Breanna. "Aye, let's ride!"

They circled the yard a few times as a warm-up before shooting through the open gates of Dun Uisneach. Eimar flew like the wind, with Breanna feeling her mount's determination not to be outdone by a mere stallion. She belonged to Erin's Hero, after all!

They headed west on the High King's Road, pounding along the road. After a time, Breanna, proud of Eimar's heart, reined in her mare outside a settlement, saying, perplexed, "One of mine is here."

Croí Dàn informed her, *"Yes, he fought you during the Comórtas in the before-time. There's more, but you should reacquaint yourselves."*

"If he remembers me."

Her Heart offered a mental shrug. *"You did beat him."*

Bre nodded toward the settlement, saying to Eoin, "Let's see if he is about."

She nudged Eimar forward, and Eoin's stallion followed her. There was a hint of an old fort that had once been, with a berm facing the High King's Road and a set of open gates. With Dun Uisneach nearby, the need to maintain separate ringforts so close to each other had relegated this one to a settlement.

As they approached the gates, a pair of guards stepped forward, taking in Breanna, clearly armed to the teeth. Looking at Eoin, wrapped in his Prince of the Blood cloak, one asked, "May I help you, my Prince?"

"Indeed, I believe you may," Eoin answered. "My Champion here, Breanna Ban Morna, battled a lad from this settlement during the Annual *Comórtas* Games last summer. The final round was for the overall championship title, which Bre won. Since we are guests of Faolán and Falyn at Dun Uisneach, she would like to pay her respects to Bradaigh and ask him to dine with us. Is he about?"

"Ahh, that's why I recognize you two," the other guard commented. "That was a tremendous display of blade work. Long blades bested a sword for the first time in eons, with a woman winning to boot!"

As Breanna tipped her head to acknowledge the compliment, the first guard said, "He's out working with others in the fields for the final harvest gathering. While we have many redheaded lads, he's pretty easy to spot as the brawniest. It's behind the settlement's huts and lodge."

"Hard work," Eoin commented. "I'm sure we'll find him."

They nudged their mounts toward the fields, weaving around the huts before dismounting at their edge. Knowing hers would not stray, Breanna took the reins of Eoin's horse and tied them to Eimar. She and her Prince then strode past the expansive vegetable garden. Further on, they found fields of wheat, barley, and oats that had already been scythed, with people working in unison to gather the cut stalks and pile them into wagons.

When Breanna caught sight of her *Comórtas* opponent, she called out, "Bradaigh! A moment, if you will."

The big lad looked up, nodded, easily hefted a large pile of cut barley into the wagon he was loading, and then marched toward the one who had defeated him last summer. He yelled, "Breanna Ban Morna, my fierce and fiery maiden! As our gods give us life, what are you doing here?"

As the big lad approached, Eoin offered his forearm in greeting and said, "We're looking for you."

Aside from his hair being red, his face was a bit softer than she remembered, and his smile was broader. It was as if he didn't carry the weight he had in the *before-time*. She offered her arm. "We are—wait, what are these sigils?"

Bradaigh raised an eyebrow. "I don't truly know. They appeared a few days back, and I now have many times my normal strength. Maybe they are a gift from our gods. That's what our Healer Druid said."

Breanna looked at Eoin knowingly before she said to Bradaigh, "Yeah, we had similar ones appear on some of us at Dun Arrogh. Our Druids said the same thing."

"We are visiting with Faolán and Falyn and wanted to see how you're getting on," Eoin said. "Perhaps consider joining us for a meal at Dun Uisneach. I'm sure you'll be able to find out more about those sigils from their Druids."

The big warrior raked a hand through his sweaty hair. "Well, the harvest is nearly in. We will probably finish by tomorrow afternoon. I could join you after that. The suppers at Dun Uisneach are always worth the ride, that's for sure."

"Excellent!" Eoin exclaimed. "There's some news to share with you, and we look forward to catching up."

As she and Eoin turned away, Breanna said, *"Croí Dán, while he's certainly more easygoing, I'm not sure he remembers our other timeline at all. Let's plan to go easy on him."*

"I believe you are correct, my Hero, yet Lugh also provided a gift, so he must have a role to play. That said, everyone in the before-time whom Danu pulled into this time will experience that change differently."

"At least he should be able to seize the void, as he did when we battled last summer. Maybe we should start there."

Later that afternoon, Corbmac and his men surrounded Breanna and Eoin as they finished their match in the yard, with the spearmen thumping their weapons on their shields in approval. The old *fian* leader proclaimed, "That was fabulous! When you two dance like that with your blades, it is simply poetry in motion."

Eoin bowed his appreciation and winked at Breanna. "My partner makes me look good."

Bhruic, the Dun Uisneach Master Tanner, and Kyle, the Master Woodwright, stepped forward, each with a towel. Fergus stood nearby, smiling his approval.

As the slightly winded warriors wiped the sweat from their brows, Bhruic asked, "Breanna, how is my leatherwork provided after the *Comórtas* holding up for you? Nothing is binding you from making an easy draw of your weapons, right?"

Finished with the towel, Breanna tossed it in an empty bucket. Then, she shrugged into her harness, sliding *Lann Dán's* hafts in place, and accepted her cloak from Eoin. She reset her six dirks, spear, and bow before answering, "All is well, Bhruic."

"May I check the leather straps?" he asked.

Breanna smiled, feeling feisty. "Maybe a demonstration is needed instead. Eoin, please take my cloak back, as it might get in the way. Ruaidri Mac Ciarán, I require your shield for a moment. Please hand it to Bhruic."

The old warrior questioned, "My Lady?"

"Humor me, Ruaidri." Breanna chuckled. "Now, Bhruic, stand here and hold the shield before you."

She stalked twenty paces away from him and turned. "Now, observe closely and tell me if you see any of my weapons binding because of your work."

The Master Tanner choked out, "My Hero?"

Breanna seized the *void*, and each dirk was rapidly in flight, one after the other, thumping home on Ruaidri's wooden shield in a perfect circle. A moment later, her spear landed between Bhruic's feet, followed by three arrows that hit the shield's center inside the ring of dirks. When she released the *void* and lowered her bow, she asked impertinently, "Did anyone count how many moments that took?"

Eoin offered, "Well, I'd say less than ten. That included stringing your bow, so I'm unsure how you want to count that."

The *fian* warriors roared in approval as she approached a pale-faced Bhruic and took the shield from him. Turning it around to admire her aim, she apologized, "Sorry if that was too fast for you. Were you able to follow my movements to see if any hindrance to my weapons was due to your work, Master Tanner?"

Fergus marched toward the tanner, laughing as he slapped his friend on the back. "She got you, Bhruic! She got you good!"

As the Master Tanner shook his head, Ruaidri stepped forward, took the shield from Bre, and began extracting her weapons. "Let me help you with this, my Hero," he said, handing them to her one by one. "I prefer to limit the damage to my shield."

Breanna smiled at Bhruic. "Apologies, my friend. I'm a bit, well, not myself. I know you treated me with kindness in the *before-time,* and for that, you'll always hold a special piece of my heart. Especially for this fine cloak you gave me."

The tanner offered softly, "I understand our gods have newly returned you to us. Yet we believe in you—you're a link to them that we haven't had in ages. Our people will look for you to right the wrongs of our leaders."

"Och, I know, and it's a burden I'm still trying to understand."

"We believe in you because your claim rang true."

"So, you felt it, and for that, I assure you, I'll do what I can."

"It's all we ask, Erin's Hero. Yet, to us, you're just our Bre."

A large wagon rolled into the dun's yard, clanking with weapons hanging from its sides. A very tall man with massive arms pulled the team of good-sized draft horses to a stop. Gus turned and exclaimed, "Goibbi!"

The substantial man climbed down from his wagon, and the two grabbed each other in a bear hug. "Aye, Fergus, aye! It's been too long."

"What brings you to Dun Uisneach?"

The mighty man shrugged. "An order to deliver."

"An order? I placed no order."

"Nay, you didn't. It was made for her." He nodded at Breanna.

Bláth walked from the main hall with Beatha and Ulicia, each Druid gazing narrow-eyed at the arrival of the smith.

Croí Dàn put in, *"Stop playing games. I know you!"*

"Aye, you do, my Heart. And I know you. Your Mother asked me to convey that she misses you and has complete confidence in you to support Erin's Hero."

"Huh," Croí Dàn huffed. *"I hadn't expected that from Mother."*

Goibbi sighed. *"My Hero—"*

Breanna, as always, heard her Heart and grated out, *"I am not your hero! Who are you?"*

He ducked his head. *"Goibnui, and my brother is Dagda."*

"*My new father? The one who saved me and then abandoned me?*"

"*Och, no, my Hero! He's been dealing with your, um, new status. I am here with a special delivery from Badb Catha, thanks to my brothers and me. The Dark Goddess thought Lugh's long blades, which Erin's Hero wielded in the before-time, needed enhancing. Dagda, Danu, and Lugh contributed new aspects that you might benefit from. So, I'm here to deliver the upgraded rendering of Lann Dàn to you.*"

"*Lugh just gave them up?*" Ćroí Dàn asked, incredulous.

"*He has a soft spot for Breanna, as we all do.*"

"*Goibniu—Eoin is listening, you know.*"

"*It's good to know he's in the loop, but I expected no less. Nice to meet you, Eoin. My Hero, I hope you like our improvements.*"

"*I'm sure I will, Goibniu,*" Breanna answered with a raised eyebrow. "*Do they know you are the smith of our gods?*"

"*Well, I'm Goibbi to them. Let's leave it at that. Now, to keep up my appearance as a human, let's use human words.*"

Breanna answered, "Well met, Goibbi," as if no internal mind-to-mind discussion had occurred. "I am, indeed, Erin's Hero. Thank you for making this trip and for delivering this. I am confident you'll be able to tell me how the royal family will support me with this delivery, which I assume is a weapon."

Goibbi winked at her subterfuge. "Of course, my Hero."

Looking around at the assembled audience, Breanna caught the eyes of the Seneschal. "Keegan, is the private meeting room available?"

"For you, my Hero, yes," he answered. "If you, Eoin, and Goibbi will follow me. I assume Bláth, Beatha, and Ulicia should join you."

The smith pulled an oblong sack from his wagon and trailed all of them. Once everyone was in the meeting room, Breanna asked Keegan to have someone bring them ale and mead. Then she turned to Goibniu. "Now that we are relatively alone, what is this about?"

Goibniu sighed, placing the bundle on the table. "As I said, our gods and goddesses want you to have these upgraded long blades."

"Cut the double-talk!" Breanna demanded.

"Dagda would be better explaining what we changed," Goibniu stated, sweeping the cover from *Lann Dàn*. "These diamond blades, gems that Badb Catha called from a volcano at the south end of the Isle of Ice and Fire, make up the Blades of Destiny."

They blazed a bright blue in the room's reflected light.

"These are now yours. Not Lugh's, but yours. A gift for truly ending the evil spirit of his grandfather, Balor of the Baleful Eye. Not to mention helping Mannanan Mac Llyr remove the God Tethra from the Fomorian pantheon. Lugh was pissy about that for a time, as he could not accomplish the deed himself, but he's over that now."

"My lack of clear memories makes me doubt your words," Breanna said as she gave the smith a tight look. Then she gripped one of the magical long blades, and it hummed to life.

As she snatched her hand back, Goibniu continued. "While *Lann Dàn* were created for a different time and designed to use magic to fight against magic, they can now help you face both magic and physical weapons. In addition to Eoin, they will be a part of your protection as you work with Dagda to defend the Isle of Erin and ensure your Gaels will not be ruled."

As a server brought in the ale and mead, Breanna circled the Blades of Destiny, somehow knowing she had wielded them magically and in battle. While they sang to her, she stated, "There's always a price with a Tuatha gift. What is Lugh's price?"

Goibniu raked a hand through his hair. "You misunderstand, my Hero. Those prices only apply to humans who ask a boon of the Tuatha. As one of them, Lugh only said he would hold and protect your family's long knives. The Tuatha will treasure them as they treasure you for the sacrifice you made for them, your land, and your people."

Breanna gave the smith a narrow and skeptical look, but pulled her long knives from her harness anyway. Then, she laid them on the table and picked up the lighter *Lann Dàn*. They buzzed in her hands as if knowing her, claiming her. They were familiar, yet different.

"Who will teach me about what's new?" she asked. "What did you call these new capabilities? Aspects?"

"Knowing All-Father, it will be me, as I understand the magic Badb Catha tinkered with to make the new aspects work. Yet, they are not that much different than how you used them to battle demons in the *before-time*."

Breanna sighed. "Again, I lack those memories. When?"

"Now," a heavier voice answered. "Daughter."

Breanna turned to find an even more massive man than the smith standing before her, his arms wide, allowing her to decide if she would embrace him. It took a moment before she tried to wrap her arms around his massive frame while holding a Blade of Destiny in each hand. "You came for me."

"Aye, my daughter," Dagda answered. "When you cast the magic of the *Triple Dáns*, there was much upheaval across the pantheons of the various gods we treat with. Many of them were afraid of the magic you could wield. Now that you are my daughter and a goddess, all are even more concerned. They fear what you can become."

Breanna released her father and set her new blades back on the table. She looked to Eoin for support, who gave her a firm nod. "Beyond apparently being a gifted warrior, I wield no magic other than that of the *void*. I'm just, well, me."

Dagda chuckled. "That concerns them most, especially when you are being yourself. There have been few new gods or goddesses in eons. They don't know what you'll be able to do. The Isle of Erin will be a power once more in the world."

"But, Father, I don't know what I can do."

"Och, Daughter, that is the fun of it all. Nor do I. And neither do the gods of other pantheons. So let's surprise them. You have already reclaimed your land and its people as Erin's Hero! I felt that through the mighty black oak that Ulicia attached you to. You did something similar to that in the *before-time*, but now your claim is immortal, as you are mine. Even Danu has been roaming our land as the Silver Huntress, howling your name with her pack, ensuring the land knows your claim."

With wide eyes, she questioned, "Immortal?"

"Let's leave that for later. First, we will discuss how the improved *Lann Dàn* can help you. Goibniu is best suited to show you these new aspects, but I know bringing *balefire* into this realm was the main goal."

"I have memory flashes about that power from the *before-time*."

"Aye, Badb originally crafted the Blades of Destiny to fight the magic of the Fomorians with her *dark matter*. You used that magic to end Balor, Lugh's shadow of a grandfather, once and for all. Magic that helped Mannanan Mac Llyr end Tethra, a Fomorian god. It was your heroic act, by the way, that made it possible. Our Sea God concurs. The way you used his lance and spear was very—creative."

"Wait!" Breanna demanded. "If I changed the timeline and removed my birth father and his Norvegr followers, would not all of my actions in the *before-time* be wiped away? Tethra and Balor could be alive once more!"

"No, the magic of the *Triple Dàns* does not work that way. Only your Heart can cast your vision of a new time. Your fury over the acts of violence those dark gods made against you and yours ensured that their part in that time did not change. Those two won't be back.

"Back to the Blades. Badb and Goibniu tried to create shields that react to earthly weapons and projectiles, but they cancel out casting *balefire*, so we'll have to see if they can work around that issue. If the shields react to a threat, the *balefire* will be nulled for a time."

Eoin interjected, "Keegan, we will need a private meal tonight. Save for Faolán and Falyn, it will be just us."

With that, as the Seneschal exited, Faolán and Falyn entered the room. Breanna noted their surprise at the two giant men. The Chieftess questioned, "Goibbi, as always, a pleasure to see you at our dun. That said, I know Gus has not ordered any new weapons."

"Aye, my lady, I'm here to deliver something to Erin's Hero."

"New long blades," Breanna said.

Falyn commented, "Magical ones from the looks of them."

Faolán asked, "And who are you?"

All-Father shrugged. "Chief Druid of Erin?"

Falyn scowled. "And is there a name we can call you?"

"Breanna's father?"

Croí Dàn injected, *"Dagda, please, stop with the teasing!"*

"Yes, Father, stop. They can accept that All-Father is standing before them, as they have done nothing but support me, both now and then."

All-Father sighed again. "Please, call me Dagda."

"That's my father. I insisted he drop the façade, as you've been like an aunt and uncle to me," Breanna added. She couldn't help grinning over the two leaders' raised eyebrows.

"As in *the* All-Father?" Faolán questioned.

Breanna shrugged.

Falyn asked wryly, "And I suppose that means you, Goibbi, are Goibniu, the God of Smithing?"

With a duck of his head, the big smith said, "Aye, ma'am."

The door opened again at that moment, and Keegan led a series of servants carrying platters of food into the room. As they placed them on the sideboard cabinets, Goibniu said brightly, "Oh, it's time for supper! And, of course, ale!"

Bláth, Falyn, and Breanna said in unison, "Mead!"

It was time for Keegan to sigh. "Of course, my Ladies. There is mead. After seeing how Bhruic landed on the pointy end of Breanna's jest, I can assure you I would never forget whatever dressing down she envisioned for me had I forgotten."

"Oh, Keegan, I wouldn't make it that bad."

"Och, I'd rather not take the chance, if you don't mind."

Eoin chided, "Hmm, I'll side with the Seneschal on this one and say it's best to keep her happy."

Breanna elbowed him in the ribs.

As Eoin let out an oof of breath, Dagda chuckled and sat on the most oversized stool in the room. When it groaned under his weight, he waved a hand to magically strengthen it, stating as he tore apart a massive haunch of boar, "I hope you had fun with your jest."

Eoin grumbled as Breanna answered, "I did, Father."

The meal with the gods wasn't what any of them expected, especially with two very tall—as in just over eight feet for Dagda and seven for Goibniu—heavily muscled men consuming massive amounts of roasted boar, so much so that Keegan had to request additional platters.

Faolán and Falyn ate quietly, watching the two gods as if unsure how to engage them. The ice finally broke when Dagda sighed. "That was mighty fine. I thank you for your hospitality."

"As do I," concurred Goibniu. "A feast fit for—royalty. Such hospitality does us honor."

Falyn, elegant as always, added, "Of course, we honor esteemed guests such as yourselves. While not our royalty, you are *Tuatha Dé Danann* royalty. It will be the talk of the country, especially since our gods have withdrawn from us for many cycles."

"Och, my Lady," Dagda answered solemnly. "We have. Perhaps too much. No, not maybe—we *did* withdraw. However, we now have a reason to renew and strengthen our ties to your land and people. We saw what can happen when we grow too distant from your realm. As Taoiseach, your knowledge of our history, people, and land means you must have a deep understanding of this.

"And I believe you now know Breanna paid a price and made the ultimate sacrifice for your people and ours. She is the bridge between the Gaels and the Tuatha now. As she learns what it means to be Erin's Hero and our Goddess of Time, I ask you both to look after and care for my daughter as you do with your children."

Falyn nodded sagely. "Of course, All-Father. She has already earned that place in our family."

With that, something caught Dagda's attention, and then he appeared to nod inwardly. He rose and bowed toward Breanna. "I am sorry, Daughter, I have to go. The Olympians and their Roman counterparts are in uproar over your ascension, as are the Sumerians and Persians. And, of course, there's the Asgardians, who your former father followed, and they're a miserable bunch when someone gives them a black eye, as you did.

"Anyway, Danu and I must attend to this, probably with Badb Catha and Lugh. These other pantheons don't have anyone destined to do what you'll soon be able to accomplish—you are a threat to them. Yet the other surviving Gaelic and Celtic gods will support us. In the meantime, Goibniu will help you learn how to use *Lann Dàn's* new capabilities. And I think you have a task in Tara that you already know of."

"Father, wait!" Breanna exclaimed. "Goddess of Time?"

"Aye, Daughter, but I have no time to explain. I apologize. That was a poor choice of words. I will see you as soon as I can. Yet I can do one thing before I leave," he added, moving to face her. He placed a finger on her forehead. "Remember all of you. Know that you are one with your land. When you touch it, reach out to it, and your land will respond. Come morning, it should become clear."

With that, he was gone. Goibniu swore. "If that's not shite timing, nothing is."

Breanna glared at the smith, but Eoin stepped to her side, saying, "Hush, my love. He said you'll have some clarity with the sunrise. While there's much to understand about this evening, we know that your band will soon be essential to support you."

Though she wanted to rage at her father, Breanna took a deep breath. Her gods were infuriating, and she was now supposedly one of them!

Goibniu handed her *Lann Dàn.* "Tomorrow, we will explore the new aspects of your blades."

Breanna asked again, "Goddess of Time?"

The big smith shrugged. "Sleep well, Breanna. I think you'll have a clearer picture in the morning. I'll see what I can do to fill in the blanks so you can better understand how Erin's *Cycle of Time* works and what you set in motion by wielding the *Triple Dàns.*"

That evening, after their bath, Breanna lay in Eoin's arms in their royal hut. She asked, "Did any of that *Cycle of Time* or Goddess of Time exchange make sense to you?"

"Sorry, my love, not really," Eoin answered. "Other than the *void*, the *sight* and the *Cycle of Time* are related, and you can touch them with your mind."

Croí Dàn said to both of them, *"Sorry to impose. They are indeed related. The void you both use is a few moments ahead of real time, and the sight shows possible future and past timelines. Yet the Cycle of Time is governed by Lia Dàn, the Stone of Destiny. As your father mentioned, you used the combined magics of the Triple Dàns to alter your original father's timeline and make it so that he had never arrived here."*

"What about me being their Goddess of Time that Dagda mentioned?" Breanna asked.

"That's where it gets complicated. No one has ever used the magic of the Triple Dàns, only individually. You and I are now intricately woven together, as are others who joined your cause in the before-time.

"Because you ate All-Father's apple and wielded the three magics woven together by Badb, it linked you deeply to the Triple Dàns, which means you no longer need to touch Lia Dàn physically to access the Cycle of Time as all Tuatha Gods do, save for Danu and me."

"And that means?" Breanna demanded.

Croí Dàn answered brightly, *"You and anyone touching you at that moment can travel forward or backward through time to any place where a Gaelic or Celtic God has been before, and they have visited everywhere that people worship other gods. It follows that few places on Earth are out of your reach."*

Breanna shivered. *"Mo Chroí, that is—truly frightening! Why would I need to do such a thing?"*

"You must change time itself so the Gaels can ensure they rule their destiny. The Romans have already enabled their successors across the sea to crush your Gaels. Only you can change the future by changing the past."

She railed, "That is a hefty weight you just laid on me!"

"I know, cousin. I couldn't tell you before, seeing you as shattered as you were. I had to protect you! When you used the magic of the Triple Dàns, we unknowingly unleashed a Goddess of Time. It is why your father and my mother are working to appease the gods of other pantheons, assuring them that they will somehow restrain you."

Unable to contain herself, Breanna erupted, "So I don't become corrupted? Become dark? Be a tyrant?"

Eoin interjected, "Bre, stop! I believe in you. We will bear this burden together, and that will not happen."

"They can take it back," she demanded. "I don't want this power to change time!"

Cróí Dàn whispered, *"It can't be undone."*

Breanna sighed heavily. "What if I get it wrong and mistakenly alter something in the past that changes our future badly? Gods, what have they done to me? This burden is too much!"

"Aye, my love, you're right. It is a hefty weight. We will need much wisdom to manage this responsibility together. "

"I should never have eaten that damned apple!"

"Aye, likely, but done is done."

"By the stars, what other surprises are in store for us?"

"We are in this together," he insisted.

"Hmm, we are," was all Breanna could say as she snuggled her head into Eoin's shoulder, thinking his arms felt right wrapped around her, and quickly fell asleep despite her troubled mind.

Apprentices

⊶⚜ Breanna ⚜⊷

Breanna bolted upright in their bed as the sun rose to brighten their hut, a strangled sob escaping her lips. "I remember it all. By the stars, this flood of memories is intense! Losing Toal crushed me, yet I bore it with the weight of my *geas* and this strange new destiny I found upon me. Then we lost Fergal. When I lost you, I thought I could not go on without your love to support me! Yet, no matter the cost, I had to stop my father and end his possible rule of our Emerald Isle!"

She shuddered out a breath. "And so I cast the *Triple Dàns*. I did not know that it would lead me here, to this point, this burden! Gods, Eoin, what have they done to me?"

He lifted her chin, making her look at him. "You did what you had to do, as you've always done. Since we first raised wooden blades against each other when you were five and I was seven. It is what you've done your entire life, fighting against your father, even when you did not know it. Now fighting for your Gaels."

As tears fell, she murmured, "So much lost. How can I stand against the tide of time? I don't even know what that means."

Eoin held her gaze. "Don't be what others expect. While our gods have led us here, you feel your land deeply inside you. Let's fight for that, for our Gaels. Be you, my love. The one whose heart I know better than my own."

Breanna clutched Eoin tightly. "Can you still love this monster I've become?"

"Not a monster, Bre, never that. We can work together. All-Father said you'd remember your life from the *before-time* when you woke up, and that happened. Look at me. Share what you can."

A shudder ran through her. "Okay. When Toal died, I battled Balor's demon form and killed him—the rage I felt was like a storm. Then, I helped Manannán Mac Lir make Tethra no more. Yet, by then, I was little more than an empty vessel as I carried Toal's body onto the deck of Wavesweeper. And we went to Falias. And—"

"Hush," Eoin whispered, pulling her into his arms and running his hands through her hair. "Let it all settle into you. Based on your words, there's too much to take in all at once."

"Aye," she confirmed and held him close. Then she shivered over her memories of the Dreadlord. "My original father was a terrible man! He and his Norvegr warriors killed our fathers, and he raped my mother. How she kept it to herself, I'll never know! He did the same to Bradaigh's and Braoin's kin. There are likely many more. They were brutal savages."

"Well, you have a great father now. Just allow it to sink in."

They were quiet for a time when *Ćroí Dàn* interrupted, *"I can show you how your father restored your memories so you can help Eoin."*

"*Really?*" Breanna said a little more brightly. "*Well, please do so.*"

A moment later, Breanna exclaimed, "Och, it was through touching the *Cycle of Time*. I hadn't thought of that!"

"*Yes, reach for the sight while focusing on Lia Dàn. Then find Eoin's final moments, pull his memories through your mind, and pass them through your touch.*"

Breanna did as her Heart instructed and touched his forehead with a finger, commanding, "Remember all of you."

"Was that it?" Eoin questioned.

The Heart of Destiny informed him, "*Like my Hero, you need to sleep for those memories to emerge.*"

Eoin leaned in and kissed Breanna's forehead. "Are you ready for the day? We have much to do."

"Aye, my Protector," she answered. "We should. Yet I also now remember us and the love we shared, especially our first time in Falias. When you have your memories of us back, I'll expect more than a kiss on my forehead."

Eoin grinned and then kissed her lips softly. "That will have to do in the meantime."

On their way to the main hall, they encountered Bláth. With her memories of the *before-time* restored, Breanna knew why she liked the woman. She asked, "Will you join us for breakfast? Goibniu is alone, and he is expecting us, as we have a few things to learn from him. And I have a gift for you."

A surprised Bláth croaked, "Really?"

Given her usually melodious voice, Breanna raised an eyebrow at her discomfiture. Eoin added, "You were once part of Breanna's Band. We need you back."

The pair led her to where Goibniu sat. He was inhaling massive quantities of food as he had the evening before. When Breanna and Eoin sat without an invitation, he raised his mug of tea. "Morning, my Hero! And my Prince, and the pleasant Master Bard."

"Good morning, Goibniu," Breanna answered. "What do you have planned for us today?"

"Well, my Hero," the big smith answered. "The Sun God believes your Prince here needs a weapon upgrade to be Erin's *Cosantóir*. Lugh commanded I loan Eoin *Claimh Solais*—what Nuada called the Sword of Light."

Breanna sucked in a breath of astonishment. "I remember watching Lugh wield that weapon against the Fomorian demons! It was when I used *Maorgairme* to summon help, and we first battled Tethra's demons and his grandfather, Balor, on the banks of Loch Aillionn. He taught me how to use the *balefire* within my blades! By the stars, that was an awful battle, but a mighty sword it is!"

With eyebrows raised, Eoin sighed doubtfully. "It's hard to believe Lugh would just loan me *Claimh Solais*. It's a blade for gods."

Goibniu smiled. "Aye, as my Hero has just recalled, it is a mighty weapon, lost for a time but recently reappeared when Lugh needed it to battle as Breanna's *Cosantóir* in the *before-time*. Maybe it was waiting for both of you. Fitting blade for Erin's Protector."

"Are its legends true?" Breanna asked.

"Aye," Goibniu said. "Opposing warriors cannot resist a command you deliver while holding *Claimh Solais*, as it can fill minds with indecision. It will also cut through any opposing weapon or armor, magical or otherwise."

Eoin suggested, "We should test its powers with the *fians*."

"Aye, you should," the smith offered with a grin. "Now it's time to focus on the *Lann Dàn*. While Breanna is a goddess, she can die in the mortal world. Just as Lugh slew Balor, Breanna used the power of *Lann Dàn* to finish off his demon soul.

"At this time, the concern is about launched weapons. There will be even greater projectile weapons in the future than Rome's ballistae. We took a broad approach because she will walk Erin's *Cycle of Time* in both the past and the future. Going into any potential battle, *Lann Dàn* should always be ready to lay her hands on them.

"One thing you do not know, my Hero," Goibniu added. "When you wielded the magic of the *Triple Dàns*, Danu included a veil over the Isle of Erin to prevent future invasions. If you die, Erin's Veil will collapse. Thus, our interest is in preserving you, my goddess."

"Hmm." Breanna sighed. "So you all want me protected, but Dagda wants me out there fighting to change the timeline in favor of us Gaels and our gods. Fighting for us."

"Aye, that is our conundrum. To protect and enable you."

"It feels like Danu has put a chain around my neck," she rejoined harshly. "She had no right to shackle me like that. Her veil was not in my vision of Erin when I cast it."

Goibniu ducked his head without argument.

"I need a break from all this talk," Breanna declared. "I need action. Let's eat and then test these new weapons. Keegan!"

Seneschal answered, "Yes, my Hero."

"Let Corbmac know I request his *fians* be ready for a mock battle with Eoin and me in a half span. We have tasks to set our minds to.

"Goibniu, please fetch *Claimh Solais* for Eoin while he and I have breakfast. We have work to do."

Goibniu stiffened at her order, but then he nodded. As she turned away to talk with Bláth, the smith mumbled after her, "Dagda's daughter is much like her father."

With that, Breanna looked over her shoulder and saw the smirk fade from the smith's face. Then she focused back on Bláth. "Now, as for you, my friend, the gift I mentioned is about memories you once had but lost when I wielded the magic of the *Triple Dàns*. I understand you saw some of what happened, yet not all of it. As a Master Bard, I know they would be precious to you."

"Aye, My Hero, they would be. But how?"

As she'd done with Eoin, Breanna seized the *sight* and touched the Bard's forehead with a finger. "Remember all of you."

Eoin added, "Now, we both need to sleep before we know what we have been missing. Only Breanna has all of her memories back."

"Ha, I knew there'd be a catch!" Bláth exclaimed.

Breanna chuckled. "Once you remember, you'll know why I'm not sure whether to call you a Bard of Destiny or a Warrior of Destiny."

After their morning meal, they walked into the yard, and Breanna informed Corbmac, "I have much trust to ask of you and your *fians*. I once more have *Lann Dàn*, and Eoin now wields *Claimh Solais*. We need your warriors to help us test our use of these weapons and hone our skills."

"Us against *Lann Dàn* and *Claimh Solais*?"

Breanna sighed. "Do not worry, Papa. No harm will come to you and yours. We need to learn how to use these weapons. Will you help me, help us?"

Corbmac's protest crumbled, and he sighed. "Of course, my Hero. Your wish is my command."

Breanna stepped closer to the older warrior and hugged him. "Oh, Corbmac, it won't be that bad. Believe in me."

"Aye, I do."

"Thank you," Breanna said with a bright smile. She turned to the *fian* warriors. "As you now know, I am Erin's Hero, and you are all my *cosantóirs*—my protectors. We have magically enhanced weapons that could frighten some, but we must understand those powers to best use them against those who challenge our right for Erin's Gaels to rule their destiny. You are all going to help us. Do you accept my challenge?"

As undoubtedly they all knew the legend of the Heart of Destiny, each warrior thumped their spear on their shield in unison for several heartbeats.

"Thank you, my Warriors of Destiny," she said humbly, bowing.

They spent the next two spans testing how the Sword of Light could command the *fian* warriors. Breanna held back her *balefire*, now available to strike against any opponent, not just magical ones, though she set a few hay bundles on fire as she worked to control her aim from the tips of her Blades of Destiny.

After a while, as the *fian* warriors hurried to put out her fires, Breanna determined she needed to practice in an open, wet field. *Balefire* was a potentially horrific weapon, especially if it could sweep an expansive area. She could cut down hundreds of opposing foes in a moment. It was almost an overwhelming weight of responsibility. Yet, generally, she was pleased, and Eoin concurred.

Chief Faolán approached them, asking, "Breanna, could your blades always do that fire-shooting thing?"

Goibniu answered for her. "No, that's new. Well, sort of. It would only work on Fomorians when they used their magic in ancient times. Now, anyone who stands against Erin's Hero in the human world is at risk of death. I suggested they practice with it."

"That's incredible," Faolán responded, looking at Breanna with a raised eyebrow. "Preferably, you'll be practicing outside my dun, yes?"

"Of course, my Chief."

"Excellent. Now, I have news from Tara. My *Taoiseach* is with Beatha now, working with the Master Fáidh assigned to the High King to ensure Niall's message is clear. Maybe it's time for a break and the midday meal in my private meeting room. Keegan, make it so."

With Erin's *Cosantóir* and the Tuatha God of Smithing, Breanna trailed after Faolán. She said to Goibniu, "You wonder who is in charge?"

Croí Dàn chuckled to her fellow God and Goddess. *"I am!"*

Eoin and Breanna laughed, and Goibniu could only shake his head and mutter, "Only in my world could a heart-shaped ruby magical construct be Danu's daughter and lead a Goddess of Time."

They greeted Falyn and Beatha in the meeting room as servants brought food and drink for the midday meal and placed them on sideboard tables. Faolán commanded, "Eat. Then we talk."

Falyn sighed when Goibniu rose to return to the platters for a third time, so the big man sat back down with a grunt. The Chieftess asked, "What is the word from Dun Tara?"

"New One God followers arrived to seek sanctuary," Beatha said. "The High King's Council is unsure what to do. The King of Connachta suggested a remote island on Loch Corrib might be a good place for their leader and his followers. Or maybe the forbidding Aran Islands off the coast."

"It is dangerous to let this religion spread," Falyn commented.

Breanna proposed, "I can escort him and his entourage through Connachta. And, of course, corrupt his belief in the One God being the only one in the world by providing evidence that our gods exist."

Croí Dàn said confidently, *"They will believe or maybe lose their minds when they experience our reality."*

"Your Heart has the right of it," Beatha confirmed. "I also have a private message for you, Breanna. A young warrior about your age has newly arrived from Galicia. She is asking where to seek out Erin's Hero. Of course, only our gods should be aware of that. How she knows about you is a mystery, as she would have had to set sail weeks ago to be in Tara now."

Cróí Dàn privately said, "*Cousin, word is spreading about a new goddess being born. The Galician and Tuatha Gods are close, along with the Cymru, Pictish, and Albion Gods across the Sea of Erin. People often fail to realize that they are mostly the same. I expect Dadga will align them with us to quell concerns among the various other pantheons.*"

Breanna told the Fáidh, "Convey that I will meet this lass soon at Dun Tara, as we are heading there shortly."

Beatha let the *sight* take her and nodded. "Done."

"What word of High King, Niall Noígíallach? Is he at Dun Tara?" Breanna asked.

With her eye caught in *sight*, the Seeress said, "He felt you claim your land as Erin's Hero, but he chose a path of cowardice and sought the seas, even during the dangerous Samhain season."

Breanna put her hand on Beatha's shoulder. "Share your vision with me."

Following her into the *sight*, she watched a possible future play out, where Énnae's son, Eochaid, would avenge his clan and ensure the *Ard Rí* would not return alive from his voyage. Breanna lifted her hand and growled, "That's some ugly blood between them."

"Aye, Eochaid trails Niall on his voyage and will likely attack when he lands where the River Lorie empties into the great sea on the mainland. Change is coming for the land of Erin."

Eoin suggested, "If he succeeds, Eochaid will contest for High King, as Énnae is too old. We need to know whose side he is on."

Beatha let the *sight* take her once more. "Énnae will challenge you, Breanna, on behalf of his son."

"I welcome that challenge," Breanna stated flatly, "as the time of High Kings and Provincial Kings will soon come to a close in our land. Patriarchs have too long supplanted matriarchs. We must create a great council and let the people have a say in their lives."

"And if the kings oppose you?" Falyn made a cautious query.

She turned her eyes to her adopted aunt, answering firmly, "I have no choice. They support me, or they are against me. Anyone who stands against Erin's Hero will have the opportunity to challenge me to personal combat. Eoin will be my Champion. That is the way we decide such things in Erin at this time. I hope we can eventually change such barbaric practices."

The Chieftess raised an eyebrow but did not answer, and Breanna turned her gaze to Faolán. "Are we clear on this?"

The Dun Chief answered, "I think it's deadly clear."

"Good." Breanna offered the word as a command. Then, to ensure her adopted aunt and uncle understood she was not seeking conflict or power, she added cautiously, "Yet if I am to go back in time and change how the Celts of Pretannia respond to Rome's invasion, that will likely impact Erin in ways unknown, including which clans rule there and here. I hope to reestablish the Great Council concept in both lands so that kings do not rule their people."

Falyn looked surprised. "I had not thought through how the ripples in time could wash out from your efforts across the Sea of Erin and the impact they could have on our land."

Eoin added, "Well, at least we have some confirmation that Erin's leadership is uncertain before we start mucking with time. We will always have to check in with our *home* time to see what we've wrought and make adjustments, but we need some leaders here in Erin working toward the Great Council goal."

Breanna sighed. "It's a heavy weight on us all. But there's nothing to be done about it today. I need time to be a warrior and work off some energy. Eoin, let's practice outside the dun."

A short time later, Breanna, Eoin, and Goibniu walked through the gates of Dun Uisneach to perform what she thought of as open-field tests using the new Tuatha magic to see what it could inflict.

As they approached the High King's Road, the smith said, "Before you try using *balefire* across a distance, Badb Catha got the notion for a new capability from the meeting with the Asgardians, in which Thor could call his Warhammer, Mjolnir, from anywhere. Lay your blades on the ground over there and walk back beside me."

Breanna drew *Lann Dán* from their harness, and Eoin freed the Sword of Light. Then they did as ordered by the smith, though she jammed her blades into the turf.

As they returned to his side, Goibniu said, "Seize the *void* and call your weapons, but remember to hold out your hand or hands to catch them."

With her hands stretched before her, she seized the *void* and used her mind. *"Lann Dàn, to me!"*

The Blades of Destiny slapped into her hands as Eoin did the same with *Claimh Solais*. "I'm glad the sword knows it has a pointy end!" he commented.

Goibniu chuckled. "Indeed. Now try *balefire*."

Calling on the strange power, Breanna envisioned the crackling fire sweeping across the green mounds on the far side of the road as she remembered doing to Balor's demons with Lugh. The tips of each diamond blade exploded with a tight, lightning-like flare, churning up the moss-covered earth. The scorched and ragged line stretched for fifty yards to each side.

Eoin breathed. "By the stars, that's terrifying."

Goibniu added, "You have impressive control already, my niece. It must come from your using *balefire* in the *before-time*."

Breanna nodded in agreement, as the strange lightning did seem familiar. *"Balefire* seems quite powerful. Where does *Lann Dàn* draw the energy from? It certainly isn't a drain on me."

"It comes from *dark matter* in the *void*," he replied.

"Dark matter?" Eoin questioned.

Goibniu shrugged. "The Dark Goddess is one of the few who understands it and can harness such energy. Brigid might be another, as she possesses a deep understanding of the connection between the realms of Erin and Tuatha. Yet, back to Badb Catha. She had to alter her original construct so that *dark matter* would impact the physical world in this realm, not just the magical one."

"I don't remember the shields," Breanna stated. "I recall Tethra's demons wounding me when I fought them with Lugh at my side."

The smith nodded. "The Mórrigan saw this in your battles from that time and constructed the shields that used *dark matter*. Neither power will drain you, but you can only use one or the other at a time. There's a cycle time between. If the shields activate, you can't use *balefire*."

"What about *Claimh Solais*?" Eoin asked. "Can you shed any light on its powers?"

"As with *Lann Dàn*, Badb Catha created the Sword Light for Lugh to fight the Fomorians, so it had offensive capabilities similar to the blades from that time. The Dark Goddess made the same changes to your weapon, *balefire*, and shields. Draw the blade, seize the *void*, point your tip toward the mound Breanna just struck, and command that *balefire* flow."

Eoin did as instructed. Breanna was surprised when a lightning bolt like hers streaked across the road, churning up the ground as she had while he swept the sword from left to right.

Goibniu clapped his back lightly. "I think you've got it! Yet, there's a cycle time of some moments between *balefire* and shields. "

As the pair shared a smile and turned back toward the dun, Bradaigh rode up to them, slipped off his mount, and exclaimed, "Eoin, Breanna! What in the name of the stars was that?"

Her former half-brother pointed at the scorched and churned-up mossy mound as Breanna slipped her blades back on her shoulders.

Eoin answered, "A gift from Badb Catha, I think, Bradaigh."

As Eoin sheathed the Sword of Light, she said, "Exactly! It's called *balefire*. And we must talk, as I'm rebuilding Breanna's Band. I remember when you joined us in the *before-time*. We fought together in a desperate cause, which you swore yourself to. I need you again. Come, let's retire to our Chief's private meeting room."

"You mean in Chief Faolán's meeting room?"

"Aye," Breanna confirmed with a wink. "I've adopted him as my uncle and Falyn as my aunt. It's mutual, as my new father is often busy and lacks a home in Erin."

Bradaigh looked to Eoin, who shrugged and said, "It's complicated. By the way, this is the Master Smith, Goibbi."

The smith towered over the big, redheaded Gael as they exchanged a warrior clasp. Then they passed through Dun Uisneach's gates, with Bradaigh leading his old horse. A stable boy rushed out to take the reins from him as the Seneschal emerged from the main hall.

Breanna waved him over. "Is the meeting room available, Keegan?"

"Aye, my Hero. Do you need a private dinner as well?"

"I think not," she answered. "Just ale and mead for now."

Keegan left them in the private meeting room with a bow so he could see to their drinks. Bradaigh seemed astonished. "My Hero? Does he mean Erin's Hero?"

Breanna pulled the Heart of Destiny from her tunic. "Aye, that one. It's just a part of the tale. Let's wait for the drink, as that might help us through the telling of it."

Goibbi excused himself, cryptically saying he had to report to his Chief. Breanna knew that meant Dagda. Then the Seneschal returned with a server, as Breanna shrugged her harness off. She asked, "Keegan, please ensure you stow these safely."

"Aye, my man, same with this blade," Eoin added.

After Keegan deposited their Tuatha-enhanced weapons in Faolán's office, which was opposite to the door to the door that led to the hall, they had drinks to raise and toast to their reunion. Breanna summarized what she had learned and remembered, including that Bradaigh had once been her half-brother. She finished with, "I will close by asking if you'll join me, join Breanna's Band once more, my one-time brother?"

Bradaigh took a deep pull from his mug of ale. "So we didn't contest for the *Comórtas* Champion last summer?"

Breanna laughed. "Aye, we did, and in this timeline, I beat you. I guess that's the duel that counts now."

Her half-brother from their previous timeline looked at her momentarily before saying, "Och, I see the truth in your eyes, my sister, and grit. I'll join you, aye, I will!"

Breanna rose as *Croí Dàn* said, "*Kneel before Erin's Hero and Goddess and swear to the following: My Hero, I pledge my blood and bones to you and promise to accept your orders and protect you no matter the danger to my own life. If I fail to fulfill this oath, may my heart cease to beat.*"

He seemed nonplussed by the Heart of Destiny speaking into his mind as he took Breanna's hand. He knelt and repeated the oath.

"Rise as one of Breanna's Band, Bradaigh, and know I will treat your blood, bones, and mind with care and honor. You are now one of us, with the title of *Laoch Dàn!* Welcome as a Warrior of Destiny. Tomorrow, I'll teach you how I seize the *void* using my way. In the meantime, remember all of you."

As Breanna removed her finger from his forehead, Eoin informed the big lad, "Sleep on that. It will make more sense in the morning. Now, let's eat. I'm starving."

They left the meeting room behind and entered the main hall, only to find the serving staff scurrying about as they prepared the evening meal. When Breanna seized a seat with the *fian* warriors, they all rose and began thumping their dirks in time on the tables as they had the night before.

This night, she would not sit at the high table; she would rather spend it with the men and women fighting at her side for Erin. For this, she greeted them, ate with them, and danced among them as Bláth led her fellow Bards to spin songs about Erin's various heroes.

Breanna and Eoin put on a show for all with a dance where their minds were in the same *void* space. She could see how Eoin wanted to lead her, including during their final move when he flung her high in a triple pirouette, making her look like a spinning knife, only to land in his arms with perfect timing so he could grace her with a passionate kiss.

After a spectacular dance with Eoin, Breanna found herself in Corbmac's arms. She sighed. "I remember you were the first to trust me. Sometimes, I can barely remember the *before-time*; other times, it is obvious. I now think of Faolán and Falyn as my uncle and aunt, and I want to think of you as my grandfather. Not too different."

A tear rolled down Corbmac's cheek. "I am honored, my Hero. Yet I do not fully remember it."

Breanna smiled and touched his forehead with a finger. "Remember all of you."

Eoin said, "You'll understand in the morning, our papa."

"So it is I who honors you, papa. Let's dance!" Breanna offered.

And with that, the pair claimed the dance floor, and Corbmac spun Breanna about as if he were thirty cycles younger. Though he was not as showy or physical as Eoin, he danced proudly with his granddaughter.

When the song ended, Corbmac hugged Breanna and whispered, "I welcome you as my granddaughter and know I trust you with my life."

"As I trust you with mine. We have a long walk through time before us, but we will make it count."

Eoin moved to Breanna's side. "I'd also like to adopt you as my grandfather if only to ensure you look after my Hero all that much more closely."

"Yet you're her Protector, Erin's *Cosantóir*."

"Aye, who better to help me guard her than our papa?"

Croí Dàn chimed in with, *"My heroes, well played."*

Breanna countered stiffly, saying, *"It was not a play."*

"Och, you misunderstand!" her Heart rejoined stridently. *"We need supporters, and you're recruiting them skillfully and from your heart, with whom I can easily bond as I am your Heart. Yet, that is not why I interrupted your train of thought. Since you'll be required at Tara soon, I subtly summoned Braoin so you don't need to seek him out at his settlement near Loch Síleann."*

Breanna sighed. *"Sorry, cousin. It has been a trying day."*

"Aye, it has, yet Braoin will be here by tomorrow evening. You can leave for Dun Tara the day after. There are other fian warriors we need to recruit along the way, and some of them are at Dun Eadan, as we cannot take all of the fians stationed at Dun Uisneach to Tara. I'll wager Chief Conn will have a fit when you commandeer one of his!"

"That may be, but now I need to restore these fian members' memories of the before-time."

Later, as Eoin and Breanna lay in each other's arms, she whispered, "Eoin, do you find *balefire* as frightening as I do? We could kill hundreds in a few moments. Most wouldn't know what they were facing if we struck without warning."

Eoin sighed. "Yes, it is an incredible power to wield."

"I remember cutting down Tethra's demons in the *before-time*, but they were not people," she said. "We must give quarter where possible. Yet, we must give none to those who threaten us."

"Romans will not hesitate to kill you because you're human. Warriors with hubris about their skills often perish, while their leaders typically escape such folly. *Balefire* will ensure that doesn't happen. It will cause those leaders to bend their will, and we must ignite support among the free Gaelic and Celtic people. That said, I agree, we must act judiciously."

"What if there's no alternative? What if we have no choice?"

Eoin kissed Breanna's forehead. "That may come to pass where we have no choice. People will die. Yet they'll die anyway if we do nothing. It may be that we need to use time, in either direction, to take our Warriors of Destiny to where they and we need to be to change time in a way that will limit deaths."

"Yes, but I'll need physical contact for something like that."

"Aye, you will, my love," Eoin confirmed. "I'm sure our smith can help with that. As to the non-magical issues like creating a Council of Erin or changing the practice of hostage-taking and how long Chiefs hold them, we will need plans to implement those ideas."

Breanna stated, "Our Lawgivers will need to change their decrees on the latter. The Chiefs won't listen to me. I'm just a warrior, but they will heed our Breitheamh Druids."

"My love, who are you?"

"Uh, Breanna Ban Morna, Erin's Hero and the Goddess of Time?" she asked doubtfully.

"Hmm, for your desire, you are forgetting the most valuable aspect of who you are to see your wishes become your actions."

Breanna screwed up her eyebrows in frustration.

"Hush, my love. As Dadga's daughter, the Chief Druid of Erin, you're his apprentice. You used his name on Goibniu, and he is a Tuatha god who folded like a leaf in the wind when you asked if he wanted you to involve him in the discussion."

Breanna smiled and kissed him fiercely. "That's superb!"

The next morning, Breanna heard Eoin groan before he said in a hushed voice, "By the stars, the fight with Tethra and his demons pitted against you and our Sea God was heroic—and I felt Toal's crushing loss inside you. The battle with your father and his Norvegrs warriors was so brutal that it makes me shudder now that I've relived it. I failed you. I should never have let him defeat me. I was better, but I underestimated his skill with the *void*. While I lay dying on the ground, I heard his last words and somehow felt you break. It crushed me completely. I failed you!"

Breanna ran her fingers over his tight brow, seeing his eyes glisten. "My love, that's behind us. What we did is now written on the *Cycle of Time*. We cannot escape it. Just embrace the fact that you and I can be together now. We can reflect on the insanity of the *before-time* later, but I need you here and now."

"Aye, my love, I never knew how much those two words meant. Not until now, as I witnessed your loss, of Toal, and me."

"I know that deeply," she cooed, "Tonight, we bond as one. But now we have new Warriors of Destiny to see to."

Breanna and Eoin greeted Corbmac, Bradaigh, and Bláth for breakfast. Each confirmed they had memories of the *before-time* and confirmed the experience was indeed unsettling.

The Bard was the most shaken. "With my bloody knife in my hand, I saw the moment you called on the *Triple Dàns*."

Breanna offered, "I know, my Warrior Druid. You were brave."

"As were you, to call on magic that nearly destroyed you."

Bradaigh added, "All we could do was watch your courage."

"And not know what happened," Corbmac agreed solemnly, "as that was where everything ended, and I was recast. Without you."

Breanna and Eoin looked at each other, not knowing what to say.

Afterward, the five of them headed to the yard, where their *fian* warriors practiced Breanna's approach to the *void*.

Next, the pair met with the Dun Uisneach leaders in their private meeting room to discuss borrowing a *fian* for the trip to Dun Tara, another from the River Bronsa settlement, with a stop along the way, and to collect another from Dun Eadan.

Falyn chortled. "Chief Conn will swallow his tongue!"

Faolán agreed. "That means you must be there to see it, my *Taoiseach*. And you do have the High King's ear. Well, the High Queen's, as he is abroad once more."

"Aye, he is soft on me, if only because I support his Ulaidian mate and queen. She is more intelligent than most of those at his court. And, Eoin, she'll love hearing about your Ulaidian ancestors' lineage."

Breanna asked in surprise, "You'd do us the honor of traveling to Tara together?"

"Aye, of course!" Falyn exclaimed. "I can make your reception with their Court go more smoothly. On our return, you can drop me off here as you escort the One God followers to the west of our Isle."

"That's brilliant, my love," Faolán said as he put his arm around his mate's waist and pulled her close.

Falyn added, "I could not be apart from my children longer."

"If you're coming with us, then you need to know about the *before-time*," Breanna added. It was becoming second nature as she seized the *sight* and the *Cycle of Time* and touched each of their foreheads with a finger, commanding, "Remember all of you."

Her words seemed to startle the pair, but Eoin interjected, "You'll need to wait until morning for that to make sense."

Dáithí, their eldest son, asked, "Mother, may I join you?"

"Aye, it'll be good for you to see your cousins again," Falyn agreed. "It will also be good practice for your riding skills."

"Maybe you can convince Eoin to help you with your sword skill training," Faolán added.

Breanna saw Dáithí turn hopeful eyes to Eoin, who said, "Aye, lad, I can do that, but you'll need to learn how to seize the *void* first!"

Dáithí whooped and ran from the room to fetch his sword. His brother, Oisín, complained, "Why can't I go?"

Teagan, their youngest daughter, demanded, "Me too!"

Faolán answered firmly, "When you're ten, Oisín, you can go on such an adventure."

Teagan demanded, "What about me?"

"It will be the same, young lady," her mother informed.

"That's not fair!" Teagan cried and stomped her little foot. "If Dáithí gets to be taught sword skills from Eoin, I want to learn how to wield the long blades. Will you teach me, Bre?"

Breanna looked to Falyn, who could only shrug, so she smiled. "Aye, but you'll need your father to ask Kyle to make a pair of wooden blades for your size. I'll show you some forms to practice while I am away. Eoin and I battled with such at five and seven."

As Teagan squealed in joy and wrapped her little arms around one of Bre's legs, Eoin turned to address the dun leaders. "If you'll excuse us, we need a word with Tadg."

Leaving the co-leader's meeting room, Breanna could hear Oisín complain, "But what about me?"

Eoin whispered, "See, I told you what they have is special. We could have something like they do one day."

"Aye, you did, and we can as long as you're my *Taoiseach*."

That made Eoin smile as *Croí Dàn* added, "*Leannáin, Cosantóir, Taoiseach!*"

Breanna pulled the Heart of Destiny from beneath her tunic. "Since we are waiting on Braion, let's do as you said. Keegan! I must discuss changing a law; only your Master Breitheamh can address the issue. Would you find him for us?"

"Aye, my Hero! It would be my pleasure."

A moment later, with Keegan at his arm, an older, portly man approached them. "I am Tadg. I understand you have a question about our laws."

"Aye, Master Breitheamh, I do," Breanna answered. "It is regarding the length of time any Chief of this land can retain a hostage once taken in battle or traded for another. It seems each Chief interprets this period liberally. Would you concur?"

Tadg assessed Breanna, looking her over, and then his eyes widened as he saw the Heart of Destiny hanging around her neck. "Are you asking as Erin's Hero?"

She smiled coyly. "I am. The one and only."

"Hmm," he mused. "Usually, warriors do not concern themselves with the law."

"Really?" Breanna questioned. "What if All-Father was concerned about this disparity?"

"He has left that issue to his Breitheamh Council."

"He may have, but I'm not happy with the council's handling of the matter," Breanna countered with narrowed eyes.

"Erin's Hero should work within her Laoch Druid Council."

"And if I'm not asking as Erin's Hero?" she queried.

"In what role would you be asking?"

"All-Father's new apprentice, of course," she said brightly.

"His what?"

"I am Dagda's daughter and, thus, obviously, his new Chief Druid's Apprentice. I'm also known as the Goddess of Time, which is irrelevant in this discussion," she added. "Now, I could bring this up with my father, as I'm sure he will be as concerned as I am that the Breitheamh Council has not addressed the issue. Do you think I should bring it up with him?"

Tadg looked at Keegan, who bent over in a full belly laugh. The Seneschal finally straightened, still chuckling. "Sorry, that was masterful. Tadg, I've seen Breanna put various people in a corner, but this was just perfect!"

"She's serious?" Tadg asked doubtfully.

Keegan nodded. "I'd say deadly. Just say you'll address the matter."

Tadg turned back to a smiling Breanna. "Of course, my Hero, er, uh, Chief Druid's Apprentice."

"Thank you, Tadg," she acknowledged. "Your *Taoiseach* and I will soon travel to Dun Tara to discuss urgent matters with the High King and Queen, but I'll return by the next full moon. I'll expect an update on this matter by then."

"You will have it."

Breanna turned to Keegan as the Lawgiver left. "As I need your continued support, I want to give you something. First, I'd like something from you."

"Of course, my Hero. What can I do for you?"

"Please, call Bre or Breanna, at least when we are alone."

He nodded, which made her smile. Like with others, Breanna did what was becoming her otherworld nature, seized the *sight* and the *Cycle of Time*, and then touched the Seneschal's forehead with a finger. "Remember all of you. That's a bit of magic my Heart showed me so that you can remember the *before-time*— you'll recall them come morning."

"Thank you, my—Bre," Keegan said. "I think."

Later, she and Eoin greeted Braoin, who had arrived from Loch Síleann riding a black stallion fit for a prince. To Breanna, he appeared more thoughtful than she remembered, and the sharper angles of his face were softer. It was as if he was more at ease with his life while still wearing justice in his blue eyes. Seeing his sandy hair reminded her that they no longer carried their father's Norvegr blood in their veins, yet he still wielded two medium sword blades. How Danu wove her magic through the *Cycle of Time* to filter various aspects of what made them unique was beyond Breanna's ken.

Still, his lighter frame looked like a taut spring, though he was not as muscled as Bradaigh. That would likely make him faster in a blade dance. Breanna couldn't wait to find out as she greeted him in the yard. "By the stars, you're looking good! That's one fine mount!"

"Aye, he is," Braoin answered, slipping from his horse's back. "Our Horsemaster, Epona, insisted I take him when I told her the summons was from a strange Tuatha Goddess's voice in my head."

"Very wise of her, as I have news about that voice."

After calling a groom to take his mount, she escorted her one-time half-brother to the private meeting room as she called for ale and mead. On the way, she noticed he also had Lugh's sigils on his forearms; they seemed more like Toal's than Bradaigh's or Fergal's and likely reflected Air and maybe Fire. When she saw her father again, she'd have to ask how the sigils were chosen for each of them.

Once she informed Braoin about the *before-time* and their connection, Breanna introduced him to *Croí Dàn*. She then went through the same rituals with him as they had undertaken with Bradaigh, restoring his memories and having him swear to the oath. She was pleased to have him and Bradaigh sworn with the *Laoch Dàn* title!

Only then did she feel close to tying up the loose ends of her past and could get on with her new life.

The following morning, after a hearty breakfast, Breanna and Eoin emerged from the main hall with Braoin and Bradaigh in tow to find Goibniu packing his wagon. She demanded, "Where are you going, Uncle?"

"My Hero," Goibniu stuttered. "I need to get back to Falias."

Breanna blew air to push a white-red lock from her face. "Why?"

"Just thought I could move on."

"Did you just tell your niece and Dadga's daughter, who assigned you to support her in every way, that you want to move on?"

"Well, no, but I was—"

"Not thinking!" Breanna stopped him with her fists clenched in frustration at her hips. Eoin put a calming hand on her shoulder.

"Aye, my Hero," Goibniu responded as he ducked his head. "I am not used to dealing with mortals for lengthy periods."

Breanna's expression softened as she grabbed his waist, hugging him awkwardly. "Och, I understand. I'm not used to being a goddess! This journey is unbelievable for me, too, but I need you, Uncle. Only you can envision what we need to turn the tide. Think about Rome. Their offensive power laid waste to the Celts on the mainland, and they pushed deeply into Celtic Pretannia across the sea, even reaching into Dál Riata. While they've retreated during this time, I will bring my Warriors of Destiny into timelines where we will be overmatched, especially in numbers. I need you! Do you understand this?"

"Aye, my baby goddess," Goibniu answered. "Yet we've never ventured so far into the mortal world, never truly needed to interact with humans, only their worship."

"I'm not sure what we can do or say to let you set aside your concerns," Eoin said. "Yet, think about what *balefire* could do to an opponent, as the Romans did when they cast fire spears with their ballistae on the mainland to make our fellow Celtic tribes break. Since Breanna is the Goddess of Time, she and her warriors need weapons that can devastate her opponents in key moments. She will not have overwhelming numbers, so she needs overwhelming strength to achieve Dagda's goal that the Gaels will not be ruled."

Breanna added, "Of course, only when needed. Dagda clarified that this power is not something I can leverage for myself, only if it is for our people, for all Gaels, and all Celts, for that matter. I need your support, Uncle. Do I have it?"

Goibniu finally smiled, answering with a sigh, "You're what we need. We have been avoiding responsibility for too long, sticking our heads in the sand. It's time to move forward."

"Excellent!" Eoin said. "Then we need offensive weapons for the *fians* who support us, as I must change their tactics to defend us. The same goes for those sworn to my mate. My first thought is *balefire*-tipped arrows and spears. I understand that the new *balefire* and the shields cannot yet coexist, but I'm sure they'd appreciate better physical shields. They will encounter the larger physical shields of Rome that they use to form their shield walls. What am I missing?"

"Maybe my *Cauldron of Plenty*?" Goibniu asked, smirking.

"Be serious!" Breanna chided as her fist pounded into his shoulder, and Eoin laughed at the big god's jest.

The smith ignored the punch and scratched his chin as she added, "What Eoin missed is I need to take anyone through time or space, so think of something long to connect both the willing and possibly unwilling to me so I can pull them into whenever and wherever as needed."

Goibniu informed her, "I need to consult with Badb Catha and my brothers."

"You do that," Eoin said. "Then we will head for Dun Tara."

Braoin, staring at the trio as the strange conversation unfolded, was surprised to see the large man rise and disappear. He asked, "Was that our smith god?"

"Aye, my uncle," Breanna answered with a shrug. "Yet, the more vital question is, do you have your memories back?"

"I do, previous sister-mine!" Braoin answered! "It was a rather intense awakening. We certainly had a shite father. I can't say I miss him, though I have fond memories of our time together, save for that brutal battle at the end. Watching you sacrifice yourself was hard."

"I know, everyone told me the same." Breanna sighed. "But, now, I can truly welcome you as one of my *Laoch Dàn!* I still need to find Bradaigh a proper mount worthy of that title while we wait for the smith to return, as he rode in on a weary old horse."

Dagda flashed into the yard a moment later with a hearty laugh. "Damn, but I love you, Daughter! As audacious as I've ever seen. You're already touching the *Cycle of Time*, restoring memories, and wielding *Lann Dán* with its new *balefire*. You easily outmaneuvered Goibniu and have been recruiting your *Laoch Dàn*! And now you've declared yourself the Chief Druid's Apprentice!"

Breanna raised an eyebrow, stating flatly, "You're back."

"Aye, my daughter!" her father said unabashedly.

"And did you deal with the other outraged pantheons?"

Dagda sighed. "Mostly. The Asgardians are still furious."

"As am I with them," she rejoined. "They best not cross me in my quest to stop Rome from conquering the Celts of Pretannia."

"Speaking of that," Dadga added, "we must meet with my fellow gods and goddesses to plan how to do that. Will you and Eoin join me in Falias?"

Cróí Dàn concurred, *"My Hero, we need their support."*

Breanna nodded in agreement. "Braoin, help Bradaigh make sure the Horsemaster assigns him a worthy mount. We will be back soon, and then we must head for Dun Tara."

All-Father said, "You take us to our realm, Daughter."

"And I do that how?"

"Connect with the *Cycle of Time* through your *sight*, and then imagine Danu's throne room as you remember it from the *before-time*. That is your intent. I'll join with you, and we'll all go together."

Breanna extended her hands to her father and Eoin. Then she touched the *Cycle of Time* with Dagda and led them into *Tír na nÓg*. Moments later, they flashed into Danu's throne room in Falias. It was the same place her Mother Goddess had commanded Breanna to take the Stone of Destiny to complete the magic of the *Triple Dàns*—all so that she could remove her birth father, along with his Norvegr invaders, during that time from her Emerald Isle.

Around them sat Danu, Badb Catha, and Lugh.

Badb Catha stated flatly, "Erin's Hero and her *Cosantóir*."

Breanna saw Dagda cringe before he stated warily, "The pair have bonded tightly, and he's wielding the *balefire* of *Claimh Solais* with skill. Yet, while he has a sharp mind, he needs more to be her true Protector. He needs tools and capabilities to understand cultures and languages, knowledge of war, political tactics, and strategies."

Danu shrugged. "An adequate plan. *Croí Dàn*, while growing, is too centered on Erin's Hero to help him."

Croí Dàn huffed in her mother's mind, *"I am not that narrow! Give me some credit for my time with Erin's Hero and her mate. We've bonded!"*

Breanna said darkly, "I care not that you're the Mother Goddess and her true Mother. Do not insult *Mo Chroí* in my presence again! And do not insult my Protector or me with your condescending attitude. That shite is no better than what Erin's *Ard Rí* and his Chiefs dish out to their people!"

Danu looked intently at Dadga's new daughter, as if assessing her, then shrugged. "Apologies to our new Goddess of Time. It's been eons since a moment like this. I, for one, am unsure how to proceed. That said, *Maorgairme* again could be of assistance."

Breanna raised an eyebrow. "Maybe ask me what I think. Or what my *Taoiseach* needs. What are our concerns?"

"If I may," Dagda interrupted, "let's address the help we have in mind. While offering *Maorgairme* again is a start, more is needed. First, I believe my great-grandson can help. He's most capable in the areas of history and cultures, something that Eoin will need."

"Ecne? Brigid's and Tuireann's spawn," Lugh spat.

"Aye, but you can't hold him accountable for the sins of his three fathers," Danu admonished her Sun God. "You settled that issue of revenge over Cian's death long in the past. Let. It. Go!"

Lugh nodded, but his expression was still surly.

Danu pulled the ring named *Maorgairme* from her forefinger and extended her hand to Breanna. "In case you need her."

She took the ring and slipped it on her right index finger. It glowed brightly as if recognizing her as Erin's Hero. She passed to the magical construct, *"I welcome your acceptance of me as Erin's Hero."*

As the ring flashed again, Danu said, "As one of us, there are no limits on how many times you use the summoning magic. Call, and one of us will answer. You can now be more specific about which of us will help you most."

"Then that is settled," Breanna said.

It seemed a rare moment of genuine agreement.

Badb Catha announced, "I will gather Ecne, Brigid, and maybe his daughter, Sinéidin. Dagda's great-grandson might be able to help me with the magical aspects of creating the new capabilities Eoin needs. And, light sister, your daughter, Brigid, might be able to assist us in reversing the downward spiral of teaching our Gaels Druidic principles in daily life.

"The Cymru Druids have done better than our own in passing down knowledge, especially in the ways of the Elements. I have already asked my sister, Agrona, to send us someone to join Breanna's band. I did the same with our Gaels in Dál Riata across the sea. Elemental Druids are strong in those lands. All would do well with amulets for their Elements to boost the sigils we recently gifted. I assume Goibniu will assess their skills and needs?"

Dagda nodded. "I will also help Ecne create pathways inside Eoin's mind to accept and process inputs from books, manuscripts, and scrolls he will likely encounter on our Hero's missions.

Languages are more difficult, but his daughter, Sinéidin, might be of help."

"What is the first mission to be?" Lugh asked.

Dagda said, "More followers of the One God have newly arrived at Tara and seek sanctuary. Breanna plans to upset their worldview about various gods and the existence of other forms of magic."

"And then?" Danu demanded.

"A true test," said All-Father. "Save the Pretannia Celts from the Romans, starting roughly six centuries ago. She may have to go further back than that, but too far will not make Rome a real threat."

Lugh whistled through his teeth. "You don't aim low. I'll say that for you."

Breanna saw her father's grin as he added, "We'll need to get our Gaelic Dál Riata and Cymru alliances behind our new Goddess of Time."

Goibniu appeared with a flash, saying, "Apologies, Danu. Dagda's daughter has sent me to request Badb Catha's aid in creating new *dark matter*-based weapons to withstand the Roman numbers, as she will only have a small force."

Then he noticed Breanna and Eoin standing beside his brother.

"Does she now?" the Dark Goddess asked drily.

Dadga smiled at Breanna. "That's my daughter, quick on the uptake! We will visit together on their way to Tara, and I will prepare Eoin to be more so he can truly be her Protector across her travels on the *Cycle of Time*."

Then, Goibniu pulled a golden rope from his belt. "As you requested, my Hero, a device to tie you together with your sworn band. It will respond to your commands like Danu's ring, *Maorgairme*."

Breanna snapped the thin rope out, commanding with her mind, *"Be straight!"* The fifty-foot cord became rigid before her, though it did not feel like it weighed more than a feather. Then she ordered, *"Coil!"* The rope returned to her hand. Then, her eyes landed on her Goibbi, and she whispered, *"Capture!"* The rope whipped out to wrap around the smith's waist. Seeing his startled expression, she quickly demanded, *"Coil!"*

As the rope settled back in her hand, she added sheepishly, "Sorry, Uncle, just practicing. What is its name?"

The smith smirked. "Um, Rope?"

When Breanna scowled, he sighed, "It does not have a name like *Maorgairme,* as it's not worthy of one. It's a simple construct that can only understand your intent. You only need to think what you want it to do—no need to use mind-speak."

"Very well," she stated. "If there's nothing else, we'll take our leave of you."

With that, Breanna nodded toward the smith, reached out to Eoin, and flashed them back to Dun Uisneach. "It seems my fellow gods are a bit stuffy."

Eoin chuckled. "Aye, they are, but we need their help to defeat Rome."

"Aye, we do," she agreed.

Under a sky of broken clouds and sun, Breanna led Corbmac through the gates of Dun Uisneach with one of his *fians,* her initial Warriors of Destiny, with Eoin as her Protector. Beatha and Ulicia rolled beside them in their chariot pulled by Dun Arrogh's hill ponies, and Bláth and Falyn were on their mounts, her son riding just behind them. Trailing after them was Goibniu in his wagon.

Once on the High King's Road, her *fian* escort marched in time as they struck their shields to keep the beat.

She blushed again over their devotion to her as Eimar whickered her approval. Then Breanna dropped back next to the smith. "What updates do you have from All-Father and Badb Catha after we left?"

Goibniu stated, "You were there."

Breanna scowled. "For a Tuatha god, you are either very good at deflecting or rather dense. I can see it on your face. Again, I feel underestimated. It is getting old, fast. I decided to leave that awful little party early."

"Apologies, my Hero, but I'm just a smith."

Breanna's eyes narrowed. "You are not just a smith. Stop playing the simpleton role with me, Goibniu! You have held counsel with the Tuatha gods for eons. I see through you!"

The smith ducked his head. "I know you do, my baby goddess. After you left, Dagda and Badh Catha argued as they usually do, but finally agreed on a plan. Brigid and Ecne agreed to help."

Croí Dàn injected with a pout, "*I was there, and Mother dissed me again. She questions how much I can help you.*"

Breanna sighed. "*Mo Chroí, I care not about her opinion of us.*" Then she asked the smith, "Just tell me their plans."

"Daughter, leave the smith alone," Dagda said as he appeared at her side, his size making his head even with hers while mounted on Eimar.

Breanna turned her head toward her father, saying darkly, "So, you have decided to grace me here instead of ambushing me."

"Och, Daughter, you have a spicy tongue."

"No, Father, I have a demanding one."

"You know, many have cowered before me."

Breanna gave him a wry smile. "But those many were not your daughter. Given that I am, I will have answers. Shall we dispense with banter?"

Dagda laughed heartily. "Good to see you're, well, being you. I wouldn't have made just anyone my daughter, you know."

Eoin dropped back to ride next to Breanna and All-Father as his giant strides easily kept pace with their mounts. "What updates do you have for us, All-Father?"

"Many, my son. First, this is for you. Something to eat now," Dagda answered and tossed a golden apple his way. "That will give you space in your mind for more knowledge of languages and cultures as you travel through time to advance our cause. Along the way to Dun Tara, we have arranged for one of our lesser gods, Ecne, to stop by and convey his cultural wisdom and negotiation skills."

Bláth let her mount circle around where Breanna and Eoin rode, and asked, "Ecne, as in Brigid and Tuireann's grandson? The one whose three fathers were slain by Lugh?"

"Aye," Dagda answered. "It was a terrible time, but Ecne is wise and knowledgeable about other cultures and customs. We often assign him to diplomatic missions. He will share what he has learned about the world."

Eoin took a bite of Dagda's apple. "Wow, this tastes good, but that is a lot to assimilate. He must have a library stuffed in his mind."

"He does, and with that fruit, so will you as Ecne's knowledge fills you." Then Dagda turned to Bláth. "We wrote a song together in the *before-time*. Do you remember it?"

"Aye, All-Father. Breanna restored all of my memories."

"Then let's make a new song tonight," he insisted.

"You'd do—do that with me?" Bláth stuttered uncertainly.

"Lady, please, recover your voice—you're one of my Master Bards, after all," Dagda declared with a chuckle. "My daughter made sure you have the memories of the past. You know what happened, who she was, and what she sacrificed. We created a great song together, even though we were working together from our respective realms. This time, we can create a deeper one in person."

Bláth trembled. "But—but you're All-Father."

"Tonight, I'll just be another Master Bard like you," Dagda responded with a huge grin. "Let's have some fun with our music and voices; make something to lift Breanna as Erin's Hero and their Goddess of Time. We need our warriors to know she is their leader, not to mention their Chiefs—especially them! Be a Bard of Destiny!"

Bláth said firmly, "I accept the challenge, but I reserve the right to ensure Breanna agrees with our rendition of, hmm, I think the title should be True Hearts Beat."

"And so, it shall be named," Dagda agreed.

As they rode on with Dadga lumbering beside her, Breanna asked, "And what of my request for weapons needed to face opponents who will surely outnumber and outmatch us?"

"Badb Catha is working on the problem," was his answer. "Our smith must go to her when we stop for the night."

"Okay, no update yet. Then tell me something about the sigils that appeared on us just after I changed the timeline."

Dagda recounted what he and Lugh had envisioned for each of them, blending Elements and each sigil's intent: speed, strength, accuracy, stamina, and conviction. With that, Breanna reached into the well of knowledge her father had bestowed upon her, and each sigil she had seen came to her mind. Hers and Eoin's would allow them to retain vast amounts of cultural knowledge, as Ecne did, to prepare to engage those seeking to subjugate her

Gaels and Celts properly. The others differed on how each warrior could best leverage their natural skills. She knew she had to dive deeper into their meanings with each of them.

After a while on the road, they approached the settlement maintained by the leaders of Dun Uisneach at the ford of River Brosna. As the *fian* leader approached, Falyn hailed him and commanded the serving staff to assemble lunch as Corbmac dismounted. The Chieftess also ordered Corbmac to create a new *fian* out of the two they stationed at the settlement to prepare to march for Dun Eadan within a span. Then she set about introducing Breanna to everyone.

As the others also dismounted, Corbmac started to hand-pick another nine warriors who would join them. Since the weather had held, the servers brought out a large cauldron of leek and fish stew, along with trenchers of boar chunks, cheese, and warm bread. Only the two big Tuatha gods returned for a second bowl and a third trencher of meat. Breanna saw Falyn roll her eyes again at those requests for more meat and grimaced at her plight.

After that, they were off again, fording the River Brosna and heading east until they came upon the ford at the River Boyne. Crossing via a rope-based raft system that the warriors worked, they followed *Slighe Mor* for a while before taking a path south and heading east to Dun Eadan. With the sun setting, they crossed through the ringfort's gates.

Falyn again took command, ordering the gate guards to fetch Chief Conn and the stable hands to look after their mounts.

The dun's Seneschal, Tynan, appeared promptly, bowing to Chieftess Falyn. "My Chieftess. While we are honored by your appearance, we had no notice you'd be arriving, not to mention with such an entourage."

"Unfortunately, there was no time for that, my good Tynan."

Corbmac stepped to her side, asking, "Where are my *fians*?"

Tynan raised an eyebrow. "Chief Conn's *fians* should be returning from their patrols shortly."

"Tynan." Falyn sighed. "You and I know who commands all of the *fians* in this part of Mide, and you're standing before him. Do not be obtuse. Do I need both my cousins and my mate's at Dun Tara, where we travel to next, to confirm our authority?"

"Och, no, I think that is unnecessary!" Tynan answered.

Breanna asked, "Don't the High King and Queen rule? Should I not let Conn know why we're here? We also have High Tuatha Gods on this journey, so look sharp!"

Tynan paled as he turned away.

All-Father smiled. "Well said, both of you."

A flash of light brightened the area around them, and a figure coalesced into the form of a red-haired lady with the look of a beautiful fairie made of light and air. She exclaimed, "Dagda, you've made a goddess!"

With Breanna standing beside her father, he whispered, "This is unexpected, but I'll handle it."

Turning to the evident goddess, he said, "Áine, good to see you. Your appearance is, well, unexpected. It is not your typical season to visit Erin."

The Goddess of Summer answered with dismissal, "I am here as Erin's Sovereign. Your new goddess will impact my land."

"Áine—"

"It is my right to rule above ground, as our pantheon agreed."

Breanna interjected, "Father, please. I will greet Áine myself."

Eyebrow raised, he asked, "Daughter?"

Breanna held up a hand to stay his protest. She strode toward the fairie goddess who claimed dominion over her land, extending her arm to offer a traditional warrior arm clasp. "Welcome, Áine, I am Breanna Ban Morna, Erin's Hero and newly cast Tuatha Goddess of Time. While I am inexperienced in these roles, may

I ask, as you are my land's Sovereign, what did you do to stop the Norvegr invasion? What did you do to prevent my mother from being raped by the one who became my Norvegr father in the *before-time*? The one I removed from our timeline using the magic of the *Triple Dàns*, making me the Goddess of Time.

"What did you do about this, as my *Sovereign* Goddess? What will you do to save our Gaels from doom? In the *Cycle of Time*, I have seen how Romans and their One God followers infected most of Pretannia, and now their remnants are here to infect us. Gaels must rule to control this mess."

Áine looked nonplussed and turned to Dagda. "I see you have chosen your daughter wisely. She is who we need, one who could have prevented those events if she'd already been Erin's Hero."

With that, Áine disappeared.

Breanna turned to her father, demanding, "What was that?"

Dagda shrugged. "A test. Many will challenge my choice of you as my daughter."

Breanna grunted. "Not a helpful answer. How can she help?"

Croí Dàn put in derisively, *"She's always been pretentious."*

Her father heard her Heart and chuckled. "I am not sure. Yet she has many who worship her—and countless lesser gods in her circle, some light, some dark. I will meet with her when there's time. Speaking of time, Ecne will be here tonight to meet with Eoin, and I expect Brigid, his grandmother, will join him as well."

Eoin asked, "He's the one who knows cultures and languages?"

"Aye, and it needs to be a closed discussion," Dagda confirmed. "Falyn, please make Conn's private room available to us."

"Certainly, All-Father," was her answer.

Croí Dàn intruded, *"Hmm, he would be fine with Dagda."*

Startled, Falyn countered. *"That is way too personal!"*

Breanna commanded, *"Mo Chroí, leave her thoughts be."*

Croí Dàn huffed, and Falyn laughed as she added, "Breanna, it's okay. I'm beginning to like this mind-speak with your Heart."

As *Mo Chroí* beamed at Falyn, Conn strode into his courtyard, his posture stiff, as if it would help him look more regal; it made him seem somewhat comical. "Highly unusual and unexpected—"

The Chieftess cut him off. "Close your mouth. We need to discuss recent developments one-on-one. Now."

With that, he whithered as the pair retired into the main hall.

Bláth commented, "That was interesting."

Dagda sighed but said no more as he stomped away.

Breanna turned to Goibniu. "Are you all full of shite like this?"

"Aye, we are."

"Eoin, I need a word with you away from these arrogant arses," Breanna demanded as she strode toward the stable to look after Eimar. Joining her, he offered, "Whatever you desire, my love."

As Breanna curried her mount, Eimar wickered her approval. While Eoin did the same with his mount, Breanna asked, "Were you as troubled as I was about that exchange between those two gods?"

"Aye," Eoin answered. "It's like one hand doesn't know the other exists. It is as if they assumed the world would go on without their direct presence. Like we'd worship them regardless of how little they helped us."

Breanna snorted. "My thoughts exactly. Let's claim our sleeping quarters and have a bath. I'm tired of these games. Ecne can wait on us!"

Croí Dàn proclaimed, "*That's my Hero!*"

Eoin

Eoin found Tynan shortly after. "We have not met. I am Eoin, Erin's *Cosantóir* to our Hero. As you may have surmised, the Tuatha gods are amongst us again, and you and your Chief must keep them in your favor. One of those goddesses is, indeed, Erin's Hero. While she is now also the Tuatha Goddess of Time, she is still one of us."

"I see," said Tynan dourly. "And what does she expect?"

"Och, man!" Eoin exclaimed. "It's simple. Respect!"

"And how can we respect our Hero and new goddess?"

"One of your noble huts for the night and a bath."

"The huge guy, her father, already made that clear."

"He did, now? Well, that's—interesting."

Tynan sighed. "It is all quite trying."

"Why, because we are not your typical *nobles*?" Eoin asked, his tone hard as his hand went to the Sword of Light's hilt. "They would take your head for such an insult. Shall I?"

Tynan blanched as Eoin added darkly, "Fortunately, I'm not like your privileged *nobles*. I'm a true Prince of the Blood who holds to the old ways. Your Chief is less so. Thus, you should know we will ensure his days holding such a title are limited. There will be a new Council of Erin that serves the people, where Chiefs who put their people first are welcome, and those who do not are, well, not. Is that clear? Make it a wise choice on which side you fall."

Tynan nodded. "Aye, my Prince. Follow the path behind the main hall. It is the last hut on the left. The baths are on the way. I already ensured our new Hero and goddess will not be disappointed."

"Breanna will appreciate your attention to those details."

Later, after Breanna and Eoin bathed and worked off some bound-up energy as mates and bathed again, they strode hand in hand to the main hall. Tynan anticipated their presence and escorted them to Chief Conn's private meeting room.

Dagda and three people Eoin did not recognize were waiting for them. Aside from Bláth, Beatha, Ulicia, and Falyn, no one else was in the room; the smith had left to confer with Badb Catha about *dark matter* weapons and shields. Platters of food awaited them, along with jugs of ale and mead. He whispered to Breanna, "I remember this place from the *before-time*, and this puffed-up and stuffy Chief Conn that Falyn diverted earlier today."

Then her father rose, saying, "Daughter, I would like to introduce you to my other daughter, Brigid, and her grandson, Ecne, and his daughter, Sinéidin."

Brigid rose and circled the table to embrace Breanna. "Sister, so good to meet you in person. Many of us have seen what you did in the *before-time* and witnessed your sacrifice. It was, well, unexpected and brilliant. You've shamed us into realizing we've been placing our heads in the sand when we should have been helping our people, as you did. Something we were seemingly not ready to do. Yet, here we are, now as sisters."

Breanna hugged her kindred goddess in return and stepped back. "I welcome you as my sister. To save our Gaels and the Celts from ruin, we must have a deep understanding of the cultures and languages that you, your grandson, and his daughter understand. First are the One God followers. Second would be the Celts from Pretannia, now called Britons, and most importantly, their fading Roman invaders."

"Indeed," Brigid concurred. "While we gods can touch Erin's *Cycle of Time* and travel to other places and times, we cannot travel with mortals. All we can do is try to influence people, as individuals, on this plane at this time. On the other hand, you are unique, as wielding the *Triple Dàns* bestowed upon you the gift to take mortals wherever and whenever you go."

Croí Dàn put in, *"Cousin, we face daunting odds."*

Brigid smiled. *"Do not fear, Danu's daughter. My father chose her, and that's good enough for me."*

Then Brigid directed at Breanna, *"I sense strength in you. And I am also proud to call you sister!"*

Then Ecne and Sinéidin were introduced, and Breanna said, "Welcome, Ecne. My father told me that you focus on cultures and history. And, Sinéidin, thank you for joining us. I remember you from my brief time in Falias, in the *before-time*. I only just learned about your skills with languages."

Eoin noticed Sinéidin blushed, and a discussion ensued about Romans, Pretannia, versus Roman-influenced Celts. Then came the Saxons, Angles, Norwegians, and followers of the One God. It was a long evening. Ecne was well-steeped in how the Romans had evolved the pagan religion of the vast empire to include their leaders as deities, how the One God beliefs recently changed their ruling class structure by adding a new religious hierarchy, and how they impacted Pretannia over the past five hundred plus cycles, and how Cymru and Dál Riata were now both trying to fill in behind the Roman retreat.

While Ecne's daughter was fluent in every language they would travel to, her magical skills allowed her to assimilate spoken words after hearing just a few sentences. It was her gift from somewhere unknown in her lineage, yet that was how Tuathain magic worked.

While Eoin found this enlightening, he knew only personal experience would tell whether they would be successful in changing the trajectory of the Gaels and Celts. Yet, having a new part of Dagda's essence, he quickly absorbed what the god and goddess conveyed about those cultures, asking many questions.

As they wrapped up the evening, Breanna asked, "Father, I need you to show me how to walk the *Cycle of Time*. I can touch it, feel it moving, and see things past and to come. Like knowing how the zealots of the One God will impact our land. But I don't understand how to move through it, to walk it as you have mentioned."

"Of course, my daughter," he replied. "In the morning, we will start with the wherever in this realm before attempting whenever."

"Once I can do that, I want to take Ecne and key team members to see how Rome's Legions work, how they win their battles."

Dadga smiled. "That's wise of you. Understand your enemy!"

⟡ Breanna ⟡

Breanna awoke in Eoin's arms and found him staring at her.

He whispered, "My love, I don't think I've even mentioned how beautiful you look when sleeping. It's like you're at peace with time."

"Hmm, you haven't, but I like your thoughts. And I don't believe I've told you how settled I feel wrapped in your arms."

"That pleases me," he said. "Will you join me?"

Given the double-entendre, she smiled, answering, "Never ask."

"Hmm, I was thinking of rising. We have much to do."

Breanna purred. "Think again, my *Cosantóir*."

A half-span later, Breanna stretched like a tigress. "Now we can rise. I must learn to walk the *Cycle of Time* in this realm, and you need to learn how to guide our band and me to avoid disaster with Rome. Then, tomorrow, we are off to Dun Tara."

Eoin kissed her lips softly, as if savoring them. "Aye, my love, there is much to learn to fulfill our roles in this strange dance with our gods and the destiny they have us pursuing for our people. Let's break our fast before we start the day. You've made me hungry!"

As Eoin headed to the baths, Breanna dawdled a bit, asking, *"Mo Chroí, about babies. I know what happens when couples mate, but I'm not ready. Given our healers have tisanes to prevent such potential life from taking hold, I should chat with Ulicia."*

"No need. Through our bond, I have already provided such protection. Only when you deem it so will you conceive."

Relieved by that news, she pursued Eoin to get cleaned up.

After they had their fill in the main hall, Eoin went off to meet with All-Father's family of gods and goddesses, and Breanna met Dagda, her *Lann Dàn* strapped in her harness on her back, and her dirks sheathed about her body. All-Father just smiled at her need to bring her weapons and led her outside the dun. Then, with a massive hand resting lightly on her shoulder, he led her into the *sight*, directing that she seize the *Cycle of Time*, find Dun Tara, and have that power take them there.

She protested, saying she'd never been there, and her father responded that she did not need to know, only to command. The *Cycle of Time* would know her intent. And then she did just that, and they both stood looking over a wide golden vista of cut wheat and barley fields to the west that Dun Tara commanded.

Breanna said, "It's a beautiful sight. Yet all inside the dun behind us are ignorant of what's to come. Is now the time to inform them?"

"That can wait," Dagda answered. "Now, take me to the western shore of Erin, to a place called Dun Bhun na Gaillimhe. The High King's advisors proposed that we settle these One God followers on an island off its shores, or maybe the island in Loch Corrib."

"Again, I've never seen it," Breanna said.

"It's all about intent. Use it!"

A moment later, they looked toward three islands off to the west, over a gray sea. "The Aran Islands," Dagda stated. "What does the *sight* tell you if we start with them out there?"

"The taint of the One God will spread across our land if we leave them anywhere without our influence."

"Exactly, Daughter. We can only leave them here for a time. Again, Loch Corrib might also be an option, but containment is the goal. When you settle them on one of those islands, Chief Connall Cas Ciabhach and the Druids of Dun Gaillimhe will have to oversee any travel they plan to undertake."

Breanna said, "Having the Uí Maine Dynasty looking after them is a sound plan. Especially once *Mo Chroí* swears Chief Connall to me."

"Very well." Dagda nodded. "Now, since you handled those initial spatial relocations so easily, let's try something more challenging. We must meet a Druid Seeress in her land who will support you. Her name is Livie, and she commands both Earth and Water Elements. You'll need her support in Pretannia. Focus on Cymru, where we must arrive two weeks before our current time so she can join you at Tara around the time you will be there."

Breanna asked, "That is my intent?"

Her father nodded. As she placed a hand on his arm, she reached for the *Cycle of Time* as he requested. When she opened her eyes, they stood in a small clearing, surrounded by strange, misty woods. The midday light was heavily filtered, and before them stood a beautiful young woman wrapped in a deep green cloak. With brownish-red hair falling about her shoulders, she held a staff that had a glowing crystal captured at its tip before her.

The young Druid said, "I had foreseen your arrival here only briefly before this moment."

"You're a Fáidh?" Breanna asked.

"In this part of Cymru, we use the Cumbric word Gwelet for such a Derwyddon title, but I speak Gaelic. So, yes, to you, I'm a Druid Seeress."

Breanna, who was familiar with Beatha's glassy expression when she seized the *sight*, noted the same look on this Seeress. Then, the young woman continued, "It is as if something unforeseen happened to you. No, it was not unforeseen. There was doubt among some. Yet you prevailed, and it was glorious. Or it will be. It is strange, as you seem outside of time."

"Aye, in a way, I am, Seeress," Breanna said. "I am now both Erin's Hero and, through the essence of my father and by wielding the combined magics of the Tuatha *Triple Dàns*, also the Tuatha Goddess of Time. As such, I pulled us both across wherever and whenever to be here. In Erin, my band is two weeks behind us now."

The Seeress raised a finely arched eyebrow before closing her eyes as if seeking the *sight* again. When she opened them, she said, "Agrona, our Goddess of War, has informed me I must support you, and so I will. I am Livie Ferch Myrddin. How may I help?"

"First, where are we?"

"We are near the hillfort of Pen y Dinas on the north coast of Cymru," Livie answered. "Not far from the settlement of Llandudno."

"Thank you for that." Breanna smiled and stepped forward with her arm outstretched in greeting. "Though being from Erin, that means little to me. I am Breanna Ban Morna."

Livie gripped Breanna's arm, asking, "And he is Erin's All-Father? As in the Dagda of the Tuatha?"

"Well, I was going to say he is my father," Breanna countered as Dadga graced her with a big smile. "But, sure, you can use either name for him. He is a big softie, at least with me. Now, as to how you can help, that's a bit complicated."

The Seeress inquired, "How complicated?"

Breanna shrugged and leaned into the Seeress, their heads almost touching. "This might sound like I'm *duine craiceáilte*, as we would say, but I am assembling a band of warriors and Druids to protect Celts and Gaels from Rome. If we can forge them into something more unified, they can fight off those who now rise in Rome's wake and Rome itself."

Livie offered, "Our word for being crazy is *gweiadur*."

Breanna chuckled. "Well, to do that, this is even more so *gweiadur*. We will need the support of this island's Celtic and Gaelic tribes. The challenge will be determining the most effective way to influence more than twenty tribes in the first century before the common era. Well, maybe even before that. Getting them to work with us to create an army and defenses against Rome will not be easy. If we're too early, they'll forget; if we are too late, we will not be in time to unite them. I still don't have a clue how to go about it."

Livie looked perplexed. "Wait! Us? We all know that our respective gods can move through time, but not with mortals."

"Wielding the magic of the Tuatha *Triple Dàns* bestowed that unique capability on me." Breanna shrugged, countering the concern. "Thus, the title Goddess of Time. That's what makes things a bit complicated. Either way, I want you to join us. I also understand you're more than a Seeress. A Water and Earth Element Druid under your Seeress self. Those skills would be invaluable."

"Aye, they would," Livie agreed with a smile. After briefly hesitating, she said, "As my goddess commanded, I will join you, but I suggest we take a trip through time so I know what to expect."

"I need some intent to target a time and place," Breanna said.

"Caesar wrote a journal about his travels," Livie suggested. "I read about one engagement he had in the spring of fifty-eight, six centuries back, where his legions faced Ariovistus, the king of the Suebi, a Germanic tribe that had settled in eastern Gaul.

Caesar defeated him and his forces at the Battle of Vesontio. Is that enough?"

Dadga nodded, and so Breanna held out one hand to Livie and one to her father, and they vanished in a flash. She had to steady her new Seeress for a moment, as her father had done with her. They were now perched high on a hill overlooking a valley somewhere in eastern Gaul, with Germanic tribes arrayed against Caesar's Legions. It was clear that the latter had a battle plan, and the former was just a little more than rabble.

Breanna stated, "By the stars, this will be a slaughter! Don't they have any gods to help them?"

Her father offered, "Aye, it will be a ruinous battle. The tribes have numbers but don't know how to use them effectively. Having fought off many enemies, these four legion commanders have become more sophisticated in how they deploy their legionnaires.

"Regarding your other question, Esus leads the Celtic pantheon, working alongside Teutates and Taranis. The latter is their God of Thunder and Storms. Yet they have faded in the mortal world, much like we had before you came along."

Breanna grumbled over that news before asking, "Can we help with this battle?"

"Nay, you need to seek a different timeline. Not this one."

Then, the carnage began as the disjointed tribes tried to rally against the more organized Romans, who marched in squares of nearly five hundred men, with ten cohorts per legion. Breanna stated somewhat dejectedly, "It seems like a missed opportunity."

"Aye, but to change the outcome, you'd have to arrive a cycle earlier to convince King Ariovistus to adopt a different strategy to fight Caesar."

Breanna, watching the Suebi-led tribes battling at the edges while the brutal Romans advanced through the heart of their opponent's warriors, had to grimace over how efficient the legionnaires were. Recognizing Caesar mounted behind his men by way of his helmet plume, she suggested, "We could assassinate the general. My *balefire* could take him even from this range."

When she saw Livie's look of alarm, Breanna groused, "What?"

Dagda put in, "They have too many good generals to change a timeline this vast by just removing one of them. It is better to teach their enemies to fight as efficiently as Caesar's men do, not to mention providing them a means to make equal weapons."

"So that's what we need to do in Pretannia?" When Dagda nodded, Breanna asked Livie, "Seen enough?"

With the clashing of steel and tribesmen's dying screams in the air, the Seeress answered, "More than enough. It is nothing like a vision. We are in this time—I need not watch men die in battle."

Breanna flashed them back, once again having to steady Livie, and inquired cautiously, "Are you still willing to join me?"

"Aye, Rome left us a shattered country. It's time to fix that."

"That's so good to hear," Breanna responded with a sigh, pulling the Druid into a surprised hug. "I can't do this alone. Yet, I think we're going to become good friends. Now, I have to return to my time of two weeks, as another Gaelic warrior from Galicia is waiting for me at Dun Tara. Meet me there as soon as you can arrange passage."

Dagda countered, "Hmm, Daughter, we have one more place to seek before returning. Badb said there is another Warrior Druid in Dál Riata we must recruit, an Elemental *Laoch Druí*, and that we also need to recruit in those Gael-held lands."

Livie rolled her eyes. "You mean Lotte! She is nothing but a savage!"

"I'm not sure, lassie," Dagda replied, while Breanna was surprised by the venom in Livie's voice. "Badb Catha, our Goddess of War, suggested her. You seem to know something of this warrior woman."

"Know something!" Livie growled. "Know something! She's my half-sister!"

Breanna pleaded, "Please, calm down and tell me your story."

Livie released an explosive breath. "My mother, a Seeress like me, spent time working with the Dál Riata Druids when she was younger. She had a child there before returning to Cymru, where she met my father, Myrddin. She left Lotte to be raised by her warrior father as a Gael. Their Druids allowed my sister to train as both a Fire and Water Elemental and as a *Laoch Druí*. By two cycles, she is my elder sister and a savage, wielding her Elements in battle against anyone who opposes her as the challenge demands!"

"Fire and Water, you say?" Dagda asked. "Together?"

"Aye, she is a barbarian who often tests limits."

"Limits?" Dagda questioned. "Those two Elements have rarely been bestowed upon the same Warrior Druid. Not since the old times when the Tuatha and the sons of Mil crafted the Great Agreement! Only a *Laoch Druí* could master multiple Elements. Yet they are all but gone in Erin."

"What does that mean, Father? Are not the Dál Riata Druids yours like ours in Erin?"

Dagda seemed to ponder the question. "First, yes, they are mine. I don't know what it means for Lotte to control both of them. As I said, only a *Laoch Druí* master could manage such Elements together, yet she is too young for that. Fire and Water normally do not mix well. It could make her unstable without a master to teach her. Unless she has a touch of Aether."

Breanna turned a concerned look to Livie. "I hope you'll still join us even if Lotte does as well. Against the Romans, our *balefire* will not be enough without help."

"*Balefire*?"

Breanna sighed. "Along with my mate, Erin's Protector, I will show you what our Goddess of War has wrought. These blades on my back and Eoin's sword are truly terrifying weapons. But the Romans have similarly terrifying weapons and more of them, along with countless men, to assail us. We need your sister's Elements to help us repulse Rome's invasions when we travel in time to meet the invaders centuries before now."

"That's so long ago. I can hardly believe it!" Livie stated.

"I know this is a lot to take in. It's been even harder for me to accept this burden, as I don't know who to trust to help me make the right choices for your land and mine. I truly need your help."

Livie nodded confidently. "You'll have it—see you soon."

Breanna gave her another hug, whispering, "Thank you."

"One more thing," Livie added. "Lotte loves her Water more than her Fire and typically resides at Dhun a bheartaigh. It is near the Erin Sea, across from the northeast province of Ulaida, and not far from here either, as the crow flies. My mother, Eigyr, ensures we visit Lotte each summer, though my sister never makes time to come here."

Breanna turned to her father on that somewhat bitter note, stating, "Off to Dál Riata and this place called Dhun á bheartaigh. With her name and that place, I expect it will be the correct intent?"

Dagda just grinned.

Then Breanna turned back to Livie. "Thank you again. I need you more than you know."

With that, Breanna and Dagda flashed away.

 **Livie**

A short time later, Livie approached her mother. "How could the *Cycle of Time* deposit the Tuatha All-Father and a young woman called Breanna Ban Morna, who happens to be Erin's Hero, at my feet?"

"You know that answer," Eigyr admonished. "There is power in your blood from both your father and me."

"Did I forget to mention she is their new Goddess of Time?"

Her mother smiled the way she always did when she had a unique insight from their gods. "Agrona might have whispered that fact in my ear. Either way, Breanna will need your help to accomplish our mutual goal of rewriting the history of the Gaels through her new skills. As our gods are miserly about sharing their power, it is remarkable that their All-Father would be so generous and give her a piece of himself. Yet, he has seemingly done just that."

"As to his new daughter, it was clear he had a soft spot for her," Livie added. "Yet Breanna has been instructed by Badb Catha to seek out my half-sister, too. Breanna hopes to change Rome's and Pretannia's timelines, which we currently suffer under, starting five or six centuries ago.

"She explained the Roman Legions invaded our land and changed the many Celtic tribes so much that they have turned into worshipers of the One God, and then they left us to face the Angles, Saxons, and Norvegrs. By forging our many Gael and Celt tribes into a loose army that can withstand those invasions back then, our time now will be different, and we will rule ourselves."

"A noble cause," her mother stated.

Livie said excitedly, "Aye, it is! I promised to join her and meet her band at Dun Tara within two weeks."

"Then that is what you must do, my child."

"And what of Lotte?"

"It could be an opportunity to bond with your sister."

"She's a savage!"

"Yes, but do you see this Breanna Ban Morna taking any stance other than an iron hand regarding your sister? Who will prevail?"

"Breanna, for sure," answered Livie with a smirk. "She is a force like none other I've encountered. She's young, like me, but takes charge. That draws me to her. She earnestly said that she needed me, and I believed her. And believe in her. I don't know why."

Eiigyr sighed. "Maybe because she is a warrior who fought for her land against Norvegr outlanders and sacrificed all for her people to be free. Such a sacrifice sealed her to her Tuatha gods, yet she still owns her soul. Or maybe her land owns her. From what I foresaw, she will not let others mold her easily. A worthy leader to follow."

"Aye, I think she is," Livie put in. "Even if I must put up with my savage sister daily, should that come to pass!"

Her mother smiled slyly. "Then make plans to set sail and save a seat for your sister. But before you leave, take a moment to connect with your father. Myrddin is the most powerful Druid Seer in our lands, perhaps across every one of our island's tribes. He sees history and the future like no other and could help Erin's Hero."

Livie flinched. "Och, he's so hard, um, to talk with."

Her mother laughed. "Daughter, he will be stunned that an Erin God and Goddess appeared to you, asking for your help. He will envy your position. Yet, he will want to participate in the expedition."

"Do I want that?"

"If I have things correct, Breanna needs to convince the many clans of this island to band together so they can face the Romans united before they invade. As you described, she must create a shared army out of the twenty-plus tribes at that time. Myrddin is first a diplomat. Next, he can be an ambassador. Yet, most importantly, he is a conniver. Therein lies the challenge of his involvement. Yet you know him well. Between you and Breanna, you can both keep him in check and limited. I believe he will meet his match in your Goddess of Time."

"Hmm, maybe," Livie responded.

—◆◈ Breanna ◈◆—

Breanna and Dagda arrived at the fort called Dhùn a bheartaig, where Lotte resided. Given it was the same time of day in Cymru, the sunlight did not change, save that they were no longer in misty woods. The sun sparkling off the water painted a pretty picture. The guards at the gates seemed stunned by the flash of light that preceded them.

"What's your business here?" one guard demanded, drawing his sword.

The other did the same. "And where did you come from?"

"Lotte's sister, Livie, sent me to seek out her sister," Breanna answered, pulling her blades over her shoulders, each crackling with magic. "We've just come from Cymru, where she lives."

Dagda stood nearby, letting his daughter take the lead, with his massive club resting casually on his shoulder. Breanna watched as the guards took in the giant and then her. Yet she did not threaten the pair; she showed them her god-given blades.

The first said, "But you speak an odd Gaelic."

"We are from Erin. Our common language is diverging."

The other guard asked, "Lotte, you say? The savage Fire Druid?"

"Aye, that's what her sister has called her, a *Laoch Druí*."

The pair looked at each other, with the first guard asking, "Are you sure? She's more than a handful and truly a savage."

"That's pretty much what Livie called her," agreed Breanna.

The other guard shrugged. "Yeah, Livie's visited here. A true and elegant lady, she is. But her sister? This one is on you."

He left the first guard to look after the travelers as Breanna sheathed her blades.

"Is this Lotte that much of a savage?" Dagda asked.

"Aye, she is. Nothing is ever easy with that lassie."

A moment later, a young woman about the age of Breanna strode through the hillfort's gates, her blonde hair streaming, woading on her brow and streaking back from the corners of her eyes, a spear in each hand, both crackling with her Fire Element. "Why would my sister send you to me?" she demanded.

Breanna said, "It's a matter of our gods working together."

"Your gods or mine?"

Dagda laughed. "We are both the same, child."

"I am not a child!"

"Father, please, let me handle this." Breanna held up a hand. "Lotte, your sister did not send us to you. Badb Catha, our mutual Goddess of War, commanded it of me, and the Cymru War Goddess, Agrona, concurred that Livie should join us as well. We are of Erin, from where all of Dál Riata originated. The Mórrigan suggested I seek you out, as we have a mutual enemy—the Romans, especially in the past, and now with the new Britons."

"The former is now history in Pretannia."

"The Romans may be gone, but the puppets left behind are not. And they will invite Angles, Saxons, and Novegrs to our mutual shores. They will rule Celts and Gaels, and many more will die."

Lotte asked, "Yet, you say you need me? Prove it!"

"How?" Breanna asked.

Lotte sneered. "Let's battle. Beat me, and I'm yours!"

Breanna shrugged, pulling *Lann Dán* over her shoulders. Then she removed her leather harness and otter-skin cloak, handing both to her father. Her Blades of Destiny sparkled with *balefire* as she seized the *void*. "Are you sure? I'll give no quarter."

"I want none!" Lotte hissed, her spears flaring with fire.

Breanna smiled darkly, still holding the *void*, and took her stance. Her long blades whirled and then slapped onto her forearms.

Lotte did the same, her spears spinning, and then lunged as fire spat forth. Breanna side-stepped the spears with their flames, only to whack her opponent on the shoulder with one of her long blade hafts. That infuriated the Fire Druid, and her spears turned to an even brighter flame as she let fire shoot forward from the tips, only to have Breanna command *Lann Dàn's balefire* to swallow the Elemental flames as if they never existed.

Lotte growled, raised her spears, and again released her Elemental fire with even more fury. Still, Breanna did not flinch as she consumed them once more before spinning with a cross-slashing motion, calling *balefire* from her blade tips. That ended the contest as Lotte's spearheads fell to the ground, now just smoldering chunks of metal and wood.

The Fire Druid protested, "That was unfair! And what was that?"

Breanna chuckled. "Unfair? You didn't define any rules in your haste to battle. And it's my advantage, called *balefire*, something our Goddess of War created, which made your Elemental Fire useless against me."

Lotte grinned, demanding fiercely, "I want it."

"Only if you earn it," Breanna commanded with equal iron.

"And I will have to endure my sister?"

"Aye, you will."

"Gah!" Lotte exclaimed. "Fine! I'm yours, as I promised."

Breanna narrowed her eyes. "I'll ensure that promise."

Crói Dàn interjected smugly, asking, *"Shall I seal that promise with the oath that all Laoch Dàn must take, my goddess?"*

Lotte's eyes widened like full moons as she heard the Heart of Destiny in her mind. She questioned dubiously, "An oath?"

"Aye, each Warrior of Destiny must take the oath."

Crói Dàn commanded the Fire Druid's attention, saying, *"Repeat: My Hero, I pledge my blood and bones to you and promise to accept your orders and protect you no matter the threat to my life. If I fail to fulfill this oath, may my heart cease to beat."*

Lotte hesitated for a moment.

Then Badb Catha said into their minds, *"Swear it, my Fire Druid. It will be glorious!"*

Breanna was surprised that their Goddess of War spoke directly to them. Yet she smiled, hearing Lotte say, "Gah! I do so swear to be a Warrior of Destiny!"

Croí Dàn commanded, *"Say the words, as they will bind you until your death!"*

As Lotte did so, *Croí Dàn* said, *"Welcome as our Laoch Dàn!"*

Breanna added, "Seek out your sister and meet us at Dun Tara as soon as possible."

With that, she and Dagda flashed away.

As they left Dál Riata and settled outside of Dun Eadan, Dagda said, "It is time to feel the pain of our Gaels and the Celts under the thumb of a Romanized Pretannia, influenced by the One God followers. With your permission, I'll lead with your power of time, walking the *Cycle* to guide us."

"Father?" Breanna asked. "When and where are we talking about?"

"Everywhere and anytime that various aggressors have oppressed Gaels and Celts. Skipping through time is like throwing a flat stone across smooth water. It is just a glimpse of each splash. Let it flow, as it will not be a linear experience. Just absorb the impact of what will take place if you do not lead your Warriors of Destiny through time to change our Gael's destiny."

"Then, lead the way, Father," she agreed as she reached for the *Cycle of Time* as only she could and led the way with his intent.

After a somewhat chaotic skip through the last six hundred and the next thousand-plus cycles, the *Cycle of Time* deposited her and Dagda back where they'd started in Dun Eadan.

Breanna staggered a bit as Eoin caught her on shaky legs. His smile warmed as he wrapped her in his arms and asked, "So, you've mastered walking the *Cycle of Time* but not standing?"

"Well, the word *mastered* is a stretch, especially after that last series of skips through time my father led me through," she answered. Once she felt steady enough, she shrugged out of her weapon harness. "It was awful! Yet, we accomplished our goal. We have two more *Laoch Dàn*: one who swore our oath after a brief duel of wills and one who plans to join us willingly. The first is a Water Druid Seeress, who also commands Earth. Then came the Fire and Water Druid Warrior. They should arrive at Dun Tara soon."

Dagda proclaimed, "Eoin, I must say, my daughter has excelled at her new craft of walking the *Cycle of Time*! It would be best if you practiced that together. Yet I am needed in Falias for some urgent matters. Daughter, I'll see you in Tara."

With that, as her father vanished, Beatha sighed with relief, muttering, "It's about time—a young Seeress is what you need. My bones are too old for all this nonsense."

"We appreciate your support as our Fáidh," Breanna said with a smile, "but you are right in what you say. These missions of ours will be for our generation. We will drop you off with Falyn at Dun Uisneach. Yet when we get to Dun Tara, I expect your assessment of this Water Druid Seeress who will be my Seeress of Destiny."

"Aye, easily done."

Breanna turned to Eoin. "And what have you been learning?"

"The Romans are formidable," Eoin answered. "Or maybe a better term would be they were, but now they are in retreat.

They always start with trading and then move on to conquering. As we discussed, we need to sow distrust of them among the Celts before Rome's first invasion. To get the myriad of tribes to organize an army, not unlike our *fians*, will not be easy. Yet, while it will help to prepare them, it is the Roman invasion that only our band can stop. Celtic defenses were non-existent in that timeline, and collaborators helped the Romans."

"Hmm," Breanna said, "Let's discuss after we eat."

Eoin laughed. "Better yet, in the morning, my love!"

Later, as they sat at Conn's high table after dinner, her *fians* welcomed her by thumping the butts of their dirks on the tables.

Breanna sighed. "I suppose they want a dance."

Bláth laughed, agreeing, "Of course they do!"

"Not tonight," she decided as she rose. "Corbmac, have you selected your warriors for our two *fians*?"

"Aye, Bre," he answered.

"Then have them kneel and swear the oath as *Laoch Dàn*!"

As the eighteen men and their leader, Corbmac, jointly sank to a knee, *Cróí Dàn* said the oath in their minds, and they answered in unison, thumping their chests. "Aye, we so swear to Breanna!"

Breanna stood proudly, offering, "Welcome! I pledge to treat your blood, bones, and minds with care and honor. Each of you now bears the title of *Laoch Dàn!* You are my Warriors of Destiny!"

They all pounded on their tables or shields.

"And I swear to you, as those committed to me, my Warriors of Destiny!! We will ensure Gaels rule and are not ruled!"

Bláth whispered, "I think you should dance tonight."

"Aye, I think so, too, my love," Eoin concurred.

Expectant eyes at the moment won her over, and she nodded.

Bláth rose with her harp to ascend the stage, where Conn's fellow musicians joined her. Then, Eoin led Breanna to the floor. When a lively reel started, Breanna found herself flying through the air as gracefully as a falcon, with Eoin tossing her using more strength than she remembered him having. It seemed he, too, was becoming more than her Protector.

Later, as they lay in each other's arms, Breanna asked, "Is this a dream?"

Eoin could only say, "Yes, it is mine. Now sleep, my love."

"Not yet," she said. Then directed *Croí Dàn*, "*Mo Chroí* One last command for the night. Send word to Fergal—he and Toal should leave Dun Arrogh with my band for Dun Tara in the morning."

"*Aye, my Hero.*"

Then she let sleep take her, cradled in Eoin's arms.

Livie

Livie knocked on her father's door. "May I disturb you?"

Myrddin said tersely, "You already have. But enter. What is it?"

"I had a visit from two Tuatha Gods today," she said.

"Tuatha Gods," he blustered. "What nonsense is this?"

Livie clenched her fists and questioned derisively, "Nonsense? Erin's All-Father and their new Goddess of Time requested I join her *Laoch Dàn* and Druids to change our timeline and ensure Rome does not conquer this land. Mother told me you should know this, but if you don't think this is worth your time, I'll leave you be!"

As Livie turned toward the door, her father said, "Daughter, stop! Tell me about this new Goddess of Time. And why does she want you to join her Warriors of Destiny and Druids?"

Livie gave Myrddin a dark look. "Maybe she needs a Seeress and an Element Druid with Water and Earth. She is also seeking my half-sister, saying her band will challenge the invasion of Pretannia by Rome in the century they came to our shores."

"Lotte," Myrddin murmured. Then he asked, "How?"

Livie fumed, "How! How! She saved her land, wielding their *Triple Dàns*. She's their new Goddess of Time and can take mortals with her as she walks the *Cycle of Time*! She can cast powers harnessed by Badb Catha called *balefire,* and who knows what else!"

Her father sighed. "Why do you think I can help?"

Livie raised her chin, calming herself. "I do not know because of how you scheme and plot to ensure the futures you foresee are validated. I am here only because Mother suggested I tell you this before I leave to join Breanna."

"And why does your mother think I can help?"

"You know the Celts. We need to rally them to stop Rome!"

"When?"

"Before the Romans invaded the southern part of our land."

"Centuries ago. Interesting," Myrddin muttered; Livie knew the *sight* had taken him. A moment later, he added, "Maybe this will work. Go to this Goddess of Time, my daughter. I'm sure we will all meet soon."

CONVERSIONS

⟶⊰⟐ Breanna ⟐⊱⟵

Morning came with shouts of alarm, and Breanna poked her head out of the door of their hut. She found the *fian* warriors scrambling to muster under a cloud-covered sky and turned to Eoin. "Something's afoot!"

"Then we'd best dress quickly," he answered as he rose.

Moments later, armed and ready, the pair marched into the yard. "What is all this ruckus?" Breanna demanded of Braoin and Bradaigh.

Braoin answered, "It seems a king is at the gates with his warband, demanding Chief Conn open them."

Falyn and Dáithí appeared beside them next, with the Chieftess adding, "Énnae Cennsalach is assuming his son will be successful in killing Niall. This area was once Laigin territory before Niall's father created Mide, and Dun Eadan would be a logical spoil to try and claim for Eochaid."

Breanna grated out, "Not on my watch, he won't! Falyn, send someone to get Chief Conn out here now. Eoin, arrange the *fians* to defend the gate."

Moments later, a stricken-faced Conn arrived. "We cannot open the gates. His men will overrun us!"

Breanna commanded, "Hush, you stupid old man. See that your *fian* warriors follow my *Cosantóir's* commands. I will handle King Énnae. Eoin, when the men are ready, you take up a position on the right watch platform."

When she turned to the gates and climbed the left-hand stairs to a small watch platform, she demanded of the guard, "Stand aside!"

Then, Breanna saw a man mounted on a warhorse before a hundred warriors and drew her Blades of Destiny. Out of the corner of her eye, she saw Eoin climb to the right watch platform, the Sword of Light held high. She gave her mate a nod as she took in the aging Laigin king. He appeared to be in his mid-forties, with graying hair at his temples and in his beard.

The old warrior eyed her. "What is this? Just a lass and a lad to challenge me?"

She commanded in mind-speak, *"Croí Dàn, Mo Chroístand ready. I could cut him down, but maybe restraint will be more fruitful. We are likely to be taking a trip to the Cuilcagh Mountains. Eoin, we will take him in this time!"*

With her voice amplified by her Air Element, Breanna rejoined and purposefully did not use his title, "Énnae Cennsalach of Laigin, you challenge Erin's Hero and her *Cosantóir*! You stand against our Tuatha Gods."

"They are no longer our gods," Énnae declared, "and you are nothing but a dream of the past!"

Breanna countered, "So you admit you are a traitor to the Great Agreement with the Tuatha?"

"They have no sway over me!" he declared.

Breanna grimaced and sheathed her blades. *"Eoin, sheath your blade and seize the void. In time, we will appear beside him and, with the rope, take him on a tour of our mountains."*

A moment later, Breanna and Eoin were no longer on the watch towers and appeared on either side of Énnae. As her rope touched his chest, she swept him off his mount and into wherever, yet still in this whenever.

Énnae stumbled, muttering, "Where have you—"

Breanna spun away, snapping her golden rope into a coil and drawing *Lann Dàn* again. "Shut your trap! I command this realm, which you have openly rejected! You are now in Ulaida territory, which already backs me as Erin's Hero. You have set Laigin against me. Who do you think I will support as the next leader of our land?"

The king exclaimed, "You just want power!"

"That I already have. Not to rule but to change who rules and how. I can demand change! While you want to hand your son the title of High King, I will end such a role in our land. There will not be another *Ard Rí*! I will form a new Council of Erin, where men and women will be in charge of our Isle, not kings."

"You're just a lass with no power to proclaim such!"

"Not any lass," she answered. "You heard my claim as all did."

Énnae sneered. "Then I challenge you to a duel!"

Eoin stepped in, drawing his sword. "That I cannot allow. I am Erin's *Cosantóir*! I protect Erin's Hero, as she cannot engage in single combat. But know you stand against *Claimh Solais*!"

"It is just a blade in the hands of a feckless man," Énnae declared.

Eoin smiled and raised his blade. "I am not just any man; this is not just any blade."

Énnae raised his blade in response, lashing out with a quick slash. The motion missed, and Breanna watched Eoin spin away as the Sword of Light ignited and swept in, shearing the other's blade in two just above the hilt. With his sword edge resting inches from his challenger's throat, Eoin added, "You have a choice to make—live or die! Through *Claimh Solais*, I compel you to pick your side wisely."

"You kill me, my warriors will rise to slaughter you all!"

Breanna sighed, wondering how they had sunk so low with rulers who cared only about power and not their men. "Énnae, I think not, as your warband would be dead in moments if they attacked. Yet I prefer not to take any Gael lives unnecessarily. We will demonstrate what our Tuatha-enhanced weapons can do to your men, as their Laigin leader thinks more highly of himself than the men he commands. They are as much my Gaels as yours."

She watched Eoin lower his blade and deftly flick the sheared blade hilt from Énnae's hand. He took the old warrior by the arm some distance away, saying, "My Hero, have at it."

With that, *balefire* erupted from *Lann Dàn*, arching fifty yards in each direction, passing a foot in front of Énnae and Eoin. The former flinched, and the latter could only chuckle. The King of Laigin had to whip off his cloak to keep it from catching fire, yet Eoin's shields protected him.

Breanna demanded, "Time to live or die, Énnae. What will it be? Bend the knee to me now, or Eoin will end you as the challenger."

The King of Laigin appeared to be utterly stunned at the display of magical power. Accepting defeat, a knee sank to the ground, saying, "With the magic as you wield, I do so swear."

"Not enough. *Mo Chroí*, make Énnae as one of my sworn."

Croí Dàn Mo Chroísaid in his mind, *"Repeat after me."*

With the King of Laigin's commitment to Erin's Hero in place, Breanna informed Énnae, "I expect Eochaid to take that same oath."

"Och, of course!" he agreed. "With you bringing me here in the blink of an eye, your *balefire* display, and the Heart of Destiny speaking in my head, I could do nothing else. The One God followers' contention that various old god pantheons were fading across many lands was incorrect. We've had our share of their zealots come ashore over the cycles, all spreading their One God lies around Dun Fearna."

"Aye, but we should not forget our gods, which are only as strong as our Gaels' belief in them," Breanna reminded him.

Eoin turned to Breanna, adding, "That now includes you."

With Énnae's surprised look, Breanna said with a shrug, "I am their new Goddess of Time as well. I guess I'll be needing some worshipers, too. Hopefully, that will not be for very long. It's hard to think that I'm truly one of them."

With that, she touched the *Cycle of Time*, and the three reappeared outside Dun Eadan moments after they had taken the king away. Énnae swayed in his saddle as he held up his hand. He demanded of his men, "Followers of the One God have misled us. Our Tuatha gods are back! Erin's Hero is back!"

The Heart of Destiny repeated the procedure of swearing Énnae's Warband to Breanna Ban Morna.

She turned to the King of Laigin. "I will call on you soon. Whatever happens between Eochaid and Niall is between them and you. I'll make no judgment, as that's old bad blood. Get it out of your system. Our real enemy is the Rome of the past and their religious One God leaders. Gaels will not be ruled!"

Breanna set off for Dun Tara with her Warriors of Destiny more than two spans later than expected after the Laigin incident. It was a cloudy day, with rain threatening. Eimar was spunky as always, having told her in Hero in no uncertain terms how much she had missed her the evening before. They headed east for a time before turning north toward the High King's Road. Beatha and Ulicia rode in their chariot, with Corbmac and Falyn clopping beside her; Dáithí was once more mounted on his small mare, staying close beside his mother. Goibniu rode in his wagon again. Dagda strode beside the smith. Yet Breanna did not ask either one about the weapons she had asked them to seek from Badb Catha.

As she stroked Eimer's neck, contemplating the developments of yesterday and this morning, Brigid, Ecne, and Sinéidin rode beside Eoin, chatting about Rome and its history of conquering countless peoples.

She knew Egypt was one of the lands Eoin and Ecne were very interested in, as it had greatly enriched the Roman Empire through that conquest. Brigid and her grandson seemed to revel in the depth of their knowledge. Yet, to Breanna, they all seemed like opportunities lost to the Gaels and the Celtic tribes of the mainland—opportunities their gods and goddesses shied away from in the face of Rome's relentless drive for more conquests, territory, and power.

Breanna passed the time testing her Elemental control, first snapping her fingers to create Fire, then using Water to douse it. That brought the two Druids across the sea to mind, and she turned to Goibniu. "I have an Elemental Fire Druid with Water and a Water Elemental with Earth joining my band. We lack Air and likely Earth."

"Such Elemental powers are rare," the smith commented. "At least, with any battle skills. I assume they are the pair of half-sisters from across Erin's Sea. They will need special weapons, ones that can harness their powers. I'll need to visit with Badb Catha once more."

"I believe she already knows of them," Breanna conveyed. "I felt her when I battled Lotte for her oath."

Dagda commented, "From what I know of her, Livie's father would be a powerful ambassador to help get the southern Celtic tribes to band together and make an army."

Breanna shrugged. "Only if he swears the oath. He is also a powerful Seer, like his mate and daughter. Livie advised that he not be left unchecked."

"I agree," said Brigid. "Myrddin has an alternate goal. He is already plotting to put forth a hybrid son of Rome and Cymru as the new High King of the islands to the east."

Breanna shook her head. "I'm tired of kings and kingmakers. The people must rule. Ecne, this must happen sometime, aye?"

"Aye, Bre. Well, I guess you're my Great-Grand Aunt," Ecne answered bashfully. "Strange. You're so new to us."

Sinéidin gushed, "Och, this is all so exciting!"

"Gah!" Breanna exclaimed, "Just answer the question, Ecne!"

The youngish god cast a scolding look at his daughter, and his grandmother stepped in. "What my grandson was going to say is, yes, there will be something known as the Magna Carta, written in the thirteenth century. It will be the first document to ensure people's rights, while maintaining the concept of kingship. Then, in the late eighteenth century, a colony from what would come to be known as the British Empire, far across the sea to our west, would also reject the notion of monarchies. After that, kings and queens mostly become ceremonial over time."

Breanna was stunned. It would take eight centuries for a king to grant essential people's rights, and six hundred more for one colony to throw off the yoke of kings! Then she said darkly, "Eoin, we must develop a plan for the Celts in the isles to our east to not let this kingship concept take hold, especially seeing the mess Niall has made of Erin with it—a king who cares little about his people."

"Aye, my love," he agreed. "The Celts and Gaels have managed mainly without such centralized rulers until recently. Perhaps we could have the Clan Chiefs gather the people's will. What is that called?"

"Each person has what they will call a vote," Ecne answered. "Given that men of privilege in the new world created the concept so that only those men could vote, and women and enslaved people could not."

"What?" Breanna exclaimed, then held up a hand as if she did not want an answer. She turned to Brigid, "Sister-mine, we cannot permit this atrocity to evolve as your grandson has foretold. Please work with Ecne and Eoin to develop a plan to change this course of action. Women will have this right!"

Brigid smirked. "As always, you're refreshing with your insights about improving the general state of average mortals."

Breanna stared her sister down, spitting, "No one is average!"

Dagda stepped in. "Daughter, please let me handle this, as I understand your passion and desire for your Gaels to have equality between patriarchy and matriarchy. We have removed ourselves from the daily lives of our people, clearly too much so—*some* of us do not care enough. I will take the lead on this. Does that appease you?"

"If you make it so," Breanna confirmed with a stiff nod. "Keep Eoin informed. The Breitheamh, Tadg, is already working on another issue I raised. The Chiefs have too much leeway on hostage terms. My *before-time* father held many of our clans as hostages for cycles on end, and no one called him out on that. Make it a law that all must follow."

Dagda sighed. "Daughter, I will address both points."

After a brief rain shower, they merged onto the High King's Road, east of the River Boyne crossing, with everyone, save the *fians*, grumbling about being wet. With the way now more manageable, they decided it was time to dry off as they stopped by a stream to rest and take their lunch. The horses drank their fill as the warriors distributed buckets of oats and hay to them, then took a moment to wash up. After that, Corbmac set about distributing Chief Conn's midday provisions.

Breanna approached Falyn with Dáithí in tow. He carried his plate and cider mug, while Breanna juggled two plates of boar, bread, greens, tubers, and two cups of mead and asked, "Can I join you?"

"I'd be honored," the Chieftess responded, taking a plate and cup; she motioned her son to sit beside her. "Before we start on our meal, I have to say, when you and Eoin whisked Énnae away, I thought for sure you'd kill him and not convert him."

"Aye, it was a near thing, but the magic of our gods is now manifest in me. Somehow, I reached him through the poison the followers of the One God had planted. He knows my plans to reintroduce our old way of no High or Provincial Kings. There will be a Council of Erin, comprised of Chiefs and Chiefesses. There will also be seats for the Druids, artisans, crafters, and traders."

Dáithí asked, "Auntie Breanna, who will be on this council? Who will appoint them?"

Having discussed options with Ecne, she knew any path she chose could pose challenges, yet she liked the notion of all having some say. Breanna answered, "Good question, young man. Initially, Eoin and I will select those we have sworn in, but soon, the people will cast their votes for their leaders and provide input on key matters.

"You, young man, are fortunate to have a wise father. Not all of our patriarchs are so inclined in this way. Matriarchs must return."

"That's an excellent idea," the lad declared. "My mum is brilliant! She always knows best."

Breanna beamed, seeing that her point had taken hold. After eating some of her meal, she continued, "You and your mate are part of the High King and Queen's family. I realized that my proposal to end the practice of Provincial Kings and High Kings in Erin might not align with the position of your family."

Falyn shrugged, pausing as she was about to put a handful of food into her mouth. "I am first a *Taoiseach*, then we are Chief and Chieftess, and last are cousins to the High King and Queen. Your plans have merit. But we have bigger fish to fry, I believe, first with these One God followers. Especially given that you had to address the Laigin incident today. From what I understand, there's Rome and Pretannia. After that, it appears, saving Egypt from Rome?"

With a twinkle in her eye, Falyn stuffed her mouth full.

Breanna did the same. After swallowing, she said, "Yes, but first, the Roman invasion of Pretannia, then helping Egypt deny Rome its breadbasket resources, at least not for no cost. The fate of the mainland Celts is also a concern. After that, maybe the power-seeking faithful followers. If time doesn't help us, we will address our rights and equality issues. Yet that raises a question. The state of our governing structure. What can you share?"

Falyn thought momentarily. "With the bad blood between Niall and Énnae Cennsalach's Clan in Laigin, there will be battles between the provinces for who becomes *Ard Rí* afterward. If he ends up slain, as Beatha foresaw, I know his mother, Cairenn, expects Niall's son Eógan to follow in his footsteps.

"How the Connachta clans lean will likely make a difference in who wins the title, and Fiachrae's son Dauthí is in firm control there. He should be able to sway the northwest to get behind Eógan.

"Now, in Mummu, that's another story. Coirpre Luachra holds a tight rein in the southwest from Dun Cashel, and there's an ugly history between the Eoganachta dynasty and those of Connachta. Yet the critical factor will be with Énnae and his Dun Fearna warriors."

Breanna sighed. "What a mess."

Falyn just grinned knowingly. After a moment, she sighed. "Let's not mention this notion of equality to the High Queen, as she envisions her eldest son following in his father's footsteps. Such is the case with those who have absolute power. Yet, I am fortunate to have a forward-thinking mate. He will support this concept. I find him strangely wise most times."

Breanna rejoined, "Aye, I find the same with Eoin."

They chuckled in unison, then Falyn added, "Speaking of the queen, I brought a dress for you to wear for the evening gatherings. I'll see that a page brings it to you."

With that, Falyn turned to Dáithí. "We have discussed what to say about public and private matters. It is a private one."

"I understand, Mother. Auntie Breanna is special. So is Uncle Eoin. He's been teaching me warrior forms and how to seize the *void*. He told me I needed to keep that knowledge to myself, as it is private, too."

Eoin

Later in the day, with the sun breaking through the clouds in the west, Dun Tara and its western golden fields came into view. The band rode, walked, and rolled into the High King's massive fort and seat of power. There were more than enough strange looks at the two giant men, but Eoin watched Falyn take charge by ordering guards to billet the *fians* and servants to prepare huts and ready the baths for her esteemed guests. With that in motion, the Chieftess arranged for them to prepare a feast. No one questioned Falyn, who seemed to be a known force among them.

Eoin insisted that he take care of their mounts, allowing Breanna to seek out their hut. When he found her lying face down on the bed, she groaned as he gently massaged her back, shoulders, and neck. As he worked the knots out of her muscles, he asked, "In this skip through time with your father, what happened?"

"Och, Eoin, it was so very dark. The times ahead are awful. Dark leaders slay men, women, and children by the thousands to gain the upper hand in the battles for more power over others. With Dál Riata Gaels, then known as Scotti Highlands, the successors of Rome, called Britons, brutally killed our Gaels and then subjugated them so they could use them to fight their battles against others. At each skip, after they conquered Erin, they starved us, and many were forced to flee our Isle for the massive land across the sea.

"That was just our Gaels. There were glimpses of worse, but Dagda stayed clear of anything that did not impact our Gaels. If what I saw is the same across the world, I don't see how we can matter."

Eoin pulled her close to his chest. "Somehow, we will prevail."

Breanna answered, her voice quivering, "I can only hope so. But it gets worse—so dark and ugly. In the name of the One God, thousands marched to the area around Egypt to fight a variant religion, where tens of thousands died in a fruitless, extended war. Then there were World Wars, where millions of men, women, and children died at the hands of various leaders whose quest for power knew no bounds. By the stars, the cruelty was crushing!"

❧ Breanna ❧

After settling their belongings in their little abode, they stepped out to see the sun setting over a golden vista of harvested wheat and barley fields. It was a glorious sight. Yet it was a short-lived bliss as the half-sisters she had recruited from across Erin's Sea approached her.

The more reflective Livie said, "My goddess, as you requested, we have arrived at Dun Tara, ready to swear ourselves to your cause."

"Well met, Livie and Lotte," Breanna greeted. "Any troubles with the sea crossing?"

Lotte said stiffly, "He kept the sea smooth for us."

"I'm pleased it was so," Breanna added. "Let me introduce you to Eoin, Erin's Protector."

Eoin bowed. "Your support of our mission is welcome."

"Indeed," Breanna added, "for this evening, we will greet Erin's High Queen. Ready yourselves appropriately. Even I have to wear a dress."

"Gah, we have to dress up?" Lotte protested.

Livie glared at her sister and muttered, "Of course, my goddess."

As Breanna and Eoin left the half-sisters hissing at each other, they turned to fetch their clothes for the evening. Eoin insisted that Breanna go straight to the baths, saying he'd fetch her blue dress.

That was when a lithe mixed-tribal warrior with almond-shaped brown eyes approached her. She was about the same size as the two half-sisters, yet she had long, straight brown hair that hung loosely about her shoulders.

She asked, "Are you Erin's Hero?"

"Aye," Breanna answered. "I assume you're the warrior from Galicia, whom my Fáidh told me about?"

"I am," the diminutive warrior answered with a strange and foreign bow. Slightly curved swords poked over her leather pauldron-covered shoulders. Beneath it, she wore a deep green tunic and leggings wrapped in knee-high boots. "Our Seeress, my mother, foresaw your accomplishments and sent me to find you."

"Why you?"

"She thought I could help you so you could help us."

"And how could you help me?"

"I was trained as a Far East warrior by my father and his father," she answered. "Both were sellswords who fought their way from home on a large island in the far east—so far away I can't believe the distance. Their travels took them across Asia, India, and the Byzantine Empire. Then, through Roman-influenced lands. That was where my father met my Druid mother; they fell in love, and I was born and raised by both sides.

"While my mother's father taught me how to use the *void* and the *Laoch Druí* way with the Elements, my father and his father taught me their Far East warrior ways, and my mother taught me her Elemental healing skills. Unfortunately, my father's father passed, but my training continued through my Druidic side.

"Later, my much younger brother was born, and my surviving grandfather is raising him as a *Laoch Druí* as he did with me. Yet my mother would not let the healing and vision aspects of my Druidic skills rest until I could seize the *void* and *sight* at will. Commanding Aether is still hard, so I rely on my other Elemental talents to heal.

"Anyway, my brother shows great strength in Earth, Water, and Aether. We have been somewhat sheltered from Rome, but now the One God followers are closing in."

"Interesting." Then Breanna stated, "Your grandfather is *Laoch Druí*? Though some might exist in Dál Riata to our northeast, they've all faded out here. Yet, Galicia is where we Gaels came from, yes?"

"Aye, you are correct. It is where the sons of Mil first set sail more than a thousand cycles ago. They were known as Milesians, but you all turned into Gaels when you agreed to worship the Tuatha gods."

With a touch of the *Cycle of Time*, she saw the brave moment when her ancestors sailed north to Erin. Breanna knew this lass would become a Warrior of Destiny. "What is your name?"

"My father calls me Izzy, but my mother's father strangely calls me Bee. That's not right, as he often uses a possessive, as in *my Bee*, and only he ever uses that honorific with me. He is our Clan *Laoch Druí*, a Master Warrior who fully commands Water and Air Elements, though he can manage Fire and Earth if needed. He easily lives in the *void* as he fights. He insisted I be able to command a myriad of weapons, including long blades like yours. Yet, my father's side taught me these dual-bladed skills from the Far East.

"Anyway, I think it was due to my size that my grandpa named me Bee. He taught me not to fear my stature, as bees can strike a giant with many stings and conquer such a beast, and thus I was trained. I know I must sting a lot to win a battle against a warrior of greater size than I. A thousand cuts are as deadly as one."

Lifting her chin proudly, Izzy added, "I have done as he taught me, and I have never lost, even against many Roman legionnaires who were half again or more my size as he and my father fought at my side. Mighty men have fallen to my katanas as I sting them repeatedly. As to your question, my true name is Isobel."

Breanna smiled warmly. "I welcome you to join us as Bee, Izzy, or Isobel. Be called what you like. And your Elements?"

"My mother is Fire and Earth, and I naturally control Air and Earth, but my grandfather makes me try to work with Fire and Water. It is unnatural to me, but I do what I can."

"And also, a Healer?"

"I have some skill, mostly used to patch up my father and grandfathers if they get wounded fighting for our clans. Or myself when I am overmatched and have not stung enough to defeat my opponent outright. That said, I prefer Izzy—unless you're a man who wants to court me. Then my proper name is my preference."

That statement made Breanna laugh, as the lithe Air and Earth Druid Warrior with Healer skills perfectly fit her band, trained by a long-lost Master *Laoch Druí*. She said warmly, "Izzy, it is. Welcome, as a Warrior of Destiny, no matter how many times you must sting to be victorious. We will have some formalities for you to complete before joining my band tomorrow, but I am heading to the baths now. Will you join me?"

"Hmm, of course, my Hero," Izzy answered shyly.

"Enough of that! I'm just Breanna! You're just Izzy. Let's go!"

Croí Dàn said in her mind, "*I welcome you as well, Izzy!*"

Izzy froze. "Wait! What!? Who is this thing that can speak inside my head? And female at that?"

Breanna assessed the layout as they entered the bathhouse and offered with a shrug, "That was *Mo Chroí* using her mind-speak. She enjoys welcoming those who wish to join us. This way."

"Wait, only the royals use this section!"

"What, do you think I'll accept common baths as Erin's Hero and the new Tuatha Goddess of Time? If I hope to end their rule, I must play their game and be one of them."

Izzy's eyes widened into saucers again. "You're what?"

"Och," Breanna said, "It's nothing—I'm playing at being royal. Just grants me access to the private baths."

Izzy muttered something about evasive answers, but she ignored the warrior from Galicia as she found a big tub for them. As Breanna washed her hair, Izzy asked somewhat bluntly, "Where'd that shock of white come from?"

Breanna touched it self-consciously and then tied the mass of hair back with her green marbled leather tie. As Izzy dunked herself in the big tub, leaving her dark brown hair flowing free, Breanna answered, "I lived another life in what we call the *before-time*. I wielded the magic of *Triple Dàns*—Blades, Stone, and Heart of Destiny—to end my original Norvegr father's reign of terror in my land. When Danu pulled all affected by him and his ilk into a new timeline, she likely missed a piece of his tainted blood when she filtered out that half of me, leaving me with my white shock. That act also resulted in me becoming the Goddess of Time."

Breanna found Izzy's dumbfounded expression a bit humorous as she climbed out of the tub. Her new band member followed her and asked, "How can you be so matter-of-fact about all of this?"

"I admit it's not easy, especially when I wonder if I'm losing the human side of me. Frankly, that troubles me most."

As the two wrapped themselves in towels, a man knocked at the door. "Ladies, may I use one of these tubs, assuming you've finished?"

"Aye, we have. Eoin, please meet Izzy."

"My Lady." Eoin bowed. "I heard about you via our Fáidh."

"I'm no lady," Izzy demanded. Then her eyes widened. "Wait! You're Erin's Protector to Erin's Hero! Her *Cosantóir*!"

"Aye." Eoin smiled. "Though every day, she's more the Tuatha Goddess of Time as we go on. Either way, she's still my Bre."

Izzy blushed, stating, "Och, so lovers."

Both answered together, "That we are!"

Eoin countered. "Please, just call us Bre and Eoin."

"Let me give you some space," Izzy suggested.

Breanna faltered for a moment with her mate's comment that she was becoming more god-like, and then declared she was just Bre. With a shudder, she demanded, "Nonsense! Eoin doesn't need me to clean him up tonight. We all have a High Queen to meet, and Falyn will help us look our best. Come, Izzy. We sit at the highest table tonight!"

As Eoin handed Breanna her dress and shoes for the evening and bid them farewell, Lotte and Livie appeared in the doorway. "Is this bath free?"

"No!" Breanna said sternly.

Eoin countered, "Ladies, I can find another. I'll make sure Bradaigh and Braoin are presentable."

Breanna sighed. "I know you will."

Then she turned to the half-sisters, adding, "You two, get cleaned up and behave yourselves. We dine with Erin's High Queen tonight and require her to support our mission. If you need anything to make your dress appropriate or lessen your warrior stench, let Chieftess Falyn know. Just say you're with me."

"Gah!" shouted Lotte. "That command to dress up rankles!"

"It may," Breanna snapped back. "Yet you swore an oath to me!"

Croí Dàn asked Lotte, *"Shall we see what pain that oath can inflict?"*

Livie heard the exchange between the Heart of Destiny and her sister and questioned, "You've already sworn her oath?"

Lotte growled. "Aye, she easily beat me in a duel and ruined two of my favorite spears. That is what my rashness cost me."

Livie laughed heartily. "If only you gave it freely, but that's you, sister-mine. Let's promise to behave when we meet Erin's High Queen as we share a meal. Breanna needs our support for her mission to ensure our people are safe. Keep that foremost in your mind."

Lotte groused once more, "Gah!"

Then she started to strip down even before Eoin had stepped out of the door. Livie could only shrug at Breanna and started to do the same as her sister after Erin's *Cosantóir* had left them.

Breanna stepped into the Grand Hall of Dun Tara. It was magnificent, with a soaring beamed ceiling hewn from massive black oak trees and a western wall with many side-by-side sliding doors that let in the warm breezes when opened in the summer.

The woodwork had whorls of Druidic Power Sigils carved on the edges, which she drank in like a massive glass of mead. Each offered variations of different Elements, giving her purpose, power, understanding, and command. Even though she was waiting for her father to grant her control of all the Elements, that power sank into her. She was the Chief Druid's Apprentice and somehow pulled on each of the etched carvings in the hall. They seeped into her body and bones, and she somehow understood them all. The lower Elements fell away in a surge of power—and she knew Aether ruled them all. A *Laoch Druí* must have created them long ago, when Dun Tara was first constructed, likely by *Tuatha Dà Danann* artisans. Maybe Eoin was right that she was becoming more like her fellow gods and goddesses. That was a troubling thought.

A moment later, the carvings were just polished wood that looked like bronze casts. Large chandeliers hung in rings around the hall, brandishing hundreds of candles to light the massive room. Yet the Sigils added to her nascent understanding of how they worked in unison to support the ruler of this magnificent place.

Queen Rignach oversaw the high table with Niall's mother, Cairenn, as the customary nobles sat at the second level, and all others took to the main floor tables. Falyn had told Breanna that while Rignach acted as her mate's representative when he was abroad raiding and trading, as was currently the case as he fled facing her claim as Erin's Hero, she always did so with Caireen beside her. Her son, Eógan, slightly older than Eoin, sat beside her.

Falyn guided Breanna and her band to either side of the High Queen and her mate's mother, but Breanna was not surprised that Brigid, Ecne, Sinéidin, Dagda, and Goibniu were now absent. Her two *fians* had settled at a few lower tables with Corbmac, as they preferred. Minus them, Breanna's Band was now eight, plus herself, and she had more arriving soon from Dun Arrogh.

As Niall's representative, Rignach said, "Welcome, Chieftess Falyn. You have quite the entourage with you."

Falyn smiled. "I do, my Queen! And what I have to share is momentous. The Tuatha gods are back! And they plan to ensure Rome does not conquer our Gaels and Celts across the Sea of Erin in the past."

"In the past?" Rignach asked with raised eyebrows.

"Aye," Falyn answered, "Let me present Breanna Ban Morna, recently All-Father's daughter and the Tuatha Goddess of Time. Not to mention, she is also Erin's Hero, who you heard claim her land."

Breanna was pleased that Falyn had thought to bring the blue dress she had worn in the *before-time* to a Céilí that the Chieftess arranged. She bowed, saying, "Very newly, my Queen, on the first two fronts. As to being Erin's Hero, that first happened in the *before-time*."

"*Before-time*?" questioned Rignach.

Breanna shrugged. "It is something you do not remember, as I changed the flow of time to remove a nearly twenty- cycle-long Norvegr invasion of our land."

"Changed the flow of time?" Niall's Mother asked with an arched eyebrow. "Did I hear that right?"

She pulled out *Croí Dàn*, ensuring they saw it was the Heart of Destiny that lay above her breasts. "I know, it's hard to believe. Yet maybe we can sit and eat first and have a less formal exchange."

The High Queen rubbed her brow, looking to Caireen, before she said, "Aye! A fine idea!"

Bláth added, "May I suggest, as we set up to dine this evening, that I present a song I've been working with—well, the best Bard in our land. Yet, to play this new folk tune, I need a moment with your Bard and his musicians. There are no lyrics yet, but I need to hear it played to lay the vocals down."

Rignach nodded with an absent wave. "As you will."

As Bláth left to consult with her fellow Master Bard at Dun Tara, Breanna said, "First, as Erin's Hero, let me introduce my sworn: Eoin Mac Cairbre, Erin's *Cosantóir* and a Prince of the Blood from Ulaida. Next, I present Bradaigh and Braoin, once my half-brothers, both sworn as Warriors of Destiny, who supported me before I changed our timeline to remove the Norvergr invaders from our land.

"Last, I'd like you to meet Livie, Lotte, and Izzy. I recently walked the *Cycle of Time* to summon these Elemental Druids to Tara—one from Cymru and one from Dál Riata. Izzy is from Galicia. Her Seeress mother sent her to me while I was still in the *before-time*. How she knew why I would succeed, I know not."

Only Livie and Eoin managed to make a presentable bow.

Trying not to roll her eyes at the others, Breanna added, "With support from my band and fellow Tuatha gods, no Romans will be able to invade Pretannia. If we succeed, Gaels and Celts will rule those lands, keeping Erin free to rule itself."

Cróí Dàn interjected, *"Words of truth!"*

The High Queen and her mate's mother staggered, and Breanna had to catch Rignach's arm to steady her as Falyn did the same with Caireen. She said, "It seems the Heart of Destiny has spoken to all of you."

Cairenn nodded. "This is now more real than a moment ago."

"I had the same experience," Falyn said. "Especially when Breanna used her powers to help me remember the other timeline. Oddly, Faolán and I knew we had supported Erin's Hero in her quest to remove her Norvegr father from our land. Our gods were likely influencing us. And here we are."

"Hmm, indeed, here we are," Cairenn commented. "How to assimilate the impact of these revelations is the question. Either way, we honor your devotion to Erin and our Gaels."

As Breanna sat on the Queen's left side and Falyn on her right, the Chieftess added, "I'm sure it was even more disconcerting to have All-Father ask our Bard to create a song to sing the praises of their new Goddess of Time and her Warriors of Destiny. Their dances are divine."

Breanna interjected, "That's us! How embarrassing!"

"Hush!" Falyn admonished. "I've seen you dance with Erin's *Cosantóir*. It is truly magical. Perhaps we might request they dance before dinner."

Breanna narrowed her eyes at Falyn while the Bard slid from the High Queen's side. Yet then Eoin was at Breanna's other side, commenting quietly, "We are at the High Court, and we should show them we are more than just two rough warriors from the midlands."

Breanna turned to Bláth. "You did this to me when you presented Erin's Hero Rising during the Céilí Falyn arranged before I used the magic of the *Triple Dàns*. In the *before-time!*"

"Aye, my goddess. At least I won't be singing, not yet anyway."

"Enough with the titles!" Breanna demanded, fuming, and then she and Eoin swept through the crowd, greeting their *fians* warmly. As she moved about one table, the other table thumped their dirks.

At the same time, Breanna noted Dun Tara's Master Bard was quickly assembling the players needed for the song Bláth intended to use to introduce the pair to the court. As Breanna's Bard of Destiny—for Bláth, it was indeed just that—she introduced the players to the melody of a song written only days before by her and All-Father, something none of them knew.

Bláth led them into the song she had ascribed a title of "True Heart's Beat" as Breanna tugged Eoin through their growing band of warriors. Their Bard introduced the composition with her harp. When they finally had it, she began to play. Then, Eoin swept Breanna into his arms, and he whispered with meaning, "Let's fly in time, my love!"

With that, they seized the *void* together, pulled on the *Cycle of Time*, and twirled and spun around the dance floor as if gravity did not exist for them. In the first few sections of the song, they amazed the audience with their dancing. If they had blades and opponents, it would have been deadly. With only each other, they spun out their love.

As the music built toward its epic end, Eoin flung Breanna into the air, her body pirouetting through the air like a knife. She went so high that those in the Grand Hall gasped—how could her *Cosantóir* catch her before she crashed to the floor? Yet, following her through time, Eoin met her at the apex of her arc, appearing in her arms together some fifteen feet in the air. In the next moment, with another touch of the *Cycle*, they were settling onto the wooden-planked floor with Breanna cradled in Eoin's arms as he knelt over her. When they kissed, *Croí Dàn* let their love for their land and each other flood the room and her land.

There was a murmured collective sigh of longing. Eoin rose, extended an arm, pulled Breanna gracefully to her feet, and once more into his arms as they spun to face the crowd. They bowed to their audience, with Eoin whispering, "Now we know I don't have to touch you to move through time with you."

Breanna agreed with a wry smile. "Likely due to our link in the *void*. I have to say that I like your style!"

When they crossed the floor toward the high table, their *fians* chanted more quietly, almost worshipfully, in a way that made her uncomfortable, using hushed and reverent tones, "Bre! Bre! Bre!"

As they approached their seats, Izzy asked Breanna, "What magic caused that flush of love throughout the room? When Eoin kissed you, it was like everyone felt it."

Eoin answered, "That was the Heart of Destiny. As Danu's daughter, she can influence the people near Breanna to love and support her."

"Gah!" Lotte spat. "Who needs love when you have blades? Yet, I want to know what you did at the end of your dance. What magic was that?"

Breanna smiled knowingly. "Part of it you already know, part of it your sister can touch as my Seeress. Yet only I can wield both aspects in a dance or a battle, and Eoin can wield them with me. Yet, more on that later. I will teach you all that I can."

Livie whispered to her sister, "It was the *void* they used to dance as if they would do in battle, and she can use the *Cycle of Time* with anyone who touched her."

Izzy overheard her and countered, "But they weren't touching when Eoin followed her into the air! That is one of my Elements, and while I could do that, I could not pull someone with me! "

Breanna sighed. "Ladies, maybe you'd do well to train using blades and Elements in the *void* with Bradaigh or Braoin to use it as we do. It is a dance among our blades where Eoin and I control our moves, strikes, and parries not to win but to grow together, to trust our partner in a battle, and to know we have each other's backs. You need to know your partner better than you know yourself. One who would die to protect you as you would them."

With a raised eyebrow at Lotte, Breanna held up a hand to stave off any more questions and turned to face her High King's mate and his mother. "Sorry about the interruption. I have new members in my band who have not attended such formal events.

Well, neither have I, save for meetings with our gods. Now, let's get back to the matter at hand."

As the servants bustled about to set up the feast Falyn had arranged, Cairenn asked drily, "Indeed, and what would those matters be?"

Breanna narrowed her eyes. Before she could utter a retort, a giant eight-feet-tall man appeared with an arm lying lightly around her shoulders, saying mildly to the woman standing before them, "Those matters would be your support of the plans your Tuatha gods have set in motion to save all Gaels. With the help of many fellow deities, my daughter and I are contributing to this cause. Your support is needed to ensure that your son, Niall, will be privileged enough to possibly still lead our land once that happens."

Breanna sighed. "Please meet my father, Dagda."

The room gasped at their god's appearance, as Cairenn drew in a breath with All-Father towering over her. She looked up nearly three feet to see his face smiling down at her. Niall's mate, Rignach, looked, well, even smaller as the pair both took in the meaning of his words. Cairenn said, "Of course, All-Father, we would not want to imperil our clan's legacy of worshiping our Tuatha gods. Breanna and her band will have our full support."

"Excellent," Dagda proclaimed. "*Mo Chroí* will ensure you and your mate's mother are sworn to Breanna before we leave. Yet, we are just in time for the feast Falyn arranged. It seems we need to make arrangements for a few more chairs."

Breanna bent around her father's big frame to see Goibniu chatting with Eoin. She rolled her eyes and said to Falyn, "More slabs."

"Already anticipated this turn of events," she said with a wink.

Bláth cried, "Let us celebrate the return of Erin's Hero and the Tuatha gods and goddesses who support her in our lands!"

Everyone rose to cheer as ale and mead flowed. Then, servants passed out trenchers and bowls of stew.

Breanna turned to her father. "Quite the appearance."

Dagda shrugged. "Influence helps. Anyway, your dance with Eoin was masterful. Continue to touch the *Cycle of Time* several times daily, especially with the *void* in mind. It will hone your skills."

"We will be undertaking battle training tomorrow."

"As I would expect," Dagda responded casually, then turned back to the High King's mother, his arm still hanging lightly over Breanna's shoulders, spinning her in that direction. "My Lady, apologies for the sudden appearance. I am utterly taken with my new daughter these days. She is just a wonder to behold, and I need to ensure support for her."

While their height difference was unmistakable, the High King's mother attempted to stand proud in the face of not just any god but All-Father. Yet that was impossible, so she bowed. "Aye, as I said, you have it."

Dagda smiled serenely, as if reading her mind, and turned to Breanna's Bard. "The instrumentals sounded good. Very hopeful, and all Gaels should love it."

Bláth blushed. "Thank—thank you."

All-Father added, "Yet, we need to construct the lyrics. Perhaps on the road back to Dun Uisneach as we travel with the followers of the One God. After that, you'll be off to Dun Gaillimhe, but I believe the song must be ready before you all depart for the west."

Breanna gave them both a dark look, knowing they were planning something, likely another Céilí! Yet, she had another question. "Father, if I'm the Chief Druid's Apprentice, I must control all Elements. Who will teach me that?"

"Och, Daughter, as you have a part of me in you and with your heart sigil, it takes only this!" he answered, pulling her into his arms and pressing his forehead to hers. A moment later, he said, "There, now you can control the Elements as if they were always your own. I also opened your mind to the Druidic language of Ogham and their Sigils of Power, much like my gift beneath your Heart. I should have thought to do that earlier."

Breanna sucked in a deep breath as all of the Elemental knowledge her father possessed bloomed inside her mind through the sigil between her breasts. What followed was their language and how they used spiral drawings and tattoos to enhance their powers to command the five Elements. With eyes wide open, she whispered, "That's—a lot to take in. Especially the *Eitear* Element, which our Druids never mentioned. It is a daunting responsibility for someone of my age to hold such power."

"The sigil I marked you and Eoin with will make assimilating this knowledge easier. Aether underpins and powers everything in the universe. It is life's energy, mainly leveraged by Ollamhs and Fáidhs. Few can truly manipulate that Element, though. Access it, yes. Maybe blend it with other Elements. But creating life with it is another matter. Badb Catha understands and uses *Eitear* better than any of us. I'll arrange for her to convey its nuances somehow."

Breanna protested, "You think Badb Catha would take the time to teach me about Aether?"

"As the Chief Druid's Apprentice, you have access to all of my Druids or any of our Tuatha deities to help you," her father rejoined with a wink. "And, of course, those who are your Warriors of Destiny. Yet, I'm always available to fill in any holes they can't. Goibniu is also very skilled, as he is my second in Druidic matters, Elements or not. As to my on-again, off-again mate, she's intrigued by the possibilities you represent to bring war to our opponents."

Breanna just nodded, processing this weighty new knowledge. She felt the Elements stir within her, caged yet flowing through her blood, and the knowledge of how to power them through sigils to ensure her manipulation of each one could continue long after she cast any given Element. A moment later, a thought struck her. "Wait, you said a Fire and Water Elemental Druid like Lotte is very rare. How is it that I have all of them?"

"Och, it is because you're my goddess-daughter and not just a Druid," All-Father answered as if it should be apparent.

"And I can do this with my sworn? Gift them an Element?"

"Aye, within limits and only if the command of their existing Elements is strong," he answered.

As servants brought trenchers with ale and mead to the high table, Dagda summoned two magical stools for himself and Goibniu to support their weight. Cairenn, Nial's mate, stared with wide eyes at the open display of magic. Eoin and the smith joined them as Breanna's father relinquished his hold on her and said, "Son, your dance with my daughter was masterful. As I told Breanna, practice this more, as manipulating such moments in battle will matter. But enough talk of taking our war to the Romans."

Eoin pulled Breanna close and spun her to face the tables where their warriors sat, saying as he held his mug aloft, "Aye! A cheer for Breanna's Warriors of Destiny!"

Her warriors paused to take a break from drinking ale and consuming food, and the first *fian* pounded on their table and chanted loudly, "Bre! Bre! Bre!" And then the other *fian* responded louder with the same, "Bre! Bre! Bre!"

While Bradaigh and Braoin joined in the cheer, one at each table, Breanna's newest members looked about in wonder as if unsure of what they had gotten themselves into. She gave them a reassuring smile and turned to Goibniu, asking, "And you, my uncle, what news do you have for me?"

The big Tuatha God of Smithing was just about to stuff his mouth full of roasted boar and had to pause with a sigh as he said, "Rest assured, you will be pleased in the morning!"

Breanna chuckled, "I see I'm standing between a man—a god—and his stomach! Eat, Goibniu, eat!"

Later, settled in their hut, Breanna asked, "Eoin, when you said earlier in the baths that more and more I was becoming the Goddess of Time, what did you mean by that? I'm just me and still your mate."

"Och, Bre!" he rejoined. "I meant you're growing into your new reality. What makes you—well, you will always be what guides you."

She whispered doubtfully, "I hope so."

When Breanna and Eoin appeared in the courtyard the following morning, Goibniu was hefting shields and spears from his wagon and handing them to Corbmac, who oversaw their disbursement to her *fian* warriors. They marveled at how light the long spears were as they took them in hand. While similar to their current long pikes, the gleaming spearheads were more spade-like.

The silver metal shields were also lightweight, especially compared to their old wooden counterparts, each painted a deep, Gaelic green, with a brass boss covering the handhold at the center of the crest. The design showed *Lann Dàn* crossed, with *Lia Dàn* to the right of the axis and *Croí Dàn* to the left of it, and a sizeable golden Gaelic Ouroboros with its fierce dragon head devouring its serpent tail to circle the *Triple Dàns*. And last came the Sword of Light, the magical blade cutting the crest from bottom to top. Breanna thought it was a crest for the ages.

Livie and Beatha stood off to the side, deep in some conversation. Nearby, Lotte and Izzy were standing with Braoin and Bradaigh, watching the warriors accept the new spears and shields. The latter four appeared envious, especially Lotte, who looked ready to demand one of the spears from a *fian* warrior.

Breanna called to Corbmac, "Grandfather, have you selected two more *fians* from the High King's men?"

Finished with his task, the grizzly warrior strode to her side. "Almost. I only have a few more to sort through."

"Do they know the stakes? Know what I will ask of them?"

"Aye, my Hero, they do and are proud to be so chosen."

Goibniu inserted himself. "My brothers, Credne and Luchta, and I have been busy with Badb Catha. Our Goddess of War is strangely happy. Anyway, I assume outfitting four *fians* will be sufficient?"

Breanna shrugged, indicating it would depend on future needs. Then, the big smith continued, "That leaves those four and the Seeress, yes?"

Breanna shook her head. "Not quite. I have one more blooded warrior and a band of archers on the way. Eventually, I'll need enough to outfit five more *fians*, one for each Province. Once trained as Warriors of Destiny, they need to build a unified army to withstand invasion in case our efforts to change time fail to take hold."

Croí Dàn reached out to Fergal and Toal's minds and said, *"My Hero, I just confirmed they are only about two spans away."*

"They should arrive before midday."

"Very well, then, before we see to the Elemental Druids," Goibniu said, "I have another gift from Lugh for Erin's *Cosantóir.*

He claimed it would be a waste for his favorite spear to lie fallow in Falias. Thus, he has offered to lend Eoin *Gáe Assal*. His treasured spear follows a path through its enemies once cast and returns to its caster's hand, wreaking destruction both ways."

Eoin sucked in his breath. "I'm surprised by Lugh's generosity."

"You'll not need much practice, as it is somewhat self-aware of your intent. Just seize the *void*, focus on your intended target, and throw it."

As the God of Smithing handed him the spear and a leather strap to secure it over his back, Eoin examined the intricate sigils that wound their way along the shaft. "Please tell him I'm honored."

Chuckling, Goibniu slapped him lightly on the back. "You'll make a fine demi-god, Eoin, or more. Now, on to your new Druids. I must learn more about them before my brothers and I can develop effective weapons for them."

Breanna motioned for the three to approach and said, "I saw your looks of envy at the weapons for the *fians*, but know they are there to have your backs. You and our other *Laoch Dàn* will be the tip of our ability to pierce our opponents quickly. Our smith, Goibniu, has questions for you. He will customize weapons for each of you."

The big smith smiled at Izzy. "Tell me about your skills?"

Izzy gave a bow of reverence and said formally, "It is an honor to meet the Tuatha God of Smithing. Will you meet me in the *void*?"

He nodded, and then Breanna, Goibniu, and Izzy were one in the space between the realms. The smith sensed her excellent blade skills and more than capable Air and Earth Elemental abilities. Breanna's uncle shared his musings about using Badb Catha's sigils to enhance her Katanas with *balefire* and shields, yet he seemed puzzled over strengthening her Elemental skills.

"Very well, Izzy. I will need your blades for the day to *sharpen* them with magic. I can do little to strengthen your two Elemental abilities, but Danu will likely have a suggestion or two. As to your spark of Aether, I'll need Badb to brighten that Element for you."

Izzy was wide-eyed. "I thank you—that's truly an honor."

"Aye," Breanna said as she stepped in. "Yet, Goibniu, we must also address her Healer skills. Do we need Father's help with this? Druids are under his command, after all."

"Aye, that would be wise, and I've already considered this. My brother will likely suggest Dian Cécht, his son and a Master Healer."

"You'll summon this Dian Cécht?"

Goibniu chuckled. "He's your brother. You do it. Just reach for the *sight*, call his name, and command his presence. You are his equal, though he might not like it. He's sometimes prickly."

Then the smith turned to Livie as she stepped up, and Goibniu said, "Ah, the Water and Earth Seeress. You're not a warrior, but you'll need to support your fellow warriors as if you were one. Like with Izzy, I'll also need your staff for the day to enhance it with our Dark Goddess's sigils. We must also strengthen your Elemental control—your amulets or sigils will come from Manannán Mac Lir and Danu. I'll need Badb Catha for Aether, as you'll need that to more deeply sense the impact of what the *sight* reveals when you touch the *Cycle of Time*."

Livie bowed as she handed over her crystal-topped staff.

Breanna commanded, "Goibniu, Bláth will need a similar staff."

The smith gave her a nod at the request as Lotte stepped forward, the Fire Druid barely controlling her Elements as Goibniu towered over her. He shook his head. "Lotte, ever a trial, ever a challenge. I will also call on Manannán Mac Lir and Danu to enhance your Elements of Fire and Water.

"Your Goddess of War, Badb Catha, knowing your preference for spears, has beseeched the Sea God to loan you two of his magical weapons, as Lugh has done so with Eoin already. Our God of the Seas has agreed—you will wield Red Javelin, *Gáe Ruadh*, and Yellow Spear, called *Gáe Buide*. While they always fly straight and true, the Morrigan will oversee the addition of balefire, as she envisioned this capability from the moment of their creation. That same issue applies to recall, which she included in *Gáe Assal*. They will now always return to you as Lugh's spear will to Eoin. When I suggested the idea, there was more than a bit of glee in our Dark Goddess's eyes."

With her father being a Dál Riata warrior, Breanna expected Lotte to be steeped in Gaelic lore and a lover of the sea—she would know the significance of the weapons her uncle had mentioned. Bearing the legendary spears would be a great honor, and glory was already shining in the Druid's eyes.

Seemingly in awe, Lotte breathed out. "Manannán Mac Lir has always been my favorite. To wield such weapons!"

Breanna nudged Lotte. "I can attest to how well those spears cast true. In my previous life, I helped him kill the Fomorian God Tethra with those spears. They are all that the legends claim."

That news seemed to surprise Lotte, but the moment was lost as Breanna turned away. She ordered Dun Tara's Horsemaster to bring out mounts, each an attempt to match her *Laoch Dàn* blooded warriors and Druids. It took them nearly a span to determine who was suited for the horses presented. Sometimes, a match did not happen, and the horse or the rider sought a new partner.

When Lotte bonded with her mount and rode around the yard in a wild ride while yelling war cries, Eimar opined to Breanna, *"She will always be a handful!"*

"Aye, she will," was all Breanna could say with a groan.

Fergal and Toal rode into Dun Tara with eight archers trotting behind them, including Toal's second, Cilla. Fergal had commandeered the only real horse Dun Arrogh had and sat atop a hill pony. The two looked around in surprise to see such a large gathering, with Fergal exclaiming, "Eoin! When our Heart called, we arrived as fast as possible. What did we miss?"

Eoin grinned. "Much, but we can fill you both in later on such details."

When Toal slipped from his mount's back, Breanna hugged him tightly, happy to verify he still lived when she had seen him die with a dark demon blade taking him in his lung. "You, my favorite cousin, look well, and I am so happy to see you whole and strong. We are picking new mounts for our Warriors of Destiny, including all of you. And then we will deal with special weapons needed for you two and our archers."

"Warriors of what?" Toal asked. "What of Breanna's Band?"

"As Eoin said, you missed a lot!" Breanna confirmed and touched each of their foreheads. "This will be clear in the morning, but remember all of you!"

Once they completed the mount selection process, with Eimar prancing before the line of horses and their riders to make sure they knew their leader rode upon her back, Eoin introduced those from Dun Arrogh to Goibniu, and the smith went to work.

A short time later, Breanna raised her arms to get everyone's attention. "All who would pledge to be part of my band who have not done so, the Heart of Destiny will now accept your oath to become *Laoch Dàn!* To become a Warrior of Destiny!"

Cróí Dàn said in their minds, as well as those already sworn, so they could feel her power once more, *"Kneel before your Hero and Goddess and swear to the following:*

"My Hero, I pledge my blood and bones to you and promise to accept your orders and protect you no matter the danger to my life. If I fail to fulfill this oath, may my heart cease to beat."

The Heart of Destiny confirmed to Breanna that all were so sworn and then let a wave of courage and love for their Hero, land, and all Gaels sweep over everyone, allowing a wave of confidence in Breanna to engulf them. Of course, with her support for and pride in their oath-taking.

Breanna exclaimed, "Welcome! I pledge to treat your blood, bones, and minds with care and honor. Each of you is now a Warrior of Destiny! Across nations and times, where there are Gaels and Celts in peril, we will defend them! We will ensure that Gaels and Celts are free to rule their lands!"

Eoin put in forcefully, "And never be ruled!

They all roared in approval, shouting, "Gaels will rule! Gaels will rule! Gaels will rule!"

Fergal

Sinéidin spotted Eoin's cousin and marched toward him. "I know you, Fergal Mac Conall, a charmer from this land who came to Falias with our new Goddess of Time."

Fergal looked down from his mount and sputtered, "Excuse me, my lady. I know of no such thing."

"Know nothing!" she hissed. "You cur! You lay with me, sharing such passion, and now have forgotten I exist?"

"Time changed when Breanna wielded the magic of the *Triple Dàns.*"

Breanna put in, "Sinéidin, Fergal did indeed die, as did Eoin and I. For him, Norvegr Dreadrider killed him by taking off his head—it was a fierce battle by all."

Croí Dàn interjected, saying, *"Sinéidin, settle down. The Triple Dàns rewrote history and memories. Some, like Breanna, Eoin, and Fergal, only survived because Danu and Dagda wove them back into this time with great skill after Breanna invoked that magic. Even Badb Catha would not wield Triple Dàns, as she knew not what it would wrought."*

She appeared perplexed. *"So Fergal does not remember me?"*

"In time," the Heart of Destiny answered firmly.

Sinéidin implored, "Apologies, Fergal. I did not know what became of you when you left Falias. It sounds horrible."

"Fergal, I have already done what I can to help with your memories of the *before-time*," Breanna added.

He stammered, "You said 'remember all of you' when we arrived and touched my forehead. Is that some magical thing?"

"Yes," Eoin informed him. "But those memories will not surface until the sun rises for that bit of magic to work. Then you'll fully remember your lass here, along with losing your head."

Fergal shuddered at the thought before he stretched his arm out, saying, "Come, Sinéidin, ride with me." She took his arm, and he slung her up and behind him. "Have you ridden on a horse?"

"No, we have no such animals in Falias."

"Do not worry. Just hold me tight around my middle."

Sinéidin did so and sighed. "I do not worry, as you might think. I realize you did me no wrong, yet I'm glad I found you in this new time. We have much to discuss."

They rode out through the dun gates, and instead of taking them to the road, Fergal led them into the harvested fields to the west and stopped in the middle of one. He sought the *void*, asking, *"Croí Dàn, I know I must wait until sunrise to have my memories restored. Can you help me with just those with Sinéidin?"*

Then, in a flash, some of his memories of her returned. They'd had a tryst in Falias. He said, "My Goddess, I just asked our

Heart to restore some of my memories of only us in the other time. She has done so, and I remember you fondly. I apologize for this lapse, yet I cannot control what happened to me. I can hardly believe I am alive."

Sinéidin tightly squeezed her arms around him. "I am glad you are alive and remember us."

Fergal looked over his shoulder. "Why? You're a Goddess, and I'm just a Gael."

"Not just any Gael. You're one of Breanna's sworn. That means you're one of us or will be soon."

"Why is that important?"

"Because Tuatha females cannot have children with our males."

"Say again?"

"Our long fight with the Fomorians sapped our ability to procreate. We have been dying out. Well, until now."

"Until now?" Fergal asked, looking at her over his shoulder.

Her voice trembled. "I carry our child."

Cocking an eye, he asked, "And you would have me as your mate? I am just a Gael warrior. In the *before-time*, before the Heart of Destiny chose Breanna, I was a non-believer."

"Och, yes, my brave warrior! You will be my mate and lover," Sinéidin said. "You are tender, passionate, and will fiercely fight for us. I have lain with you and know this deeply.

"Having a baby grow up with Breanna as an aunt, Eoin as an uncle, and with our Warriors of Destiny to protect her, our child will make a glorious young goddess to support our new leaders. As the father of our daughter, you will ensure the Tuatha live on."

"But will *your* father think the same?"

"I will make it so," she answered firmly, and Fergal saw her glittering irises dancing dangerously. "My father is off doing research for Eoin but will be here tomorrow—we will know more then."

──◈ Breanna ◈──

Later, Breanna met with her blooded warriors in a private room, one that was much like Chief Faolán's at Dun Uisneach. A sideboard table held dinner and drinks for her sworn Warriors of Destiny. Casting her gaze across them, Breanna sensed they were a guarded group, unsure of each other, a disparate collection that needed a common bond.

Croí Dàn demanded, *"My Hero, allow me to use my magic."*

A moment later, Breanna felt her Heart spread the need for each of them to introduce themselves to one another, whether warrior or Druid, who made up her band.

Of course, being across from Toal, Lotte had to ask derisively, "Aren't you a bit young to be here?"

Toal smiled smugly. "Unlike you, I understand I died for my cousin in my past life at the hands of a Fomorian demon who buried a foul black blade in my lung, so I think I have earned some right."

Being next to Toal, Cilla added tightly, "And given he can put your eye out with an arrow at over a hundred and fifty yards using the *void*, I'm all good with him being the youngest and best here."

Breanna chuckled. "Nice, Toal, Cilla. Very nice. And good work with the archers as well. We will need them."

Cilla beamed. "Now that we all have suitable mounts, we can train a unit. Hitting a moving target is one thing, but hitting a target while moving is another. Right, Toal?"

"Aye, Cilla," he said, "we need such practice as you say, and I'm sure Lugh's sigils will help us somehow."

"That's the kind of creativity we need," Eoin commended.

Breanna moved on. "Izzy, meet Toal, my cousin. Toal, Izzy is *Laoch Druí*-trained and an Air and Earth Elemental. She might be able to help you enhance your god-gifted sigils."

Toal presented his forearms.

"They do look as if *Laoch Druí* etched." Izzy grinned at the lad and then turned to Braoin with a curious tilt to her head. "I see you have a similar sigil and wield two blades at once like me."

"Aye, I do, as my blades suit my frame and speed," he said. "Much like yours, I think. A blade dance between us might be entertaining."

Izzy took the challenge, responding with, "It would."

Breanna turned to Fergal. "Cousin, you've also missed a fair bit of practice with us, but now that will be not just with a sword blade. We now have magically enhanced weapons, and then there are Elements. You, Braion, and Bradaigh need to learn control of one or more Elements. Since we are light on Air, Izzy and I will try to teach you."

Then she turned to Lotte. "Since you opened your mouth first, you go next. And you get to suss out Bradaigh's other possible Elements while we work on their training."

Breanna grinned at how Lotte steamed over her command, ready to rise in protest, but when *Croí Dàn* delivered a zing of her oath magic at the Dál Riata warrior, Breanna felt it as Lotte yelped, "Ouch! Okay, fine!"

Breanna chided in mind-speak, *"You two, rein it in. We are supposed to be getting to know one another and learning how to work together."*

With that, Croí Dàn added contritely, *"Lotte, apologies."*

Given the broken ice, each told their tale of how they had become one of Breanna's *Laoch Dàn*. The mood had lightened when each had finished their introduction. Breanna announced it was time for dinner and drinks, which lifted everyone's spirits. After that, she would share more about their first mission.

Corbmac waited with Breanna and Eoin as the others lined up at the sideboard to load their trenchers and fill their mugs. "Impressive band you have pulled together, my lassie."

She shrugged. "Part luck, part gods injecting themselves, and part pure hearts that believe in our cause."

Corbmac smiled. "I believe in you, my granddaughter."

Once they had their fill, Breanna rose, quieting the room with her presence, and said, "My *Laoch Dàn*, our first mission is to escort some newly arrived One God follower seeking refuge. Our High King's advisors do not trust these new immigrants, as they will eventually seek to convert Gaels into One God followers, turning them away from our Tuatha gods. Our goal is to subvert them, ensuring they learn the true nature of our gods and goddesses and that their One God is not the only one."

Yet again, Lotte protested first. "No battles?"

Breanna confirmed, "No battles with them. We will train daily with our new Tuatha-enhanced weapons each morning and evening, showing them real magic at work. We must become a highly honed band capable of raining death with *balefire* as we escort them to an island either off Dun Gaillimhe's coast or the island on Lough Corrib. While we do that, we need to practice our new skills and discover hidden ones, such as Elemental capabilities buried in our burly men.

"After that, we must travel roughly six hundred cycles into the past to convince all of Pretannia how dire their fates are. At that time, Rome invaded the island across the sea. They must create a unified military force among twenty-plus tribes, as our *fians* will do for us here in Erin. Since they are primarily an agricultural society, we will likely need to teach them how to fight in units as we convince them of the threat Rome poses.

"Our first engagement with Rome will come next, as we must turn away any attempt to create a foothold on that island. A man named Julius Caesar, who would eventually become the Emperor of Rome for a short time, led that effort as their general, as he did against the mainland Celts.

"Once we ensure our Gaels and Celts can defend themselves, the real battle will be for us to stop the Roman Legion's armadas from landing on the shores of Albion. Historical records indicate that the first expedition comprised two legions, approximately ten thousand legionaries, one hundred transport ships, and thirty galleys. The cycle after that, the next invasion was much larger."

Bradaigh coughed. "That many against us?"

And Braoin asked, "Armadas? As in, there is more than one."

"Aye and aye," Breanna answered. "Ecne says that the first wave was only two legions, but the second was five with twenty-five thousand warriors. Yet, who knows what will happen after we blacken Rome's eye, as I plan to punch Julius Caesar in the face. When we sink their fleets with *balefire* and Elements, they may raise another army to sail against our cousins across the Sea of Erin. Only by creating a new history can we control our destiny, telling us how we will be needed whenever or wherever!

"I know that's a lot to take in—such as moving back in time, using Tuatha magic—and some of you might find it confusing. If you have questions, ask Eoin or me, and we'll do what we can to clarify them."

As her *Laoch Dàn* dispersed to marvel over their new weapons, Livie approached her, asking, "My Goddess, might I have a word?"

"Gah! Livie, call me Bre! Stars, now I sound like your sister. What is it that is troubling you?"

Livie looked momentarily surprised, but then relaxed and chuckled over the comment about her sister. She took a deep breath and sighed. "Okay then, it's Breanna. Maybe in the future.

My father can help influence the southern Celts in Albion and Cymru to prepare for war. He is more skilled in the *sight* than anyone I know in our land."

Breanna narrowed her eyes. "Yet you do not trust him?"

"Aye, you're correct," Livie answered cautiously. "He has a vision of putting a Roman and Cymru half-blood on the throne and then making our land the seat of the island's power. We must meet with Myriddin to recruit him to our side, as my mother foresaw that we would."

"What will that take?" Breanna asked.

"I'm not sure," Livie replied, gnawing at her lower lip.

"I am." Breanna grinned. "What if I teach you how to access the *Cycle of Time* as effortlessly as I do? You will not be able to walk the *Cycle of Time* and take others with you as I can, but if you're to be our *Laoch Dàn* Seeress, you must access it and advise your leaders—advise me—on what you discover beyond prophetic visions. You will see what has been and could be when we change various timelines. It will be complex, but Tuatha will help us with interpretation questions."

"You would do me that honor?"

"Of course," Breanna confirmed firmly. "As much as I need you to be my Seeress, I also need you to be an Elemental Warrior. As I said, we are short on Air. I know you're Earth and Water, but we need to find a way for you to add Air as one of the Elements you can control. Maybe Fire, too, as each *Laoch Druí* used to do. As our Chief Druid's Apprentice, I'll ask my father how to help my chosen ones to hold all of the Elements, and we will work together. He said it was possible."

Livie appeared to shudder. "I'm not a Warrior Druid like Izzy."

"Not yet." Breanna winked, then surprised the Seeress by pulling her into a hug. "As my heart beats, so does yours. Look at the gods and goddesses around us. Do they look old? Do you think they age? It is a thought that only recently coalesced in my mind. We must have influenced our people for hundreds of cycles to ensure they can stand strong.

"Kingdoms will rise and fall, yet we will still be here or there, or whenever, ensuring one simple destiny—that Gaels and Celts will rule, and we will not let others subjugate us. My Heart says you're the one I need as my Seeress to make this so."

Croí Dàn added, *"I do, and you'll be more significant as a Seeress than your father could ever be in his current timeline!"*

Livie's eyes bloomed like full moons. "Thank you both for your confidence in me. That is a lot to take in."

"Aye, I expect being immortal will be a boon and a burden. I'm still trying to internalize that immense responsibility of changing time and history. That's why I need you to be more than just a Seeress. In time, you will be both a Warrior Druid and Seeress."

Livie questioned, "Why me?"

"When one knows she can inflict incredible destruction as I can, I know your temperament will guide you toward restraint," she answered. "I need someone to balance my rage at injustice, be it against Gaels, Celts, or others. I don't want to lose what it means to be human and no longer care about my people. If my closest companions can be brutally honest with me, it should ground me and the power I wield."

"So I am to be your conscience?" When Breanna shrugged and nodded, the Seeress asked, "So you'll teach me how to reach the *Cycle of Time* on command, and I must contribute my Elements to your battle needs?"

Breanna answered, "Aye, we must work on the latter part. With Goibniu's help, we'll ensure it's not too much for you."

Then she turned to Izzy. "I need a word with you, too. Like Livie, you have another skill besides your blades and Elements.

You told me your mother taught you to be a Healer. My father has a son, Dian Cécht, who can enhance that skill, meaning battle cannot always be your first response, as you may have to save one of us if a Warrior of Destiny is injured. Will you be our *Laoch Dàn* Healer, like Livie is our Seeress?"

Izzy answered, "Of course, my Hero. I'll be whatever you need me to be. Yet, I must ask one thing. You just stated we may live for many cycles?"

"Only if we ensure Gaels rule!" Breanna answered wryly.

Izzy looked perplexed, as that was not the answer she expected.

Breanna clarified, "While we may live a long time, we can die, which is why we need a good Healer or two."

Izzy and Livie nodded and moved away, whispering to each other. Then, Eoin stepped in. "Nicely done."

She wrapped an arm around his waist, cherishing his touch as she pulled him close. "So many moving pieces—keep me sane!"

"Certain. Yet, here's another puzzle to work on."

Breanna groaned and turned to see Fergal and Sinéidin approach them, the former asking, "May we have a word with you both?"

Breanna asked her Heart, *"You know what this is about?"*

"Aye, but you need to listen first," Mo Chroí answered.

Eoin said, "Of course, cousin. And, Sinéidin, you're more radiant than when we first met you in Falias. I'm so glad you could be here with your father and a great, several-times-removed grandfather. I heard about your language skills. If you're willing, we will need that ability."

Sinéidin offered shyly, "Of course, Erin's *Cosantóir*."

"Och, nothing so formal, please. It's just Eoin."

Fergal cleared his throat. "We have a bit of a dilemma."

"Such as," Breanna asked with a cocked eye.

Sinéidin blushed. "You remember your time in Falias?"

"Hmm, yes."

"Fergal and I got, well, frisky like you two did. Given that no Tuatha has ever been concerned about such couplings in over a thousand cycles, I didn't either, as you can imagine. Yet, now I'm carrying a daughter goddess."

Fergal added, "We'd like your help breaking the news to Ecne."

"And my great-grandpa, not to mention Brigid, his daughter."

"Wait! What?" Breanna demanded.

"We want to have a Druid's hand-fasting ceremony," Fergal said, "and hope your father will officiate for us."

Eoin scratched his beard. "I didn't see this coming."

Croí Dàn imparted, "*While unexpected, I know my Hero will be happy to help Sinéidin. She is part of our family, so you need to believe that you and Breanna can smooth the waters.*"

Breanna grumbled silently. Then, a bright thought struck her, and she asked, "Sinéidin, as Eoin mentioned, we require your skills for our success. I can think of only one way to ensure my father's support and, therefore, your father's support. Would you consider becoming a Warrior of Destiny and traveling with us?"

"I'm no warrior," Sinéidin replied, her expression concerned.

"Neither is Livie, yet she is my Seeress. And Bláth is my Bard, and she is also sworn while she walks the line between her Bard and Warrior roles, for she became blooded in the *before-time*."

Sinéidin protested, "She is an Elemental Druid, not a Goddess. Same with Bláth."

"Yet I am blooded, clearly now a Seeress who walks the *Cycle of Time*. Still, I am just an apprentice directly under your great-grandpa. I will never put you in danger, especially not with my niece at stake!"

"Hmm, let me discuss it with Fergal further."

The following morning, in the yard of Dun Tara under a sky of gray clouds that threatened rain, Falyn introduced Breanna to Phátric, the leader of the One God followers seeking refuge. Surrounded by her sworn Warriors of Destiny, she was fully armed and armored as she looked the man up and down. Unwilling to touch him in greeting, she crossed her arms, saying distantly, "I remember you. I watched you be cut down and die in another time by Norvegrs, a time when I sacrificed myself for my land."

"Pardon, but we have never met," Phátric countered. "I have only just come to this land."

"Ó, but we have met," Breanna said with certainty. "And you lie with your words, as I know you were once held hostage by one of our Chiefs. For several cycles. Is that not so, one who calls himself a leader of the One God?"

Phátric looked aghast. "You cannot know my history!"

"Och, I do," Breanna said darkly and held out her hand. "Shall we see what I know about you?"

"My lady, that would be improper."

"For whom?" she demanded. "You, a liar and a coward, slinking away from your land when it needs you? Or me, Erin's Hero? You seek refuge in my land. I will know you, and you will know me. Or, I will order you and your pilgrims to be put on a ship and sent back to Albion or Cymru."

"You don't have that authority! The High King—"

"Again, but I do," Breanna calmly interrupted with narrowed eyes, her hand still extended. "He now answers to me as Erin's Hero, even if he is a coward and ran away to raid the mainland so as not to meet with me."

Phátric sputtered, "Erin's what? That's no Kingly title!"

Breanna's smile did not waver. "Take my arm, and we will see. While I am no King, I will ensure my Gaels rule."

The One God priest looked doubtful but offered his arm. When Breanna clasped it, she made sure to touch his skin. *Ćroí Dàn* interjected, *"I am the Heart of Destiny, and I chose Erin's Hero. She is now a Tuatha goddess. Be respectful or be dead!"*

Phátric was stunned. "Was that one of your demons in my head?"

"No, I'm not a demon, but a Tuatha goddess! Like my chosen Hero, Breanna Ban Morna, just not corporeal."

Breanna continued to smile at the pale and now trembling man as he tried to pull away from her, but her firm grip held his muscled arm firmly. Then she said into his mind, *"My Heart speaks true. To grant you refuge, I must accept your terms. But we can wait on that for now, so let's see how you died when you last sought shelter from Cymru or Albion. And why will I not allow you to roam our land, seeking a place to spew your foul lies about our gods being dead?"*

Breanna pulled Phátric into the time vortex she created, letting him watch in horror as he emerged in that *before-time* at a river ford where white-haired Norvegr warriors rode him and his fellow faithful down while they battled a white-haired Gael woman who fought them. His eyes popped open as they reappeared, and he exclaimed, "We all died at those Norvegr's hands!"

"That you did," Breanna confirmed. "I could not save you, as I was just learning who I was then. Yet I killed three of those five."

"But how am I alive?"

"I wielded the magic of the *Triple Dàns* and changed Erin's timeline so that the Norvegr never appeared in our lands. You are alive again because my fellow gods, who saved me and mine, somehow saved you for a reason only they can fathom."

"If our gods are at odds, why would you help us?"

"You ask the wrong question. What if your One God and mine are not at odds? What if the Roman religious leaders corrupted your beliefs about my gods with the notion that we are either dead or evil?"

"Hmm," Phátric answered. "Yet, I am half Roman."

"Indeed, you are," Breanna concurred. "And a follower of the One God. Why Erin?"

"Why flee Cymru and seek refuge? As you already know, I lived as a *daor aicme* for six cycles and was taken hostage in a raid. I learned your language and know the ways of your people. Albion and Cymru are in tatters, and the rest of Pretannia is balancing on a knife-edge."

"And you know my people are ripe for your message about your One God," she rejoined; the priest shrugged. "Well, against my better judgment, I have agreed to my *Ard-Banríon's* request that my band escorts you and your followers to the west side of Erin, where you can create a settlement on an island. So, while we travel, I will reasonably consider your One God's tenets if you accept the same from me and mine."

Phátric commented, "Of course. Based on what I've seen of you and your warriors, we will not be killed by savages this time as we travel through Erin."

Breanna laughed as she turned to wink at Lotte. "I wouldn't count on that, as my Fire Druid Warrior from Dál Riata is quite the savage!"

Lotte offered a dark smile as flames appeared on the tips of the dual-pronged Red Javelin and single-pronged Yellow Spear. She pointed them at the priest and cackled, "*Gáe Ruadh* and *Gáe Buide* might like a taste of your flesh and that of your faithful."

As the Fire Druid turned away, water rushed from each hand and up her spear shafts to douse the flames. She sheathed the two magical weapons across her back while grousing about weak Roman half-breeds. When she launched herself onto her unsaddled stallion, the beast reared, but Lotte had already clamped her thighs around his withers and grabbed a handful of mane. "Someone join me in a race!"

Lotte kicked her mount forward, leading him in a circle around the dun yard, whooping battle cries. Bradaigh took up the challenge, ran to his stallion, leaped into the saddle, and soon met Lotte at the gates as they shot out onto the High King's Road, shouting out calls for battle, challenging each other.

Breanna could only shake her head at the pair. Before turning away, Eoin said, "You look after the matters needed for Izzy and Livie, and I'll take the rest of them out for a day of *balefire* drills and improving their access to the *void*."

Then he turned to their band and declared, "Get ready to ride or march!"

While Eoin taught her Warriors of Destiny how to use the *void* to command *balefire*, Breanna used a similar link—the *sight*—and touched the *Cycle of Time*, letting her mind skip through the days ahead to check the weather. Then she looked at Phátric. "It will rain later today and into the night, but it will be fair while we ride to Dun Uisneach. Have your group be ready to leave early tomorrow."

With that, she left him speechless, knowing she had a Tuatha god to summon for Izzy. It was time for her Healer to have some genuine powers to wield when something went awry in battle. She also had to teach her Seeress how to seize the *void* and the *sight* in her way, not to mention how to walk the *Cycle of Time* in spirit, but, unfortunately, not in person. That power was hers and no other.

Breanna turned to find Falyn striding at her side. The Chieftess offered, "I heard we are leaving tomorrow. I'll send a rider ahead to inform Faolán that he should expect us, as we have no Faidh to message."

Croí Dàn told her, *"No need—I passed the word to your mate."*

The Chieftess shook her head. "With all this mind-speak and such, I will miss such interactions when you leave me behind."

With a sigh, Breanna said, "Falyn, you are a knowledgeable and wise leader. Our land has much to repair, given the direction our male leaders have taken us. Some of this is due to our Druids, many of whom no longer truly believe in their gods—in our gods, or even believe in me. Or our High King, the coward!

"The Provincial Kings have become a law unto themselves. Our matriarchs are all but gone. My progenitors were not like that! And, as one of those goddesses, I will not condone accepting male-dominated leadership just because they say so. Many are foul, taking hostages for themselves or in the High King's name! A High King who has run away on yet another raid rather than meet me! Because of his actions, we ended up with these One God followers at our doorstep. I hate the idea I might have to remove these kings by force, as it makes me no better than the vile ones I'd replace."

Croí Dàn huffed her support mentally.

"Hmm," Falyn said reflectively.

"And?"

"It will take time," Falyn shrugged. Then she added, "But, you have time on your side, do you not? Use that. You can't solve everything at once. But you can solve many things using your convictions and time. Focus on that. Outsmart them."

"You mean I should use my ability to change how things are?"

Falyn smiled. "Here's a simple idea. Ask Dagda to order his Breitheamh to introduce an updated version of the Magna Carta that includes women as equals in the text, making it the new law of our land. They are his Druids, after all."

"Yet, Druid influence is waning. The Provincial Kings will resist."

"Aye, they will resist. Yet, they don't have what you have."

Breanna looked perplexed for a moment. Then she exclaimed, "Time! I will crush their notion of any King ruling when I change the timeline and stop the first Roman invasion! I can ensure men do not rule at the exclusion of women! As has been our way for eons."

Falyn just grinned. "You can also rally your people in this. Recruit them. There are plenty who are unhappy. Use that."

"I will," Breanna agreed. Then she frowned as another thought struck her. "I need a *Taoiseach*. I need you."

"You have one in Eoin," Falyn countered.

"I do, but he needs a *Taoiseach* to guide him."

"That I can agree to be for him."

Breanna smiled brightly, thinking she had addressed yet another issue. Her mind swirled with ideas, concerns, and challenges, leaving her dazed at times. Yet the notion that her powers could draw her into taking darker actions lingered.

As Eoin organized the morning drills, Breanna pulled Izzy and Livie aside, saying to the former, "You can train with your warrior skills any time. It is time to expand your Healer skills. That starts with teaching you my approach to seizing the *void*, as I have yet to share the entire method with you. You'll need it for battle, along with your Healer skills.

"And you, Livie, need the same so you can access the *Cycle of Time* to use your *sight* more fully."

"Then show us," Izzy said.

Breanna led Izzy and Livie to one of the High King's private meeting rooms, with Beatha and Ulicia trailing behind them. Once they arrived, *Croí Dàn* added, *"Open your minds and seize the void, each in your way, then I'll help tweak your approach. You two as well, my long-time Druids."*

While the old Seeress huffed at the command, the Galician-trained Warrior Druid did just that, as did the Cymru Seeress, with Beatha doing so reluctantly; Ulicia shrugged and joined them. Then, the Heart of Destiny helped them see Breanna's path. A moment later, Livie said, "That was unexpected. Unexpected, but brilliant."

"Indeed," Izzy added. "It's like you blew away a mist."

Beatha remained silent, looking curiously at her young charge.

"I'm glad you think so," Breanna responded. "Now, Livie, find a place nearby to practice seizing the *void* and calling on your Elements to ensure you have no questions. Later, I'll show you how to do the same with the *sight* and the *Cycle of Time*. Beatha, please join her. It would be best to impart your wisdom and lore of the Irish Gaels. Livie's Cymru upbringing means she might need some color about how Erin's people evolved compared to her own."

With that, Livie smiled at the old Fáidh, took her arm, and the pair left the room. Breanna turned to Izzy and Ulicia. "Are you ready?"

"Ready for what?" Izzy asked dubiously.

A moment later, Dadga appeared in the same meeting room with his son, the primary Healer of the Tuatha gods, at his side. Izzy, who was now somewhat used to the appearance or disappearance of the Gaelic gods, sucked in a breath of awe at the beauty of the All-Father's son.

All-Father, noting this, grinned. "My daughter, at your request, I'd like you to meet your brother, Dian Cécht. You requested

Healer training for a Warrior of Destiny. Ah, I assume this is your chosen one."

"Aye, Father, she is; Ulicia has been teaching what she knows about being an Ollamh of Erin, but more is needed.

"And welcome, Brother," Breanna added, nodding to the relatively slight man standing next to All-Father. Well, if one could call six feet plus of bone and muscle slight.

Dian Cécht bowed with reverence. "Sister-mine. Your recent exploits have shattered the distance between the Gaels and Tuatha, which crept between us over the last thousand cycles. I only understand your planned missions will be in distant lands to ensure our Gaels' rule."

The Healer God of the Tuatha turned to Izzy, gesturing for her hand, and then bent to kiss her knuckles. "Your commitment to my sister is appreciated."

With eyes wide, Izzy just nodded.

After touching her forehead, Dian looked perplexed for a moment before he declared, "Given your command of Air and Earth as an Elemental Druid is strong, you'll need a Water Druid beside you for my Tuatha magic to work in the lands you'll travel to."

Dagda interjected, "My Son relies heavily on Water and Aether for his healing."

Breanna narrowed her eyes. "My Seeress is an Earth and Water Elemental. Will she need to divide herself between her foresight and healing to help Izzy?"

"Aye, that would be wise," Dian agreed.

Breanna sighed. "That is not the best strategy, as I'll need Livie during battles to command her Elements and *sight*, as she will need to touch the *Cycle of Time*. Father, there must be another option."

Dian and Dagda looked at each other, eyes locked for a moment, and then said in unison, "Airmid!"

Croí Dàn added, "*Yes!*"

At Breanna's raised eyebrow, Dagda said, "Dian's daughter is strong in Earth and Water, unlike my son, who is mainly Water and Air. Her ability to draw healing magic from the Earth, although not as strong as from Water, would provide a blended approach. Hopefully, my Son and Granddaughter can impart their knowledge to Izzy and Livie through the *void*. There should be enough time between the two, especially since you plan to share your ability to wield the *Cycle of Time* with the latter. You can always tweak any timeline by shifting back to see that a warning is needed to change the future and avoid grievous injuries."

Breanna nodded. "I'll have *Mo Chroí* fetch Livie while you summon Airmid."

A moment later, Livie returned, holding her crystal-topped staff, with Beatha trailing. As the older Fáidh moved to sit next to Ulicia, Breanna said, "We have a slight dilemma, which will be clear shortly."

Then there was a flash of light as a golden-haired woman appeared, huffing, "Father, Grandfather, that was rather rude of you both to demand my immediate presence!"

As the relatively diminutive goddess crossed her arms sternly, Breanna strode toward her with an arm extended in peace. "My apologies, Airmid. My Father and Brother should have been more tactful. Yet my need is urgent."

The goddess took the offered arm and said with bright eyes, "You're my aunt, our new Goddess of Time! Och, all they had to do was say you needed my help. Speaking of which, what can I help you with? You have powers far greater than mine."

"That may be, Airmid, but I have a much greater need to lead battles, not take time healing injured Warriors of Destiny during a battle."

With that, she briefly outlined her plans to save Pretannia from the Romans and, in turn, save Erin from the fate that lay ahead. Then she went on to explain their problem about the capabilities of her two Elemental Druids and the need for them to be able to heal battle wounds. "Thus, meet two of my sworn, Izzy and Livie. Our Healer Druid, Ulicia, has been training Izzy, but more is needed."

Dian's daughter greeted both. "I see the conundrum. You need both to be able to focus on contributing their unique skills as a warrior or Seeress while commanding Elements and rendering aid to the injured."

With that, Airmid held her hands out, commanding, "Izzy, Livie, form a circle with my father and me. I assume you can seize the *void* so I can join us."

Croí Dàn confirmed, *"Rest assured, they know my Hero's way."*

Airmid stiffened as if the Heart of Destiny had raised hackles. Breanna breached her niece's mind effortlessly. *"Tread carefully."*

"Apologies, Auntie, but Croí is Danu's troublesome daughter."

"Again, tread VERY carefully, Airmid! I will not tolerate this!"

Dagda's voice was tight, yet not quite a mental shout: *"Shut it!"*

Airmid blanched, and her father shook his head at her, signaling silence. With that, the Druids all closed their eyes and joined Dian and his daughter in the place that bridged the Tuatha realm with that of Erin, and the latter two let their healing knowledge flow into each Druid's mind as appropriate. Then Dagda joined them, putting his hand on Dian's shoulder, and Breanna and Ulicia did the same with Airmid.

With the initial knowledge transfer completed, Breanna turned to Airmid, commanding darkly, "Your penance for such a lack of discretion regarding *Mo Chroí* is that you must travel with us as we escort the One God followers to the west of Erin. It will ensure my Druids can fully absorb your skills. Going back to your realm is off-limits until then!"

With a snort of displeasure, Breanna snatched up her long blade harness and stormed out of the meeting room with her four Druids close behind.

After Breanna left the Seeress Druids to practice their craft, she walked to the stables with Izzy. Needing to burn off some steam, she ordered their mounts saddled. Eimar was pleased that her mindful Hero had brought her an apple to munch on after their ride as they crossed Dun Tara's gates.

Looking at the sky, Breanna guessed they had a little over a span before the rain she had foreseen moved in. Then she caught sight of her Warriors of Destiny sparring with their *balefire*-enhanced weapons under Eoin and Corbmac's watchful eyes, and her mood lightened. She turned to Izzy, saying brightly, "We have yet to test our blades against each other. Let's have a match!"

"You and me?" Izzy squeaked.

"Why not? After all, you need to practice with the *void*."

"I know I need practice, but you're—you're my Goddess!"

"Och, no!" Breanna chuckled. "I may be the Goddess of Time, but first, I'm your leader. We need the practice. I hope we will be friends soon, as we are about the same age, and we can put that goddess thing behind us. Remember, I come from a dirt-poor back hills dun and grew up with a conceited boy born of royalty. While I love Eoin dearly, he and I are as new to this"—Breanna just waved her hand around—"as are you. Well, maybe I have a few months of experience with the Tuatha gods on you. Anyway, let's dance with our blades!"

As they arrived at the field Eoin oversaw, Izzy looked doubtful but slipped from her saddle and drew her katanas. Breanna shrugged out of her cloak and harness and pulled *Lann Dàn* into her hands.

She reached for the *void* and was unsurprised to see Izzy in that otherworld space with her. She conveyed how their blade dance worked and set out to engage the lithe warrior. She noted how the slightly curved oriental blades could inflict grievous wounds, as, like most swords, they had a more extended range than her diamond long blades.

Yet, as they danced in the *void*, careful not to inflict damage but keeping each within reach while respecting the other's skills, they tested one another. When Breanna pressed, Izzy bent but did not break, flowing through the forms her father and grandfather had taught her. Then, Izzy would go on the offensive, and Breanna would have to give ground.

The Galicia warrior's exquisite skills matched her petite frame; she could launch high or roll low and sweep up. She constantly turned, spun, and changed the angles of her two katana blades as she whirled through her forms. When Breanna went low herself, Izzy used her Air to flip over Breanna's head, twisting as she did so, letting crossed katanas touch her shoulders.

Sweating, Breanna proclaimed, "Match point to Izzy!"

After a heavy breath, Izzy folded into herself with a bow. "That was exhilarating!"

"Indeed!" Breanna answered. "You have much to teach us."

Around them, the Warriors of Destiny had gathered to watch their blade duel. Then Lotte demanded, "I want to be next!"

Ignoring the Fire Druid, Eoin proclaimed, "Let's switch to one-on-one battles like Breanna and Izzy performed! Controlling the *void* while you fight is the experience you'll all need!"

As various warriors paired off, Lotte looked at Bradaigh with a feral smile, saying, "Are you ready for me?"

Bradaigh returned her smile. "Always! Seize the *void*!"

Breanna reminded Lotte, "No Fire or Water Elemental skill use allowed."

With a frown, the savage Druid nodded, and the battle began. Neither Bradaigh nor Lotte ceded an inch to the other, sword blade against spearheads, swirling, tangling, jabbing, and deflecting. Yet, when they came dangerously close to injuring each other, Eoin demanded, "Stand down!"

When Bradaigh obeyed the command, and Lotte did not, her spear pressed against his heart, *Croí Dàn* demanded, *"Freeze!"*

Breanna knew her Heart had used the oath to seize control of the Dál Riata warrior's muscles.

"Lotte, Bradaigh is not the enemy," Eoin commanded.

"Yet, he has desires!"

Breanna stepped in, seized Lotte by her collar, and demanded, "Your oath binds you to me. Shall I have *Croí Dàn* end you? Stop your heart?"

Bradaigh stepped aside, saying, "Breanna, enough. Lotte is just passionate about winning any battle. A draw does not suit her."

Lotte glared at her opponent and angrily jammed her spears into the harness on her back. "It is as he says!"

Breanna leveled a narrow-eyed look at the pair. "Do not let this happen again. Work it out, or I'll strip you both. Is that understood?"

Both warriors nodded, and after they left, Breanna looked at the sky. "There'll be rain any moment. Time to seek cover."

With that, she threw herself onto Eimar and rode off.

⚜ Lotte ⚜

Bradaigh turned to Lotte. "What was that?"

"I felt your lust for me!"

"First, how?" he demanded.

"I'm not sure!" she shot back.

"Have you considered that you might be feeling it through Aether?" he asked. "I've had some discussions with Eoin about how we men should find our Elements. He explained them all, including Aether as the Life Element, which you could have some control over."

"What has that to do with what I felt from you?" she demanded.

"You do not think you're magnificent in my eyes? We battled equally, yet you wanted to run me through," Bradaigh fumed.

"It's not right!"

"Why?"

"Men don't accept women as equals!"

"You think Eoin doesn't accept Breanna as his Hero and Goddess? By the gods, woman! You think that low of me?"

Lotte stood, arms crossed, eyes narrowed, saying nothing.

"Well then, Lotte," Bradaigh rejoined as he flung himself onto his mount. "Think what you will. To me, you're nothing short of magnificent! And, yes, I do have feelings for you."

As Bradaigh rode off, Lotte growled, rain spattering her face. The savage side of her felt he might be worthy, as no other male had ever been brave enough to breach her feral, fiery walls. Maybe he was someone to consider.

As for her controlling Aether, she would have to discuss it with Breanna.

──◈ **Breanna** ◈──

Back at Dun Tara, Breanna announced to the High King's mother, Cairenn, that she and her Warriors of Destiny would depart for Dun Uisneach in the morning as they escorted the One God followers to the west of their lands. As always, Cairenn graciously suggested a farewell evening meal and music. Yet, when the time came, it was a subdued affair, with talk among warriors focused on their new weapons, battle training, and some of the other gods' deference to Breanna. It was something she noted—uncomfortably—as well.

She and Eoin milled about the tables where the Blooded Warriors and Elemental Druids sat, with Corbmac, Beatha, and Bláth doing the same. Shunning the Royals was a slap in their face. Bradaigh and Lotte sat somewhat stiffly next to each other, with loaded trenchers set before them and ale in their tankards. Braoin and Fergal sat with Izzy and Livie among the *fian* warriors. Toal and Cilla sat with their seven archers, three of whom were lasses. All seemed to shun the high tables.

Then Dagda and Goibniu appeared next to Breanna and her Warriors of Destiny, with the former booming, "Daughter! Son! Can I assume all goes well?"

"Aye," Breanna managed to smile. Her new father was always so full of himself that it was hard to resist his cheerful nature. Then she turned to Goibniu and asked, "What news of weapons have you for me?"

Goibniu sighed. "Your doubt wounds me, my Goddess."

Breanna crossed to the big smith-god and hugged him. "Sorry, uncle—too much stress and challenges you're all putting on me. Given our mutual relations, I know you want the best for me, but I'm a young goddess compared to you."

Goibniu smiled and sighed as he wrapped his big arms around her. "Okay, my baby goddess, I have good news. All is ready. Thanks to Livie, I found a new weapon for the future. My brothers and I have developed crossbows with *balefire*-tipped bolts. These new weapons should be devastating to the Romans."

"Thank you, uncle," Breanna murmured, squeezing her hug.

Standing beside her, Eoin asked, "Will you train with us?"

"Och, of course!" Goibniu concurred. "Dadga wants to ensure his daughter has what she needs to challenge the Romans. And I'm working with Badb on a new *dark matter*-enhanced hauberk for you."

"Uncle," Breanna replied, looking up sheepishly through her lashes. "Your efforts are appreciated. I've been skipping through time and saw the Romans use weapons called ballistae from their ships and on land. At that time, those weapons could cast an iron-tipped wooden spear, with and without fire, five hundred to a thousand yards, and now it's nearly three times the lower number. I need something like that, mounted on carts that can be pulled by a horse, with a plan that woodworkers can build fix-station versions for ports and forts."

Goibniu groaned and then sighed. "Of course, my niece."

Breanna smiled brightly as she touched his forehead, adding, "See what I have seen. It's like the 'remember all of you' gift my father gave me."

Dagda grinned, then turned to tuck Bláth under his massive arm, adding, "Master Bard. We have a song to finish, ensuring all Gaels and Celts learn about their new Goddess of Time!"

"Father, no!" Breanna protested, aghast.

"Sorry, Daughter, we must embed you deeper into our Gaels' memories, especially over time."

Bláth looked uncomfortable, as though unsure if she should say anything more.

Later, after they retired to their hut, with Eoin's seriously muscled arms wrapping around Breanna, she thought about the future and past, Elements, Ogham, sigils, time in general, and her talk with Falyn. She whispered, "I requested Falyn act as your *Taioseach* as you act as mine."

"Hmm," rumbled from Eoin's chest. "Wise of you, as always."

With their bodies skin-to-skin, their passion took them into a blissful state. Then, before it should have been, Breanna woke the following morning, and things seemed right in her world. After all, she had time on her side.

The pair shared some playful moments while bathing, as Breanna practiced with her Water Element, making it dance for her. When Eoin turned away to grab a soap cake, she sent a squirt of water at his back, and he turned with two hands, scooping a wave of water at her, only for her to turn it back with her elemental power, drenching him.

He proclaimed, "I surrender!"

"Och, 'tis but play," she countered.

Eoin pulled her to him, saying thoughtfully, "Aye, it is, and it is all about you, my love."

Breanna looked deep into his eyes. "I know that. Yet, I need to share what my new father granted me. Seize the *void!*"

She shared how her father conveyed control of the Elements. Eoin sent her a thought with a chuckle. *"Och, but that's a lot to take in! Yet, now I am the apprentice to the Chief Druid's Apprentice!"*

"Gah!" Breanna rejoined.

Croí Dàn added, *"My Hero, 'tis but play!"*

With that, Eoin pulled Breanna in tightly, saying, "Hush."

She calmed her racing thoughts and sighed, letting his love sustain her.

Arms of Magic

⸺⸱⚜ Breanna ⚜⸱⸺

As Breanna had foreseen, the weather was with them as they set out under partly cloudy but dry skies. Goibniu had already distributed the latest weapon, rapid-action crossbows with *balefire*-tipped bolts, to the *fians* and Toal's archers. Practice with non-active bolts would have to wait, though, as it was time to march back to Dun Uisneach.

Breanna turned to her young cousin. "You're in charge of all crossbow training, unarmed bolts only for now. I need details on trajectories and distances once your archers test them. Then train the next *fian* in your rotation. We also need the same with any *balefire* shot from their spears. You, cousin, are a Warrior of Destiny!"

"Aye," he answered proudly. "You'll have the results you need."

Cilla asked, "Can we try some riding formations as we go?"

"Aye, my lassie," he confirmed. "Best use our time on horseback."

"We should also practice more with that *void* dance thing."

"Good idea, Cilla," Toal agreed. "We'll do that on horseback."

Then Goibniu turned as he held up silver-laced vambraces, pauldrons, and a chest plate that wrapped over Breanna's breasts. "These are for you—Badb Catha's idea—if you get separated from *Lann Dàn*, you need personal *dark-matter* reactive shields. The reaction time between casting *balefire and canceling your shields, and vice versa,* is still an issue. Yet you can now cast *balefire* from your blades when not in your hands."

Breanna raised a skeptical eyebrow. "To confirm, I can command *Lann Dàn* while they sit in my harness?"

Goibniu answered, "Yes, but the time to switch between the two aspects—offense and defense—is still an issue, as you know. Yet, your vambraces can feed your fingers, though not as powerfully as your Blades of Destiny."

Eoin smiled. "Excellent progress, especially given we will travel to other lands where we must show grace and wariness together."

Breanna was doubtful. "While I appreciate that capability, it would be better if I could command *Lann Dàn* while they sit in my harness."

As she pulled off her blade harness and leather pauldrons made by Dun Uisneach's Master Tanner, Goibniu exhaled heavily. "If the blades are on your back, they should be able to cast *balefire*."

After she unlaced the forearm leathers and handed them to Eoin, Breanna donned the silver armor replacements, doubtful they would fit. When the arm guards and intricately fashioned, gleaming pauldrons with spaulders atop each shoulder fit better than her leathers, she settled into them. Of course, her uncle would make it perfectly. Then came a complexly wrought breastplate covered in sigils of each Element, especially Aether. After shrugging back into her harness, she checked the draw of her blades. Not surprisingly, all of the armor was a perfect fit. Breanna let out a pleased breath. "It is exquisite."

Lotte brazenly demanded, "Goibniu, I need something similar!"

The Tuatha Smith started to protest. "You—"

"Will do as my Warrior of Destiny requested," Breanna cut in. "The same applies to those I've sworn, save for my *fians*, as they already have big shields. Make it so. Ensure you include harnesses appropriate to their weapons. Last, I want small, *dark-matter* reactive arm shields for my sword-wielding blooded warriors."

Goibniu could only nod. "Aye, my goddess."

Hands-on hips, Breanna demanded, "Enough of that. I have stated a need and, yes, a requirement. If you repeat *my goddess* like that again, I might snatch you from here and drop you off on a mountaintop! In another century or four from now, or maybe before!"

The smith chuckled, seemingly amused by the threat.

"Yet, my favorite uncle," Breanna sighed coyly, "I know you will make it perfect for me, your niece, Dagda's new daughter. You know I need you. Even if mortals are troublesome and make you uncomfortable, you can lean on me."

Goibniu smiled wistfully. "My baby goddess, know I love you. We all love you, especially your spunk and sacrifice in the *before-time*. Many will try to judge your words and actions. You'll have opponents. Just believe in yourself as I do."

"Thank you, Uncle," Breanna said, pleased by the comment. She swung herself onto her mount and looped the golden rope on her saddle horn. She could feel that Eimar was delighted and proud that her Hero was dressed in her brilliant, lacy, shimmering plate and riding gloriously atop her before the lesser trailing stallions and marching *fians*.

Corbmac rode beside Beatha and Ulicia in their chariot. Behind them came Goibniu in his war wagon, with a sour-looking

Airmid sitting between him and her father; she would not look Breanna in the eye as she rode by. Bláth took place next to the smith on the other side, and Dagda's giant stride chewed up the road beneath his big feet on the other side as he easily kept pace with the horses and carts. Falyn nudged her mount beside Breanna, with her son at her side, riding before their entourage, leading them back to Dun Uisneach.

Her blooded warriors and archers followed. Pulling up the rear came two wagons full of One God followers, who looked anything but comfortable as the trotting *fians* bracketed them.

After encouraging Dáithí to use the time to learn more about the *void* from Eoin, Breanna dropped back beside the faithful leader. "We have an agreement to exchange beliefs."

Phátric eyed her skeptically. "I'm senior to you by fifteen cycles! Why should I listen to such a young one, and female at that?"

Breanna smiled darkly. "Maybe because I can end your life with a thought? Shall we see? My Heart, let's give our Phátric a fright."

With that, the One God leader clutched his heart and collapsed in his seat as a stone falls to the ground. Then Breanna waved a hand, and the One God leader sucked in a deep breath.

"Well, we have time, and, as I promised, the weather will be kind to us during our journey to Dun Uisneach," she continued nonchalantly, calling a gentle breeze with her Air Element that swirled dust from the road around her even though the ground was wet. "We should do so during our midday break."

Phátric stared at her wide-eyed as he sat up. "With a near-death moment like that, I'm finding it hard to deny your—powers. You are strangely one with your land. More than just a warrior-lass, and you command—something more."

Breanna shrugged. "Even as a hostage, you became one of us. I sense how you feel about this issue. As Erin's Hero, I am one with my land and people. Know that I am serious about changing the future in which you say your god will *save* us."

Phátric asked, "Who are you, truly?"

In a calm voice, she answered, "More than you or your brethren could know. I was born in a back hills hillfort, raised by my clan without a true father. I was born to a Norvegr father who invaded my land and raped my mother. A Gaelic warrior who believed in her gods and fulfilled a destiny—a sacrifice that made me a goddess."

"He was the one you ended?" Phátric asked.

"Aye! And I see you are no different—you intend to end us."

"No, we can save you!"

"From whom? You? Your One God? Your One God leaders? We don't need to be saved by you. We have our gods, and you have yours. I thought I was getting through to you about what that meant, and then you fall back on your *I can save you* shite!"

With that, Breanna commanded Eimar to seek her new father's side. "I have been thinking about how all of us can train to use the *void* and the *Cycle of Time* in battle."

"As you should, my daughter," Dagda said.

"Are you being obtuse?"

"No, just proud. Whatever you have in mind will be brilliant!"

That left Breanna nonplussed. *"What did that mean?"*

Ćroí Dàn offered, *"That he trusts you, cousin."*

When Breanna grumbled, her Heart thoughtfully added, *"My Hero, that's how I sometimes feel with my Mother."*

"Indeed, and I'm sorry that's the case. At times, it's all too much."

With that, Breanna decided to ride alone at the head of their caravan and urged Eimar forward to displace Falyn and her son, letting her mind settle. Without thinking, she called her Earth

Element through Eimar's hooves and pulled that energy into her beast. Her mount whickered in approval as Breanna felt the flow of the Elements around her, now easily at her beck and call.

At midday, Falyn nudged her mount next to their leader. "It might be a good time to take a break."

Breanna nodded in return. "Of course. Make it so. I'll spend more *time* with Phátric to discuss his beliefs in his One God versus our Tuatha pantheon."

Falyn smiled. "I'm happy to take on logistical matters and make appropriate arrangements. Dáithí, assist me."

Breanna's adoptive aunt and her son quickly arranged the middle meal, and Breanna picked up two baskets as she left her mount behind. As she passed Airmid, she commanded, "Just don't sit there! I'll not tolerate an idler! Go! Work with Izzy and Livie on their healing skills!"

Airmid stiffened as if to protest, but her father laid a hand on her shoulder. "No, daughter. Accept your penance."

Airmid fumed, stepping down from Goibniu's wagon with Dian as the pair sought out the two Elementals. A short while later, Breanna watched the three lassies draw energy from the Earth, creating a bloom of flowers around them—flowers not usually seen in the late fall season—with Ulicia nodding approvingly.

Meanwhile, Breanna brought a basket to Phátric. "It is time to follow up on our previous chat, but please eat first."

He accepted the basket with a nod. "My thanks."

Moments later, Breanna asked, "While the flowers my Druids have summoned from the Earth are pretty, let's start with a question."

At that moment, the Tuatha God Ecne appeared with his daughter, Sinéidin, a basket of food in his hand as if he had just plucked it from the food cart. He stated, "Apologies, Auntie.

I hope we are not disturbing you two, but this conversation is important."

Breanna grinned at them, nodding in agreement. "Indeed."

Phátric paused. "Your appearance is—disconcerting."

Ecne shrugged. "Yet, I am the God of Knowledge and History for the Tuatha, and I assume you want the truth about how your One God leaders crafted the narrative you follow or will soon.

"We all understand what we see and hear, and my daughter, our Goddess of Languages, will act as our translator. I believe that was the bargain you negotiated with our new Goddess of Time, aye?"

"That was the agreement," Breanna confirmed.

Ecne placed his hand on Breanna's shoulder. "Excellent! Please finish your meal before Breanna takes us to witness a moment that will illuminate your leader's shady side. I think I have a great place to start, which is just a little while in the future."

"You can do that?" Phátric asked, clearly awed.

Ecne smiled. "Me, no, but she can. I'm just a guide."

"Can't wait to see this," Breanna chuckled and filled her mouth.

Eoin joined her. "Sounds like you'll be our escort."

Finished with the meal, Ecne took her hand, then Sinéidin's, and she took Phátric's as Breanna touched the *Cycle of Time*, with Eoin laying a hand on her shoulder. They jumped into the mid-sixth century when the Second Council of Constantinople, led by Emperor Justinian, was underway. The four from the past, transported by Breanna, watched a private meeting of senior One God clergymen, during which they debated whether the teachings of Origen should be banned. She used the cloaking sigil her Father granted her before the time, as she knew she needed to bend sound and light with her Elements to keep them hidden.

Even though Phátric understood Latin, Sinéidin, using mind-speak, translated their words into Gaelic for Breanna and

Eoin. Then the clerics finalized their arguments to prohibit the teaching of reincarnation—that a soul transitioned from life to life based on given experiences, as the Gaels believed each *anam* sought the *Cycle of Time* over and over, and instead ascended to the One God's realm.

The internal argument ended with comments about how their faithful followers of the One God would only be under the papal leader's thumb. He would control who ascended to heaven and who did not. The hierarchy could not truly control their followers if they believed in the possibility of any rebirth of their *anam*. Then, those same high clergy members strode in with Emperor Justinian into a larger chamber where their gathered lesser clergy were assembled. They declared the writings of Origen to be anathema and that teaching a doctrine of spiritual rebirth would be punishable by death.

Ecne, Sinéidin, Phátric, Eoin, and Breanna lurched back into their current time. "What did you hear versus what were you taught?" Breanna asked. "You grew up in Cymru and here, in Erin. You speak Latin, so you can't blame the translation on Sinéidin."

Phátric sighed. "I cannot—her translation into Gaelic was perfect, as I speak that language fluently. Yet, it was, well, disturbing."

"And of the magic that took you there?" asked Ecne.

"Even more so," Phátric answered.

"And which question is more important?" Breanna asked.

Phátric answered, "Their decision was wrong. Or should I say it will be wrong? That goes against our scriptures—and the early writings of scholars like Origen—which portray the prophet Elijah being reborn as John the Baptist. Many Gnostic sects, such as the Essenes, use this as their basis for believing in souls living more than one life."

To which Ecne said, "Yet your clerical leaders will outlaw that belief. I would happily find more such acts for you to witness."

"Indeed!" Breanna commanded. "I say we have frequent excursions through time to see what other twists and turns your religion will wreak upon our world. With my father, I have witnessed witch trials led by your priests, roughly twelve hundred cycles in the future, where they burned women at the stake! Their screams of pain were blood-curdling, and the smell of their flesh burning made me retch. I hope you have a strong stomach."

Giving the cleric a dark glare, she turned away to seek out Eimar and rounded everyone up to get them on the march. She heard Ecne say proudly to Phátric, "I'd say our new goddess is one fiery woman! Best to try and stay on her good side."

Phátric groaned as Breanna glared at him. "What do you expect of me?"

"Seek the truth, and don't hide behind your false tenets!"

As Phátric looked conflicted, Breanna offered a grim expression. Once they were underway after their break, and she calmed herself, she slipped her horse next to Ecne's, where Sinéidin rode behind him, asking, "May I borrow your daughter?"

"Of course," Ecne said somewhat suspiciously. "Shall we stop to switch mounts?"

Breanna waved a hand, letting her Air Element carry Sinéidin over to Eimar. The lithe goddess squealed in outrage as she settled gently behind Breanna. "Sorry, my niece. That was more expedient."

To Ecne, Breanna added, "We will be back."

With that, she rode ahead, Eimar proudly strutting into the lead point of their line. Then Breanna said, "We must talk about your request and your father."

"Aye, we do," Sinéidin agreed.

"And what did you and Fergal agree on?"

"Well, we want this child, this daughter goddess."

"And?"

"She will be the first of us born in over a thousand cycles. Well, except for you and maybe Eoin. But you two were not born as babies. That will make our little one important to our family and everyone."

Breanna confirmed, "Which means he'll be overprotective."

Sinéidin grumbled, "Aye, he will. It is the way with our male gods, including my father. That is why we both want to do this, right?"

"You did well today, which bodes well for my arguing about you being a part of my band. Are you ready for that?"

"Aye, Fergal and I agreed," Sinéidin replied. "We must address my father's security concerns—namely, my security."

"Of course—the safety of all sworn will always be my priority. Your father will not be happy, but we must make you a Warrior of Destiny before revealing the daughter in your womb. Agreed?"

"Aye."

"Shall we do it now?"

Sinéidin nodded.

Breanna commanded, *"Croí Dàn, please swear in our fellow Goddess of Language as a Warrior of Destiny, minus the piece about her heartbeat stops, as my father wouldn't stand for that, nor would her father."*

As *Croí Dàn* confirmed the oath was complete, Breanna placed a hand over her niece's hands that had settled around her middle. "Okay, then. Now, we need to find a time to announce this development."

No longer hesitant, Sinéidin said, "Thank you for supporting us. We were not sure how you would both take this."

Breanna wanted to smile, but held it back. "Hush, you're family. Always believe that. Fergal was pretty annoying as we grew up, hating all things magic. Yet, he came around and then lost his head for me after he met you."

"Hmm, I'd like to know more about him."

"You have all the time in the world—I'll ensure that!" Breanna informed her. "It would be helpful if you could determine what Elements he may be able to control."

Sinéidin nodded. "Of course, for it will help protect my mate. And our little goddess will have a most excellent aunt and uncle."

"Aye, she will!" agreed Breanna. "And I asked Goibniu to address your security as he has done for my other sworn. You can cast *balefire* with your new vambraces, and a breastplate like mine will provide shields. I'll let you know as soon as Goibniu has them ready."

With that, Sinéidin said fiercely, "I am ready to cast death where needed to protect me and mine!"

 **Toal**

With Breanna riding alone once more, Toal signaled to Cilla and his archers to follow him and urged his mount next to his cousin. He said, "Cilla suggested you show us how to dance in the *void* with time, not just us two. Yet, instead of practicing on a dance floor, we would do so on horseback."

Breanna pulled her rope from her saddle hook. "Cilla, that's a brilliant idea! Since touching each of you while riding would be awkward, take hold of this and follow me into the *void*."

As the rope snapped out, they did just that. Toal felt them all in their shared space between the realms, with Breanna leading them through how the *void* and the *sight* were similar. Then, by combining the two, one could move with the *Cycle of Time* in space and in small bursts of time.

With that, Toal and his band pulled their bows off their shoulders and charged off at a gallop on their new mounts, following the High King's Road southwest. Up ahead, the forest drew close, and he called them to a halt. Cilla quickly had them set up cloth targets on a half-dozen trees. Once in place, they charged up and down the road, shooting to the left one way and then turning around to shoot from the right, arrows thwacking mostly dead center repeatedly. While their archery skills were excellent, their riding skills needed work. Fortunately, the Horsemaster had assigned mares to each of them—their only riding experience was on hill ponies, and never in a coordinated way—knowing they would be easier to manage.

Toal and his band were retrieving their arrows and targets when Breanna and her convoy caught up to them. He approached Breanna and said, "Well, your instructions helped, but we need more practice on our riding skills!"

Breanna paused. *"Eimar, let these mares know their riders only have experience on hill ponies."*

"Aye, my Hero," she answered, *"I suggest Crói Dàn link them."*

Her Heart told Toal and his band, *"Seize the void with me and touch your mount between its ears, offer your name in your mind as if you were speaking to me silently, and then ask for their name."*

A moment later, smiles bloomed across their faces, with Cilla squealing, "My mount told me her name is Luathán!"

⟶✦⟶ Breanna ✦⟵

The caravan arrived just before sunset at the River Brosna settlement. When the *fian*-in-residence saw Breanna leading the approaching disparate group, they once more marched in time to the beat of their new spears on their new shields. Then their counterparts in the caravan joined in, taking up the beat as well.

Goibniu appeared, looking pleased with himself. She assigned Falyn and Dáithí to get the evening meal served and find everyone a place to sleep, while she and Eoin took the hut they had used when she had been the Dreadlord's daughter during the *before-time*. It was remarkable that she could remember the first time she had slept next to Eoin in this very place.

All the while, Dagda and Bláth worked on the lyrics to the melody that had emerged initially from the latter's dreams at Dun Tara, though Breanna suspected her father had a hand in that effort, helping her new friend. Goibniu told her he would be leaving to work with his brothers so they could fill her most recent request for small shields and armor.

Yet, before the Warriors of Destiny took leave to find their beds, Dagda said to Livie, "Stay a moment, Seeress, as I have a favor to ask. Bláth and I find ourselves challenged to create the epic sounds we need for our new song. Our drums are not large enough at this time. We are sure someone in the future will create something more powerful and so full of deep bass that it stirs the soul. Can you find this for us so Goibniu can recreate it?"

"Aye, All-Father, I will seek it in the *Cycle of Time* while I sleep."

"Thank you, lassie," Dagda said with a big smile. "While you will find a burden in your seeking eye throughout time, it will grow within you to be a strong and deep part of your *anam*. The burden will be heavy at times. Yet, it can also bring joy to many."

As Livie nodded and turned away to seek her bed, Breanna said, "Thank you, Father, for giving her this task. She is adrift."

"Not for much longer, Daughter. It is already written in a thread of the *Cycle of Time* that you will pursue with her, one that will tie those of Cymru and Erin nearly as tight as the Dál

Riata and Erin are. Now, you look like you took a beating. Get some sleep."

Eoin said, "I'm glad you said that and not me. Now, come, my love. They will bring us food as we get ready for the night."

Breanna was too tired to think about anything profound as they ate the supper that Falyn had arranged. That night, she let her back nestle against Eoin's chest as his arm wrapped around her, and a heavy sigh escaped her lungs.

Breanna started awake at sunrise, having dreamt of Julius Caesar's invasion of the Celtic tribes on the mainland, whispering fiercely to herself, "We must know more about how he defeated all of the various Celtic tribes there!"

"Hmmm?" Eoin asked, now awake.

"What were the first tribes that Caesar's Legions battled in Gaul? We need to understand how he won so many battles in Gaul. With my Father and Livie, we saw how he beat the Suebi, a Germanic tribe. It was with numbers and skill. It can't be the only way he did that."

"In that same time, he beat the Helvetii, Germani, and Belgae."

Breanna declared, "We must better know how Caesar managed to beat them. Understand what battle strategies he used beyond might."

"Another skip through time?"

"No, something deeper, more personal," she answered. "A small band for a mission in time. We'll need Livie, Lotte, and Izzy."

Eoin suggested, "Ecne and Sinéidin would be helpful."

"Only after we secure the meeting points," she countered. "Let's break our fast and get this done."

Within a span, Breanna had assembled her team. Ecne advised, "The first Chief you'll seek was named Divico, leader of the Tigurini and Tougeni Helvetii tribes, who faced Caesar in the fifty-eighth cycle during the Battle of Bibracte, a hillfort on the slopes of Mont Beuvray, which was under the control of the Aedui tribe, allied with Rome."

"That should be enough for my intent," Breanna said as she extended her hand for the others to cover. "Everyone, be ready to draw your weapons."

As she reached out to touch the *Cycle of Time*, they disappeared.

Breanna and her chosen four materialized in a copse of oak trees that hid them from a large camp of warriors. Beyond them was the massive hillfort of Bibracte, to which it appeared these warriors were besieging. She cast her *sight* across the mass of fighters below them, sensing their unease over any potential traps laid for them.

Breanna motioned to Izzy, with fingers from her eyes to the warriors, knowing her Galicia-born warrior would best understand the Helvetii tribe's proto-Celtic language.

 **Izzy**

Izzy nodded and moved silently from the woods, stepping like a whisper on the wind, using her Elements as a mask. She walked among them, unseen, no more than a ghost, until she found a group of captains around a fire. She settled among them and slowly unwound her cloak.

Finally, one said, "Girl, why are you amongst us?"

Izzy looked up with feral eyes. "Warrior Druids know of your peril. Inform Chief Divico that this is a Roman trap. Our Seeress has foreseen your defeat."

One protested, "The Aedui retreated to resupply! We strike!"

"And the Romans will fall on you from either side. You're dead already, and those who survive will do Rome's bidding."

"And what of you?" another asked.

"Just a Warrior Druid who answers a higher power. Seek me with a signal fire when Divico is ready to meet my Celtic goddess, one who can save his tribe."

With that, she cloaked herself in her Elements and disappeared.

 Breanna

When Izzy returned to her band, she released her Elemental mask. Breanna hissed quietly, "What did you do?"

Izzy cocked her head as she weaved Air to muffle their voices, stating, "What I've always done to keep my family alive—fight Romans with every ounce of my life force. You're now also my family. I've not been just training to face Rome—I've been living amongst Celts trampled by Romans my entire life. I planted the seed for you to meet Chief Divico and maybe save his tribe."

Breanna and Eoin looked at each other, with the former saying in mind-speak, *"Hmm, Izzy is more capable than I thought."*

She said, "Sorry to have underestimated you."

Izzy grinned. "I understood your intent."

"And now?" she asked.

"We wait for the word to pass up to Chief Divico," Izzy answered. "I suggested to his captains that they light a signal fire to accept your meeting request. They will try to lay a trap. Yet we must ensure your safety. You and Livie need to seek out our near future."

Breanna sighed. "Izzy, you didn't tell me all about you, did you? When did you begin infiltrating other tribes and the Romans?"

Izzy shrugged. "I started training with wooden katana blades at three, and had a blunted one at five. My mother's father taught me ways of stealth, and by nine, I could command my Elements. I was ten when my grandpa sent me on my first intelligence-gathering foray and eleven when I earned my great-grandpa's katanas. While I still struggle with the Aether Element, my grandpa recently proclaimed me *Laoch Druí*."

"So that was how you disappeared?" Breanna queried.

"Aye, I was the unsuspected young spy in my tribe."

Eoin asked, "So now what?"

Izzy suggested, "Wait for their signal fire."

Breanna commanded, "Livie, seize the *sight*. What is to come?"

She did just that before saying, "Romans lay in wait on the far side of the Aedui hillfort, but I caught an echo of them on the edge of Divico's camp. There is a small group dressed as Helvetii tribesmen who reek like the Romans behind the fort."

As Livie pointed them out, Izzy turned her eyes on them. "As I expected. They have a trap planned, likely to attack the Helvetii's flank when the tribesmen try to take the hillfort. That will signal the Legionnaires to sweep into the battle. It is a classic Roman tactic."

Breanna cursed, "Shite, my targeted intent did not include this."

"No matter," Izzy said. "Exposing them as Romans or traitors will get the Chief's attention. Give me a moment."

With that, Izzy disappeared into her Elements.

Lotte muttered, "By the stars, how does she do that?"

Moments later, there was a brief battle at the edge of the camp, one led by their warrior from Galicia. After some *balefire* flashes, it was over quickly, with several dozen dead. When Izzy returned, blood dripped from her katanas and splattered across her tunic.

"You've been wounded!" Livie exclaimed. "Roll up your sleeve."

Izzy did so. "It's just a scratch."

Lotte growled. "Gah, that's not a scratch. It's bleeding deep."

"I've had worse," Izzy rejoined nonchalantly. Livie knelt beside her and placed a hand on the ground and the other on the wound, pulling on her Earth Element to heal Izzy's arm. A shallow slash across Izzy's ribs caught Breanna's attention, who drew Livie's focus to it. "A stupid fecking Helvetii mistook me for an Aedui after I released *balefire* on the traitors. The shields were gone. Ah, that's better—thank you, Livie."

Breanna frowned. "That was reckless."

Izzy countered, "I have survived tighter spots. I left the Romans a message and arranged new terms with Divico's captains."

Seeing Izzy in a new light, Breanna asked, "Which are?"

"To trust us, or the Romans will kill them. They chose us."

"Where?" Eoin asked.

"A place in the hills above us," Izzy answered. "Come morning."

"And here I was thinking we'd need Ecne and his daughter to help us talk with these tribes," Eoin muttered.

"Indeed," Beanna agreed. "Let's find water so Izzy can clean up. Lotte, please use your Element to locate a stream on the way."

Lotte guided Izzy as they climbed through the hills to a stream along their path. While Izzy stripped down and worked to remove the blood from her blades and clothes, Breanna asked, "So, my *Laoch Druí*, have you hidden this side of you?"

Izzy shrugged. "I think not, as you did not truly ask. Yet also know that when I swore to you and your Heart, I did so fully. You'll have to trust me. It is the life I've led for nearly ten cycles. I know how Roman and Celtic men play their games of power. Now, follow me. We need to find a place to camp until sunrise."

The next morning, Izzy introduced Breanna to Chief Divico and took him on a brief trip into the future, which convinced him to alter his plans.

The Chief stated, "You have saved the lives of tens of thousands of my people, not to mention mine. I don't know how to repay that debt. I will lead my people back into the hills and seek out other tribes I've allied with. My previous Chief had made a pact with the Aedui, which was clearly at an end. Yet I must ask if you and your Warrior Druids can further help us?"

Breanna sized him up before answering. "Maybe. Do you know of Ariovistus, the king of the Suebi? I know Caesar attacked them earlier this cycle."

"I heard as much," Divico said grimly. "Bad news, that was."

"Maybe cast the word that the remnants of them are welcome."

"Aye, that I will. Any other assistance?"

"If I can, I will bring ballistae and plans for it."

He nodded. "That would be welcome. Then farewell, Breanna Ban Morna. You and your Warrior Druids saved many this day."

With that, the two Helvetii tribes retreated, ensuring they held the high ground as they sought help from other tribes.

Breanna's next stop took them north into Belgica, where a battle raged across the River Sambre between Caesar's Legions and the Nervii Tribe. This time, they saw ballistae in action. Without those weapons, the Celts would have likely held their ground. After that, a naval battle broke out between the Romans and the Veneti. Once more, ballistae played a role in delivering fire spears from ship to ship, along with their ability to cut the sail-power rigging, leaving them dead in the water. Having seen enough, Breanna took them back to Erin and their time.

 **Julius**

When a Centurion reined in his horse before the gates of the sprawling fort known as Bibracte, Julius Caesar halted his pacing. "Report!" he demanded.

Marcus, the Centurion whom he had assigned to lead three flanking cohorts, dismounted and answered, "The Helvetii tribes have disappeared into the hills, and our infiltrators are now dead."

"How did this happen? Were they somehow found out?" another asked. Caesar looked at his friend, a Tribune named Gaius, and realized he should have thought to ask that question.

Marcus took a deep breath and answered, "They were, indeed, discovered, and based on the state of their bodies, it was likely two days ago. The tribes appear to have started their withdrawal yesterday morning, as moving tens of thousands of people out of this valley would take at least that much time."

"Any sign of how they knew we had planted those Aedui?"

"Only one clue—words carved in Latin on the foreheads of six men, each laid side-by-side. The message said: 'Warrior Druids are coming for Rome.' The other troubling sign was seeing limbs separated by fire, something that cauterized as it cut through flesh and bones. It is like nothing that we have ever seen."

Caesar demanded, "Who are these Warrior Druids?"

Marcus shrugged. "Unknown rumors, like a mist in the night."

"Not an answer I can accept," the general declared.

⎯⎯◈ Breanna ◈⎯⎯

Breanna's band returned to Erin and found everyone was ready to head for Dun Uisneach. Their band of warriors, gods, goddesses, and Druids left the River Brosna settlement behind, marching and riding steadily west, with Falyn leading the way.

Breanna and Eoin rode between Ecne and the smith, who asked, "I take it you learned something useful about Roman battle tactics?"

"Aye, we did," Eoin replied. "They used their hardened numbers and ballistae to defeat the Celts, but not all battles were easily won."

"And they appear to use subterfuge to recruit traitors to their side," Breanna added, looking over her shoulder at Izzy, Lotte, and Livie riding behind them. "Izzy discovered the Roman plans at our first stop, and we possibly changed the timeline of the Helvetii."

The *sight* took Ecne for a moment before he said, "The Helvetii eventually merged with others instead of being wiped out, which caused Rome some minor issues in Legionnaire deployments."

"We'll have to do more next time," Breanna groused and reined Eimar in so she could follow up on a possible next step for the Helvetii. "Their leader asked for help, so I set Kyle and Fergus to making a few ballistae. It might help if the tribes are better armed."

Ecne could only say, "Maybe. It's a mighty river you're trying to change. Yet, who knows what one thing will have an impact?"

Walking beside Goibniu and his wagon, Dagda asked Livie, "Speaking of the *Cycle*, I know my Seeress had an exciting time in, well, time. Yet I must know what you found in the future in the way of drums to help our song?"

Breanna chucked at the puzzled expression her Seeress cast her way. Then Livie countered, "I thought I was your daughter's Seeress."

"Och, hers, mine, ours." All-Father sighed. "It's all the same."

Livie cocked her head at Breanna, who had nothing to add to that comment. "Well then, about twelve or thirteen hundred cycles from now, Gaels will create what are known as kettle drums. They have a big, deep beat, especially when the Gaels march with them into battle, but the sound was bigger when players used them at a Céilí, as they were larger and in a stand, twice the size of the marching kettle."

"Livie, that sounds perfect for our needs. Pass your vision to Goibniu." Then he turned, commanding, "My mighty smith, make haste to create some standing kettle drums for us."

Goibniu handed the reins to a startled Airmid. "Little goddess, there is nothing to it, as the horses will follow everyone else."

Then, he jumped from his seat to land on the ground next to the Seeress and took Livie's tiny hand as she sat in her saddle. Breanna felt him seize the *sight* as he received her vision; then he disappeared.

Airmid grumbled in clear annoyance.

Breanna chortled. "Enjoying your time with us? Once we arrive, you'll have time to train Livie and Izzy in your magical healing arts. Make good use of those moments."

Airmid snarled in response, and Breanna smiled broadly.

Dagda added, "Livie, please also pass on your vision of these future kettle drums to our Bard of Destiny so she can hear how they are played in that time."

Bláth, who was riding beside the Seeress, took her hand. Moments later, she exclaimed, "Och, that will be marvelous!"

Toal and his archers rode ahead to practice their mounted targeting runs, and by the time the caravan caught up, the nine riders were smiling; they and their mounts were one.

They arrived at Dun Uisneach just after midday, with everyone still dry and in good spirits. Breanna was somewhat irritated that preparation for a Céilí was underway in the yard, as Chief Faolán had planned for it to occur the following day. Her mood lightened at the thought that this celebration might shift the focus more toward her Warriors of Destiny and less on herself as their new Goddess of Time. At least, she hoped that as she swung down from Eimar's back. She found Eoin at her side a moment later.

Faolán greeted Falyn with a passionate kiss, then wrapped his arms around her and held her tight before turning to his son to offer a warm hug. The yard paused during their reunion, and all cheered when their leaders parted to pull Breanna and Eoin into a joint embrace.

Dáithí said excitedly, "Uncle Eoin showed me how to seize the *void*, and we had a blade dance!"

Faolán and Falyn smiled, with the former saying, "Maybe, one day, you'll be one of their Warriors of Destiny."

With that, one of the *fians* started chanting, "Bre! Bre! Bre!" Then the other two chanted, "Warriors of Destiny! Warriors of Destiny! Warriors of Destiny!"

When those gathered ceased their chants, Bláth, Master Bard of Dun Uisneach and now their Bard of Destiny, stepped forward, pulling All-Father behind her. She utilized her mastery of the Air Element to amplify her voice. "Our *Ceann-feadhnas* has organized a Céilí to celebrate us and our land. Not only have the Tuatha gods returned to us, but their magic has, too. The Heart of Destiny has claimed her as Erin's Hero! More importantly, Breanna Ban Morna is now our Goddess of Time. As such, she will ensure the Romans do not corrupt the Celts of Pretannia, and the One God worshipers will not rule the Gaels in Erin or anywhere else! Spread the word!"

Beside her, Dagda's voice boomed, "Gaels rule!"

The *fians* chanted, "Gaels rule! Gaels rule! Gaels rule!"

Bláth exclaimed, "Prepare for a celebration!"

Breanna was pleased to see the diminutive Bard standing proudly beside All-Father, her father. He had undoubtedly claimed her as his voice, their voice, throughout the times they would travel. With that idea in mind, she commanded her Heart that it was time to make the dun's Master Bard one of her sworn as her Bard of Destiny, not just a Warrior of Destiny!

Croí Dàn confirmed, *"I will make it so, something special."* And thus she did, ensuring Bláth swore an additional oath to

Breanna. She saw the lithe Bard tilt her head as if listening to her Heart before looking up with a big grin.

Later, during the evening meal in the main hall, Eoin and Breanna took to the floor to dance. Bláth led her fellow musicians in a jaunty tune, and the pair used it to cement their support of their people in her cause as Erin's Hero. Their dance, which leveraged their magic and aided the Heart of Destiny, did just that.

A short time later, Goibniu returned with three large kettle drums that his brothers helped him create. Yet, the night was long when Breanna finally pulled Eoin into their royal hut.

After Eoin and Breanna rose and prepared for the day, the former headed to the barracks to arrange more battle training for their Warriors of Destiny and work with young Dáithí again.

Meanwhile, Breanna spotted Ecne and signaled him to join her in seeking out the leader of the One God. When they found him in the main hall, Breanna commanded, "Phátric! It's time for our first discussion of the day. Note that means another one could take place later. I want to discuss the natural world and who controls and commands it.

"Like what makes fire, who commands the winds, how our earth provides for us, and the core nature of water that sustains us all. Tell me your thoughts before I share mine."

"Er-ah-my—"

"Just call me Breanna. All the titles, like Erin's Hero and Goddess of Time, do not matter in this discussion. It is your beliefs versus my reality."

Phátric stammered, "Beliefs and reality?"

"Phátric, please, you're not that dull, are you?" Breanna asked with a frown. Then, she snapped her fingers, sprouting fire between them. She added, "Fire, the heart of our world, the sustainer of life, the grantor of death."

"It is a powerful part of our One God," Phátric answered.

"Show me how—how does he control it, gift it?"

"We just believe. Lucifer in Hell controls fire on Earth."

"Not your all-knowing god?" Breanna asked derisively, bringing a hand up again. This time, it swirled with water at her command. "What of Water? Does your god gift that element to others? Like this?"

Breanna let a small fountain gush from her hands into a bowl on the table, putting out the flame. "Then there's Air, which I could combine with Water to make a mist or ice."

With that, the water in the bowl rose, and a gentle breeze turned into a mist in the air before them, then chilled. Ice crystals dropped onto the table and into their bowls of porridge. "Oops! Sorry if I cooled your breakfast. I probably shouldn't use 'Earth' in my demonstration at this point. Cold, watery porridge mixed with dirt would not be tasty."

One of Phátric's brethren asked, "Are you a sorceress?"

"Och, nay!" Breanna denied it in surprise. "I am but a lowly Druid apprentice. Well, maybe 'lowly' isn't the right word. Maybe an inexperienced Druid apprentice would be better. Wait, I must be honest. I'm the Chief Druid's Apprentice, who happens to be my father. Aye, as in All-Father, as in the Tuatha god of many things."

Phátric shook his head. "I learned about your gods from the Druids while I was a hostage, so, yes, I know of All-Father in your pantheon and have seen him about during our travels."

"And you know about Danu?" Ćroí Dàn asked excitedly. *"She's my Mother!"*

Breanna noted that Phátric seemed startled by her Heart speaking in his mind. She said, "My Heart can hear through me."

He sighed. "Of course. I know of your Mother Goddess."

Breanna growled. "I'm an idiot. I should have known you were playing stupid. So, you know all about Druids and Elements?"

"Yes and no," Phátric answered. "Druids, yes. Yet, your gods and goddesses, I never met one until recently. As to your Elemental powers, I have never witnessed such a thing. The previous Druids I met did not display such skills to me. You are a first for me, for us. What I don't understand is why you fear my god."

"You forget that I am also the Goddess of Time. I don't fear your One God. I fear what the followers of your One God *will* decide to do with the power they've seized and what they *will* do with those who do not believe as they dictate.

"And it is not a fear of what they may do. It is a fear of what they *will* do. I have traveled through time and have seen it. I have seen it as the Goddess of Time when I roamed the world with my father, across many timelines that can take shape in our future.

"Unfortunately, it does not get better, and religious wars and persecutions by the men who lead the world over the ages by claiming the divine right of their One God will cause hundreds of millions of deaths—added together, over the cycles, billions of lives will be lost.

"All of this will cause more deaths in the names of other such omnipotent gods, pushing their followers to prefer those who *give* those men the right to rule. In a few short cycles, another Abrahamic-based religion will rise in the same region where your fellow followers claim is the birthplace of the One God's son. Battles over unbending religious doctrine by these various righteous leaders will make Might is Right the motto of our world! Leaving women and children to suffer. Your rulers and mine seek to cut out what ordinary people desire. So, I might be the one to tear it all down, and I plan to ensure our people rebuild it. Failure is not an option."

Breanna took a deep breath before saying darkly, "I cannot let that happen. I just can't. I can't let all the suffering I've seen take place. And it will not just be my people who will suffer. Across the world, we will grow to billions of people, the majority oppressed by wealthy, powerful men who seek only more power, more control."

"How can one person change what you have seen?"

"How can one person not try to change it, knowing this. Even one who believes in a merciful god that yours is supposed to be?"

With that, Breanna rose, looked down at Phátric, tears in her eyes, and said fiercely, "While I will weep over those I cannot save, I will fight fiercely for those I can. And I will not be merciful while doing so to those who've brought the battle to mine. I cannot be!"

⸺⚬⚭ Breanna ⚭⚬⸺

Breanna marched toward the stables, knowing she needed to be one with her land, and only by riding Eimar could she make that connection. Her mount demanded, *"My Hero, who has upset you so?"*

Cróí Dàn informed Eimar, *"It's the burden of the past and future she must change that arose from her discussions with the One God leader."*

"I'll trample him!"

Breanna smiled at Eimar's notion that such an action would help. Then she passed through the gates and rode east for a half-span or so. There, Breanna veered south into higher climbs of the ridge that ran east and west. It was time she sought another mighty black oak. When she found one that seemed old and gnarly enough, Breanna dismounted, crossed over to it, placed her hands and forehead on its rough bark, and let her troubled mind still before reaching out to its spirit.

Through her Earth Element, she let herself merge with the ancient one. After a long moment, the response was a low yet still female chuckle. Breanna found that a surprise. Then, the tree astonished her even more, saying, *"My brother told me about Erin's Hero walking the land once more. He said you were troubled, as you've been Erin's Hero recently. Yet, now you have a deeper concern, one that is different. You saved your land at no small cost and need our support, your land's support. How may we help?"*

Breanna hesitated, then answered, *"What's coming is much worse than what I faced in that past time you referred to. You know I'm now more than just Erin's Hero, yes?"*

"We do, our Goddess of Time. We also now feel Erin's Veil cast by Danu during your sacrifice and transition. And if you die, the Veil will fall. Again, how may we help?"

"I don't know," Breanna answered as she sank to the ground, her back against the mighty tree. *"The weight of what I must do lies heavily upon my mind. If I succeed, billions of lives could be better off. Yet, if I fail, those same lives will be lost."*

The tree somehow smiled at her. *"Yes, billions of people can be lost if you fail, but they would be lost anyway, with or without you. Change what you can, accept what you can't, and fight for what you desire to be and believe in. Be one with your land. Find your past! Rely on your Taoiseach!"*

Breanna sighed, letting her land seep into her, comfort her, renew her. *How could a tree make it so simple?*

A moment later, Eoin dismounted next to Eimar and then knelt beside Bre. "My love, you escaped Dun Uisneach without telling me. *Croí Dàn* led me to you, as she always will. Please tell me your troubles. I am, after all, your *Taoiseach*."

Breanna barely held back her sob. "It's about what I've seen in the future. It's terrible—no, it's beyond terrible. My skip through time with my father has been wearing on me. The future will be horrific if we fail. I sought the trees and the land for direction and solace. They told me to find my past."

Eoin knelt beside her in contemplation and nodded. "I think I know who you must seek in time to find your past. We must first travel to Maeve's time and draw out her wisdom as the *Banríona* of our land in that time. After that, we can seek out Macha Mong Ruad, our first *Ard-Banríona* of Erin. Each was a strong woman, a strong warrior, and a strong leader. While in time before ours, each may provide insight into how they ruled. Our Heart chose them and will know how to guide us."

The tree **she** had joined with said, *"My Hero and Goddess, listen to your Taoiseach!"*

Breanna looked up at Eoin. "Thank you, my love."

Eoin pulled Breanna from the ground and into his arms. "I have strong shoulders, *Mo grá*. Lean on me."

Eoin

Back at Dun Uisneach, with the Céilí celebration preparations well underway, Eoin suggested Breanna get something to eat and led their mounts to the stables. On his way back, he caught Ecne's attention in the yard. "We have a mission in two past times before this afternoon's events get underway. Breanna needs to know how Maeve and Macha managed their roles, each as Erin's Hero in their time and as matriarchs of their land."

"Interesting concept," Ecne said. "I'm in!"

"Breanna missed breakfast, and I did the same because I had to help her manage this burden, so let's grab something to eat and be gone."

Ecne grinned. "For a mortal, I like you more and more. Something about you says you're more than you let on."

Eoin tilted his head, then paused momentarily, a frown crossing his face. "I was there when she sacrificed herself to save her land and people. Yet, by then, I was all but dead at the hands of her father. I would not change anything except that I'd rather have killed him myself. Yet, I guess I'm no longer just truly mortal. Aye?"

Ecne could only nod as they turned toward the main hall. Eoin sought out Breanna and found that thirty-plus Warriors of Destiny had already surrounded her. Having sensed her distress, Eoin knew they would have surged to her side when she returned, each letting her know they believed in her.

Eoin proclaimed, "My Hero!"

Breanna shifted her gaze to him. "My *Cosantóir*."

"We have a mission, first to visit with Meave, as we discussed," Eoin declared. "Ecne will join us, along with Sinéidin. I recommend that your blooded warriors and one *fian* join us. Our destination is the stronghold known as Cruachan of the Enchantments in Connactcha. The timeline is when Maeve held the Heart of Destiny as Erin's Hero."

Breanna nodded. "That is enough intent to find her. Corbmac, pick your chosen *fians*. We leave as soon as they have their weapons and shields ready. We must assume the guards will be hostile. The rest of you gather the same. We'll meet in the yard in half a span. I certainly do not want to be late for the Céilí!"

Izzy barked a laugh. "You can always be *on time*."

Breanna chuckled, only to have Bláth ask, "I am not blooded, but I have sworn the oath."

Eoin answered for her, "Actually, when you ensured Runa was dead with your knife in that past time, you became one of our blooded, but you must have forgotten that nuance. Of course, you'll be joining us. Bring your staff and knife, and be ready to challenge what you see versus what your legends tell you."

Bláth accepted Eoin's command, saying, "Aye!"

⟶✳❧ Breanna ❧✳⟵

In the yard, Breanna looked around at their assembled band and was pleased. She said to them firmly, "We are about to travel back many centuries to seek advice from Erin's Hero of that time. We seek Queen Meave, once Erin's Hero, ruler of Cruachan of the Enchantments in Connactcha. We do not challenge, only parley."

Seizing and snapping out her magical rope, Breanna commanded, "Form a chain by touching this rope until you're all linked to me. Remember, we bow to no one. Gaels Rule!"

A moment later, just over twenty Warriors of Destiny and a god and goddess suddenly appeared before the gates of Maeve's fortress, which had more formidable stone barriers than Breanna had ever seen, barring the way into the place known as the magical Cruachan of the Enchantments. Her *fian* warriors, with their Roman-styled shields, fanned out in a semi-circle before her, forming a shield wall that bristled with the otherworld metal spears Goibniu had provided.

Breanna could sense that Maeve was somehow controlling the Tuathain magic. It rolled off the walls, barring the way, but she strangely knew it could not stop her. Looking closely, she found the walls woven with Druidic sigils. Yet, she knew she had to seek Maeve in peace.

She declared, "I am Breanna Ban Morna, Erin's Hero and Tuatha Goddess of Time! I seek your *Banríona*! I have come to meet with your leader about important matters regarding the distant future of our Emerald Isle."

"You have too much protection to come in peace!" a guard atop the wall stated, with several more looking down at them.

"I travel with those I trust. Maeve walks our land freely because everyone knows she is a fierce and mighty warrior backed by you. Currently, I am unknown here. Yet I am similar to your Queen and travel with protection. Again, I would only like to discuss this with your *Banríona*."

"We open the gates for no one we do not know."

Breanna huffed and groused privately to Eoin, "This is getting nowhere. Any suggestions?"

Croí Dàn said, *"Leave this to me."* Then, she directed her thoughts toward the fort. *"Maeve, I am back. We need to talk, you, me, and my new Hero. Well, not just her, as you must meet Erin's Cosantóir and two other Tuatha gods."*

Maeve answered with an astonished thought, *"How is this possible? You just left me, and you already have a new Hero? A fast rejection, that!"*

"It is a matter of time, as I will return to you when I return to my current time."

"How can this be?"

"Erin's Hero in my time is also the new Tuatha Goddess of Time. She brought us here, to this time, your time, to discuss grave matters our Emerald Isle will face in the future."

"How far?"

"Just over five hundred cycles."

Breanna heard the exchange, and moments later, the gates creaked open. Queen Maeve, dressed in her ancient warrior leathers, held her spear, *Cletiné*, setting the shaft-butt on the ground. Looking darkly at Breanna, she ground out, "You have claimed my Heart. I see it around your neck! Anyone who takes what is mine is my enemy!"

Breanna narrowed her eyes. "As my Heart informed you, she will return to you when we leave your time. As I see it, the sooner we do that, the sooner her return will assuage your wounded pride."

Maeve hissed, her spear springing to life with Elemental fire. "Pride? I have no equal!"

The *Lann Dàn* leaped into Breanna's hands, *balefire* crackling. They circled, with the queen offering a feint to the left. Breanna countered with a jab inside her opponent's spear to counter, forcing Maeve back.

Croí Dàn commanded, *"Maeve! Stop!"*

Breanna pulled back. "You have no equal in your time. Yet time has moved on, and you are history. Think, Maeve! I currently live in a time where men rule almost absolutely, and a new religion will displace our gods. Millions of women will die! Men will rule. Matriarchs will become no more. They have already faded in my time. And now the Romans have left Albion, which is about to be picked over by Angles, Saxons, and Norvegrs. Those combined victors will create a new country out of that island's chaos to our east, and they will rise to crush our Gaels and their Celts over the succeeding centuries."

Maeve proclaimed, "Never!"

"Are you brave enough to see it firsthand?"

"How?"

Sheathing her blades, Breanna stepped forward and extended a hand. "Again, I am the new Tuatha Goddess of Time. Take my arm, and you can see what I have."

"Is this a trick?"

"Unfortunately, it's not," Breanna answered sadly, still holding out her hand.

Croí Dàn exclaimed, *"Trust me, as I trust her!"*

As Maeve took Breanna's hand, they disappeared.

Then the pair returned a moment later, with Maeve saying, "That was very—disconcerting."

"Indeed. It breaks my heart. And yet, I have to fix it. Or—"

Maeve interjected, "We Gaels will be crushed! I understand now. Apologies. I thought you were here to challenge me. Yet, you're not; you need to seek solutions so you're not overwhelmed by the ugly, power-hungry men in your time and beyond."

"And your advice?"

"Show no mercy—kill them when you can! Respect is won."

"What about the cost? The deaths required to secure that win. The people lost by that decision? My actions could result in many deaths, especially for our Gaels and Celts. I have to bear that weight."

"Once you choose a path, commit to it. Trust in your beliefs, but there can be no room for pity or remorse or doubt if our land is to survive. Be merciless! Listen to your time sense."

Breanna pulled her team back to the present. Around them, the Céilí preparation continued. Eoin said, "Her message was as strong as she was. Yet we still must visit with Macha Mong Ruad."

Breanna answered, "Aye, but not tonight. Ecne, we have a private matter to discuss. You and All-Father are required to attend this meeting. It is not a request."

Ecne raised an eyebrow, saying, "Of course, Auntie."

"Eoin, Fergal, Sinéidin, with me. Livie, join us as well."

As Dagda joined them, he proclaimed, "Daughter, what is this about? I have music to make."

"First, we have a revelation," Breanna said sternly. "Yet, I require your restraint to reveal it. That includes both of you. No exceptions. Please confirm you agree to my conditions."

Ecne and Dagda looked at each other and nodded in unison.

"Swear it! Our agreement in this matter will bind you."

Ecne commented, "In what matter?"

Dagda confirmed, "Daughter, my restraint in this matter is bound."

"Thank you, Father." Then, Breanna said tightly, "Ecne, swear it now!"

Ecne said, "I cannot, cousin, without knowing why."

"Then we are at an impasse. It's my way, or we battle!"

The pair stood still, Ecne going pale at Breanna's stare, cold and indifferent; she knew he would not stand a chance against her.

All-Father commanded, "Enec, let it go."

His many-times great-grandson could only nod. "My restraint in this matter is bound."

Breanna said flatly, "Sinéidin has sworn to me."

"What!?"

"Yes, as a Warrior of Destiny, she is now mine."

Ecne's tone was dark. "Why?"

"Because she carries our future," Breanna said proudly. "Sinéidin and Fergal have made a new little goddess."

Ecne appeared stunned.

Breanna added brightly, "And they are mine."

Ecne protested, "They are our future. Our Tuatha future."

"Och, they are, and only I can assure their safety. Do not stand in my way, cousin. As an adult, Sinéidin chose this path!

"Livie, she added, "Seek the *Cycle*. What do you see of this baby?"

The Seeress did as requested, eyes glazing over. A moment later, she said, "She will look like her mother and be the first of more new baby Gods and Goddesses, all growing up surrounded by Breanna's Warriors of Destiny."

Dagda sighed. "Ecne, you are outmatched. If Breanna says Sinéidin and this new little goddess within her will be safe, they will be safe."

Ecne groused, clearly unhappy but unable to argue.

Sinéidin grinned at her new friend and fellow goddess.

Breanna winked back, adding, "Father, you'll oversee their handfasting this evening during the Céilí. It will be another thing to celebrate."

Dadga grinned. "My daughter, of course, and nicely done."

Ecne looked icily at his great-aunt many times removed, but she just blithely turned away, knowing they had at least won this battle. She was less sure what the coming war she planned would bring, but her visit with Maeve had clarified one thing: she must not give the Romans any quarter. Nor the tribal Celtic Chiefs in Pretannia, with whom she needed to draw to her side if they were to survive the coming centuries.

Back in the central yard with her Warriors of Destiny, Breanna thought about the Celts across the Sea of Erin and said, "Livie, we must plan a time to meet your Father! "

Now standing beside Beatha, the Seeress muttered to her, "Myrddin. I had hoped she had forgotten about him."

"I heard that!"

As Breanna held her Seeress's eyes, Livie added, "You know him as a diplomat and ambassador. Yet, I did mention he is also a conniver, a weaver of intrigues, conspiring with whoever he can to advance his plots, all to ensure his visions come to pass."

"Sounds like just the man we need, as long as we ensure we give him the right visions to chase."

Livie groaned, asking Beatha, "When does this Céilí start?"

"Bláth is on the stage setting up now, so soon."

Breanna raised an eyebrow at the deflection.

Livie brightened. "I hope so. I understand she and Dagda have a new song for us to listen to this evening."

Breanna grumbled to Beatha, "And here I thought Livie and I were going to become best friends."

Beatha snickered behind her hand at the pair.

Goibniu strode to Breanna's side and said, "Gather your blooded warriors. I have your requested shields and breastplates."

"*Croí Dàn, please pass the word,*" Breanna commanded. "Come, Livie, let's drop the matter of your father for now and see what our smith brought us. After that, I must change into my blue dress for the party!"

With the Céilí underway, Breanna and Eoin wandered about the dun's yard, visiting with each artisan, asking after their mates and families. There were weavers, dyers, wood carvers, and the like. They found a jeweler with polished green Connemara marble stones, similar in color to those in her hair tie. One piece called to her, a teardrop-shaped stone wrapped in a Celtic knot of silver that dangled from a silver circlet with beaded stones woven into it. The fit was so perfect that it seemed as if the jeweler had made it for her.

Eoin commented, "The green stones go well with your red hair. It is a unique piece made for my goddess."

"I'm sure it's beautiful, but certainly too much," Breanna said.

"Never too much, my love," Eoin said, handing the stone worker four gold pieces. "Will this cover the cost?"

"Nay," the woman said. "It is my honor to give it to my Hero."

Eoin smiled. "Then it is my honor to give you a boon."

As Breanna settled it on her head, they turned away to see what else they could find, and four gold coins lay on the polisher's table.

Breanna watched as Lotte and Izzy preened in their new, gleaming pauldrons and breastplates, each etched with Druidic sigils that would enhance their elemental powers. At the same time, Braoin, Bradaigh, and Fergal had small, round shields painted in the same emerald green crest their fiancés bore, which they could quickly sling on their backs. Livie's armor was more understated but no less effective, and even Sinéidin now had a short sword and a dagger strapped to her waist, with armor similar to what the Seeress wore and her vambraces.

Breanna saw that Toal and his archers each had slightly larger square shields with a slit in the upper half, through which they could shoot their new crossbow bolts while still being protected. Cilla was not pleased, grousing that they needed reactive armor and not shields—those would block his aim and limit Toal's ability to calculate trajectories. Goibniu acknowledged the oversight and said he would correct it.

Now wearing her dress that Falyn provided her in the *before-time*, Breanna strolled along with Eoin. They stopped at the artisans who had set up to offer their wares, praising the weavers and potters for their fine work. Then, seeing the Master Smith of Dun Uisneach, the pair sought him out for a chat.

Eoin held his arm out in greeting. "Gus, sorry we have not had much time to visit. It's been busy, for sure."

"Och, no worries," Gus said. "You two have got a lot on your hands, after all. Discovering that our Goibniu is the *Tuatha Dé Danann* God of Smithing was a surprise. I see he has brought you some fancy new weapons and armor."

Breanna took his arm next. "But I still have my dirks, which came in handy in the *before-time* we experienced. I'll not be parting with them."

Catching sight of the Master Tanner of Dun Uisneach, Breanna waved him over. "Bhruic! I hope you've forgiven my teasing about your inquiry on the performance of your finely crafted leather work."

"Certainly, my Hero," Bhruic said. "It was on me as I put my foot in my mouth. Yet, I saw you have my harness, belt, and cloak. Falyn told me they gifted them to you during your *before-time.*"

"Of course I do! While the Tuatha have magic, their realm cannot produce leather from animals that do not exist there. Maybe you should suggest a trade with Goibbi. It would help bring them closer to us."

Bhruic smiled. "Great idea. Let me go work on that."

As he left, Kyle, the Master Woodwright of Dun Uisneach, approached her, saying, "My Hero, I understand you have newly crafted—well, small bows. What are they called?"

"Crossbows," Eoin answered. "The larger units are ballistae."

"Um, well—er—I thought we could make them for all *fians.*"

Eoin stepped in again. "Likely a good idea, and I'll broach the notion with Goibniu, but only those sworn as Warriors of Destiny could wield them with *balefire* bolts."

"Of course," Kyle said. "If our Hero wants our guilds to swear an oath as Artisans of Destiny, we will happily do so."

Fergus put in, "That's brilliant, Kyle. Let's do that!"

Breanna looked at Eoin in surprise, and he said, "I will make the arrangements with *Croí Dàn* for an appropriate oath for the guilds."

Breanna added, "All guilds will report to Eoin and the new Council of Erin we are putting together. You two, come up with a plan beyond the oath. Gaels must rule not just this island but the seas as well. We will need better ships to do so. I'll see if Manannán can help you."

Then, as if lightning struck her, she saw a possible future that might help them with their coming battles with Julius Caesar, not this cycle but the next. *"Eoin, Ecne—we need plans to build a port and a shipyard! It needs to be near Dun Tara, where the River Liffey flows into the Sea of Erin. Summon Livie. She will show you where in time to find the plans."*

And then all was normal as Kyle and Fergus huddled to discuss their ideas. Eoin just nodded to Breanna as they continued across the yard. As they did, various Warriors of Destiny drifted to their leaders, each greeting them warmly.

"Eoin, aside from the ship thing, I've been thinking."

"Och, that can be dangerous, my love!"

After elbowing him just below his breastplate, Breanna chided, "You oaf, I am serious. Livie is now our odd girl out, with Fergal and Sinéidin matched. We need one more."

Eoin sighed, asking, *"Croí Dàn, who could match with Livie?"*

Their Heart suggested, *"Fionna Mac Cumhaill?"*

Bre questioned doubtfully, "A poet for a Druid Seeress? I'm not sure. I don't see a fit for a one-time young poet who ate a Salmon of Knowledge. Yes, he gained knowledge and rose to be the leader of all *Fianna* in his time. Who else? Maybe someone from Cymru."

"Because my Mother can touch the Cycle of Time, I can do the same. Through Livie's Cymru roots, I foresee one who is to come in the form of a powerful derwydd bardd yn nghymru, to use their language—a Seer and Bard named Taliesin."

"I have no idea who that is or where in time to find him, but he might be one to balance out Livie's father, Myrddin. I'll ask my father, as I'm not sure Ecne will help us after our earlier—discussion."

"But not now, my love." Eoin nodded toward the stage.

Faolán and Falyn greeted the assembled crowd. The former addressed those gathered, "Our people, our friends, and our extended family, we welcome you all to Dun Uisneach! For those who live in other duns and settlements, I expect you'll not know why my mate and I called for this Céilí so soon after our Samhain festival.

"I am pleased to let you know our Tuatha gods have returned to Erin to help us address the future of all Gaels. By rescuing Erin's Hero in another time, where she saved our land from an invasion that few are aware of, Breanna Ban Morna walks among us again with her Heart of Destiny. And she returns as our Hero and our new Goddess of Time. You might have seen her and her Warriors of Destiny dancing with their blades.

"Some of you have been matched against them. And, because of this, you know their warrior skills have become magical. That's because they are indeed just that. The All-Father and other Tuatha gods are here to support Breanna in a new mission to save all Gaels from being ruled by others, such as Rome and any future nations they will spawn, which will bring a plague of terror and destruction among us.

"Yet, Erin's Hero and her Warriors of Destiny will not let that future befall us!"

As the crowd cheered at their Chief's words, Faolán and Falyn motioned toward Breanna and Eoin, now surrounded by their Warriors of Destiny. The Chieftess added, "Enjoy our games, crafts, hospitality, and this marvelous weather. And take the time to get to know Erin's Hero and her sworn warriors. Celebrate that we renew our commitment to the Great Agreement, where we worship the Tuatha gods as they committed to protect our realm against all foes."

Her people bellowed their approval again as Faolán and Falyn climbed down the steps to greet all, milling among them with their Druids, answering questions where they could. All welcomed Breanna and her warriors, thanking them for accepting the mantle they had taken up to protect their fellow Gaels and Celtic cousins.

Soon, trenchers were in hand, each taking their fill of boar, venison, fish, roast sicín hens who had stopped laying eggs, tubers, boiled cut wheat, and bread. And ale and mead flowed into mugs and cups. While that was happening, Dagda, Goibniu, Ecne, Dian, and Airmid appeared amongst the Warriors of Destiny, causing a stir in the gathering. Her father waved a hand, and two sturdy stools appeared for the two large gods, who then sat at a nearby table with their trenchers and mugs. Others around Breanna and her *Cosantóir* also took their trenchers and mugs to that table.

Airmid and Dian sat stiffly across from Breanna. Her brother said wryly, "Sister. Interesting that you have chosen that seat."

She beamed. "Just wanted to enjoy some time with your daughter. And, of course, Ecne!"

"Auntie," Ecne acknowledged, his voice a bit tight as she sat next to him. "You did well with Maeve, I believe. She was certainly volatile, yet you managed her."

Breanna shrugged. "I missed the minor fact that *Croí Dàn*, being sentient, cannot exist in both times simultaneously. I should have thought of that. Maeve was quite unhinged when she saw *Mo Chroí* around my neck."

"I expect it will be the same with Macha," Eoin agreed.

Dian commented, "Aye, that must have been a shock. Lugh mentioned Danu is rather proud of your Heart, especially over how you've bonded and are working together. It is good to see that mother and daughter are no longer at such odds."

Airmid snorted on a mouthful of food, making her father scowl.

Breanna grinned at her niece. "That is good news, brother."

Then she turned back to Ecne. "We will have to think of something to prepare Macha, but that can wait. What is not is that we still have a challenge with our Seeress from Cymru. She must excel at touching the *Cycle of Time* and feeling its nuances and shifts among the timelines that might take shape when we impact history. She is critical to our success."

"Och," Ecne said. "I saw she was previously working with Fergal, but that is now problematic with Sinéidin in the picture."

Breanna sighed. "Not just that—Livie does not relate well with warriors. I need to find one more compatible, such as a Bard or Seer, either from history or the future. Balance is key, as I see teams of two working together as friends or lovers. I'll never send any of us into time alone. My Heart has suggested a young poet from Cymru named Taliesin. He will rise as a noted Seer and Bard, but I'm unsure where or when he will live."

Armid muttered, "Mortals are too sentimental."

Breanna ignored the Healer. "So how do we find him?"

Ecne held out a hand. "Auntie, take me to the *Cycle of Time*."

Breanna took it and seized the *sight*, pulling them into the *Cycle's* flow. She watched Ecne deftly pick at various threads of time across the Sea of Erin, swiftly culling through the Celtic region called Cymru. Then he skipped ahead many centuries, finding historical scholars who had written about the man to hone in on when and where Taliesin had lived.

A moment later, Beanna felt her cousin push an image to her and release her hand.

"Found him," Ecne said. "He will be born early in the next century – say, within fifty cycles, near the town of Caer Guricon. At that time, Cymru will be shifting from worshiping their old gods to the One God more dramatically, so you'll need to approach him while he's young – before those forces can influence the lad."

"Thank you, Ecne."

"Of course. Yet, when it comes to Sinéidin, I will not forget your pledge – I expect you will keep her safe."

"Goibniu has already seen to it that your daughter has the same enhanced shields created by Badb Catha that all Warriors of Destiny bear. Yet, know that I am not planning to take her into battle, so it is just a precaution. I assure you, I only plan to engage her in language translation."

"You moved quickly, Auntie, enough so you were confident there was no question of the outcome of that discussion."

"Exactly," Breanna said drily, raising an eyebrow. "I believe that's partly my father's influence, as I do not plan to fail. I will not let anyone rule my Gaels! Just as I will not sacrifice us, the glorious Tuatha, to the long night where the Gaels forget us!"

"With every such interaction, you're making me a believer."

Breanna gave him a surprised smile. "Come to the stage for your Daughter's handfasting when it's time. Dagda will be presiding. And please, no more calling me auntie. I'd rather be just Bre."

Evening fell, and the Céilí continued, and Breanna watched Dagda and Bláth make their way to the stage as her Bard's players finished another reel that had drawn people to dance. When All-Father sat on his sturdy stool, his massive harp, Uaithne, appeared before him. One of her players handed her a smaller harp.

Bláth projected her voice with her Air Element, calling out, "Here's a new song for this special occasion we have been working on with Dagda's help, one to memorialize our Goddess of Time and her Warriors of Destiny. It's called *True Hearts Beat*."

Then, following the song's opening hopeful introductory notes, her soprano voice, joined by All-Father's bass voice, merged with the song's hopeful introductory notes. And soon, the kettle drums from the future joined in the mix.

We rise as one
We stand as one
We call out as one
We fight as one

In the Cycle of Time, where sacred souls are lost
Our Goddess defends all with true hearts
With the sound of silence, we're no longer afraid
To fight with Erin's Hero and protect all who she aids

We pledge our blood and bones across the ages
We pledge our blood and bones as chaos rages

With the Heart of Destiny, such miracles to divine
No more myths, no mysteries, no more hiding from our fears
Remember all of you, our words, and all our truths
We shall return with our Hero with true hearts

We rise as one
We stand as one
We call out as one
We fight as one

We rise as one
We stand as one
We call out as one
We fight as one

With true hearts, we fight as Warriors
To protect all our people and the future they seek
We don't walk this earth alone and speak out as one
Seize the *void*, trusting our Goddess, we live on through time

We rise as one
We stand as one
We call out as one
We fight as one

The crowd roared once more with approval, and all on the stage, including Dagda, rose and bowed in appreciation. All-Father let Uaithne fade back to Falias, leaving the stage with Bláth to make their way to Breanna, Eoin, and their Warriors of Destiny.

"Our very own song!" Izzy exclaimed.

Lotte said sourly, "Yet, I've done nothing—won no battles like you. Taken no heads. I've defeated no one."

Breanna groaned. "Father, maybe that was premature?"

"No, Daughter," Dagda answered as if disappointed. "It will take time to spread. You all need to focus on what you must do now while you take the One God followers west. Your ability to dance in time is still suspect. Your Warriors of Destiny—well, one of them, at least—are over-eager for battle."

Lotte appeared to wither under the gaze Dadga cast at her.

Then he added, "Yet, others are tentative in their abilities with the *void*. You all need practice, much more practice."

"Point taken, Father," Breanna said. "My warriors, it is time to dance among our people. Bláth, give us a tune to show our people."

As they paired off, Livie asked, "And what of me?"

Breanna said firmly, "While I have a plan for you that will take time, you focus on tonight. With this song, Eoin will carry you through *time*. Trust in me."

"But he is yours," Livie protested.

Breanna corrected, "Aye, he is, but he is also your protector like he is mine, and he is both my *Taoiseach* and yours."

Then, the pair joined hands, and Eoin led Livie through the music Bláth was once more conducting. And somehow, Eoin could guide Livie through the *void*, lifting and twirling her in *time*, not challenged by her robes in the least bit.

When the song ended, Eoin returned Livie to Breanna's side. "There we are. You did well, Seeress."

Livie said, slightly out of breath, "That was—more than I expected. I'm not sure how you did that."

Eoin bowed. "My Seeress, I'll leave you to my love to say more."

Breanna agreed. "He has a gentle side that warms me, a side that hides the warrior in him. I think that's the problem. You don't need a warrior but another Bard or Seer, maybe one from Cymru."

Dagda put in, "That is my brilliant daughter at work!"

"How can that be?" Livie asked, clearly astonished.

"He is about to be born, but time favors you because you're with me." Breanna shrugged. "Taliesin is destined for greatness and must meet you."

"He's not even born yet?"

"Correct, but he will be our age when we visit him."

"Why would you do all of this for me?" Livie asked.

"You are My Seeress. I will do anything that's needed for you."

Livie was stunned by that commitment, tears brimming as Eoin stepped beside her again, saying, "If that answer is not clear, know my love feels deeply for those who have sworn to her. Everyone counts. All are needed for us to succeed. She has foreseen it and has shown me the horrors that await the Gaels and Celts if we fail."

Livie stiffened, saying more confidently, "Then, as my Goddess of War originally commanded of me before I met you, I will do my best to see we do not fail!"

Breanna gave her a hug of thanks and turned away. "Fergal! Sinéidin! Time for your Hand Fasting!"

With that, she took her Father's massive hand and Eoin's arm and led the way to the stage. Along the way, Sinéidin snagged Ecne's in the same motion. When the next song ended, the six climbed the steps and motioned to Bláth that they needed to command the stage. After Breanna managed to get Eoin to stand behind Fergal and Ecne behind his daughter, each with a hand on a respective shoulder, they were ready.

With All-Father looking out over the crowd, the people quieted. "My Gaels of Erin!" Breanna called out. "Tonight, we do not just celebrate the return of the Tuatha gods walking amongst us Gaels once more. We celebrate the joining of two Warriors of Destiny! One who is a Gaelic warrior and one who is a *Tuatha Dé Danann* goddess. We gather to bear witness to their handfasting ceremony this night!"

As the crowd drew in a collective breath, Dagda's voice boomed out, "Before you stands one Fergal Mac Conall and my Great-great-Granddaughter, the Tuatha Goddess of Language, Sinéidin. Both present themselves to you, desiring to confirm their handfasting, with Eoin, as his Chief, and Ecne, as Sinéidin's father, who is the Tuatha God of History and Culture. Both are here to confirm their support of these two as mates."

With that, Dagda motioned for the two to clasp hands, wrist to wrist. Then, magically, a glittering golden sash appeared, dangling from his fingers as he began tying their arms together. All-Father commenced with, "In unity, as your hands are bound together now, so your lives and spirits are joined in a union of love and trust."

Fergal and Sinéidin answered jointly, "To my mate, I bind myself to a union of love and trust."

"In strength, may these hands give you support as you need it."

They answered, "To my mate, I grant all my heart and strength."

Dagda guided, "In commitment, you swear in peace and passion to stand with each other, heart to heart, and hand in hand."

"To my mate, I promise, in peace and passion, to stand with you, heart to heart, and hand in hand."

"In love, may your hands be clasped in friendship and your hearts and souls be joined forever in love."

"To my mate, I pledge my heart and soul forever in love."

"In wisdom, may you always have the insight to cherish this precious love you share."

"To my mate, I vow to cherish our love as we join our souls."

Dagda announced, "As the Chief Druid of Erin, I present our newly mated Fergal and Sinéidin to you!"

The pair then raised their joined hands to the crowd, embraced each other with their free arms, and shared a passionate kiss.

Croí Dàn pulled a thread of their love and, using her power, let it wash over the crowd, and there was a collective sigh of joy.

In the morning, Breanna lay in Eoin's arms and sighed.

"My love," he said. "That is not a positive way to approach a new day. Do I need to please you, my fierce warrior mate?"

Stretching like a cat, she turned to him with a smile. "You sense me so well."

Eoin said nothing more as their lips met in a passionate clash, and they found pleasure in their heated embrace. Once sated, they lay back, their bodies sweaty, pressed close together in a tender embrace.

Eoin coaxed, "Now, tell me what troubles you."

"It's the Christians. We must ride west with them today, wasting our time when we need to focus on Rome."

"True," Eoin concurred. "Yet, it will not be time just spent traveling with them. We still must educate them on what their leaders will do in the future—make them see the damage being caused in the name of their One God. We should make an excursion with Phátric somewhere in time during our lunch break."

Breanna was thoughtful momentarily before adding, "Maybe a witch-burning trial would be good after our pious monk has something in his stomach to lose."

Eoin chuckled. "That is a cruelly excellent idea. And we will make some other excursions, like seeking out Macha and Mong Ruad, not to mention finding Taliesin for Livie and visiting with her father, Myrddin."

"True," she confirmed. "Then let's bathe and join our sworn."

The pair brought their breakfast trenchers to a long table that her Warriors of Destiny had claimed in the main hall. Breanna noted that Ecne, Fergal, and Sinéidin clustered, their mood upbeat as the *Tuatha Dé Danann* and the Gaelic Warrior of Destiny learned more about each other.

Breanna headed to that end of the table, saying, "Sinéidin, I see Goibniu provided your shield plate and vambraces. It is a most becoming look for you."

"It is strange but not uncomfortable."

"So how does it work?" Ecne asked.

Breanna suddenly flicked a dirk over his daughter's shoulder, and, with a flash, it bounced off her otherworld shield.

Ecne sucked in a breath. "What was that?"

She bent to retrieve her dirk and answered, "Badb Catha has been busy. She's using her *dark matter* to make her formerly magic-only weapons and armor work in our world. Your daughter's breastplate has shields to protect her. And her vambraces can cast *balefire*. But she needs to be careful with using that when she needs the other, as there's a cycle time between the two powers."

"I see," Ecne said drily. "You could have told me that before we—argued. Or before you just did that!"

"I could have, but what fun would that have been?"

Her something-removed nephew laughed at her jest. "Indeed!"

Breanna's tone turned serious. "I hope you'll stick with us a bit longer, as I have a few more jaunts through time I'd like to take with you."

"Of course, Bre, as that will keep me close to my daughter while her little goddess grows within her."

"A good thing," Fergal said, handing Ecne a shield.

"What's this?"

"Similar to your Daughter's breastplate. We all have them."

Ecne took the round shield with its new crest of the *Triple Dàns*. "I should have known. Blades, Stone, and Heart of Destiny are etched in power sigils like the breastplate you wear and on this shield. It is powerful magic—*dark matter*—one that only Badb Catha can manipulate so that it can be invoked or imbued in an item like this. She truly is invested in you and yours."

"Aye, very much so," Breanna confirmed, beaming.

"Och, my great-grandfather could have let me know. But enough about Badb and her vast abilities. I have a surprise for you." Ecne handed a scroll to Eoin. "As requested, here is a revised version of the Magna Carta you asked me to find for you. It is written in Latin for now and opens with:

"'By the grace of our chosen gods, whoever they may be, in our desire to ensure justice and equality for all people, we hereby grant and declare the following rights and liberties to be held by all individuals, regardless of gender.'

"The revised version goes on to provide sections covering equality before the law; the right to fair trials; protection from arbitrary actions by those holding power; reasonable punishment for transgressions of the law; the right to hold property; freedom to choose one's mate; rights of widows and widowers to prevent seizure of assets; protections for families and children; equal access to learning and training; freedom of speech, assembly, and protest; equal participation in governance; protection from discrimination based on sex, race, or skin color; freedom to believe in one's gods or goddesses; and additional rights for the vulnerable and less well off.

"It closes with: 'This Charter of Rights and Liberties is granted in perpetuity to all people, without race, gender, or age distinction, and shall serve as the foundation for a just and equal society of all Gaels.'"

Breanna scanned the document over Eoin's shoulder while Ecne provided the summary. "Ó, but that's a lot to take in!"

Eoin commanded, "Seize the *void* with me, my love."

As she did, Eoin said, *"As you once shared your knowledge of the bow before the battle with the Norvegrs, I share my now more thorough knowledge of Latin with you. I know I taught you how to read it, but now you'll speak it."*

A moment later, Breanna said, "That is amazing! I like many of these provisions based on those words, but learning and training are at the top of my list. Teaching them Latin would be an abomination. We need a common written language for our people."

"Aye, but it is a start. We will confirm a path forward after consulting with All-Father regarding this proposed text. Additional changes are likely needed to enshrine these rights fully, but we'd like to thank you for your help, Ecne. Maybe Sinéidin can help us create a written version of the Gaelic language to teach our people."

Sinéidin tucked an arm inside Breanna's. "My Hero, I would love to help with this effort. Maybe we need a new Druidic Sect of Teachers."

Breanna called with her mind, *"Father! Sinéidin suggests we need a new Druid sect to create and teach a written form of Gaelic. Our people must be able to read the Chairt Mhór to understand their rights! Maybe here is where we can use Áine? To influence the Chiefs!"*

Dagda answered, *"Daughter, this request is a marvelous idea. They will be known as Múinteoir. Ecne and Sinéidin, you will lead this new sect of my Druids, as they will need a council. I'll speak with Áine."*

Ecne blew out a great breath. "Well, that's my Great-Grand-father—decisive as always. Daughter, we have work to do."

Sinéidin smiled broadly. "I will not only bear the first Tuatha goddess in over a thousand cycles to have a child, but we will head up a new Druidic sect of teachers—the *Múinteoir!*"

Breanna called, "Keegan, a brief word, please."

"Um, Bre," he answered. "How may I assist you?"

Breanna caught his eye but said nothing. "Please fetch Tadg for us. Your Breitheamh will join us on our march west as Eoin has a new task for him to work on."

Eoin agreed, "Aye, we do. Like the Great Agreement between the Tuatha and Gaels, our Gaels need a Great Charter between our leaders and our people to define their rights.

"In the meantime, I have a task for you and your Chieftess, Falyn. All-Father has created a new sect of Druids to teach our people a written version of Gaelic. Dun Uisneach will have the first *coláiste* in Erin. We will need a building for this school where our *Múinteoir* can teach written Gaelic to the people."

"Impressive," Keegan declared. "I'll work on this with Faolán and Falyn while you're all in the west."

Breanna took the Seneschal's hand. "Thank you, Keegan. Speaking of heading west, let everyone know we'll ride out in a span."

"As you command, Bre."

A moment later, Goibniu rode his wagon through the gates with two gleaming ballistae on wheels tied behind it. Breanna clapped, excited to see the new weapons she requested, as her uncle exclaimed, "Bre. I have two prototypes of the long-range weapons you requested, but you will need to find the horseflesh to move them. They have a range of about one thousand yards. You have live spears and practice ones."

Breanna demanded, "Stableboy! I need our hill ponies hitched to these new weapons. Please have Kyle and Bhruic help make it so.

"And speaking of which, please find Fergus."

Goibniu climbed down from the wagon. "Here are the plans. The secrets are in the new sigils. Study them. I will see you along the road to the west as needed. Good luck, my baby goddess."

"Toal!" Breanna called out. "I have an assignment for you!"

Her cousin and Cilla were quickly at her side, along with Fergus, Kyle, and Bhruic. Breanna said, "I have plans here for Roman ballistae. I need portable sample versions produced for our Celt friends in the past. We must provide them with a sample unit and written plans so that they can build more on their own. Can you all do it?"

"How many?" Kyle asked. "And should we make crossbows?"

Breanna said firmly, "Yes, ten of each will do for now."

With mounts ready and two wagons loaded, they set out. Then, the followers of the One God rolled behind them, along with another wagon carrying supplies. Her *fian* warriors prepared to march behind Corbmac's chariot. Their caravan included their two new rolling ballistae. Eimar pranced proudly at the head of the column. The weather threatened rain, but it held off. They reached the ford at the River Shannon some two spans later, manned by a lad named Crogher, who had fought Breanna, Braoin, and Bradaigh in their *Comórtas* this past summer.

Breanna dismounted and approached the lad. "Well met, Crogher! What news do you have for us? We have a mission to escort these One God believers to Dun Gaillimhe."

"Also well met, Breanna! By the gods, it's good to see you!"

"Same here," she answered, offering her arm in welcome. She gestured to the robed men behind her. "Yet we need news of the west, as that's where we lead these One God followers."

Crogher looked at the wagon. "The Connachta clans know the High King is distracted. Their leader, Dauthí, supports Niall, but his Chiefs and Commanders press him for more. Those of Mummu are also on the move, looking to sow their doubts about the High King."

"They are likely to oppose me as well," she commented carefully. "I am planning a change in how we rule ourselves, with a Council of Erin replacing kings and common folk having a say."

"I'd like that, but it will be a big hill to climb," he responded, at which Breanna could only nod. Crogher then looked curiously at the glowing long blades in her harness. "Those are mighty ancient-looking weapons you have there. Not the ones you beat me with."

"Aye, they're not," she answered brightly. "Our gods have smiled upon me. Pass the word—Erin's Hero walks the land once more, and she will fight for her people."

Croí Dàn commented, *"A loyal and devoted Gael. Let's swear him to us."*

"Erin's Hero from our myths and legends?" Crogher croaked.

"The same. While I have already claimed all in my land, I offer you the opportunity to be sworn to me."

"I felt you a few weeks back, aye?"

"Indeed, it was me. Will you join my cause?"

Crogher nodded and sank to a knee as *Croí Dàn* instructed, *"Repeat after me."*

With that, he was sworn. Breanna commanded, "Stay vigilant. Those in Ulaida, Mide, and Laigin will back me. It is unclear if Connachta and Mummu will do the same."

"I will check with others who use this ford and let you know their sentiment when you return," Crogher told her. "Now, let's get you and your formidable force across the river!"

She then commanded all to prepare to head west. Breanna informed them they would need several ferry trips to cross the River Shannon. She also reported that the Connachta clans would likely pose trouble. Corbmac put two *fians* forward, and Eoin did the same with half of their blooded Warriors of Destiny. The head of the caravan bristled with weapons. The dark green forest opened around them and drew closer from time to time as they followed the road west. The weather was partly cloudy, though it was somewhat chilly when they were in exposed meadows with little foliage to block the breeze blowing in from the west.

Breanna signaled Ecne to join her and nudged her way between Tadg and Bláth. "I assume you now know why you're riding with us?"

"Indeed, my Hero," Tadg answered, yet clearly uncertain.

Bláth laughed at her fellow Druid. "Tadg, first and foremost, Erin's Hero prefers just Bre or Breanna."

"On that, we agree, my Bard of Destiny," Breanna rejoined. "Yet, I must ensure that you, Tadg, know how to do your task. Thus, Ecne and Eoin will represent my requirements for the eventual people's rights charter you will produce for me and my Father's review."

Ecne said, "I look forward to working with you on this endeavor, Tadg."

She asked in mind-speak, *"Ecne, any update on the ship-yard plans?"*

He just smiled. *"Coming along, Livie is most helpful."*

With that, Breanna retook the lead with Eoin as the forest drew in again. She commented, "With Crogher's warning, I'm feeling prickly. There are eyes upon us. Join me in the *void*."

As they entered their shared space between the realms, she said, "*I remember the skill of seeing auras of living things hidden behind trees and in the brush. I will show you.*"

When Eoin's eyes widened, Breanna knew his altered vision flickered to life alongside hers. She added, "*Note that wildlife differs from humans in size and color. Most animals have a green or golden shimmer, while men are often red or orange when riled or excited; conversely, they are bluish or purple when calm.*"

Eoin said, "*It is an interesting vision state. There, ahead on the north side of the High King's Road, men loping through the woods.*"

"*Aye, I see them, and as well to the south. Slip back and alert the others. I want Braoin, Toal, and Cilla on point with me, bows ready and nocked.*"

Eoin nodded. "*I'll have the other archers ready their bows as well and have half of the fian warriors do the same with the crossbows. The remaining fians will be ready to form a shield wall in front of our non-combatants. Our blooded will have their balefire weapons ready for a demonstration.*"

"*Then I want you back with me, as we might need to take their leader on a jaunt into wherever as we did with Énnae.*"

Still holding the *void*, Breanna looked to the briefly open sky above when the forest pulled back and saw a falcon circling above. She reached out and directed with her Aether Element, "*Be my eyes!*"

With that, their life thread merged, and she and the raptor were one as they swooped over the forest, then down along the road, shooting forward as if they were a lightning bolt. Catching sight of those waiting for them, the falcon twisted through an opening in the canopy, and they were back in the sky. Breaking contact, Breanna said reverently, *"My thanks for sharing your eyes, fierce one!"*

A span later, the forest formed a tunnel over them, and fifty Connachta warriors swarmed onto the road before them.

Corbmac ordered, "Shield Wall! Pike's out! Crossbows ready!"

As his *fians* took their formation, the Connachta leader commanded, "We control this road. By what business are you here?"

Flanked by Braoin, Toal, and Cilla, each with their bows nocked and ready, Breanna nudged Eimar slightly forward with Eoin beside her, saying stiffly, "By the High King's order, we escort these pilgrims to the west."

"The High King is off on his many raids," the Connachta leader said. "Rumor has it, Eochaid is pursuing him during his latest mainland raid. We will likely have a new *Ard Rí* soon."

"Old news." Breanna shrugged. "There will not be a new *Ard Rí*, and Énnae Cennsalach, King of Laigin, has already sworn to me."

The commander chortled. "Sworn to a lassie, you say?"

Breanna smirked as she fingered her golden rope. "Aye."

"We claim you all as hostages."

Eoin demanded, "On whose authority?"

"Mine, through my king," he answered.

"Do you honestly not know Erin's Hero leads this caravan?"

"We do not recognize a myth."

"I rule my land!" Breanna asserted firmly. "You heard the call of my Heart and my claim! As I have told others, I will fight for all of my Gaels. Our battle should not be with each other but with those who will soon invade us—danger grows across the sea. As Erin's Hero, I need your lives as sworn to me. Do you give them freely?"

Their leader said, "We give no lives freely. We will kill you all!"

Eoin drew *Claimh Solais*. "Idiots, you face any Tuatha magical weapons that can end you. Do you think the fire in my blade will not burn the skin off your bones?"

"Two against us all?" He sneered. "Our gods are dead!"

Then, one of the Connachta warriors cast a spear at Eoin, who let *balefire* from his sword consume it. Eoin sighed, saying to the commander, "You're an arrogant shite. We are more than two and well-armed. Yet only you will die."

"No," ordered Breanna as she reached out to Eoin and seized the *Cycle of Time*. Then, she thought the word *snatch,* and her coiled golden rope snapped out to the commander. The three of them disappeared when it wrapped around his throat. A moment later, they returned, and she proclaimed, "I will not kill one of my Gaels unless I have to. Your commander now sits at Shannon's Pot, wondering how he got there. It will be a long hike back for him. Who's next?"

The warriors looked around, unsure of what had happened. Then Izzy whirled forward, using her Air Element and letting her katana blades sweep out with *balefire* that churned up the road before their feet. She landed in a crouch, her blades held before her, her expression one of barely contained fury. "No one insults my family!"

"Which of you does not accept Erin's Hero?" Eoin demanded darkly. "If so, step forward, and Breanna will send you to where she dropped off your former commander!"

They all knelt before Breanna and Eoin as *Croí Dàn* demanded they swear the oath.

With that, Breanna said, "I look forward to a survey throughout my land after we deal with these One God followers. It would be appropriate for all the Chiefs of Erin to swear my Heart's oath before we start our campaign against Rome.

"To you of Connachta, who now live by my Heart's grace, we face a disaster in the future. Please spread the word about how we relocated your commander instead of dispatching him. Tell your king he comes next. He will bend his knee and swear the same oath to *Croí Dàn* that you have, regardless of his numbers. Unfortunately, good men will lose their lives should their leaders choose the path of fools. Be wise and good men and pick the path that unites us."

At that, one man rose in defiance even after swearing the oath, ready to toss his spear, but he suddenly clutched his heart, dropping the spear as he crumpled to the ground dead.

Croí Dàn proclaimed, *"As sworn, I own all of your hearts. If anyone doubts this, rise, and I will stop yours as I did with this misguided fool just now. Pick a new commander, one loyal to MY HERO! Pass the word. Erin's Hero walks among you."*

Breanna sighed. "As I said, we should not fight each other."

Silence reigned before one rose, saying, "I will lead them and bring word to King Dauthí, the *Ard Rí's* nephew, that Erin's Hero has returned and that you want to unite our Gaels against invaders."

Breanna nodded. "The *Ard Rí* already knows this, as his Druid Seer told him, but he has run off instead of having to swear to me. Yet, his Queen and mother have already given me their oath, making Ulaida, Mide, and Laigin mine. Tell your King he is next. I travel to Dun Gaillimhe, should he wish to meet me there to discuss the disposition of these One God followers."

As they rode on, leaving the sworn Connachta warriors behind, Breanna asked, "Why are the men of Erin so arrogant?"

Ecne answered, "It was so from the beginning, with the sons of Mil. We thought we could negotiate a peace, but it was hard."

"Well, not on my watch," Breanna said quietly. "If I am to save my fellow Gaels, we can't allow our leaders to seek positions of even more power while wasting good Gael lives to achieve it. Those are lives that should be protecting Erin from the outside world. Maybe the High King's coming death at Eochaid's hands will allow us to change how we choose our leaders."

Ecne sighed. "We did not have someone who wielded the magic of the *Triple Dans* then. Badb Catha's construct that tied the three *Dans* together lay uninvoked. Yet you did just that, and now we have a Goddess of Time. I find you refreshing."

Breanna sighed, her mood still troubled over the death of a Gael.

ACROSS TIME

⟶⟨⟩⟶ **Breanna** ⟨⟩⟶⟶

There were showers right before they stopped for lunch, but it had been dry since then as they made their way peacefully along the High King's Road, which followed the River Shannon for a time before turning west toward Dun Gaillimhe. With several spans of daylight left, Breanna commanded their caravan to make camp, stating that all warriors must practice controlling their *balefire* by calling it to life without casting it. They needed to make it an extension of their weapons.

Standing before them, Breanna drew her Blades of Destiny and called *balefire* to demonstrate what she wanted to see. Two beams of crackling fire grew at the tips of *Lann Dàn* to three feet and stopped. When she crossed them, *balefire* was like a solid extension of her blades, each spitting sparks of power when they touched the other.

"*Croí Dàn, show my Warriors of Destiny how to control the balefire their weapons contain,*" Breanna said.

With that, the Heart of Destiny did as commanded through their sworn link, and she guided them as to how Breanna controlled Badb Catha's *balefire*. Soon, all were controlling the magical fire. Then Breanna added, "Now spar!"

They tentatively engaged in one-on-one matches but were hesitant because *balefire* was a fearsome weapon. Their blade extensions hissed as the flaming bars of firelight clashed, crackling when they touched. It was a cautious dance.

Breanna sighed. "Eoin, join me in the *void*. Let's demonstrate this use of controlled *balefire*."

Eoin drew *Claimh Solais* and extended his sword blade with the Dark Goddess's strange *dark matter* to match Breanna's Blades of Destiny. And they danced with their extended blades for a time. The peculiar magical extensions collided repeatedly, sparking steel-like fire blades. When they stood down, Eoin proclaimed, "Izzy and Braoin, you're next."

The lithe warrior from Galicia exploded into action, using her Air Element to flip up and over her startled opponent as she controlled the *balefire* extending from her katanas. Braoin spun, countering her dual blades with his two swords. For a time, it was close, four blades whirling, spinning, and clashing. Yet, in the end, her speed won out, and her crackling blades crossed before his neck.

Braoin withdrew his *balefire* and sank to a knee. "I yield, Izzy!"

"Good, as I prefer your neck remains intact," she commented lightly, reining in her extensions. Then she added impetuously, "Especially with you bowing before me like this. Are you going to propose we be mates or something?"

Braoin winked at her as he rose. "Maybe I should."

"Okay, you two, clear the field," Eoin commanded, somewhat exasperated. "Bradaigh and Lotte, you're up next."

With her two spears elongated by *balefire*, Lotte had the advantage of reach and made short work of Bradaigh's defense. He even tried to lengthen his sword's fire, but her two weapons were more than he could handle. Thus, he had to do the same as Braoin and knelt, calling out, "Lotte, I yield!"

Balefire vanished as Lotte demanded, "No proposals out of you!"

Bradaigh rose, eyes narrowed at her statement, muttering, "I think you want one but won't admit it."

"Gah!" Lotte threw back at him.

Breanna chuckled over the courtship dances her sworn warriors were making. She nodded to Corbmac, who called his *fian* warriors to gather in two shield wall formations, ordering them to extend their pikes with *balefire* and march toward each other's line. As the extended tips met, thunder and lightning rumbled as they clashed.

Breanna pulled on her Air Element to be heard and called out, "Stand down. I conceived this exercise to ensure we can safely use our most potent weapon—*balefire*—in a situation like the Connachta warriors posed. If their attack had split our line, casting *balefire* amongst ourselves could have hit our own. While we all have shields, I'd rather not take that chance. Thank you for humoring me. As you swore to me, I am sworn to you."

The *fian* warriors thumped their spears on their shields in appreciation as Lotte approached Breanna. "A question, Bre. There hasn't been time, but Bradaigh suggested something outside Dun Tara after you admonished us for our spat. He suggested my sense of his *feelings* for me might be due to a potential to control Aether. Is that possible?"

Breanna perked up at the question, quirking her head to one side. "That was perceptive of him. He's likely right, as my father said the same thing. Most Druids who command Fire and Water are unbalanced. Yet, with all your rage, you mostly rein it in. Aether would help you balance the two. I can offer you a Sigil of Power if you accept it. As you are of the Fire Element, searing you with it will not be pleasant, as I must blend your primary element with Aether."

"Make it so," Lotte commanded.

Breanna reached out, taking hold of Lotte's left forearm. "So mote it be!"

Lotte hissed at the pain, but Breanna knew that it had passed as Aether flooded through her sworn warrior. After a moment, Lotte said, "Worth it. Everything is clearer now. You and I have clashed since the first day, yet you've stood by me, including now. Maybe my sister is right. There's much to learn. Aether is just one aspect."

Breanna sighed and hugged the recalcitrant warrior. "We all have challenges with life. Just live what you have!"

With that, Bláth began preparing dinner as the rest finished setting up their camp. As that took place, Eoin asked, "My love, where do we go next? To see Macha?"

"Let's spend some time with our Warriors of Destiny this evening."

Eoin said to their Bard, "Bláth, let Corbmac handle our dinner. We need some music!"

She answered, "Aye, Eoin, I'll gladly change my duties."

Corbmac groaned. "Why does the old man always have to cook?"

"Because you do it so well, my grandpa!" Breanna said fondly.

"That's thick butter you spread on my bread, my girl."

"It's lovely butter, though, right?"

Breanna saw Corbmac try to suppress his smile and hugged him when he grinned broadly. Then he set about the task Breanna had asked him to do. With that, the *fian* leader dug out two big pots to make a stew. He nodded to a few of his warriors to see what they could hunt up. Braoin, Toal, and Cilla drew their bows and set off with them, heading into the meadows of Connachta, dotted with clusters of black oaks. A short while later, they returned with rabbits and pheasants, with Cilla taking down a young buck. After they made quick work of bleeding, skinning—for which Cilla claimed the deerskin—or plucking their prey with help from the *fian* warriors, they each settled in with a mug of ale to listen to their bard.

Once Corbmac's stew was ready, Breanna skimmed through their camp, getting to know her Warriors of Destiny, carrying bowls to those waiting for the line to thin out. As she had circled through her Warriors of Destiny, she commanded Izzy and Livie, "I think you two should spend some time with Bláth to improve her control of her Air Element while in battle, stealth, and as protection. She's used it for casting her voice and not much more. She wields her knife in battle better than her Element."

Izzy nodded. "We would be happy to do so, Bre."

Her Bard looked confused until Breanna added, "You'll want better control of your Elements should you need to protect yourself. I want you with me for many cycles, so I'll not trust the Fates on this."

Breanna saw Bláth blush at her commitment as her friend.

They made camp for their first night, setting up a new contraption called tents, something her Seeress had discovered in her divining of Roman, Saxon, Angle, and Norvegr ways; she promptly had their Master Tanner make them before they departed. Small ones were for one or two blooded warriors, and larger ones were for Corbmac's *fians*. Usually, each would roll out

ACROSS TIME ❖ 267

their oiled bedroll tarps and wrap themselves up if it rained—the tents made for a pleasant and dry first evening. Breanna decided Livie needed a special gift to say thank you, as she and Eoin could lie skin-to-skin on their bedrolls, covered in warm blankets. She remembered many shivering nights in the *before-time*.

Over the next few days, they encountered Connachta warriors twice more as they headed to Dun Gaillimhe. The first encounter had a similar outcome: Breanna dropped the commander off at the Shannon Pot, and *Croí Dàn* swore the remaining warriors to Erin's Hero. When the next commander stopped them, rumors had already flowed before them. Their leader took the oath with his men this time, and she sighed with relief that no one died. Then the caravan rolled on through showers and sun breaks.

When they stopped two nights later, Breanna approached Phátric. "Events have disrupted my plan for your education, but we will get back on track tomorrow. Please rise early, as you'll need to eat breakfast before we go watch an accused woman burn at the stake."

As she held his gaze, Izzy called to Breanna, "My Hero!"

Breanna looked up from the pious monk leader and, seeing the lithe warrior's concerned expression, stated, "Remember, call me Bre, my friend. What is it, Izzy?"

"Bre, then." Izzy sighed. "I just got a dark premonition from my mother, not quite a vision. There's trouble back home!"

"Your clan is under threat?" Breanna questioned as she touched the *Cycle of Time*. Switching to mind speak, "*Croí Dàn and Livie, find her mother in space and time! Use Izzy's connection. Find her family now!*"

Livie took Izzy's hand and seized the *sight* with *Croí Dàn*—Breanna sensed it was an unfamiliar experience for the Galicia warrior—and responded, "*I have the location, and the time is* now! Roman-led One God followers are attacking a Celtic enclave upon a hill."

Ćroí Dàn added, "Remember, you can jump there, but your intent can make it before this moment. It's unclear when the attack began, so it's best to plan on arriving several spans before now—say midday."

Breanna switched to her natural voice. "My Warriors of Destiny, we leave now for Izzy's home in Galicia to protect her family! Ready your weapons. We depart in a quarter-span at most. My blooded warriors, take to your mounts. I plan to be there before the trouble starts, but we might get into a battle! Prepare to call *balefire* to your blades; only cast if the way is clear. To me!"

As they scrambled to readiness, plucked up weapons and shields, her bloodied warriors flung themselves onto their horses, just as Breanna did. Eimar whickered in approval as her Hero was on her back once more. Breanna called again, snapping out her magical rope. "To me! Make a chain along my rope or touch one who has taken hold of it."

Eoin commanded. "On three, with us!"

Only Dian, Ecne, and Airmid remained, with the baffled followers of the One God watching the warriors disappear and wondering even more so that the Tuatha Goddess of Time's magic was truly real.

Breanna's Warriors of Destiny appeared before the open gates to a Celtic enclave hillfort, where a collection of circular stone-walled huts with thatched roofs stood within timber walls. While they were ready for battle, she called, "Hold! We arrived before the Romans, and there's time to defend against the coming attack."

Izzy flipped off her mount using her Air Element and landed before a surprised middle-aged Druid. "Mother, I received your dark premonition. As you suggested, I've sworn myself to Bre-anna Ban Morna, Erin's Hero, and their new Tuatha Goddess of Time. Her Warriors of Destiny are here to defend us!

"Fionna, my mother, please meet my new leader, Breanna."

Breanna slid from Eimar's back. "Fionn—Seeress, Healer, your warning reached us through your daughter. She has sworn to me, as I am sworn to her and thus to those close to her. You are in peril, yet we have arrived before your call to your daughter."

"How can this be?" Fionna asked. "How can you know this? Our hillfort is—well, it appeared, will be burning."

Breanna smiled. "My Tuatha gods embraced me."

An older man, bearing a sigil-covered long sword and a shorter one on his belt, wearing a black kilt below it and a boiled leather cuirass above, strode toward Izzy, saying in a gruff voice, "My Bee!"

"Grandfather," Izzy pulled up short and answered with a bow.

"Enough of that. Welcome your grandpa as you should."

Izzy leaped into his arms. "I've missed you!"

He gave an oof. "As you should. Yet, you brought us warriors to fend off enemies who are coming. I am very proud of what you're becoming. Your Elemental control is impressive."

Back on her feet, Izzy turned to hug a young man with the same mixed-clan hair and features as her own. Izzy proclaimed, "PK, seeing my brother is well pleases my heart! How is your training coming along? Have you chosen katanas? Or will you choose the Gladius and La Téne as your weapons?"

In a disappointed tone, PK answered, "Father has not found a smith who can make katanas, so it will likely be the latter."

Breanna stepped next to Izzy. "PK, I am Breanna. One day, should you wish it, you'll be one of my sworn. If you want katanas, I know a smith who can make them for you."

Izzy looked at Breanna in surprise as she drew her now sigil-laced blades. "Like these?"

"Aye, of course. It has to be Goibniu."

The boy answered, "I would like that, as it would enable me to honor my father's father."

Izzy resheathed her blades and shook her head. "Grandpa, speaking of Father, where is he?"

"Trying to rouse the nearby tribes to stop the Romans."

"With my Hero, their warriors will not be needed to save us," Izzy countered. "Please meet Breanna Ban Morna, Erin's Hero, wielder of the *Triple Dáns*, and the new Tuatha Goddess of Time. As well as Erin's *Cosantóir*, Eoin Mac Cairbre."

"The one your mother sent you to seek out," Izzy's grandfather stated. Then Breanna knew the *sight* had taken him for a moment. He added, "This pair is all that and more of what your mother divined. Along with her band. Welcome to Clan Tamarici."

Breanna stepped forward, offering her arm, which the well-aged warrior grasped for a bit longer than necessary. She felt him scan her aura as she did the same with his, her Elements reacting to each of his. She asserted, "You're deeper than you present."

"Ó just an old man," he shrugged. "Call me Séamus."

Breanna narrowed her eyes. "No, Séamus, you're not just an old man, but a *Laoch Druí*—one of the lost Warrior Druids who can command all of the Elements, maybe the last, though I hope not. You're needed once more. Dagda has tasked Eoin and me with ensuring our Gaels rule their destiny. And as their new Goddess of Time, I will do just that. Even if I must recruit from the past."

"That may be, and you might hold the key to that success. Yet, we have an immediate need. One God-influenced Roman legionnaires approach from the southeast. How would you counter their numbers? As you see from those in this courtyard, we have less than half the warriors you command."

Breanna answered, "My Dark Goddess gifted me and my Warriors of Destiny her *dark matter*-driven *balefire* weapons and shields."

"Badb Catha's works are a fearsome thing," he confirmed.

"Aye, they are," Breanna responded. "Something that will protect your granddaughter. Yet, I have a challenge: I need more Gaels and Celts to believe, ones you can train in our ways—your ways."

Izzy questioned, "Grandpa, are there sons of Mil at this time?"

"Of course, my Bee. Yet only a few. Will it be enough?"

"Enough?" Breanna countered. "Yes, if we train them. You are one of the last *Laoch Druí*. Your enclave can be a beacon for Celts who want to learn our ways. I can send you warriors."

"How?"

"Through time. It is on my side, after all."

Séamus cocked his head as if he had a question, then shrugged. "I will show you how the Romans will come through the valley. With your numbers and this *balefire*, you might be victorious. Yet for how long?"

Breanna smiled darkly. "As long as it takes, Séamus. My Warriors of Destiny and I will fight for those we pledge to support! I plan to utilize my ability to move through time to achieve victory. That's my notion. We'll have to see if I can live up to such a lofty claim."

"Very well," he answered. "Follow me to the valley."

Séamus and his daughter led Breanna and her Warriors of Destiny out of the timber gate of the hillfort and down a well-worn path in the foothills where Izzy had mentioned they had built their home. His fifteen warriors in training followed.

Breanna requested, "Fionna, as Izzy's mother, please walk with me. You, as well, my Seeress. Let's touch the *Cycle of Time* together."

Fionna responded, "Of course, my Lady."

"Och, I'm no Lady, just a chosen warrior by my gods."

"Breanna had a humble upbringing," Livie said. "It's time you met the Heart of Destiny."

Croí Dàn interjected, *"Your daughter is a marvel."*

Fionna stumbled on a rock, and Livie steadied her, saying, "I had a similar challenge meeting the Heart of Destiny the first time. She's rather affectionate to those who support Erin's Hero. Yet, vengeful of those who do not."

Fionna hesitated. "Our Celtic Gods have faded here."

Livie responded, "It's less so in my lands of Cymru west of Albion. Yet, Breanna brings hope and change for Gaels and Celts."

"How?"

"First, she plans to stop Rome's first invasion of Pretannia and their fellow Celtic tribes six centuries ago."

"You think she can do that?"

"Breanna can do things I could never have imagined."

Fionna looked at Breanna with narrowed eyes.

Breanna suggested, "Livie, please focus. Take us to the *Cycle of Time*. Let's see the next day."

Livie blushed and then did as commanded. Eoin, Fionna, Séamus, Sinéidin, Bláth, and Izzy followed Breanna into time as the latter seized control of its magic at that moment, spinning forward one and a half spans when the twisted Romans would eventually crush the hillfort and into tomorrow.

Eoin said, *"They appeared to be a hundred plus strong, splitting a cohort a third of a Cohort. Where are the others? Usually, they assign three hundred to an outpost. Could they all be out on the same mission with different targets?"*

Breanna followed their threads back through time to their outpost, which they had left empty. A little further back, a One God leader had arrived with orders for them to advance on the Celts to the north and west.

Sinéidin translated the Latin they overheard. *"The Tamarici, Morcani, and Lancienses tribes are their targets."*

Then, Breanna pushed her touch back two days on the *Cycle* and cast it to the Celtic tribes in the surrounding hills and valleys. *"A Roman Cohort of Legionaries is approaching. Get ready for battle. The Warriors of Destiny will help you! Be prepared!"*

After that, she shared the vision with the surrounding Celtic tribes. Breanna released the *Cycle of Time*, saying, "I doubt we need their help, but I'd like other nearby hillforts to see what we can do. Then, they might start believing the power of Rome is dead, and the Celts can rise again. Our fight is more clearly with the corrupt power-seeking leadership in the One God followers from Rome."

Fionna staggered into Livie, who caught her again. Izzy said with concern, "Mother, are you okay? Was that one of your flashes in time, one where Breanna could change the trajectory of our homeland?"

"Aye, it was. Yet it's all just a bit too much to take in."

Sinéidin suggested, "If there are any words you do not understand, I can translate them for you. The language of Gaels and Celts has diverged, especially here."

"And you are?"

"The Tuatha Goddess of Language, but just call me Sinéidin."

"Hmm, okay, though I can't say I'm surprised by this."

Izzy added, "It's okay, Mother, she's delightful."

"What did I get you into, Izzy?" Fionna just shook her head. Then asked, "And who are you?"

Bláth, who had been quiet, objectively observing, and recording these events for future tales with her Drudic training, said, "Just a simple Bard who happened to swear to Breanna in another life."

Fionna said doubtfully, "Is nothing about Breanna simple?"

"Och, that's spot on! She creatively surprises us continually."

As the path widened and the valley opened below them, Breanna looked to each side of the hills funneling into the meadows before her. "Eoin, take charge of the battle plan. We must plan to send ourselves in time and space to address the other two parts of this cohort.

"Séamus, my *Taoiseach*, will deploy our resources. As you may have heard, I invited those from nearby hillforts to witness our victory. They will spread the word to their fellow Celts that none should hesitate to accept the havoc we wreaked upon the Romans. Now, watch what our Dark Goddess has wrought."

Breanna left Eoin to lay out the battle plan and surveyed how the hills funneled the lower meadow to the path that led up to the hillfort. It was a rough but beautiful countryside. How to keep it untainted by Rome was the question.

Then she turned her attention back to Eoin as he positioned two *fians* in the gorse to each side. Her blooded warriors stood at the mouth of the path to the stronghold, with Toal and Cilla's archers kneeling before them.

As one of her warriors attempted to lead their mounts to the safety of the hillfort, Eimar protested. Breanna turned to her. "You have one life, and I hope it is long. I need you with me. Eoin is wise. Please follow his command."

Eimar whickered her approval and trotted back up the path with their other mounts following her.

Séamus watched the strange interaction between Breanna and her mount. "You talk with your horse?"

"Ah, you missed that gift the Tuatha gods gave the sons of Mil, who became our Gaels. Communicating with animals was a key incentive that the Tuatha included in the Great Agreement. It is mostly a lost skill that our Gaels have forgotten. I'm going to revive it. My bond with Eimar is special."

Séamus chuckled. "Of course it is. Yet, I am amazed at how easily you embrace such concepts. Anyway, what can my warriors do to help? I've trained those with the Fire Element to cast it."

Eoin commanded, "Split them to either side behind our *fians*. They can pick off any Legionaries who get past our warriors.

"Corbmac! Have our *fian* warriors start with active crossbow bolts and switch to spear-based *balefire* shots if needed.

"Same with you and yours, Toal and Cilla. Should the *fians* empty their crossbow carriages that Corbmac's team wields, split to each side of the path, and use your bows at will. It will let our blooded warriors unleash *balefire* down the path with their weapons. Our blooded warriors have more than ten tips of attack using our various blades. Make them count."

Séamus commented to Eoin, "You're a good commander."

"My mate prefers *Cosantóir*," Eoin rejoined with a wink. "Speaking of which, Breanna, please ensure your sigils are distributed along the path to ensure we have leap points."

⟿⟾ Eoin ⟿⟾

As Breanna descended along the path to cast her Earth sigil upon the rocks, Séamus asked, "Leap points?"

Eoin answered, "Aye, Breanna is our Chief Druid's Apprentice. He gifted her all five Elements and enabled her to create sigils of Druidic power. Leap points allow redirection of *balefire* off each point."

"By the powers!" Séamus exclaimed. "That's ingenious."

"I have difficulty keeping up with my love's ability to leverage her Tuatha-laden powers like *balefire*."

"Och, lad, Breanna is on fire with ideas of what is right. Keep her close. She needs your counsel and grounding."

Eoin smiled. "Aye, she is on fire, as you say, and I do."

A while later, the Roman legionnaires appeared on the far side of the meadow, marching to a drum. As expected, they were indeed roughly a hundred and fifty strong. Eoin ordered, "Hold until my command. Breanna's blooded, do the same. We strike as planned."

Séamus asked, "Son, are you sure of this course?"

"Aye, I am. Trust in us. It will not matter that we are out-numbered nearly three to one," Eoin stated confidently as he and Breanna drew their blades, with the others following suit with their *balefire*-enabled weapons, each crackling. With Air, he cast a whisper, "Hold."

The Romans marched through the valley, and just before they passed between the hidden *fian* warriors, Eoin sent the command through *Croí Dàn*, "*Unleash your balefire!*"

Thirty-six *fian* warriors, eighteen to each side, let loose their crossbow bolts tipped with Badb Catha's *dark matter*-driven *balefire*, each effortlessly punching through the bronze-covered wooden Roman shields, killing those behind them. Breanna's leap points glowed in their otherworld vision as Toal, with his eight archers, did the same, aiming at the sigils on the ground as they redirected the *balefire*-tipped arrows off the rocks behind which some Romans took refuge. That was followed by another round of bolts from the two sides and another down their throats from the path where Toal's archers knelt.

Eoin ordered, "One more release!"

When that happened, the last few still hunkered behind their large scutum shields collapsed to the ground, and a hundred and fifty Roman legionnaires lay dead with smoking chests or missing heads.

Eoin turned to Corbmac. "Have our men retrieve the bolts and arrows so Breanna can recharge them."

"By the gods!" Séamus exclaimed. "That's not just fearsome. It's a power that is only to be wielded with restraint."

Breanna said, "It is, and we will. Unfortunately, I must give the Romans cause to fear us. They've killed or subjugated countless Celtic tribes over the last six centuries. I use this mighty ability reluctantly. Yet, you must also understand I've seen the future. It's one where the Romans crushed the Gaels and Celts, then left them in chaos as they withdrew to the mainland to face other threats closer to home. They left their followers of the One God behind to corrupt other conquerors who would assault Pretannia in their wake. The dark ages are coming. I have seen that millions of people, and likely a hundred times that number, will live and die under tyrannic rulers in the name of their One God religion."

"That knowledge is a heavy burden," Séamus said. "Yet, we're glad you were here to save us, even if the battle was one-sided."

Lotte grumbled, "Gah! There was no glory in that clash!"

"Bide your time!" Breanna said darkly. "It will come!"

Livie suggested, "Seek Aether, sister-mine. Center yourself."

Eoin crossed his arms sternly over his chest at the off-point chatter. "Not the time and place. Bre, we need to draw out the Celts, now."

Breanna turned from her blooded warriors, and Eoin felt her casting her voice with Air to proclaim, "I feel you in the hills! Rise, my Celts! As a *Laoch Dàn*, I welcome all who fight Rome!"

At first, only a few rose from the hills, but more followed, led by a warrior with two curved blades over his shoulders.

Even more trailed those as Breanna called out, "I am Breanna Ban Morna, and I command these fighters. My Warriors of Destiny have defended this valley! Join us in fighting Rome and its One God leaders! Together, we can win this fight! Gather later at Séamus and Fionna's hillfort. The spoils of this battle are yours!"

Izzy called, "Father!"

The man with two blades on his shoulders, similar to Izzy's, descended from the hills, holding his hand up as a signal to be silent. He bent a knee before Breanna, saying gravely, "I am Dòmhnall. Fionna, my mate, sent my daughter to you. Yet, here you are, saving what is ours."

Breanna smiled. "Rise, Dòmhnall, no one bends the knee to me who is family of my sworn. Her family is our family."

Dòmhnall rose and bowed. "Gracious of you. Our custom from my land is to honor family and clan first, my Lady."

Seeing Izzy's manner in the man, Eoin suggested, "Dòmhnall, as Breanna's mate, I'd suggest you address her as Breanna or Bre."

Breanna added, "Indeed. Izzy has sworn to me, as I am sworn to her and thus to hers. Yet, I have more Romans to end this day."

Eoin turned to their band. "To us! We have the rest of this Roman Cohort to end."

With that, Breanna snapped out her golden rope, and once all of her band took hold of it, she and they disappeared.

The two subsequent encounters with the splintered Roman Legionnaire Cohort were similar. However, Breanna used her blooded warriors to engage the enemy both times, saving time in recovering so many reactive bolts. At the last massacre, they found the commanding Bishop from Rome had held back and tried to flee the battlefield.

Lotte narrowed her gaze before unleashing her *balefire*, striking him down, and then exclaimed, "That was unrewarding! I believe I just killed a coward!"

Eoin commented, "A dead coward can't order people killed. I'll count it as a win. Now, let's return to Izzy's home. To us!"

Once they all clustered and chained along Breanna's golden rope, they were suddenly back at the Tamarici Tribe's hillfort.

When the Warriors of Destiny arrived just outside the gates, many Celts from surrounding strongholds had already gathered in the courtyard. Eoin noted the wary glances Galicia clan members cast at them. He proclaimed, "I would like to introduce Breanna Ban Morna and her Warriors of Destiny, who just crushed a Roman Cohort! As Séamus's clan has likely told you, we are Gaels from Erin, where the sons of Mil sailed for several millennia ago."

Breanna continued, "We have been gifted powers by the Tuatha gods of Erin, who laid a massive challenge at our feet. Ensure all Gaels and Celts rule over our future, not Rome and followers of the One God. To that end, the Roman Legionnaire Cohort to the south is no longer a threat! As with your tribe, I awarded the spoils of those battles to the Morcani and Lancienses tribes. There are now three hundred Roman swords in Celtic hands!"

Cheers and thanks rang from those collected before her, and her *fian* warriors beat their spears on their shields in time for a few moments.

Séamus stepped forward, holding his hands high to attain their silence. "When Fionna sent our Isobel via a ship to seek out one who would become Erin's Hero of the Gaelic Emerald Isle, I had no idea how that would help us. Yet, we now have Breanna's commitment to aid us in our time of need. For those who did not witness what happened in the valley below us, her Warriors of Destiny decimated a third of a Roman Cohort in less than sixty heartbeats, Legionnaires who would have burned down this hillfort, and likely yours. They did so with the other two-thirds of the divided cohort's numbers. So we celebrate!"

Then Fionna and the other non-combatants in the fort brought buckets and cups to the courtyard.

Izzy offered, "For our cousins from the north, here's a fruit punch called queimada fortified with orujo, a spicy liquor."

Eoin chuckled at Breanna's dismay that they had no mead and whispered in her ear, "Just a taste."

"If I must," Breanna agreed with a smile, accepting a cup and raising it to her lips, acknowledging their new Celtic allies. Eoin quickly handed Breanna a glass of water.

"Thank you, my love!" she added, raising her eyebrow at her new friend. "Spicy indeed! Nevertheless, we must return to escort our missionaries."

Eoin knew their sworn friend was disappointed, and Izzy said, "I understand. Let me give farewells to my family."

"Och, no, you don't understand," Breanna countered. "I was going to suggest you spend the night. I'll fetch you in the morning."

"Ó! Thank you, Bre," Izzy exclaimed and hugged her.

"Eoin, let's get our mounts and head back to Erin."

⸺✥⚶ Breanna ⚶✥⸺

Breanna and her band returned to Erin within moments of the time they had departed. With Airmid glaring at her, Ecne stated, "I take it you had a successful mission."

"Aye, we did," she answered. "And we have new Celtic allies in Galicia now."

Internally, she added, *"Goibniu, I have a task for you."*

The smith appeared suddenly. "My niece, you have a request?"

"Two, actually," Breanna told him as she hugged her uncle. "I was just discussing with Ecne that we have new Celtic friends in Izzy's extended family. Yet, they do not have a smith who can make another set of the Far East katanas for Izzy's brother. He is a young Warrior Druid in training who wields Water and Earth."

"That's easy enough. What is the second ask?"

"Well, I've been thinking," Breanna answered hesitantly.

"Uh-oh," Eoin chimed in and received an elbow in his gut.

Breanna continued as if he hadn't said anything. "While I don't need to learn how to craft katanas, I think I should know how to imbue an item, such as a sword, with *balefire* and *dark-matter* shields as you have done for us."

"We must travel to Murias. Take my hand and seize the *sight*!"

"Corbmac, please get dinner ready. I'll be back shortly."

With that, she and Goibniu flashed away.

When Breanna returned, not but a moment later, using time to her advantage, she held two curved blades etched with Druidic Sigils. She placed them in their tent and, now famished, made her way to Corbmac's pot. "Grandfather, anything left for me?"

"Girl, you just left us! Of course, there is!"

"Hmm," she said, "I'm still getting used to this time thing."

He handed her a bowl. "Spread the load, my Lady."

"No such titles for me, but you're right."

Then she sat next to Eoin without a word, inhaling her dinner.

Later, wrapped in his arms as they lay inside their strange new tent, Eoin asked, "How was Murias? I assume you saw Goibniu's workshop."

"It was, well, very illuminating," she answered. "My uncle and his brothers have unique sigils they attach to various items and people. In this case, one is for *balefire*, and the other is for *dark matter* shields. Using my Fire and Aether Elements, he taught me to etch those sigils into blades. It is somewhat like the leap points I cast on rocks with my Earth Element, but much more complex. Goibniu had me add them to PK's blades."

"Good, then Izzy's younger brother can cast and be protected with his blades. Yet, it's been a busy day. Get some sleep, my love."

A moment later, Breanna succumbed to the night, wrapped in his muscled arms.

The following morning, Breanna woke refreshed and ready to meet the day. She and Eoin approached Ecne, with the former saying, "We're taking Phátric to witness how his future fellow clerics make it a gruesome sight. Eoin, make sure our leader of the One God followers eats well. In the meantime, I need to retrieve Izzy from Galicia."

With that, Breanna flashed away and returned to the hill fort that Izzy called home. Standing in the courtyard, Séamus strode forward. "Breanna! Thank you for the gift of my granddaughter for the night."

She exhaled heavily, holding her hand out for a warrior clasp. A moment later, he took it. "Finally, someone who isn't bowing to me. I have these blades for PK."

Izzy was in the yard a moment later. "Bre."

Breanna held the blades. "Please, give these to PK while I have a moment with your father."

Izzy took them with a bow and raced to find her brother.

Séamus gave her a gracious nod. "I saw the sigils."

"Aye, they are what you think they are. Hand me your sword."

"You think that's wise?" he asked.

"My decision," she rejoined. "While I do this, answer one question. What of your mate?"

Séamus looked sad before whispering, "Ah, due to a sickness that her daughter and granddaughter could not heal, my mate sent her *anam* into the *Cycle of Time*, where I'm sure I'll find her, as we have before. And we will again, due to the knots of time that tie us together."

"Your roots run deep. Now, Séamus, hand me your blade."

As he did so, she sank to a knee, holding the tip down on the stone before her. Pressing her palm to the blade just below the hilt, she called her Fire and Aether Elements. The white-hot fire etched the sigil into the steel, and *Eitear* gave it life. Then she spun it around to the other side and repeated the process.

When she rose and returned his blade, she asked, "Do you see the constructs of *balefire* and *dark-matter* shields in the sigils?"

"Aye, I do. I also saw that Aether was required. It is undoubtedly a challenging Element to master. I'm still working on learning its nuances. I am not sure I could repeat it."

She shrugged. "As am I—Aether is a puzzle. Anyway, test it. It's only one of a handful of times I've used *Eitear*."

With an arched eyebrow, he did, and *balefire* shot out of the open hillfort's gates. Counting to fifteen, she felt his shields click in and tossed a dirk at him, and he raised his blade to deflect it. But the knife dropped short when it hit his shields.

"I'd say you learn quickly. You said you'd be sending warriors my way?"

Breanna nodded as she retrieved the dirk. "I will, hopefully, come this fall—after I challenge Julius Caesar."

Séamus asked, "No words of wisdom in using this power?"

"No. I believe in you. Train PK well. Protect your family." She called out, "Izzy, time to go!"

As she had done before, Breanna watched Izzy unwrap herself from her Elements to appear at Bre's side. She hugged Séamus. "I hope to see you soon, Grandpa."

With that, Breanna touched her shoulder, and they flashed back to Erin and their camp along the High King's Road. She signaled Ecne and Eoin to stand ready and commanded Phátric, "It is time for our jaunt in time. I hope you enjoy it."

"I just finished my breakfast," he protested.

"Good, we will stand clear of you once we return," she added, extending her hand to him. He took it, and when Ecne and Eoin put their hands on the shoulders, Breanna flashed them away. Moments later, they were back, with Phátric on his knees, retching up his morning meal. Breanna had known that Sinéidin could remain behind, as such a gruesome sight would need no translation, and she did not need to see the ugly, dark, and vicious scene in her present state.

Breanna commented, "Ecne, do you think our trip accomplished what we needed?"

"Aye, that was truly awful. Male humans can be such savages!"

"Good to know you understand why they enrage me."

While her band packed up the camp, Breanna set herself to the mindless task of recharging spent *balefire* bolts and arrows from the previous day's battle. They were the one thing they could fire without canceling out their shields, as the projectiles activated only upon impact, away from the shooter.

Later that day, they entered the rolling hills above Dun Gaillimhe. Breanna saw riders coming up the road, and she knew it was Chief Connall Cas Ciabhach leading his band of warriors.

"Halt," she ordered. She fingered her magical rope. "Eoin, take charge."

Her *Cosantóir* commanded, "Front *fians*, shield wall low with spears! Rear *fians*, shield wall high, with crossbows ready! Blooded, draw blades, and prepare to cast."

Moments later, Chief Connall halted his band before them. "What is the meaning of this warband caravan coming to my doorstep?"

Breanna maneuvered Eimar forward and surveyed her potential adversary. "You already know part of it when I claimed my land as Erin's Hero. Yet, I also know the *Ard Rí* sent messengers that we have One God followers, as he did not want to kill them outright, and his council decided to put them out there." Breanna pointed to the Aran Islands.

Connall nodded. "So, you're the one?"

"Aye, I am."

"I thought you'd be older," he commented.

"I am, but you just don't remember it," Breanna stated.

"Meaning?"

"In the *before-time*, Norvegrs invaded our island. I wielded Tuatha magic, known by some Druids as the *Triple Dàns*, which changed Erin's timeline. That act removed the invaders. Yet Danu, Dagda, and Badb Catha did not know what such magic would do to me, as no one had used the *Dàns* together before, not even our gods. The resulting magic returned Erin's Hero, creating their Tuatha Goddess of Time.

"My task is to use my time-travel abilities to ensure Gael's rule! I must seek out key places in time to accomplish this, starting with these One God followers. And Rome, with its invasions of Pretannia roughly six hundred cycles ago."

"You speak of things beyond my ken."

"I speak what my truth is. Tell your men not to overreact," she said as she drew the Blades of Destiny and held them high.

Connall raised a hand to quell any reaction from his men.

"These long blades are called *Lann Dàn*. Witness their power."

Breanna let her *balefire* flow, sweeping a hundred yards of destruction along the roadside. As a collective gasp rose from the men of Dun Gaillimhe, she commented, "Each of my Warriors of Destiny possesses some aspect of this *balefire*, with my blooded equal to my blades in power."

Then Breanna concluded, "We have also engaged other bands of Connachta warriors, supposedly bound to your provincial King Dauthí. When they tried to take us hostage, I snatched two of his commanders away and left them to find their way home across the Cuilcagh Mountains through Ulaidian territory. Their men selected new commanders, and all swore to me.

"The third commander heard what happened to the other two leaders and wisely decided not to attempt to take us hostage; they have also sworn to me. What do you say? Shall we battle and lose the good Gaelic lives we need for future fights with Rome and others?"

"Or we can talk," Eoin added. "If we fight, Breanna will give no quarter."

Connall sighed. "We talk, as this is deep shite you present to me."

"Wise man, Chief Connall," Breanna said.

Then she smiled brightly when she heard *Mo Chroí* say to him directly, *"Wise man indeed! We might get along!"*

With that, the startled Chief led them through the rolling hills down to the seaside fort of Dun Gaillimhe. Before them, a sparkling bay spread out, offering a breathtaking view. She nudged Eimar beside the young Connachta leader. "I thought you'd be older, too."

As Connall let a small smile slip, Eoin appeared on the other side of him. "By way of introduction, I am Erin's *Cosantóir*, and her—"

"Mate?" Connall injected.

"Aye, that is true," Eoin countered stiffly. "I was going to introduce myself as *Taoiseach* to Erin's Hero. The High Queen tasked us with finding a place for these zealots. Yet, our challenge is that they have no scruples. Their One God demands that all bow to him. We cannot allow this. Phátric must be contained. We suggest the Aran Islands."

"Brutal landscape, but I agree," was Connall's assessment.

Everything was pleasant during the evening reception and dinner, with seafood and fish as the main dishes. As the meal wound down, Breanna raised a question in a firm voice, "Connall, all who meet my Heart, as you have, are presented a choice. To support us or oppose us. Will you swear to my cause?"

"Aye, as much is wrong in our Emerald Isle."

"It is," Breanna said. "*Mo Chroí*, please swear Connall and any of his willing men to join us. We need Warriors of Destiny on the home front while our band is abroad."

"I can accept that challenge."

"Good! I have a position for you to fill. I plan to number the days of any future King ever ruling. They seek power at any cost, especially that of our Gaels. We need to end provinces fighting each other and rein in roaming bands of warriors trying to take people hostage as bargaining chips. We must focus on threats across the sea.

"To that end, I am creating the Council of Erin, initially made up of Chiefs and Chieftesses, and there will be seats for Druids, Artisans, and Tradesmen. Each Province would also have its own Council to ensure balance within each of them. Eoin and I would initially appoint my sworn, but soon, the people will vote for who will represent them."

Connall chuckled. "You are certainly a breath of fresh air!"

Fergal approached with his goddess on his arm. "I wanted to introduce myself and my mate, as my clan, which is related to Eoin's Ulaidian roots, shares a name with you. I am Fergal Mac Conall, and this is Sinéidin, Tuatha Goddess of Languages."

Breanna smiled and spun away to find Eoin, Bláth, and Livie chatting with Dun Gaillimhe's Druids about how to manage the One God followers. "Is everything settled?" she asked. "If not, what needs to be done? If yes, it's time to sleep, as Livie will go on a journey with Eoin and me in the morning. We need to have a meeting with your father."

Livie squeaked out, "Must we?"

"Aye, my Seeress, we must! But on the way, I have a surprise."

That night, Breanna and Eoin enjoyed the private hut, as their new tent could not muffle the pleasure that Eoin liked to dish out. Yet, there was no such concern here, and they mated as they preferred—with unbridled passion.

In the morning, Eoin's voice rumbled out, "I think I'd like a handfasting ceremony between us soon, as your father did Fergal and Sinéidin."

"Would you now?" Breanna questioned with a teasing twinkle in her eyes as she stretched up to kiss his lips.

"Aye, I would, so we can make some babies," he said softly.

"Someday, my love, but not now."

With a nod, Eoin said, "I understand that we have to wait on babies, but I would see us mated first. I guess it's the formality of the ritual that I want—with you and no other."

"And I with you, my rock. Once we return from Pretainna, we'll make it so. With our new friends, I'm sure it will be a spectacle! But first, we must focus on the past and the future. Let's seek out Taliesin and Myrddin with our sworn."

With that, they rose, with Eoin taking her hand and pulling her into his arms. "Let's get ready, then."

As they sought the baths, Breanna asked *Mo Chroí, "I know we discussed how you're ensuring I will not have children now, but it raises a question. What powers will our children have?"*

Her Heart answered, *"Many gods and goddesses are third, fourth, and fifth generation. Each mated pair is another level*

removed from their source. It means their powers are less concen-
trated. You are a first-generation goddess, as is Eoin."

"And that means?"

"Your children will be strong Elementals—Laoch Druí strong.
Well beyond Izzy's grandfather. And they will be able to walk the
Cycle of Time as you do. If those they mate with are of the second
generation, it will barely diminish the powers of their offspring."

"Gods, we need to tread carefully with our children!"

Mo Chroí said, *"Aye, we must. If you or Eoin are hurt or*
diminished by those of this world, they will likely retaliate on your
behalf. I have foreseen a time when there are selective assassinations
of evil world leaders. All to keep you two safe, to protect you both,
and this land."

"That must not happen," Breanna declared.

"Unless your children are wise," Mo Chroí countered.

Breanna wanted to growl but kept the conversation to herself
as they sank into one of Dun Gaillimhe's mostly empty tubs.
Once cleaned up, they headed to the main hall to break their
fast. Breanna was disappointed that sicín eggs had missed the
western part of her land, but the smoked boar, freshly fried, went
well with cheese, soda bread, and porridge.

Livie appeared with her staff in one hand and her trencher in
the other. She sat beside them, offered a morning greeting, but
then was quiet as she ate. Finally finished, she raised her eyes to
Breanna, stating flatly, "When we meet my father, remember
this above all else. He is a conniver. Do not trust him."

Breanna smiled. "No worries, my Seeress, I have ways to
ensure his compliance. Shall we go? First to the future?"

"The future?" Livie asked, clutching her staff.

"Aye," she said, taking each of their hands and flashing
them away.

Breanna used her intent as she touched the *Cycle of Time* to seek out Taliesin Ben Beirdd. They appeared in what looked to be a good-sized library that was part of a larger structure made of stone blocks, with arched beams above them similar to Dun Tara's main hall. Leaded glass windows allowed light into the large room. Around them, shelves lined most of the walls, with books of all sizes upon them.

Breanna found they were looking over a young man's shoulder. He wore his golden locks that held a shimmer of red neatly tied into a bun at the nape of his neck. Dressed in black robes, he was intently studying a book written in Cumbric, the language of Cymru, and did not seem to notice them until she cleared her throat.

He turned in surprise. "Och, and who are you three?"

Breanna smiled, answering warmly, "Friends from Erin."

He looked perplexed, yet clearly understood Gaelic as he answered in that language. "From Erin? At this time in the cycle? Few dare cross the inner sea with the many possible storms in this season."

"My Seeress can foresee the weather. The waves were smooth."

The young man rose, looking at Livie with her crystal-topped staff, and stated in a courtly voice, "I am Taliesin Ben Beirdd, Librarian, Bard, and sometime Seer in the Powys Court, here at Caer Caradoc. What may I help you find?"

Breanna tilted her head. "We are not seeking a book, but a Bard and Seer-to-be. Since we had the time, we wanted to take a moment to introduce ourselves. I am Breanna Ban Morna, now known as Erin's Hero, and this is my protector, Eoin."

Taliesin looked them up and down, taking in their many weapons strapped about their bodies. "You seek Bard and Seer, you say?"

"Aye," she answered, seeing his eyes widen when he noticed Livie beside him. "And this is my Seeress and budding Healer, Livie Ferch Myrddin. I assume you've heard of her father?"

"Who hasn't? He's a legend in Gwynedd!"

Livie rolled her eyes, snorting in Cumbric, "No, he's *bolche!*"

Taliesin raised an eyebrow. "You think he was arrogant?"

Livie shrugged. "He is as he's always been—full of himself."

"Wait, he can't still be alive. He was ancient when I was born."

Breanna interjected, "Yes, he still lives, yet with the caveat that he does so within another time, a previous one. You are in the future for us. Do you grasp the concept that time can be bent? Changed? Something more fluid than humans think it is?"

Taliesin looked back and forth between the three of them as he asked, "You're serious?"

"Aye, very," Breanna said tightly.

Livie put in softly, "Maybe we should retire from your library?"

"What would you suggest?" he asked.

"Tea?" Livie questioned hopefully. "There's much to discuss."

"Of course, my Lady Seeress. If you would follow me."

Taliesin led them through a door on the far side of the room. The antechamber behind it held a round table with four chairs and another open door across the room. He stepped to it, poked his head through the opening, saying to someone out of view, "Tea and biscuits for four, please."

He turned back to them and motioned for them to take a seat. Joining them, he settled between Breanna and Livie, asking the latter lightly, "What is a Cymru Seerees with a famed lineage doing in Erin with these two warriors?"

"Well, that's a story, for sure," Livie replied. "But before I answer your question, I must pose one. Have you ever communed with our old gods or goddesses using the *sight*?"

Taliesin responded, "Only indirectly. As a Seer, my talents are more oriented toward the *Cycle of Time*."

Livie sighed. "My mother, also a Seeress, and my father are closer to them, as am I."

"Eigyr Ferch Amlawdd. Your mother is a mystery in history."

Breanna saw Livie hesitate and wondered what the lad knew of her mother. The Seeress continued, "You'll likely meet her and my father soon. As I was about to say, Agrona, our Goddess of War, has despised the Romans since they arrived here many centuries ago. When Breanna became the Tuatha Goddess of Time, Agrona and the Tuatha Goddess of War made a pact, and I was part of that bargain. Shortly after, I met Erin's Hero and her father, Dagda. Then I swore myself to her cause."

With a twitch in his eye, he stated, "Which is?" he queried. "I assume it includes time in some way?"

"Aye, it does," was her response.

At that moment, they were interrupted by a servant with a tray of tea and biscuits. He set down the tray before scurrying away. Breanna and Livie moaned in appreciation of the earthy and subtly floral tea. Taliesin smiled, adding, "It is my blend, meant to lighten the soul."

Breanna asked in surprise, "You're an herbalist?"

"Aye," he answered with a shrug. "Yet, please continue, Livie."

Breanna heard her Seeress question through *Mo Chroí*, *"Maybe he's an Earth Elemental and doesn't know it?"*

Then Livie picked up her tale again. "Hmm, you asked about time. We must travel back to the early first century, the one before the rise of the One God's son. You might know it as before the common era. It must be early enough to convince the various tribes of Albion, Cymru, Dál Riata, and likely the Picts that they must create a united front to stand against the

Romans. Otherwise, they and their One God will tear our lands apart and turn us away from the old gods."

Taliesin looked at Breanna with an arched eyebrow. "Goddess of Time, is it?"

"Indeed, much to my surprise, after Danu and Dagda saved me as I wielded Badb Catha's *Triple Dàn* magic to remove Norvegr invaders. That act made me a goddess who could travel wherever and whenever with mortals. I'm assembling my Warriors of Destiny for our mission that Livie outlined. Yet we are unbalanced, with too many warriors and only one and a half Seeresses. Well, three, if you count me, but I must lead. That is why we are here, talking with you. Livie and I discovered that you will become an even more gifted Seer over time, and we could also use another Bard. And we could certainly help you achieve master status in both areas in short order."

Taliesin stammered, "You want me to join your quest?"

Croí Dàn added, *"Indeed, young man, we do!"*

"Wait! What? Who was that?"

"The Heart of Destiny, one of the *Triple Dàns,"* Livie explained.

Breanna said brightly, "She prefers *Mo Chroí* over *Croí Dàn.*"

"So this is all real?" came his question.

"All of our magic is very real," Livie said.

With that, Breanna said, "The tea and biscuits were lovely. Think about this opportunity. We will be back, but now we have another time to seek. The place and time where Myrddin Wyllt resides, as we are likewise recruiting him."

Then Breanna reached out to Eoin, and Livie showed her where her parents dwelt. She took them to the northwestern part of Cymru that Taliesin called Gwynedd, where they would find Myrddin and Eigyr back in their time.

Myrddin sat behind a desk in his private room. "So, Daughter, you brought your Goddess of Time to me."

"It's more like she brought us to see you," Livie countered.

As Myrddin arched an eyebrow, Breanna commented darkly, "While I have lots of time, I have none for arrogant fools. Eoin, explain the offer, and then, if he agrees, *Croí Dàn* will swear him to us."

Myrddin rose. "You—"

Croí Dàn demanded in his mind, *"Shut your mouth!"*

Breanna could only smile at his startled expression. "Livie, let's visit with your mother. A doyenne who might keep me from killing your father with the consequences be damned!"

Livie led Breanna through the home where she had grown up and to the kitchen. She found a woman she assumed to be Eigyr. Surprised, the matron seeress wrapped her arms around her daughter, exclaiming, "Livie!"

"Mother, meet Breanna Ban Morna."

Eigyr turned, pulled Breanna into a group hug, and whispered, "Thank you for bringing my daughter home for a visit."

With a big smile, Breanna said, "I'll ensure she can do that occasionally. I've left my *Cosantóir* mate to treat with your mate to see if he will travel back in time with us to save this island from the Romans and their One God."

Eigyr said without concern, "What will be, will be. But the oven is hot, and I have bread baking, which is nearly ready. You are just a bit early, you know."

"Mother, you expected this visit with Erin's Hero?"

As she shrugged, Breanna smiled. "If you're all-knowing, you'll pour the right drink for me."

Eigyr answered by seizing a jug and a mug before pouring some golden liquid into it. "A woman after my own heart!"

Then she filled cups of mead for her daughter and herself, toasting, "To Seeresses! May we rule!"

A short while later, Eoin and Myrddin ambled into the kitchen, with the Seer saying reluctantly, "I will support your efforts to change time and end Rome's influence on our lands."

"Excellent," Breanna exclaimed. Then she asked, *"Mo Chroí, did you make him swear the oath?"*

Eoin and *Croí Dàn* said in unison, *"Yes."*

Eigyr asked tentatively, "Can you two spend the night with us? So I can catch up with my daughter?"

"Of course, we can make time for such a visit," Eoin said.

"That is a special gift you offer. I'll start on dinner!"

Later, Breanna lay in Eoin's arms in a spare guest room, breathing hard as they came down from their shared passion. She chided, "Hmm, I'm thinking you wanted me to make time for us."

"Always, my love," Eoin confirmed. "Thoughts on our day?"

"Livie handled Taliesin well, as you appear to have done with Myrddin, though you didn't say how you convinced him. Care to share?"

"It was talk of gods and goddesses and traveling through time to thwart the Romans. He hates what they've done to his land, including the One God followers. It was easy to pluck his strings."

Breanna chuckled. "Yet, we must still choose our first foray into Pretannia before Julius Caesar sets foot on that land. Maybe the Iceni should be first."

"No need to visit Macha in the past?"

"I think not. I've grown into being, well, the new me."

"That pleases me, my love. I had a thought," Eoin added.

"Och, that is dangerous," she chided.

"Gah!" he rejoined. "But I'll not elbow you over it. Anyway, have you looked at how they designed this roundhouse? We should bring it to Erin."

"Aye," she agreed. "Yet we go back to see Taliesin in the morning. Time to sleep."

 Livie

After their second meeting, Breanna and Eoin returned to Dun Gaillimhe's yard with Livie and Taliesin. Taliesin staggered as they arrived in another place and time, gripping his black oak staff tightly. Livie placed her arm around his waist to steady him. "Easy there, take a deep breath. The imbalance will pass soon."

"How do you manage it so easily?" Taliesin asked.

Livie chuckled. "More experience, though only by a few weeks."

"That's—ah, revealing."

"Aye, it is," she answered. "My Hero's fervent convictions make it easy to get swept up with the rest of her band. There's not a dull moment with Bre at the helm. Her Warriors of Destiny will certainly agree."

With that, she gestured with her staff to men and women bristling with weapons and various shields that bore a strange green-backed crest, a stone, a ruby heart, and crossed long blades over a golden Oberous.

Chief Connall, who was in the yard, exclaimed, "By the gods, Breanna, my serving staff said you had disappeared in a flash, not a moment ago!"

Erin's Hero said, "Just a little side trip through time to add another Bard and Seer to my Warriors of Destiny, not to mention an ambassador as we slip back through the centuries to take on the Romans."

"While you once more speak of things beyond my ken, we must finalize what to do with the One God followers."

Livie told Taliesin, "That's the Chief of this dun."

Breanna countered, "Connall, grow a backbone! On which Aran Island do you suggest we settle them? Pick one and make it so! I have another century, a long past one, to seek. Yet, know I'll be back when needed to keep them in line!"

Taliesin murmured, "Breanna is a fiery one."

"Och, you don't know the half of it. But Bre is profoundly committed to those who ally themselves with her. She would do anything for them. I've seen it firsthand. Yet, let's take a stroll. I must show you something about the Tuatha gods' commitment to our Hero's cause."

Taliesin nodded, and Livie led him through the dun's gates, following a path to the edge of the great sea. She sighed. "It's such a beautiful sight. If only our world were so tranquil. While I cannot travel through time with other mortals like Breanna, she has taught me how to touch the *Cycle of Time*. When trying to view multiple timelines, she refers to it as 'skipping through time.' Will you join me to see how dire our fates are?"

"I don't know why, but I believe in you, Livie. Show me."

With that, she took his hand, seized the *Cycle*, and skipped through the visions of the horrid moments Breanna had shown her.

A moment later, Taliesin bent over and retched. Once he recovered, he said, "Apologies, Livie, that was unmanly of me."

"No worries, I did the same," she admitted. "So, with such stakes, you need to know the power of life and death you will wield. I have committed to using what the Tuatha gods have provided. Even though I'm a Seeress, Breanna might call upon me to defend my fellow Warriors of Destiny."

Livie held out her crystal-topped staff and let *balefire* flow across the water for a hundred yards or more. The seawater boiled, and she pulled it back in. "Every weapon Breanna's warriors wield can cast this power. On the safety side, we also have magical shields. Try and strike me with your staff—in one, two, three. Now!"

"I cannot." Taliesin seemed aghast at the idea.

"Do it!" she commanded.

Taliesin tried to tap her shoulder lightly, but her shields stopped him. "What? How is that possible?"

"Welcome to my impossible world," Livie responded with a sigh as she took his hand. "Let's return and see what Breanna and Eoin are up to. I'm sure there's something in the air!"

⸺⸙ Breanna ⸙⸺

Breanna and Eoin stood at the front of the main hall of Dun Gaillimhe, facing a room full of her new fellow Tuatha gods and goddesses, along with Connall, his commanders, and Breanna's sworn inner circle. The deities took turns peppering Breanna and Eoin with various questions about their planned foray back into the time of the Celts across the Sea of Erin to stop Rome. Dagda raised his hand, bellowing, "You all sound like these new sicín hens that squabble after their feed!"

Several of them gasped over the insult, but All-Father asserted, "Know my daughter and her *Cosantóir—also* my son—have prepared. Now, Dian and Airmid, are the Warriors of Destiny Healers ready?"

His son, Dian Cécht, said, "Aye, they are, Father."

"Good!" Dagda exclaimed. "Eoin, can all Warriors of Destiny cast *balefire* and raise shields?"

Eoin nodded. "Aye."

"Then what challenges are left?" All-Father demanded.

Breanna pondered the question. "Erin will have a leadership vacuum when I travel across the sea and through time."

Áine, the Irish goddess of summer, wealth, and sovereignty, flashed into the hall, stating, "I have been watching Dagda's new goddess from our realm. Given that you have all accepted this island as my dominion over this land, I acknowledge that our new Goddess of Time has claimed their Emerald Isle as her own. I support her proposed changes to how the Gaels should rule themselves as she seeks to secure their future abroad."

That silenced any dissent as Breanna whispered to Eoin, "I didn't see that coming."

Badb Cath raised a hand, proclaiming, "Dian and Airmid, as in the eons of old when we fought the Fomorians, you will create a new Tuatha healing pool near Dun Uisneach for grievous wounds, and it will revive Gaels near death as you both did in days of old."

Eoin noted Airmid snarled something into her father's ear. Yet he was surprised by the proclamation, and he knew he had to rein in the rabble. He rose, hands held high to ensure quiet. "Dian and Airmid, thank you for your willingness to train our healers. Ecne and Sinéidin, thank you both for taking on the role of educating our Gaels in the ways of the world and for helping ensure we can shape our destiny.

"I give special thanks to Badb Catha, Goibniu, and his brothers. They armed us as no Gaelic force has ever ventured forth before. And last, to Danu and Dagda, I thank you dearly for pulling us into this new era, where Breanna and I can lead our Gaels throughout time to ensure they rule with our gods to guide us."

Eoin pulled Breanna close, and they both took another bow to show gratitude. Danu said, "Breanna and Eoin, I must say, you two have allowed my daughter to grow as no one has before. For that, I will be eternally grateful."

With that, Dagda added, "Now, go kick some Roman arse!"

Croí Dàn added privately, *"I didn't see that coming!"*

With that, ale and mead flowed, and Breanna approached Chief Connall. He looked bewildered as she commanded, "Introduce yourself to Áine, as you are on the Council of Erin. She can help ensure that those who join you are genuine, as *Mo Chroí* will not be here to swear them in.

"And please make sure all know that any other appointments are temporary assignments until confirmed by my Heart."

"Of course, Breanna," Connall confirmed with a smile.

Breanna asked, "Eoin, please facilitate a greeting with Áine."

Taliesin stood beside her, along with Livie, saying, "I have a hard time believing this is all real."

"Aye, me too," Breanna agreed. "Yet you need a weapon and shields. Livie, take him to Goibniu. Bláth, follow along and find out what instruments our new Bard plays."

As they headed off, Breanna suddenly found herself beside Badb Catha, who said, "You have considerably more skills since our last meeting, young goddess. Dagda has you and your warriors using micro-time in bouts, which can save a life. You will soon seek the *Cycle of Time* to change the past of the Celts across the sea and their Roman invaders.

"We have never been able to impact time like this, especially in such a distant past, but when you put that new timeline in motion, you will have to set yourself and your band on a path in that given timeline. Those threads must play out. Starting over isn't an option; it would cause chaos in the *Cycle*. If you or the Celts lose a battle, it's lost. I've met the Fates of Olympus; Clotho is the life spinner, Lachesis assigns destinies, and Atropos is the one who cuts them. In our pantheon, I command all three roles, so heed my warning.

"That said, in your *before-time*, Danu, with Dagda's help, only had to rewrite less than twenty cycles in a narrow part of your land. You'll be dealing with six centuries across many lands. The difference is like rerouting a stream versus a mighty river. Stopping your changes will be challenging once you start to alter its path."

Breanna took a deep breath. "I think I understand. Once I choose a path, I must commit to it. What of the present?"

"When you start to change that mighty river, you'll feel it."

This time, Breanna just nodded. Badb continued, "Good. Now, as for you, your command of *Eitear* is still weak. It is the main Element that powers life. It is the source and signature of life. You will need to wield Aether as well as you do the *void* and the *sight*. It will help you in a possible future that may come to be—to find life strands in time for one you hold dear. To help you accomplish that, I created a Life Thread Sigil. You must master it."

With that, the Dark Goddess touched Breanna's forehead, burned a sigil into her mind, and then Badb was gone. Reaching up to her where The Mórrigan had put her fingers above and between her brows, Breanna exclaimed, "Ow!"

Eoin stepped to her side, asking, "What's that symbol on your forehead? It's glowing like fire."

"It seems to look like it feels—on fire! It appears Badb Catha has imprinted upon me an Aether sigil, one I will need to master for some possible future."

"Cryptic as always, she is," Eoin asserted. "Well, at least the fiery sigil is fading from your skin. Should I draw it before it's gone?"

"Nay, for it is etched clearly in my mind's eye," she answered as she shook her head. "Yet I can see life threads more distinctly now."

Reaching for the *Cycle of Time*, she used the sigil her fellow goddess had just bestowed on her and pulled on Myrddin's signatures through Livie's attachment to him, seeing what he had in motion and what he kept to himself. Then, the *sight* released her. "Tomorrow, we seek Celts of Pretannia."

"The Iceni?"

"No, the Seer Myrddin. He hides a Cymru Sword of Power," she countered, surprised when the *sight* seized her again. A moment later, she intoned. "Not power, but life, leadership, and heroism in Cymru, maybe the entire island. Much like *Mo Chroí*, but it is not sentient. It is called *Caledfwich*. Badb Catha's Life Thread Sigil revealed it to me. I sense E*itear* more clearly now, more deeply. We need a warrior of that land to wield this weapon, one who can lead the Celtic tribes. It is like the Sword of Light is to the Gaels. I will extract the truth from Livie's father!"

"I heard him swear the oath, Mo Chroí," Eoin confirmed.

"Aye, but he slipped in words that let him skirt the full meaning." Breanna seethed. *"Never let that happen again!"*

Eoin said gently, "Bre, calm down. I missed it as well."

Breanna snarled, "We will trap him. Be ready. Have Livie let her father know we will pick him up along the way. Then, we spring our surprise."

"After that, we seek the Iceni?" Eoin questioned.

"Still to be seen. There are twenty-plus tribes we could engage. I'm still unsure where to begin our foray into the past to save Pretannia."

Mo Chroí whispered dejectedly, *"I failed you."*

With that, Breanna heaved a great sigh. *"Och, my Heart, nay! You've not dealt with liars and connivers. It's all on me, as I should have expected, especially given my experience with my original father. I got swept up in being with Livie and her mother when Myrddin raised my hackles. I just wanted to be with women like me."*

Eoin said, *"My love, focus on the future, but recognize you have time to adjust to what's needed."*

Breanna sighed, knowing Eoin was right. *"Mo Chroí, we are done for tonight. Yet, all is well. I'll spend it with my mate."*

———◈ **Dagda** ◈———

All-Father used mind-speak to seek out Breanna. *"Daughter, before you retire, we have an issue to address with the Norvegr Gods. May I join you?"*

"Aye, we are still decently dressed."

He flashed outside the doorway of their abode, and Breanna said, "I see you brought your great club."

"Aye, it's a statement," he answered as it rested on his shoulder, magically weighing nothing to him. He informed the pair, "The Asgardians demanded a meeting with us. Well, with you. They foresee a time when they can gain a foothold in Pretannia and Erin. Thor, their God of War, wants to assess your intentions and mettle. Odin agreed, so we must accept their request for a parlay."

Breanna sighed. "When?'

"Now," he answered grimly.

"Are you serious?"

"Deadly, as they seek weakness. You must show none."

"You think I'm ready for that?" she asked.

He just nodded.

Breanna barked, "Gah! Fine!"

He commanded, "Armor up! You too, Son! Bring Lugh's spear."

"Give us a moment," she demanded.

With that, they cloaked themselves in all of the armor and magical weapons that Goibniu had provided; Breanna included her earthly dirks just in case. Tying her hair back with her green

Connemara marble thong and settling her teardrop circlet on her head, she growled, "Where's this parlay?"

"The Isle of Fire and Ice," he answered, sending an image of a snow-covered volcanic slope that led to an angry sea, with a honeycomb of hot springs between the two. With that, she held out her hand to Eoin and Dagda, reached for the *Cycle*, and they were swept into the wherever. The three appeared next to Danu and Lugh, who nodded thanks as Eoin handed the god *Gáe Assal*.

Dressed as the Silver Huntress, Danu had her sword in hand, looking as fierce as Dagda had seen her in ages. He was pleased to see their Mórrigan had chosen her magical black cloak of crow feathers, knowing it rippled with its own life, her hands moving in patterns that wove various Elemental Sigils of Power. Next to Badb stood a massive man that she suspected was the mainland God of Thunder, Taranis, whom Dagda had once mentioned. What he was doing there, Breanna had no idea.

Across from them stood the Asgardians. During their skips through time, Dagda had explained a bit about the Asgardians to Breanna, hoping she had been paying attention. He pointed out, *"As you may have surmised, Odin has the patch over his right eye, and Thor with his Warhammer, Mjolnir. On Thor's left is Tyr, their God of War. Next to him is Freyja, another key Goddess of War. The winged warrior is the Valkyrie, Gunnr."*

When she tipped her head, Dagda's voice boomed, "Odin, you requested a parlay on behalf of your son. The Tuatha honor your request, not his. Make it clear why we are here."

"As previously discussed, Dagda, you created a new goddess and maybe another demigod. Thus, as is prudent, we need to ensure we understand each other's goals to avoid personality clashes. If we do not know who your newly *born* is, we could mistakenly end up at war."

Dagda saw Breanna smile in a disarming way and countered, "Och, but that is shite, Odin. You know it, as do I. We could be in your halls or ours, drinking together, so you could meet my newly *born*. Instead, we are here, in this forbidding place, with your most capable warrior gods standing at your side, to discuss the future of those who worship us.

"Given one of our most capable sustains an Elemental Air shield on this hostile Isle of Fire and Ice, you have tied up one of us. You can imagine my concern about this selected venue for a meeting with my newly *born*. It creates an opportunity for more tension and escalation, not less. It's also a concern for our Celtic counterparts, which is why Esus and Teutates suggested Taranis join us."

Odin cocked his head. "I care not about the Celtic Gods. You created her in your pantheon, causing this potential conflict. We both know those who worship us sustain us. Your newly *born* daughter can influence those of this realm."

"Indeed, she can," Dagda agreed. "She defends Celts and Gaels, especially those impacted by Roman invasions, and those who have always been ours and not yours. Her claim over Erin and plans for Pretannia, using the magic she earned by wielding our *Triple Dàns* created by our Goddess of War, are hers to command. It's fitting you chose this location for this meeting, as this is where Badb Catha drew those diamonds for one of the *Dàns*. Blades that now rest on the shoulders of our Goddess of Time."

Breanna drew *Lann Dàn* and said darkly, "Beware, Thor, for my long blades are now much more than when I used them to vanquish your Norvegrs, the ones who raped and killed those in my clan when they invaded my Emerald Isle."

Thor turned red at the insult. "You—"

Odin held a hand up. "I would hear more from this new Goddess of Time."

Breanna stepped forward. "What do you want to hear, Ó mighty Odin? If I can make Thor's warriors no more when I was not a Goddess, know I will, as one of the Tuatha, claim Pretannia and stop Rome from destroying my Celts. I know your son is behind this *parlay*. And I know why. He's barely more than a scared little boy who thinks I'm taking away his toys."

Thor bellowed, letting lightning flash from Mjolnir. Dagda flinched but watched in surprise as Breanna absorbed the energy when it slammed into her shields, causing her to give no more than a grunt; it was a blast he knew would have killed her otherwise.

She looked up at him, her head cocked, looking through her eyelashes. She said, *"I don't want to, but I will show restraint, Father."*

He smiled proudly and noted she was waiting for her *balefire* to be cycled back after Thor's assault. He could see all holding their breath over what her response would be. Then, her shields clicked off, and *balefire* roared out of her blades as never before. The impact tore Thor's hammer out of his hand and hurled it through Badb's Elemental Air bubble.

Breanna said coldly, "Odin, we have fulfilled your request to meet Dagda's new Goddess of Time. Me. Breanna. Ban. Morna. I stand before you, defiant and uncowed by your attempted show of power. I met your kind in my *before-time*, and I cast them into the whenever. Rome will not rule my Gaels and Celts or those who follow them, be they Norvegrs, Saxons, or Angles. They will not remake Pretannia.

"I provided a controlled restraint this evening, unlike your son, who tried to destroy me. I could have aimed my *balefire* at his heart, not his hammer, and he certainly would have died. If I see Thor or his followers in my lands again, you're the one who will bring on war. Given that I dance in time, be careful with the latitude you allow."

She finished with, "When Ragnarök looms, Odin, you'll need powerful friends to face it. You have no one, save me, who can wind and unwind time. Do well to remember that.

"Taranis, know that I will fight for our mutual Celtic peoples. If one falls, so will the others. I appreciate your support and look forward to any aid you can provide."

He said, "We welcome your efforts on behalf of our peoples."

Then Breanna turned to Dagda. "Father, I assume you can pick up the pieces here. I believe I am no longer needed. Danu, Lugh, and Badb Catha, I thank you for your support."

The Mórrigan added, "You showed impressive control."

"Thank you. Yet, the weight you placed on me is hefty."

With that, Eoin took back Lugh's magical spear, and she flashed them away.

⁕⟨ᚨ Breanna ᚨ⟩⁕

As they sequestered themselves in their hut and finally settled into bed, Breanna said, "Well, that was a big pile of shite. What was my father thinking? I could have started a war with the Asgardians."

"Yet you did not, though I had my doubts when Thor attacked. I have to admit I almost lost it when his lightning bolt hit you."

"By the stars, I did want to destroy him!" she concurred. "At least we now know that Badb's shields are powerful. Yet, standing off against a bunch of Asgardians is not something I want to repeat."

Eoin offered, "I'll admit, I was more than a bit intimidated."

After a deep breath, Breanna added, "Well, it's behind us now. I've not had time to tell you the other topic Badb broached before gifting me with her Aether Life Sigil. For any effort to change the timeline, she offered a deeper explanation of what it will take to claim victory over the Romans. Danu altered our timeline by less than twenty cycles to resolve my vision, which was also in a narrow portion of our land!

"We seek to change six centuries of history. Badb likened it to redirecting a tiny stream versus a vast river. Once we start moving that timeline, that river, there's no turning back if we hope to defeat them. No matter who dies, I'll only have moments to make such a change to ensure that any such death takes hold in that timeline. Gods, what a weight!

"If someone dies on my watch, I have to decide if I can save them or I will lose them in this new river of time. And what if I have to make a choice? Who would put that burden on me? To decide who lives or dies?"

Eoin whispered, "Unfortunately, no one can but you."

"By the stars, I never wanted this. Only to end my *before-time* birth father's time from conquering our Emerald Isle. Somehow, the future of the Gaels and Celts rests upon me. Who thought that was a good idea?"

Eoin didn't answer, but instead kissed the top of her head, which she had nestled into his shoulder. Breanna could only sigh. "Just hold me until sleep gives me an escape from this nightmare!"

"Then sleep, my love. Let the worries of tomorrow be for then."

The following morning, after discussing the Asgardian incident with no clear understanding of its implications for their goal of ensuring no one rules their Gaels and Celts, Eoin readied their band to travel. Breanna stepped before the table in the main hall where Livie and Taliesin sat and asked, "May I have a word with you two?"

Taliesin rose and gave her a courtly bow. "Of course, my Hero. Please sit."

Breanna rolled her eyes. "Enough with the titles. It's Bre or Breanna. I have an urgent matter to discuss. What do you know of *Caledfwich*?"

Livie said, "Taliesin, you're a historian. You start."

"Well, our Derwyddon, what you call Druids, have long held that the Lady of the Lake, whose name is Nimuë, imbued the power of sovereignty into *Caledfwich*. She is said to choose who wields the sword. Given she dwells underwater, some have postulated she might be related to the Sea God, Llŷr, and possibly be his daughter."

"I believe I might be able to call in a favor from our mutual Sea God if that is the case," Breanna stated as she turned to Livie.

Seeing the look, her Seeress sighed. "Hmm, let me fill in my father's ambitions about the sword.

"My father has sought *Caledfwich* for much of his life, hoping to find a warrior worthy of the blade in Nimuë's eyes, one she could bestow its power upon as the leader of our island's now fractured political structure. He thinks he has found that in a lad named Artur in Gwynedd. His grandfather was of Roman descent, and his mother was born in Cymru. He now lives with his uncle, who pretends to be his father. The lad claims he's a descendant of *Teulu* Pendragon. That's Cumbric for Clan."

Breanna declared, "Your father has made more progress than you thought. Badb Catha granted me a new Life Thread Sigil to sharpen my ability to use *Eitear*. I have felt the life threads Myrddin created to connect Nimuë and this Artur."

Taliesin exclaimed, "By the stars, is that possible?"

"Aye," Breanna answered grimly. "And Myrddin slipped in some words in his oath to *Ćroí Dàn* that allow him to keep his vow to me and lie about the connection between Nimuë and Artur. I need that tie to exist when we are in the past time that we must go to! If Nimuë and Artur can do what *Croí Dàn* and I are doing for Erin, they are critical for our success."

Livie shook her head, muttering, "My father is a blind fool."

Breanna stood. "Ready yourselves. We leave shortly with Eoin. I will face down your father."

After gathering Eoin and conveying her revelations about Myrddin's hidden agenda, Breanna sought his life thread through her new connection with the *Eitear* Element. Moments later, the four arrived in what appeared to be a rocky cave with a pool at its center, with the Seer facing the water, murmuring a chant.

He turned in surprise and started to protest, but Breanna demanded, "Shut it! You tricked *Croí Dàn* and, therefore, me. We all know it, and with Aether, I can track you down anywhere or anytime. I know you are plotting to install Artur as the head of this land's leadership during this time.

"Yet, I need Artur with *Caledfwich* to be with me during our quest to rally and unite the Celtic tribes six hundred cycles ago. You did not believe in me. Why should I be surprised? *Maorgairme*, summon our Sea God!"

Manannán Mac Lir appeared momentarily, questioning with wide eyes, "Breanna? What may I do for you, my niece?"

Breanna asked directly, "Is Nimuë your daughter?"

"Hmm, strange question, one I did not expect, but she is, as my other island across the Sea of Erin needed her. Wait, we're there!"

"Aye, and there are fools in all lands," Breanna stated. "Meet the no-so-bright and conniving Seer, Myrddin Wyllt. He has created life threads between Nimuë and a warrior named Artur. Given that, with *Caledfwich*, he can unite this land, I need them in the past before Rome invades it."

"Och, that's brilliant!" Manannán proclaimed.

"Can we find Nimuë at that time?"

"Better yet," he said. "Daughter, come to me."

A sword emerged from the pool's center, followed by a hand holding its hilt. Next came the rest of the Goddess Nimuë's body, a white shift draped about her that the water did not appear to touch. She seemed surprised. "Father? It's been such a very long time. I wondered if you had forgotten me."

Manannán looked pained. "Never that, Daughter. It has, indeed, been longer than I should have let pass, and you have my apologies. The world is changing fast. We have a new opportunity to bring your magic to your land. Meet Breanna, the new Tuatha Goddess of Time in Erin. She understands this Seer, known as Myrddin, has connected you to a warrior named Artur, whom he seeks to lead your island in these dark times.

"Yet, what if these times never happened? What if Breanna took them back in time to unite the Celtic tribes and prevent Rome from causing the chaos it brought? Can Artur be that man, be that leader?"

Nimuë looked at Myrddin, demanding tightly, "I trusted you! Did you know this?"

The Seer bowed. "Only recently. It seemed improbable she would succeed, especially given that Breanna is new to her role."

"Not so new, laddie," stated Manannán. "She saved my life once before and helped me end the Fomorian God Tethra. In that same battle, she single-handedly struck the death blow to Balor of the Baleful Eye's twisted demon essence."

Nimuë cast a narrow gaze at Myrddin and turned to Breanna. "Perhaps *Caledfwich* should be yours?"

"Nay," Breanna replied. "I am Erin's Hero. *Cróí Dàn* is my Heart, *Lann Dàn* are my weapons, and I walk the *Cycle of Time* via the power of *Lia Dàn*, the Stone of Destiny. The Tuatha gods tasked me to ensure the Gaels and Celts rule their respective destinies and islands. I need to facilitate that on multiple fronts, not just here."

"Hmm," said Nimuë, clearly unsettled. Then she faced Myrddin. "You disappoint me, as I believed in your smooth tongue. Yet, Breanna, who called my father, will ensure I unite *Caledfwich* with Artur under her watch, and you will travel with him to that time when our Celts and Gaels ruled themselves. She requires Artur's support more than you, as he can be the leader we need at that time. Maybe you can earn your way back into Breanna's trust."

Turning to her father, she added, "I expect to see you in this *before-time* Breanna seeks. And you, Taliesin, will keep my blade safe until you meet Artur and can let him merge with it."

With that, a sheathed *Caledfwich* appeared in his hand. Nimuë cast Artur's life thread to Breanna and disappeared, along with her father, Manannán.

Taliesin said, "I'm not a swordsman. How do I carry it around?"

"You'll want to keep the pointy end down," Livie suggested.

Breanna, Eoin, Myrddin, Livie, and Taliesin appeared a moment later in the courtyard of a small castle in Gwynedd as she was drawn to Artur through his life threads. The young man seemed to be a few cycles older than she was as he sparred with another lad of a similar age.

He held out his hand to stop the match. "Myrddin?"

"Artur!" the Seer rejoined. "We have much to discuss. Please meet Breanna Ban Morna, Erin's Hero and Goddess of Time. She will join you with *Caledfwich*!"

Breanna stepped next to Livie's father, with *Lann Dàn* in her hands, crackling with *balefire*, and with narrowed eyes, said, "Under my conditions, Artur. I have a mission—a prophecy—to fulfill. If you swear to my cause, you shall wield *Caledfwich*! To ensure the Celts and Gaels of this land rule, not Rome, nor the various invaders they've left behind."

Artur marched forward. "How can this be?"

"Careful, my liege," his sparring partner said cautiously.

Breanna continued as if the lad had not spoken. "We will travel back in time, some six hundred cycles, to ensure that those of our lands can fight off the Roman invasions of that time. I need a leader to unite them—someone from this land who can call on *Caledfwich's* power to do what I have done in Erin."

Artur's sparring partner attempted to circle behind Breanna, but her gaze stopped him in his tracks. Plucking his name out of his mind with Aether, she commanded, "You, Lanslod, are a skilled warrior, yet you command no magic. I sense it is within you, but you buried it. You could hone these skills in support of Artur if you are brave enough. If you can master your fear of magic."

The lad's eyes widened. "Who are you?"

"More than you know," Breanna stated.

Artur asked, "Myrddin? What is this about?"

The Seer answered, "Just what she said. Taliesin carries our land's Sword of Power, and only he and Breanna can bestow *Caledfwich* to you. This Goddess of Time summoned Nimuë's father, Manannán, our Sea God, as if he were nothing but an afterthought, and the Lady of the Lake put your fate in the hands of Erin's Hero."

Lanslod cautioned, "Beware of this magic."

Breanna sheathed *Lann Dàn* as she frowned at Artur's sparring partner. "Your One God beliefs have tainted you."

Then she turned to Artur and offered her arm in a warrior's greeting. "And you, do you believe in your true gods? Or have you also been tainted?"

Artur looked to Myrddin, who nodded, and then he said, "Aye, I do believe in our land and our gods."

Breanna demanded, "Then are you brave enough to let me show you what will come to pass should we fail?"

As Artur stepped forward, his companion reached out, taking his arm. "Are you sure?"

"I am, Lan," he said. "Join me in Breanna's offer. Let's see it together. Believe as one or not?"

As Artur took Lan's arm with his right and Breanna's arm with his left, she swept them into time to see the fate of the Celts and the Gaels as she skipped through the ages. When they returned, Artur had to be supported by Livie and Taliesin as he retched on the ground before him; Lan had no support from anyone and was on his knees, letting anything in his stomach hurl on the ground.

Livie offered, "It gets better with practice. Right, Taliesin?"

"Only barely, as of now," the Seer answered.

Once Artur recovered, he lifted his head. "Lan, this is real. Breanna showed us our land in other times. It gets worse."

His friend asked, "Deceivers?"

"No, Lan, it is as real as it gets. Waves of foreigners will overwhelm our future, more than the Romans have already done. Our Celts will be conquered and transformed into something we'll not recognize."

Breanna held out her arm. "Not on my watch!"

Artur smiled. "Breanna Ban Morna, I swear to thee."

Breanna asked, "Lanslod?"

"Where Artur goes, I go."

"Good. It is not I to whom you two swear, but Erin's Heart of Destiny. Right, *Mo Chroí*?"

Croí Dàn answered in mind-speak, *"Yes, My Hero, as only I can stop their hearts if they break their oath."*

Breanna knew Artur was surprised by the voice of her Heart as he asked, "Lan, will you join me in this quest?"

"Of course, brother of another mother. Always together!"

"Artur, Lanslod —AND Myrddin—repeat precisely after me."

After they were sworn, or resworn as the case may be, Breanna commanded with her hand held out, "Before I join you with *Caledfwich*, there is a promise I must keep. Each of you to me."

When they had placed a hand over hers, they appeared again in Nimuë's cave, this time with Artur. But it wasn't in their time—it was six centuries earlier.

The Lady of the Lake rose, standing knee-deep in the pool, asking, "Breanna, why have you brought Artur here with my sword? I gave you the power to join them together."

"Aye, you did, but I think the bond with his land will be stronger if you make it here at this time," Breanna answered. "At this moment, he needs to lead all of the tribes of this great island against our enemies."

Nimuë intoned, "Wise of you, my cousin. Taliesin, hand me *Caledfwich*. Artur, join me."

The young warrior removed his boots and stepped into the pool. With that, the Lady of the Lake called on her sovereign magic as she held the hilt out to him. A moment later, with the blade in his hand, *Caledfwich* whispered its call to the people of her land with a message that Artur would unify them. It was much like when Breanna had claimed Erin, but muted.

Artur bowed to the goddess. "My Lady, I won't let you down."

Nimuë nodded and then turned to his companion. "Lanslod, you have a path before you, a deep choice to make which will hold your bond with Artur or shatter it. Know this, and your choice will decide the fate of our land. Breanna and Artur may still prevail without you, but it will be a narrow path. Choose wisely."

The warrior appeared to shudder at the weight laid upon him. As if a fog lifted, he looked at Artur and said, "I swear to be true, Artur."

Breanna looked to Nimuë, asking, *"What is this about?"*

"He can choose to betray Artur in an affair of love."

"Ahh," Breanna said. *"You touch the Cycle of Time. You see the future like me?"*

"Not as precisely, more like a Seeress without your power."

Breanna nodded to the Lady of the Lake, adding, "Thank you, Nimuë, for your insights. I will oversee this potential issue.

"Yet, a promise made and kept. Cousin, I give you Manannán."

As the Sea God appeared, Nimuë gasped. "You made him fulfill his pledge."

"Nay, Daughter, she just facilitated it. While I'd do anything for our new goddess, I am here for you."

Breanna said, "Myrddin, lead us out of this cave. We need a plan to unite the twenty-plus tribes of this land. It's time to make some changes. Farewell, Cousin. Uncle."

Emerging from the cave, Livie whispered, "We are just above Llyn Llydaw, the lake where Nimuë dwells in the Snowdonia Mountains. It is fairly close to our settlement of Llandudno in northern Gwynedd."

"You are correct, Daughter," Myrddin confirmed.

Taliesin added, "And that peak is Yr Wyddfa."

Lanslod shuddered. "This magic you've accepted has pulled you into some deep shite!"

Artur motioned for him to be silent with a gesture.

Ignoring the comment, Breanna stated, "The question is where to start. Do we rally the tribes that Artur is more familiar with, or start with the southern tribes like the Iceni or Catuvellauni?"

Myrddin suggested, "While we all share the Celtic language roots with them, I'd start with where we know the people best, where we are likely to have a greater grasp of common words. Also, I assume we can choose the time of the cycle we begin this campaign, aye? Let's start at a time that makes travel easier across the country."

She nodded and swept them back to Dun Gaillimhe.

Breanna and the others reappeared with a startled Artur and Lanslod, who had to place their hands on their knees to steady themselves. When they could finally look up, Artur asked, "Where are we, and what is that body of water?"

Livie answered, "Western Erin. We won't be here long, but give me a moment. Fergal, we may need Sinéidin to translate various Cumbric words into Gaelic for our guests."

Breanna commanded, "Livie, hold on. I need a moment with Sinéidin first."

Then she turned to Fergal's mate and found Ecne standing before her. "Bre, I might also be able to help. Before you take my daughter through time and away from me."

Sinéidin sighed explosively. "You can always visit, Father!"

Breanna said, "Indeed, I can fetch you if needed, but let's address that later. While Celtic is the root language of the land across the Sea of Erin, we may have a language problem, as six hundred cycles of divergence have likely happened since then."

"It has indeed," Sinéidin said, "as Cumbric evolved from Gaelic, which sprang from what linguists call Proto-Celtic. That's the language spoken in that land at the time we seek. In contrast, there are similar underlying constructs that will facilitate communication with them. Changes in word meanings and usage will likely cause issues, and the Chiefs might be confused by what we ask of them if we misuse their language. That will hurt our cause."

"Is nothing easy?" Breanna demanded. "Okay then. Badb Catha recently imprinted a new *Eitear* Life Thread Sigil upon me. As such, it embodies life. Can we overlay that sigil with your skills, maybe create something new to cast your translation ability into a combined *Eitear* sigil?"

Sinéidin paused, then smiled. "Aye, Bre, we can. It must be *Aer* and *Eitear*, as any human voice creates sound with air. How will you etch it into a person?"

Breanna exclaimed, "Shite! I hadn't thought of that. I burn *balefire* and *dark-matter* shield sigils into steel or wood weapons. These are people, my people. Yet my father and Lugh used woad."

"As do I," Taliesin offered. "And, if embedded with needles, woading tattoos remain mostly permanent. Many warriors seek me out for such sigils, which work until the person loses that body part."

Livie commented, "I did not need to hear that detail!"

Lotte snickered but said nothing as Breanna commanded, "Focus! Bláth, witness! Sinéidin, take my hand while we create this combined sigil of life and language. I'll include *Talamh* in the Element mix, as woad is of Earth."

She clasped Talieisin's arm in a warrior's greeting and added, "*Croí Dàn*, please capture the combined sigil marks so you can send it to our new Bard, Seer, or whatever he is."

With that, Breanna felt Air, Earth, and Aether stir inside her as Sinéidin's mind joined hers in the *void*, letting her magic of hearing a language and understanding flow instantly between them. With the marks clear in Breanna's mind, her Heart cast it out through her hand to embed the blue symbols into the Seer's skin.

A moment later, Taliesin hissed as Breanna released her grip, and he looked at the inside of his forearm to see a new tattoo. "Och, I'm an idiot. I should have known she'd pick me first to impart this new woad-based sigil you two magically cooked up."

Sinéidin said in Sumerian, "Of course, she would, though I'm not sure I agree on that first part. You're likely not an idiot."

"Wait! What? I understood that!"

Livie chuckled. "Rarely a boring moment with Bre."

"That is a true statement," Bláth added.

Eoin chimed in with, "Excellent. Artur, you're next, and then Lan. After that, we cast the woad sigil on everyone else. And, Taliesin, be assured we have more firsts in store for you. It is likely best to suggest we are from the Ordovices and Catuvellauni tribes, offering help to the Silures and Dobunni tribes."

"Well done, my lad," Ecne commended. "Good choices. Let me know if you have any questions while on your mission."

Breanna said, "Indeed, impressive. It is the best starting point we could have hoped for. Let's prepare to ink this new Language Sigil, and then we are off into the past!"

Then she turned to Goibniu. "Taleisin is our, um, ambassador across the Sea of Erin. He needs an enhanced weapon, shield protection for his staff, and something to compel truth when *Mo Chroí* cannot."

When Goibniu extended his hand for the Seer's staff, Taliesin passed it over. After fondling it for a moment, Breanna felt the smith reach out with his magic to sift out the nature of the wooden piece. "Hmm, possible. We can modify the Language Sigil you created to discern truth."

"Add it, and add *balefire* and *dark matter* shields as needed. Time to move fast, my uncle. Everything is finally in place except for the coin of the time."

Goibniu nodded. *"Mo Chroí, I'll need your help to design this new Truth Sigil. Ecne, I need your help as well."*

As others slipped away, Mrydinn asked, "What of me?"

Breanna shrugged. "I'll leave that to your daughter. I might accept you if you can redeem yourself in her eyes."

───◈ Eoin ◈───

During their midday meal, Eoin and Breanna cornered Ecne, Artur, Lan, Livie, and Taliesin. "I know Breanna needs a point of reference to focus her intent to travel back through time. We did this before and nearly landed in enemy territory. Caer Didi is too vague."

Taliesin said, "I know I'm going to regret suggesting this, but maybe we should seek that time at different points to get a sense of the land then."

Breanna finished her trencher and suggested, "Livie, let's make this happen with Ecne and Taliesin!"

When the foursome flashed away, Eoin asked Artur, "Maybe a friendly match between *Caledfwlch* and *Claimh Solais*?"

"Let's make it so," Artur agreed and rose, circling the match area. Then he asked, "No quarter?"

Eoin rejoined, "Nay, my mate would have my hide if I smote you down. Let's make the first tap."

"So be it."

Then they moved, swords crossing, clashing, deflecting, and sparking. Eoin was testing him and refused to use time, so he relied on his swordsmanship to match his opponent. He and Artur seemed to be of the same age and similar speed, yet different in style as they circled, dodged, feinted, and parried—steel ringing on steel.

After a while, Eoin changed his mind about using his special skills; this contest could be a learning opportunity. He seized the *void* and pivoted using time as he had been practicing with Breanna. When he appeared where he should not have been able to, Artur spun in surprise to evade the coming riposte. Yet the lad managed to trip himself with the move. Then Eoin tapped Artur's forearm. "Match!"

Lotte protested, "Gah! It was just getting good!"

Artur looked up at Eoin. "Well met. You certainly have skills I need to master."

Eoin sheathed his blade and extended his arm to help his opponent stand. "It's called the *void*, where you see those around you a moment in time before they do. Breanna and I use it in our blade dances. Then there's moving in time, which I also did with you. She will insist we train together, though I do not expect we can ever be as good as my mate. Either way, we have the two most powerful swords ever created in your land and mine. It was a good match."

Breanna returned with Taliesin, Livie, and Ecne a moment later. "Did you two boys wrestle over a bone?"

Eoin crossed a hand over his heart, "You wound me!"

Breanna snorted lightly. "Ever so dramatic."

Eoin shrugged. "While his sword can impart some advantages, I know what is needed—your path to the *void*."

"As I expected. And how to move in time."

Artur looked back and forth between them and questioned, "Do I even want to match my blade against hers?"

Eoin sighed. "She will have it no other way."

He watched Breanna draw *Lann Dàn*, indicated Artur should do the same, and she began her blade dance with their new band member. She whirled around him relentlessly and effortlessly, tapping him over and over again, and each time, Eoin said, "You're dead."

After more than ten "you're dead" proclamations, the match ended, leaving Artur on his knees and panting from exhaustion. Eoin extended a hand and pulled him to his feet again. "You need to understand how to battle with the *void*, as Bre and I do. We must touch your mind to convey how to seize the *void*. Understanding how to use time as you fight will take longer."

When Artur nodded, Eoin took Breanna's hand and placed his other palm on their new Cymru friend's forehead. Eoin felt the link between the three of them. The life threads Nimué had created between the lad and *Caledfwlch* echoed through Artur, and then they were in the *void* together. Eoin and Breanna spun out how to use the *void* to foresee an opponent's next move, and then they broke the connection a short time later. Eoin added, "Artur, you have much to learn, and I'll make time to do so."

"Will you teach Lanslod the same way?"

Eoin hesitated, then added, "If he can release his fear."

"Listen to Eoin—he has taught me much with subtle nudges when I would be an angry bull." With that, Breanna walked away.

Artur said, "That's one tough woman you have as a mate."

"Aye." Eoin shrugged. "From our first battle with my wooden sword when I was seven and she, at five, with her wooden long blades. When she took me on with the heart of a badger, I knew she was the one for me. It's always been that way, though it took another twelve cycles and our gods to force us to face our love for each other head-on. Never fight with the Fates."

Then the *sight* seized Eoin, a first for him, and he intoned, "While you are fated to Guinevere in your natural time, there will be another in the time to where we travel to who will be the same."

Artur demanded, "What are you babbling about?"

"Something special."

Eoin knew he would have to talk to Breanna about this. He turned after her to discover what they had found on their jaunt.

 Breanna

Breanna sought out Chief Connall Cas Ciabhach. When she found him, she cordially stated, "I have a request. Two Druids and two warriors are likely to need mounts. I can return to Dun Uisneach to acquire them. Or—"

He waved a hand. "I can supply them, my Hero. I'm sure you drew on those two co-chiefs heavily. No worries. I can do no less."

"And the One God followers?"

"Under control," he answered.

"Hmm, and Áine?" she asked.

"Seemed like a reasonable goddess." Connall shrugged.

Breanna huffed, "That's a surprise."

"You underestimate yourself."

Breanna surprised herself by admitting, "I do."

Connall offered his arm, and Breanna took it as he suggested, "Be strong. Easy for me to say, I know. There's a lot of weight on your shoulders. Yet, I saw my hall filled with our gods and goddesses, all squabbling over the leftovers you allowed them."

Breanna laughed. "Connall, I must say, after my first encounter with the stubborn commanders your King Dauthí chose, I thought we would battle. Now, you're a charmer."

Connall chuckled. "I'm just glad we did not battle, as my arse would be making its way back here from the Cuilcagh Mountains."

Breanna acknowledged with a grin. "Indeed."

"Know you have a friend here," he stated. "And many more across our land. Some will fight us, but we will triumph in the end."

"I hope so—just a back hills warrior that the Fates swept up."

"Ever the one to prevaricate. I believe many will join you."

Breanna sighed as they walked on until they met Eoin.

Livie

Livie knocked on the pole that held up the front of her father's tent, located on a field outside Dun Gaillimhe's stone walls. "Father, we must talk."

Myrddin commanded, "Enter, Daughter."

Livie did just that, silently standing before him.

He said, "So, she sent you to discuss my part in this mission."

"No, Breanna did not. As a *truly* sworn Warrior of Destiny, she left the decision to me whether to trust you."

"I see," he said sourly.

"Do you?" she asked. "All my life, you've kept your secrets."

"Visions are imprecise."

"An excuse for—dishonesty," Livie countered. "You swore to her Heart with deceit in your heart. Since I swore to her with all my heart, how can I trust you now? Even your mate, my mother, said not to trust you, even while she told me you could be helpful."

Her father winced, and she thought it odd that she did not consider him her father; it was the cold side of him speaking to her mind. Livie continued, "My advice to Breanna will be not to grant you access to her magic, which is too powerful to trust you with. I know because she has trusted me. As to imprecise visions, I can now wield the *sight* and the *Cycle of Time* as precisely as Breanna.

"If only you could have believed in me, your only daughter, that I had the skills to discern that their gods had made a new goddess who could make a difference in the joint future of our people without her ego clouding her vision as you have."

With that, she turned and left her father behind.

 Breanna

While Breanna knew that Taliesin and Myrddin did not have mounts and were assigned mares from the Connall stable, she had to take the Bard to his home in the future to fetch his travel harp and war drum. Yet Artur had a great-hearted mare named Llamrei, whom he insisted needed to be retrieved, and Lanslod's was a white stallion.

With that task accomplished, Eimar sniffed about Artur's and Lan's horses, but they seemed to agree that her rider led this band, and thus, Eimar was in charge of the mounts. While listening to the three horses engage in mind-speak, Breanna was surprised to find that they had a hierarchy based on their riders; that was another first for her.

Breanna's Warriors of Destiny gathered in the courtyard of Dun Gaillimhe."Now is the moment we go back in time to ensure the Celts of the island across the sea of Erin," she announced. "We must convince twenty-plus Celtic tribes to resist Rome. Ultimately, we will still need to face their armadas that bear legionnaires. Yet, we have the power of our gods and goddesses, our Tuatha-enhanced weapons, and now the power of an ancient Celtic goddess from the island across Erin's sea and her chosen one, Artur!"

She gave Eoin a nod, and he began to pass out a bag of coins—Goibniu chose the Catuvellauni Tribe for the source—to each of them. Then, she continued, "We will fight for our fellow Gael and Celtic cousins across time. Some will resist and betray us, but we will win them over. You've all sworn to me, and I am sworn to you!"

Each band of nine warriors thumped their spears on their serpent-embossed shields and chanted, "Bre! Bre! Bre!"

She held up a hand to quiet them as she snapped out the magical rope. A moment later, they were back in time, her fierce band looking down on an ancient fort called Caer Didi that the Dobunni tribe held.

INTO TIME

⸰⊰⊱ **Breanna** ⊰⊱⸰

The warm spring weather had transformed the land around the stone walls into verdant green beds, adorned with a riot of wildflowers, and a settlement stretched along a river that flowed into a large bay. Many merchant and fishing vessels were moored to the docks, while captains of larger ships had to anchor offshore.

Breanna asked, "Artur, given we plan to establish multiple touch points across this land, how would you advise us to approach the various Chiefs? We can't just march to their gates and say we have been sent to help build their defenses against a coming Roman invasion. And, in this case, if I'm not mistaken, some of those merchant ships in port are indeed from that country."

Artur looked to Lan, who shrugged. Then Myrddin stated, "You asked the wrong person to answer that question."

Breanna snorted, "Ó, wise Myrddin, give your sage advice. Share your vast wisdom with us."

Ecne stepped next to Breanna. "Ignore him."

She turned in surprise. "How did you manage to grab hold of my rope?"

"No need, Auntie." He chuckled. "As a fellow god, I can follow you easily through time because you have my daughter with you."

"It's back to Auntie, again?" she protested. "We agreed on Bre!"

"Technically, great-great-great-auntie," he added sheepishly.

"Gah," she groused.

Ecne chuckled. "Anyway, I suggest we go into the settlement in groups, each offering that we are sell-swords that the Ordovices and Catuvellauni have paid to help the Caer Didi Chief protect this port, as we will do so at Caer Went. The various Chiefs will send runners to other Chiefs. They typically meet twice a cycle at Beltane and Samhain. Thus, in a month or so, for the upcoming one."

"Let's make plans to be at those meetings."

Ecne nodded and then pointed toward a tavern at the center of the settlement. "We all meet there, and we act surprised that we've all followed the orders of our respective Chiefs to help them ensure the port is secure. Rumor has it that Rome will invade soon. That's not entirely true, as it will be another cycle before a full invasion happens. Then Caesar will make a concerted attack, and not just a landing. These people won't know that. Starting such a rumor will benefit your cause, hopefully uniting them in time to withstand the Romans. Given that I've spent cycles studying the Gaels and Celts during this period, we can be creative with the truth about your and Artur's mandate to unite the clans.

"With that, your blooded warriors will have roles to play. Lotte, you're a Gael leader with *fians* from Creones and Caledonia, the area known as Dál Riata and the Highlands in the fifth century. They support the Catuvellaunian concerns about Rome. Izzy, you're a mainland Celt hired by Chief Vellaunus to the east.

"Breanna and Eoin, you're from the Ulaidain capital of Emain Macha, descendants of Macha Mong Ruad. You're responding to Caledonian's warnings about the Romans. Breanna, your new title will be Guardian of the Celts, which we claim is equal to any Chief, and your blooded warriors will have the title Hound of the Celts. Translated, it is similar to Hero on our island. Eoin will still be your Protector, and eventually, we can transition to using Warriors of Destiny."

Breanna nodded as she held out a hand. "Very detailed, but we'll need to make a few minor changes and visit with a cousin goddess first. We need some magical weight. Give Eoin and me a moment with Artur, Myrddin, and Lan."

When they took her hand, she flashed them away.

Breanna took them to Nimuë's cave, saying, "Cousin, come to us. We have arrived here to begin uniting the clans of your island. Yet, Artur needs your magic to claim his role as Guardian of this land with *Caledfwich*. I will need the same via *Cróí Dàn* to stand at his side."

The Lady of the Lake rose from the pool in her cave, stating with some confusion, "I connected magic within *Caledfwich* to Artur. I felt the call go out. What more can I do?"

"My cousin," Cróí Dàn interjected, *"It might be best for me to share what happened when I claimed Erin's Hero, as I did with Breanna, and then what happened to all life when she claimed our Emerald Isle. Maybe we can combine our magic here to create something similar."*

"Cousin?"

"Aye," came the answer as Breanna drew *Mo Chroí* from her tunic. *"I am Danu's daughter, a sentient being cast into this red gem. Thus, we are kindred goddesses."*

Nimuë asked, *"How old are you?"*

"From this time, over a thousand cycles."

"Och, but you've always had a Hero, aye?"

"Nay, Breanna is only the sixth," Croí Dàn answered with a quiver, unable to keep her voice steady. *"She is the last Hero I will ever have, for I have decided to die when she does. While I can hear and interact with my kindred, I do not even have a semi-physical body to project or see with. Breanna now provides me with her eyes and ears for those outside my Tuatha realm."*

"I've at least had my father's creatures and mere folk to engage with. I cannot fathom your loneliness, my cousin."

Breanna sighed. "Nimuë, I appreciate you taking the time to bond with *Mo Chroí*. She and I have had similar conversations, but now we must focus on how to bond Artur to his land. If I need to remove my boots and join you in your pool, let's do that so you can experience how she cast her magic. It is how I claimed Erin as mine."

"We can meet at the water's edge," Nimuë said with a wave.

The three did just that, goddess to goddess to goddess, as the Lady of the Lake held *Croí Dàn* while she replayed the moments in the *before-time* and then the more recent reclaiming.

Breanna now saw the life threads between her and her land through Aether, the Life Element, with all its creatures and people. She passed on her many connections across her land to Nimuë. "I believe you are primarily a Water Element goddess, what we call *Uisce*. Yet when you combine that with Eitear, the result is much more powerful. *Croí Dàn* can do that with all of the Elements, but she mainly uses Aether to bind her chosen one to the land and her people.

"I suggest we do that with Artur. Study his life threads."

Nimuë turned to her chosen one. Then, awed, she said, "Cousin, you have shown me more about my magic than my father ever did!"

"I expect Badb Catha planted the seed," Breanna commented. "She recently granted me an Aether sigil. Let me share it with you as you take *Mo Chroí* in your hand again."

When the three goddesses joined again, Breanna melded their minds and powers. Nimuë declared, "Artur, draw *Caledfwich*, drive the blade into that rock, and proclaim Pretannia yours!"

When he did so, sparks flew, and rock melted as he roared, "I am Artur Pendragon, and this land is mine to guard and protect!"

Myrddin whispered, "What have you done?"

With the sword's length halfway buried in rock, Artur ignored the Seer and sank to his knees. His hands held each side of the pillar, where he had embedded *Caledfwich*. Artur felt his land's life enfold and welcome him. The three goddesses shadowed him with a guiding hand, first across what would one day become Cymru and its mostly gentle mountains, north to Dál Riata coastal ridges and the Highlands, then across the Pictish lands. Finally, they flowed south into Albion and west to Dumnonia.

It was all his, from the rivers and loughs teeming with water creatures to the various winged life, deer herds, and isolated bears and boars. Then, domesticated animals, particularly horses, acknowledged him, and Nimuë's ties to sealife also acknowledged their new Guardian. The people came last, most astonished, some defiant.

Breanna continued to shadow him with Nimuë and *Croí Dàn*, ensuring they were part of his Guardian claim, and then she decreed, "Rise, Artur, Guardian of Pretannia!"

Nimuë added, "Draw *Caledfwich* from the stone! If you fall or fail, the sword will return to me and can only be drawn again by a warrior anointed by Breanna or me."

Artur did just that, and the sword sang as he freed the blade from the stone where he had embedded it. He marveled at its new unearthly sheen.

Breanna dropped to a knee, commanding, "Artur, lower the tip of your sword to the stone floor before me. I have another gift."

When he did so, she placed a palm on each side of his blade near the hilt and etched two sigils into the steel with her Fire and *Eitear* Elements. She added, "I'll explain *balefire* and shields later.

"Lan, kneel before Artur so he can proclaim you as the Protector of Pretannia's Guardian! Only with that can I grant you powers as a Warrior of Destiny. Eoin, place a hand on our new protector's shoulder and show him his responsibilities."

As Artur and Eoin moved to do that, Breanna murmured smugly to Nimuë and *Mo Chroí*, "I just love working with kindred goddesses. Yet, Cousin, we could use some help from your sentinels of the sea if Roman ships are in the waters of Pretannia."

"Aye, consider it done. I'll leave the sky to you, though."

Croí Dàn added, *"Now that we are bound together, Nimuë, I'm just a thought away whenever you need some girl time."*

Breanna added, "Indeed, always just a thought away!"

Then she flashed them back to the hills just above Caer Didi, where Ecne and her band awaited them at a clearing in the woods.

 **Izzy**

Isobel let time flow around her while her new leader was away, drifting from tree to tree as the rest of the band moved to sit on the green grass beneath sunny skies, avoiding the shadows cast by strange oaks. Izzy found them to be much different than

Erin's black oaks. Her land in the rocky Galicia hills held no large trees like these.

Calling on her Earth Element, she reached into the ground through one large trunk, letting herself flow across the land around them as her grandfather had taught in the *Laoch Druí* way, feeling for discord, danger, harmony, and peace. While she found the latter to the north, the south and east yielded unsettled tension amongst the Celts.

A moment later, a wave of strength and protection washed over her, and she could feel the life signatures of both Breanna and *Croí Dàn* in their makeup—they almost tasted like a hint of Erin, along with a new one she thought had to be Artur. Her lips twitched at the notion that the tall, burly warrior could cast the feeling of a Guardian!

Then Izzy's inner senses told her that Breanna had reappeared, and she turned her gaze to find her Hero's eyes on her as she continued to hold her *Talamh* Element. Breanna motioned for Artur to follow her and approached. When she placed a hand over Izzy's, Breanna blended their Earth Elements. Only her grandfather had ever been able to do that; it was a very personal gesture that spoke to her Hero's understanding of her connection with her Earth Element.

"Well done, my friend. Deft touch," Breanna complimented. Then her Hero commanded, "Artur, put your hand on the tree trunk with Izzy and me. Do you feel your land now?"

"Aye, it's like a low buzz in my mind."

Breanna nodded. "Good. Let's wake our friend up."

Izzy saw Artur's eyes widen as Breanna used mind-speak, *"Your Guardians call you, great one, through your roots, to tell us the state of our land."*

An old, gnarled woman's voice answered. *"Guardians, I felt your claim just moments ago. And you, Fierce Little One, your* gentle touch. As to the state of our land, it is as your Druid observed. Clans to the north are mostly settled amongst themselves, with a misguided belief that they are safe. Yet, those in the south and east are troubled, as if holding a dreaded breath. There are traitors to our land amongst them, there and here."

Artur spoke with his mind. *"Rome's threat is felt more deeply in the southeast, while a taint here still needs to be dealt with."*

"Very well, my Lady of the Woods," Breanna thanked her. *"While I hope our casting that the Celtic gods have proclaimed the Guardians of Pretannia was explicit, please echo it through your brethren's tree root networks across the land. If your kind encounters Romans, alert me or my Fierce Little One."*

"Aye, Guardian and your Fierce Little One," came a raspy response. *"She is special and can draw on us and our land anytime."*

With that, they withdrew their hands. Izzy followed Breanna and Artur as they strode into the sunlit patch where the others sat on the grassy patch of land. Izzy protested, "Bre, I must say, being called a little one was insulting! Even you used it!"

Breanna turned, raising an eyebrow. "I heard *Fierce Little One!* How is that bad? A great tree acknowledged you and just said you can call on any of them anytime! Personally! Approach any tree in this land, wake it, and demand that *Fierce Little One commands your attention.* That tree will answer on behalf of all of them, as will this land's animals. Reach deep into your Earth Element. Feel it! But, if you need more, say, *'Fierce Little One commands your attention. You may call me Bee!'* There, problem solved!"

Izzy could only cry. "Gah!"

Breanna turned to her band. "We now have two Guardians anointed by the Celtic Gods of Pretannia among us, Artur and me. It's time to settle the matter. Izzy, you take Lan and Braoin. You'll lead them and the first *fian* of warriors to arrive from the west. Lotte, you and Bradaigh take the second *fian* and come in from the east with Artur. Eoin and I will take the other two *fians* and everyone else into the settlement heading in from the north. Bláth and Taliesin, as our Bards, play something courageous for us as we arrive. It would also be good if you could compose some Guardian Druid tales to spread amongst the common folk."

With that, they were each off, descending through the hills around the fort of Caer Didi and its settlement. Izzy's group sauntered along a path that led down to the estuary and toward the river settlement. They arrived at the tavern first, with the blooded warriors dismounting in the center of the *fian* warriors. The central ring of the settlement featured an inn, a smithy, and a market that sold a variety of goods, including meat, seafood, grains, bread, and vegetables. And, of course, a tavern called The Fish Head would be where they would meet. It offered ale, mead, and a seafood stew for their midday meal.

Izzy exclaimed, "Gods, it is good to find a civilized place after marching for days since we left Chief Vellaunus' stronghold at Cassi."

Lan agreed. "Sellswords don't often get lovely weather, and someone who cooked a meal for us."

"Are you implying my cooking is bad?"

Lan started to choke out, "I—"

"This place looks promising," Braoin declared, cutting him off. "My good lady—"

"I'm no lady!" the woman clearing an outside table groused.

Izzy ordered in mind-speak, *"Use your translation sigil!"*

She saw Braoin wince as he announced, "Pardon, my—server, we are from the east on an assignment from the Chief of the Catuvellauni tribe. We are here to help your people defend the port. Rumors abound about Rome's invasion intentions."

The serving maid stated, "Stop passing wind! What'll it be?"

Surprised, he answered, "Mead for my fierce mate—owe!"

Izzy stomped on Braoin's instep. "I place the orders for my band—you know that! Mead for me, ale for the boys, and fish stew for the lot."

The woman demanded, "You have the coin?"

Izzy huffed, slamming a Catuvellauni silver coin on the table. "I expect change! Send out your keeper."

The server's eyes bulged at the silver coin as she scooped it up and scurried off. Shortly thereafter, she returned with the ale, mead, and stew, followed by The Fish Head Tavern's keeper, demanding, "I am Keeper Morcant. What are you doing in our port without permission?"

Izzy scowled. "Hoping for a good meal with a drink. I paid for my order with a silver coin and expect whatever change is due! What is it with you, Dobunni? Are you suspicious of us, fellow Celts and Gaels? Yet you accept Roman filth at your tables, who will kill you all one day!"

Izzy watched his reaction, seeking hints of deception. Eyeing him, she added, "You don't seem concerned about how I know that."

He sighed. "Few see the truth before them. Yet, I have insulted a fierce warrior. My apologies, my lady."

"Like your server, I am no lady, just a blade master Warrior Druid. I like to slice and dice those who challenge me," Izzy glowered at the proprietor. "As Celtic Hounds, we do not have to seek permission, save from our Guardians, to slay insolent fools. My warriors need to eat and drink. We have tasks assigned to us. Am I clear?"

Just then, Lotte led her band into the town circle and dismounted, exclaiming, "By the gods, Isobel! How is it we meet again? When my Chief in Caledonia sent me to lead this motley crew, I didn't think a fellow Hound had also signed on. Who are you with?"

"Aye, it's Vellaunus," Izzy answered, liking her new persona. "Only did it because he assigned us Guardians and Hounds like you. Lotte, I thought this was a civilized place, but it appears they are fools whom Roman merchants have bought. Keeper Morcant, here, thinks—I don't know what!"

Lotte's spears were in her hands in a flash, their power crackling with fire. "Shall we burn it down to deny the southern bastards from Rome a foothold in our lands? No good meals for them!"

Morcant said, "No, no, Warrior Druid!"

Izzy almost laughed when Lotte turned her eyes to the man, replacing the flames with a gush of water. "Would you rather have a flood? Maybe I can pull in the tide through the Severn?"

Morcant sputtered, "That would be as bad, likely worse."

Lotte turned to Izzy, asking brightly, "Are you buying?"

"Only if our keeper gives me a discount for his insults."

"Och, I'm sure he will," she declared. "Mead for me, ale for my boys, and we'll have whatever Isobel's men are eating!"

A crowd gathered in the town circle as they ate the fish stew. When Izzy finished her meal and mead, she used her Air Element to flip herself over the startled proprietor, landing behind him, her Katanas in each hand, hovering around his neck. She said, "You can keep the change since I am paying for both parties. Please let me know if I need to make any adjustments for you. Like a Roman."

"No—no, Warrior Druid, not just now," Morcant answered and hurried to get the drinks and bowls of stew to the other Hound's warriors.

When Artur chuckled, Lotte shot him a dark look. "Want to test my control of the *void* and time while we dance amongst my ancient spears against your magical sword?"

"Nay, my—Hound. A Guardian must be above the fray."

"Gah!"

⸺❧ Breanna ☙⸺

Breanna and Eoin ambled through the low hills surrounding the river delta that led to the Dobunni port on the Sea of Erin. The path led them past Caer Didi, and Breanna had to shake her head at the lack of any defense response to their arrival. It did not bode well for their coming challenge from Rome. Yet, she'd known this and would persevere. Failure was not an option.

As requested, Taliesin beat on his small war drum, and Bláth used her lower-octave harp strings to match his beat.

When they reached the town circle, a good-sized crowd gawked at the warriors as they ate outside of The Fish Head Tavern.

Izzy called out in her roleplay, "Guardian! Good to see you! These Dobunni are suspicious of us Celts and Gaels and seem to welcome the Romans, who will stab them in the back one day soon."

"Hail, Izzy and Lotte!" Breanna called back. "Have they insulted you, my Hounds? You know tradition calls for you to claim the head of any such offender."

"Nay, close, but not that close," Lotte grumbled.

The tavern owner cried, "Guardian, we had no idea of this."

Breanna held up her hand. "Silence!"

Then, a Dobunni commander rode into the circle with his guard of ten marching behind him, five to each side. "What is the meaning of this?"

Breanna retorted, "Meaning of what?"

"Why are you in our settlement? And what are those strange weapons on your carts?"

"Och, you dare to challenge a Guardian of the Celts?"

"You're—ah, nay!" he answered Breanna with wide eyes.

She asked, "Shall I unleash my Hounds, true Druid Warriors, on you and yours? I have more behind me who will join the carnage if you choose, and the wrath my ballistae can inflict will be even worse. Even two of my *fians*—bands of nine—could obliterate your pathetic guard. Yet, that would be a waste, as I need you because the Romans are coming. The Great Council of Celtic Tribes sent us to train the Dobunni first. Our Protectors will oversee this endeavor."

"Wait, there is more than one of you?"

Artur stepped forward. "Aye, and your arrogance singles you out. We Guardians just sent our call to our land. Most have acknowledged that call, yet you did not. Nor did your Chief. Why is he not here? I should be pissing on his pants for his insult!"

He stammered, "Guardian, I—"

"Send for your Chief, now!" Artur demanded.

As a messenger rushed off to fetch the leader of Caer Didi, Artur turned to Breanna. "I've heard this before. Traitors who were invested in their machinations with the Romans even as they withdrew. We will have much of this kind of deceit. Will you grant me the right to assess judgment, fellow Guardian?"

As Breanna drew *Lann Dán*, with its *balefire* crackling along its diamond blades, she sighed. "Within limits, fellow Guardian, within limits. We work together."

A collective gasp ran through the crowd, and then Artur drew *Caledfwich*. It now also spat *balefire*. He demanded, "We called to all of you only recently, yet your Chief denied the power our gods granted us! Is that because he has already sold you to Rome?"

That started a murmur of worry amongst the crowd, with the tavern owner calling out, "We are true, but merchants buy and sell more than goods. They trade in secrets."

Standing at Breanna's side, Eoin informed the commander, "Lan and I shall represent our Celtic Guardians in everyday matters with your warriors and the building of defenses for the port. Our Hounds will lead that training, along with Guardian Artur."

"What of the Dumonii tribe to the southwest?" the commander asked. "If they fall, so will we. Not to mention the Silures, Atrebates, and Belgae."

Eoin gave the man a tight smile. "All fall in line as we topple false leaders. Caer Went in Silures is next on our list to assess."

A moment later, the Chief of Caer Didi arrived, full of bluster. "By what right—"

Artur raised his sword as if he meant to cleave the man's head from his shoulders. Then Breanna muttered *snatch*. Her magical rope snapped out to wrap around *Caledfwich's* hilt. His blade dropped with a thunk at her feet, and the rope quickly coiled around the Caer Didi Chief. With that, Breanna disappeared with him.

 **Eoin**

Eoin was surprised to see Artur's sword snatched from his hand by Breanna's rope, likely saving the Dobunni Chief's life. He suspected his mate's action was because the man would have much information about the Roman network southwest of Pretannia, regardless of whether he was a traitor.

Croí Dàn interjected, *"Eoin, she took him to the hillfort."*

Artur was certainly startled. "What the—"

Eoin commanded, "Pick up your sword and shut your trap."

He turned to the commander, saying, "Our Guardian decided she needs a private audience with your Chief. We will find them shortly at Caer Didi.

"Now, each Protector's role is to secure the safety of their Guardian and to help ensure their mission is carried out without too much collateral damage, such as what could have happened with your Chief. Be advised. Some Guardians are more forgiving than others.

"Yet, we are all Celts or Gaels here to fight off Rome. We aim to prepare this port so you can defend it with the Roman-style ballistae weapons."

Eoin, keeping his voice low, added, "Lan, you and Artur secure this port. No ships leave. If new ones dock, impound them. Make sure you meet every captain.

"Fergal, Toal, and Cilla, you three deploy our ballistae with your archers to ensure the ship captains obey our command.

"Izzy, Lotte, Braoin, and Bradaigh, you deploy three *fians* as you think best. All orders go through Izzy. No one dies without Breanna's approval. Is that clear? No further discussion amongst our new *friends*.

Eoin turned to Artur and his man. "You two, keep your heads together from now on. No rash actions. We need to win hearts and minds first."

Lan nodded as Artur looked on dubiously.

Croí Dàn added, *"Artur, you need to temper your rash reactions."*

Artur blanched at the *voice's* admonishment.

Having heard their Heart, Eoin smiled. "Good. Remember, we are just a thought away. I will ensure sleeping arrangements are readied for our entire band at the fort. We will hold a council meeting this evening."

He added hushedly, "Corbmac, deploy the remaining men around the rest of us. I know where to find Breanna. After that, we will meet other tribes and see how far the Roman taint has infected others."

With Eoin's orders cast and the Warriors of Destiny appropriately dispersed, he motioned toward Caer Didi. "Commander, lead me to your Chief's high table."

"You mean Corovius," the man answered.

Eoin nodded, "Yes, and your name?"

"Morcantix," he stated.

"You know why our Celtic Guardians are here?"

"Aye, it is because my Chief is—dirty."

"Very astute, but it's bigger than that."

Once they entered the fort, he found Breanna towering over the cowering Chief Corovius of Caer Didi in the main hall, her blades crackling. To Eoin, she looked relieved to see him. He informed her, "Guardian, the port is being secured."

"Excellent, my Protector," she said. "As always, you excel. This man deflects my questions very well. What shall we do?"

"My Guardian, we have no choice. *Croí Dàn* must uncover the truth as you use your Aether Life Sigil. Bare his soul."

Eoin thought he heard his love sigh as if she had not thought of that. Only a moment later, Corovius was babbling about how the Romans had offered him command of western Pretannia for his allegiance. With that, *Croí Dàn* picked his mind apart, including who in the other tribes had colluded with him. Some were his fellow Chiefs, and others were willing to assassinate leaders to curry favor with Rome. They had managed to corrupt the Dobunni and the Durotriges to the southwest. Still, the Belgae and the Atrebates tribes on the southern coast were staunchly Celtic, resisting infiltration, as were the Dumonii and the Silures tribes to the west.

Eoin told the commander, "My Guardian has exposed Corovius as a traitor. His fate will be sealed in the settlement circle tomorrow. You must provide for our band tonight. As for your former Chief, I assume you have a holding cell for him?"

Morcantix answered, "Aye, I do. And the other Guardian?"

Eoin's tone brooked no quarter. "He answers to us."

The commander nodded. "Based on what I heard, is there a way to test who is true to our land and who is not?"

"Not generally. My Guardian must touch someone for her Heart to know them truly," was Eoin's answer. "Once you have everything here at the fort in order, Morcantix, I think you should return to the port and let all know, including the Roman captain, that Chief Corovius has an important announcement to make at midday tomorrow, honoring those who have helped grow this settlement through trade and those working to expand the port."

Morcantix nodded. "Sound reasoning. Most of your warriors must camp in the front yard, between the fort and the bluff. And I'll need to get our cook started now on a meal for thirty-plus of you for it to be ready by early evening."

⚜ Breanna ⚜

Once the rest of her band had joined them and they were away from prying ears, Breanna stared down at Artur and said to Myrddin, "Did you teach him nothing about politics? About strategy?"

The Seer frowned. "I didn't have time, as you compressed it."

"Gah!" Breanna growled.

Livie stepped in. "Father, you chose Artur because you could manipulate him. It is not a question, but a statement."

Myrddin protested, "The future showed he had promise!"

As Artur squirmed, Breanna sighed. "Do you understand my frustration, my fellow *Guardian*? We are each of an age, but I, at least, have been tested. I DIED for my land! Eoin died!

Fergal died! Toal died! My gods brought us back. They made Eoin and me a god and goddess. Fergal mated with a goddess. Through being touched by our gods, Toal will likely match the best archers in history. All because we made a sacrifice in our *before-time* to save our island.

"And you present yourself as a co-Guardian of this land?" she seethed. "You undermined our mission! I barely contained the damage! Rome is coming!"

"We learned so much by ripping through Corovius' mind, and what would you have cost us if I hadn't stopped your blade? It would have taken months to extract that information. I gleaned details, such as the names of chiefs and captains conspiring with Rome, all of whom were complicit in their plans. They have recruited commanders to assassinate those chiefs and their commanders who plan to resist the coming invasion."

Breanna sighed. "While my fury can be dangerous, I have my Heart and Eoin to keep me mostly balanced. Your arrogance is reckless, and your Protector is your friend who doesn't know how to guide you. Only you can make him your counselor, your conscience."

Artur held his hands up in a gesture of surrender. "It was foolish. I was an idiot. Seeing his dark life threads, I knew the Chief was a traitor and thought it would be good to make an example of him. It was my first time glimpsing threads like that—since you and Nimuë had me claim Pretannia. As a Guardian, I reacted to the moment, as it was my responsibility to end him."

"That's the problem, Artur. Did you hear yourself?" Breanna questioned. "How ignorant can you be! We are not in post-Rome!"

Eoin stepped in. "Breanna is correct. We are pre-Rome, so our tactics must be different. Rome is coming for this land, not retreating from it. Everyone can be an asset, an enemy, or both. Treat them as such."

Breanna's expression was grim. "Myrddin, tell me you have some helpful skills here that you can impart?"

"Now you need me," the Seer said with a sneer.

Breanna's golden rope lashed out, and the Seer disappeared to another place and time with her. They appeared on a snow-capped mountain in a blizzard. It was now the dead of winter as Breanna held a bubble of her Air and Fire Element while the wind and snow whipped around them. She smiled. "Know where we are?"

"On top of a mountain in a storm!"

Breanna chuckled, "Not just any mountain. Yr Wyddfa, above Nimuë's cave. In your time, with your home just over there?"

She waved a hand, adding, "Fitting, I think. While I cannot unbind your oath to my Heart, I can free you from your commitment to my cause. You can find your way home and be the great Seer you think you are. Go, run along, little druid."

"That would be a death sentence!"

"Not my problem, Great Seer!"

"You mock me!"

"It's so easy with you! Either way, I'm done," she declared.

"You'll leave me here? To freeze to death?"

"You should make it, though you'll likely lose some digits. Maybe a hand or a foot or one of each. I care not. I have decided to move on. I don't need you, as you have proven to be of no worth, just a conniver for your own goals, as your daughter and mate warned me of. And now I have an arrogant Guardian sworn to this land to keep safe from your corruptive nature. With such a nature, you should survive as you find your path home, maybe somewhat intact."

As Breanna faded and the cold and snow swirled in, Myrddin exclaimed, "Wait!"

"Why should I?"

"I know subterfuge. I can help root out traitors. Sway my Celts against Rome. I know that's what you need."

Breanna reformed her bubble. "I have to bring us to this point for you to offer that now?"

Myrddin sighed. "My apologies. For decades, I have pursued my vision of bringing a new leader to our land in our post-Roman era. Then you show up, Goddess of Time and all, and take us back to pre-Rome Pretannia with a better plan, magical weapons, and genuine support from your people and your kindred gods. Then I find out our Lady of the Lake is your cousin, and your Heart ties Artur to his land in a way I could not. I should be thanking you, but I found myself churlish, wondering if you would cast me aside like this. Let's try to make this work."

Breanna gave him a tight nod. "Only if you agree to respect your daughter."

"Of course. Livie deserves better than what I've given her."

After dinner, Morcantix offered Breanna and Eoin his former Chief's quarters. After removing the skins from the bed, they rolled out their travel blankets to replace them. With the stone block structure chilly, they quickly got under the covers to settle in and share each other's warmth. Eoin asked, "So, what happened with Myrddin?"

"Just a little talk in a cold place," Breanna replied. "While he should be more helpful now that we cleared the air, I'm more concerned about Artur. Yet I think the Seer will provide him with more guidance now."

Eoin said, "Speaking about our other Guardian, the *sight* seized me after my blade dance with Artur before we left Erin.

It appears he will meet someone to keep him interested in staying here."

"You mean he has a fated one in this timeline?"

"Aye," he answered. "Hopefully, that's a good thing. Now, let's get some rest. Best let today's events sink in while we sleep."

Their breakfast was watery porridge with flatbread instead of soda bread, which Breanna grumbled about, along with goat cheese and some fatty cuts of meat from a domesticated pig slaughtered for the previous day's dinner. Afterward, as she walked with Eoin around the fortress, she found Caer Didi fascinating. The builders had constructed it of more stone than Erin's ringforts or hillforts. They used the natural bluff to ensure a view of the river, estuary, and settlement. Returning to the yard, she found her band queuing up for breakfast.

Despite her pleasant stroll, Breanna was unsettled by their first day in Pretannia. "Generally, this was not a good way to start our mission. We have much to learn, and I need to be more ruthless, especially with traitors surrounding us. Yet being so might change the timeline in ways we don't want. We need to unite these people. I feel like I'm walking on a rope tied above a raging river."

Eoin countered, "Aye, I understand, but we managed. Don't be so hard on yourself. It was a day of revelations. Whatever air you cleared with Mryddin, it had an impact. He's been interrogating Corovius most of the morning."

"That's something. At least the weather has held."

"Indeed," Eoin agreed. "Morcantix, along with Artur and Lan, are all spreading the word about a big announcement at midday in the settlement circle that Chief Corovius will make. He will supposedly reward those who have made contributions to the settlement.

"As everyone gathers, the commander will mix his warriors with ours when we announce the traitors. Morcantix also asked if we could confirm his men are true to the Celts of this land."

Breanna commanded, *"Mo Chroí*, swear them to Artur. That will expose anyone with foul intent."

"Aye, my Hero," her Heart answered. *"It would be better to scan them first. We do not want to repeat what happened on the High King's Road when we swore those Connachta warriors. I will scan them first, and that will make the Commander responsible for any punishment."*

Breanna sighed. *"Thank you, my Heart. One less burden for me."*

Artur approached them with Lan. "I heard that Corovius has confessed to being a collaborator. That's good news. My Protector, as you now call him, has an idea. My friend?"

Lan stammered, "Ah, yes, my Guardian—"

"Stop!" she insisted. "I am Bre or Breanna to you!"

Eoin suggested, "My mate gets testy with titles. Now, your idea."

"I was thinking about how to pay for the port defense improvements," Lan offered. "Currently, Rome traders pay nothing to exchange goods, or such funds go to the pockets of those like Corovius."

Eoin added, "Indeed, I've been on jaunts through time with Breanna—in the future, of course—where countries often charge a fee for the cost of the goods brought into their land, which they assess on the buyers. It usually hurts the people more than it helps."

"Yet we could assess any fees on the sellers after they agree on the payment," Lan countered. "We certainly need more of those ballistae."

Eoin agreed, "Aye, Toal has the plans for them from our God of Smithing. As I understand it from Ecne, we have more hillforts overlooking the Severn Estuary that must have been fortified. Then we move southeast along the coast."

Breanna caught the aforementioned god out of the corner of her eye. "Ecne, when are we precisely in time?"

"Bre," he answered, "we are in the cycle of fifty-five, counting down toward zero. That's how historians ended up measuring cycles before and after the common era turned—much ado about the One God and his son's birth cycle. It is this summer when Julius Caesar first steps ashore in Pretannia on the southeastern shores of what they called Albion. To the Celts, it is Albiu. His expedition fails, yet he will try again in fifty-four and has significant success at getting the southern tribes to pay tribute. Your first foray into understanding how Roman Legions worked was three complete cycles earlier.

"After that, Caesar returned to Rome and had to fight to become the Emperor. He then tried to conquer Egypt and forged a relationship with its leader, Queen Cleopatra. Yet, he was not trusted and was eventually murdered by several colleagues in the Senate. It will take roughly a hundred cycles for Rome to return and invade Pretannia again, under Emperor Claudius, who strengthens his hold on his title by taming this land and, of course, crushing its people."

"Thank you." Breanna sighed. "We have some time to give Julius Caesar second thoughts on his plans. Yet, we cannot wait a hundred cycles for them to return. We must weaken Rome's influence in Egypt and lend aid to the mainland Celts, and then we can return to take on this Claudius fellow if needed. We'll have to see what changes we can inflict on Rome in the fight over the mighty river of time."

Fergal put in, "We wait for a hundred cycles?"

Breanna countered. "We will have lots of fodder to work with."

Eoin interrupted, saying, "Back to now, my mate, we must focus on today. Artur—you and Lan are with me, as we must meet with Morcantix and our Warriors of Destiny to make sure everyone knows who they are rounding up. Can *Mo Chroí* keep Corovius from speaking out until we have rounded up the other traitors?"

Croí Dàn huffed. *"Eoin, I can hear you through your mate. Just ask me directly! I will see to it."*

Eoin gave her a mental wink. *"Sorry, Mo Chroí. I'll try not to let it happen again. We're now amongst new folks in our circle."*

Breanna heard that huff and could only shake her head in response.

Eoin

At midday, Eoin, Breanna, and Artur rode out, leading a chariot that carried Morcantix and Chief Corovius to the settlement's circle. He and the commander had sent their warriors ahead to take up their positions. Eoin noted that the chief was pretty placid, especially given he was heading to his death, and assumed it was due to *Mo Chroí*'s influence.

As they entered the circle, Eoin found that the entire settlement had gathered to hear what Chief Corovius was announcing, and whispers ran through the crowd, gradually growing louder. Fortunately, all ships from the day before were still in port, and a new one looked like it had dropped anchor; Eoin hoped it would be a Roman trader.

Morcantix raised an arm for silence. "Good folks of the Caer Didi settlement, we gather to celebrate some good news. As guard commander, you are aware that I am responsible for the security of this port, settlement, and fort on the hill. Yesterday, we received ominous details about Rome's interest in our island and this port."

With that, several captains moved to leave, but their Caer Didi guards and the Warriors of Destiny blocked them.

Morcantix continued, "Two great chiefs of our land sent us a pair of Guardians and their Hounds to ensure we stay true to our Celtic roots. To that end, I introduce Artur and Breanna."

A rustle passed over the crowd as some Celts attempted to slip away this time and were blocked. Breanna stepped forward. "Hear the truth from your former chief's mouth!"

Corovius said, "The Guardian speaks true—I sold my land to the Romans. Their leader, Julius Caesar, plans to invade our island this cycle. I have helped make that happen."

A gasp ran through the crowd.

"Likewise, Corovius has given us details on Roman captains who were part of this conspiracy—two are amongst us today," Breanna went on. "He also named traitors in other Dobunni settlements, as their chiefs plotted the same as part of their pact with Rome. If they are faithful to Celtic rule, the Romans have hired assassins to kill these chiefs or commanders, one of whom is among us today. What is your verdict?"

In unison, the crowd chanted, "Death! Death! Death!"

"Any objections?"

After a moment of silence, Breanna nodded before commanding, "Guardian Artur! The sentence is confirmed. Carry it out! The Guardian's Heart will confirm guilt. Not one escapes her wrath unless they are true. The lives of any complicit ship captains are forfeit, and their ships are ours. We will spare any crew members who were not aware. Again, our Heart will confirm all judgments for or against any accused, and she will confirm all actions with me first. Your Celtic Guardians fight for you, not Rome!"

As two captains struggled in the hands of Bradaigh, Fergal, and Lan, Morcantix seized one of his men with Braoin's help. Having already confessed, Corovius was the first to lose his head, with his body tossed into the estuary's outgoing tide.

Next came the Roman Captains, one saying, "I protest!"

Breanna snapped her golden rope around his wrist. "Speak your truth."

"I—" he croaked.

Croí Dàn ordered, *"Only truth will pass your lips."*

"I—follow General Julius Caesar, who will conquer all Celts on this island as he has done with Celts on the mainland!"

Breanna nodded to Artur as she snapped her rope back to her side. After he carried out that execution, the remaining two men followed the first three, with their bodies also stripped and cast into the sea, as was their custom. The commander demanded that their heads be placed on pikes at the gates to proclaim them traitors.

Eoin turned to Morcantix and proclaimed, "Do as you see fit for your tribe. You will serve as the acting chief of Caer Didi while we seek other leaders of the Dobunni Tribe to determine if they will accept you as we root out other traitors. Your former chief insinuated the Roman rot went pretty deep. "

"That would be Chief Boduoc at Bagendon," Morcantix said.

"Aye, we know of him from Corovius. While we do that, our armorers will help you build Roman-style ballistae to protect this port from them. From their general, Julius Caesar."

With that, he turned to Myrddin. "Ride for Caer Went and explain what happened here to Chief Corovius. Spread the word that Celtic Guardians now walk this land. If all is well, move along the coast to other hillforts, and we will catch up with you in a few days."

The Seer nodded. "Understood, Eoin. I have a horse and coin to keep me fed. See you and Breanna soon."

───◦◈ Breanna ◈◦───

Breanna spoke with Goibniu, asking whether he or his brothers could help Toal, especially since he and his archers would be staying behind at Caer Didi. The goal was to assist in constructing wooden ballistae for the port using the provided plans. She also asked Corbmac to start working with Morcantix and his men on how the *fian* warriors trained; fighting in groups of nine would better prepare them to fight organized Roman legionnaires with their orderly cohort approach. They would also likely share how to build the new crossbows without *balefire* bolts.

While they could have ridden east for two spans to reach the central Dobunni settlement of Bagendon, Breanna snapped out her rope and soon requested Chief Boduoc's presence at the gates of the tribe's main fort.

The commander stood on a watch platform, much like at Dun Eadan when Breanna and Eoin had stood down King Énnae of Laigin, demanding, "Who brings a Warband to our gates?"

Breanna said, "Peace with you, Commander. Artur and I are Guardians of the Celts, the claim of which you likely felt, regardless of your acceptance. We do not concern ourselves with your tribal rivalries. We are focused on keeping this island free of Roman domination. Having all tribes work together to stop Rome would be better, but we will leave that to you. That said, none can be allowed to support our enemy.

"We will be working with many chiefs throughout Pretannia to stop Rome's coming invasion. In fact, we just ended a Roman threat two spans west of here, where we stopped the Roman coup attempt at Caer Didi on your border. He was one of your own.

As a result of this effort, we have gained detailed knowledge of other traitors in the Dobunni Tribal lands, including those in this area and several other hillforts. We stand ready to challenge General Julius Caesar, who is preparing an expeditionary landing this cycle and a complete invasion next cycle."

The commander rejoined, "You speak well but have an accent as if you're not from this land."

"I am a Gael from Creones and Caledonia, so still my land and yours. My name is Breanna Ban Morna. And yours is?"

"I am Carovetos, the Bagendon Guard Commander."

"Well, Commander," she continued, her voice ice cold, "as I said, two Guardians of the Celts and their Warrior Druids, capable of immense destruction, sit on their mounts before your gates. I alone could level your walls and roundhouses. I suggest you refrain from testing me. Yet, we are not here to fight our Celtic brothers, as we need all Celts to prepare to fight Rome. That said, I cannot let the traitors identified by Chief Corovius roam free once he has named them. He's lost his head, but we have witnesses at Caer Didi, including the new acting chief, Morcantix."

Artur held up his hand, saying, "Greetings, Commander Carovetos. I hail from the Orkneys and am a fellow Guardian of the Celts, along with Breanna. I have fought her in hand-to-hand combat, and she is genuinely a Warrior Druid beyond compare. I suggest we trade information. If you reject her advice, we will protect the other tribes, not the Dobunni. Yet we will ensure that the areas of your land that do support us will be handed over to, say, the Silures or the Dumnonii. Maybe the Belgae or Atrebates will want to ensure the Catuvellauni do not lay claim to any additional lands. Or not."

Breanna said brightly, "Well, what shall it be?"

When he frowned and crossed his arms, she quickly had her *Lann Dàn* blades in her hands, cracking with *balefire*. A moment later, just short of the gates, the ground before her was smoldering. Her voice turned firm, "I do not suffer fools."

Commander Carovetos demanded, "Fetch the Chief!"

Moments later, the gates opened.

When Chief Boduoc arrived, he exchanged words with his commander, who gestured at the smoldering ground. The Chief turned to a still-mounted Breanna. Eoin slid off his horse and then strode forward, saying as he motioned to Breanna, "As the Protector of my Guardian, I would suggest you not underestimate her resolve. Breanna Ban Morna is more capable than any Warrior Druid you've ever encountered. It was not a good day for her, as she oversaw the execution of a Chief, one of his Commander's warriors who confessed to plotting his superior's death, and two Roman merchant Captains, who each freely admitted they collaborated with the Roman General, Julius Caesar, all to undermine the Celtic tribes of this land in support of their conquest of, well, us. Breanna abhors senseless violence but dislikes traitors even more.

"As to Rome, their effort will be slow and steady, making you think they are only playing with you and are not serious. Yet, in less than ninety cycles, they will crush nearly every Celtic tribe in Pretannia. Even so, Caesar's efforts to invade this cycle and next will have an impact, sowing the seeds of doubt that the tribes can hold the Romans back. It will change how the squabbling tribes of this island fight for supremacy. The first will be the Catuvellauni, which will take the brunt of the general's next attempts to divide the Celts. My Guardians will not allow that to happen."

A defiant Chief Boduoc asked, "And how would you stop us from choosing Roman rule over Catuvellauni?"

Eoin shook his head. "We would have to rain utter destruction on Bagendon. Assuming you just admitted to being a Roman sympathizer, that is."

"And if I did?"

"I would have to challenge you to personal combat," Eoin said. "We await your decision. We are off to meet with other tribal leaders, giving them this opportunity to join us. One possibility is that you oppose us, and Rome wins. The other possibility is that you oppose us, and the Catuvellauni tribe consumes you, where we help them drive off Rome. Be wise, Chief Boduoc, and spread the word. Guardians of the Celts walk among you. In the meantime, I have a list of traitors within Bagendon. Produce them when we return. If you cannot read Latin, I will call them out."

With that, he rode forward and tossed a rolled-up sheaf of paper on the grounds, then turned away to remount and nudged his horse after Breanna.

Ambling west, Breanna said, "A disappointing response."

Eoin countered, "But not unexpected. They've lost their way. Much like the clans of Erin in our time. Chief Boduoc is likely as dirty as Corovius was."

"Aye, they fight for scraps while raptors circle."

"They are too busy circling each other while Rome looms."

"So be it. It is time to engage other tribes. Let's try the Dobunni and Atrebates border next." She snapped out her golden rope, enabling her band to follow her to wherever her next stop was.

This time, they received a more positive response to their warning about the impending Roman invasion and their offer to help teach them how to build defenses for their hill forts, including ballistae.

The same occurred with the next hillfort on the same border and then with the next as they made contact with the Belgae.

Three spans later, the Durotriges hillfort on the Severn Estuary offered the warmest welcome on that sunny afternoon, as they had heard about the fall of Chief Corovius at Caer Didi and the building of ballistae to protect the waterway forts and settlements from a Roman invasion.

The Silures Tribe across that body of water came next. The gates of Caer Went appeared before them. The hillfort was similar to Caer Didi, though more sprawling. It also looked over a sizable waterfront port and settlement on the Severn Estuary.

A chief named Branoc greeted them with his commander in tow, informing Breanna and Artur that word about Corovius's demise as a traitor was spreading around Caer Didi, as it was on the border between the Silures and the Dobunni and only about two and a half spans' walk to the east. They told them an old Druid had wandered through that morning, saying it was the Guardians of the Celts at work.

Breanna smiled, knowing it was Myrddin who was walking the land. Of course, she shared their experience meeting Chief Boduoc with him, where he indicated he might be a Roman sympathizer. If that were the case, they would not have assisted them when Rome eventually invaded.

The Silures Chief welcomed the news that the Celtic Guardian's band would teach them to build ballistae shortly, but that would have to wait until Breanna's armorers fortified Caer Didi; then, they would do the same for the Durotriges port. She learned that the Roman Captains tended to bypass Caer Went, preferring Caer Didi and its ties to Bagendon. Either way, she would need her armorers to build defensive weapons for the three ports within range of the Severn Estuary and a fourth Dumnonii port farther west.

Before whisking her band away, she suggested, "Branoc, pass our promise to your fellow Silures Chiefs that we Celtic

Guardians will support you all, as every tribe must work together for any tribe to survive Rome's coming invasions, even with our help. Once all your chiefs are involved and you've picked one to represent you on the new Great Council of Celtic Tribes, we could use your help to get the Demeta and Ordovices tribes to organize and work with us."

With that, she snapped her rope and flashed her band away.

After circling through the northwest part of the Dumnonii peninsula, Breanna took them to the southern coast to see how those defenses could be enhanced. Finally, she pulled her band back to Caer Didi and asked for a status update from Morcantix. Even with only one day of work, he was impressed with her armorers and their progress. Then Breanna informed him of the response she received from Chief Boduoc; the commander, now Chief, was not surprised. Given that Caer Didi sat on the border, projecting goodwill with Chief Branoc would be wise, as Caer Didi might need to ally itself with the Silures soon.

Breanna was pleased to see that Toal was working well with Goibniu and that they all had time for their evening meal together. After updating those who stayed at Caer Didi that day about their various stops, she asked, "What do we know about our general, Julius Caesar, at this time?"

Ecne answered, "He's waiting in Gesoriacom, which is the town that sits above the harbor. The Morini call it Bonona Bay. That leads to Itios, the strait between Gaul and Pretennia. Caesar labeled it as Portus Itius. The Morini granted him access to the docks, in trade for his Legions not burning their grain fields before the harvest."

Breanna declared, "That *dìolain*! We must find a way to learn more about his plans and senior staff. We will be ready."

The following morning, Toal and Goibniu finished their work at Caer Didi's port, and she sent them along the north coast road toward Caer Went. In the meantime, Chief Morcantix ordered all cargo removed from the Roman merchant ships. Then, he chose the transport that needed the most repair work as a target practice for the new ballistae.

With the rest of her band, Breanna sought out the Catuvellauni Tribe and its Chief, Vellaunus, at his main ring fort, Din Dubnos. It was initially a similar conversation to the one they had with Boduoc, where distrust ruled. Then, Ecne stepped in to provide detailed information about the number of ships, galleys, transports, and warriors Julius Caesar would bring in the coming months. That got Vellaunnus' attention. Yet, when he added what would happen the following cycle, the chief commented that it looked bleak for his Catuvellauni Tribe.

Breanna, seeing his concern for his tribe, said, "All is not lost yet. Let us show you what our band of thirty-plus warriors brings to this fight. We bring *balefire* to this battle, while they bring blades."

With that, she, Eoin, Artur, and Lan marched to the open gates and unleashed their magical weapons that ripped up the turf on each side of the road. Breanna turned to their chief. "Magic created by our Dark Goddess."

Vellaunnus whispered, "That is a frightening amount of power. How do you command this *balefire*?"

"This magic is granted only to us Celtic Guardians and our sworn Warrior Druids," Breanna answered. "We also have armorers who will teach you how to build ballistae like the Romans wield in battle."

Then she promised to hamper Caesar's legions this cycle and destroy them in the next cycle before the Roman ships could get their legions ashore. After taking Vellaunnus, Artur, Ecne, Bláth, Livie, and Taleisin on jaunts through time, good and bad, the Catuvellauni leader declared he was convinced that

Rome would not win these battles, but those at Din Dubnos appeared skeptical.

He proclaimed to his fellow tribesmen, "Spread the word. The Guardians of the Celts support us; we will hold off Rome with them! All Celts must band together. We must forge a new union in which we don't squabble amongst ourselves. We will adopt the way of our fellow Gaels, where bands of nine warriors, which they call *fians*, will be formed and report to a council of tribal Chiefs we will create."

Breanna interjected, "We Guardians call it the Great Council of Celtic Tribes."

Vellaunnus smiled. "So be it! With our Guardians, we can build a new Celtic nation! Send runners to all Catuvellauni Chiefs to ready their men. No more warring between the tribes."

Breanna stepped next to Vellaunus. "Remember, you will swear to my Heart for these gifts. That time is now."

Croí Dàn presented her oath, at which Vellaunus hesitated and then nodded. Her Heart added, *"Then, as I allow it, your heart will still beat!"*

Breanna added, "We have work to do, but as promised, I will make time for us to defeat Rome and Julius Caesar together. Now, we turn to the tribes of the Icni, Cantíiací, Trinovantes, Regni, Atrebates, and Belgae. We will show them what will come with their support, and what won't. In the meantime, my Protector and I will determine the best way to blacken Caesar's eye!

"That said, my fellow Guardian, Artur, will lead our support to convince your fellow Celtic tribal Chiefs of the serious threat Rome poses. He and his advisors will be your primary resources as the rest of us plan to thwart Rome's landing this cycle."

Artur added, "Vellaunnus, as a Guardian of Pretennia, I am here to support you. Let's make an army to stand against Rome and anyone else who would challenge our Celtic Tribes.

We'll be in touch soon. Get your tribe aligned with this vision to get this started."

With that, Breanna swept her band away and back to Caer Didi, instantly calling for Morcantix to meet with her, Eoin, Artur, and Lan.

After telling the new chief about the meeting with Chief Vellaunus, she declared, "We cannot let Boduoc remain in charge at Bagendon if he defies us. How to convince him is the question."

Morcantix said, "Offer him a seat at this new council and train his men, which is planned for the other tribes. With the Catuvellauni behind this, all of the southern Tribes will want a seat, with promises to keep the current borders as they are."

"Let's see! Eoin, round everyone up for one more trip today."

They arrived at the Bagendon settlement moments later, with Breanna demanding, "Chief Boduoc, we've unfinished business!"

Commander Carovetos disappeared, and the Chief soon stood on the platform next to the gate. "Why are you here?"

"Are you being deliberately obtuse? I said I would be back."

"To destroy us?" he asked.

"That is up to you. First, I must provide you with an update," Breanna stated. "Chief Vellaunus has committed the Catuvellauni Tribe's support to our goal to stop Rome, including maintaining existing tribal borders with a new body, the Great Council of Celtic Tribes, to oversee such disputes. The Silures and Dumnonii are gathering their chiefs and plan to rally the Ordovices and Cornovíí. Next, we will rally the remaining tribes in the southeast."

"Given this, what is your answer? Will you still support Rome over your kind?"

"You hold the sword of Damocles over me!"

Eoin said, "So you study Roman literature. Interesting."

"We are not ignorant," Boduoc blustered. "Yet let us discuss what assurances you can provide."

With that, the gates opened, and they followed the Dobunni Chief to a covered, roundhouse open on all sides, which acted as a communal meeting place.

—※🛡 **Izzy** 🛡※—

Once they settled in, Izzy knelt and planted a fist on the ground, pulling Earth. She carefully surveyed the chief and his men to suss out why they felt wrong—as if they were hiding something.

Izzy paid no attention to Breanna, who coldly stated, "I can provide no assurances save what we've offered other Celtic Chiefs. We know you are trading with the Romans and seek to support Julius Caesar's invasion. Do you deny it?"

"I do not answer to you!"

"Ah, but you do," Breanna asserted.

Izzy kept her focus on the nervous chief, his eyes darting around the meeting space as if he were assessing the odds of winning. But what? She knew he saw that he was outmanned, but there was determination in his eyes. When Boduoc nodded to himself, Izzy launched herself into the air as he ordered his warriors, "Kill her!"

Izzy pushed hard on her Air Element as two of his warriors rose from the shadows and let their spears fly. Yet all fell to Breanna's *dark matter* shields as Izzy sailed through the quickly narrowing space between her and their chief. Barely a moment had passed before she hovered with curved blades crossed behind his neck, hissing, "You dare threaten my Hero and Goddess!"

Seeing their cast spears deflected aside, the Celtic warriors supporting Boduoc hesitated. Breanna included Izzy when she asked, *"Ćroí Dàn, do we end him?"*

"YES, as he is a foul one."

Breanna signaled to Izzy, and Boduoc's head rolled into the center of the meeting hall before blood gushed from his neck; she kicked his body forward and herself back. When he landed with a thud, she settled into a crouch and flicked his blood from her katanas. Izzy sneered. "Do any of you cowards want to tangle with me?"

Each blooded Warrior of Destiny let their weapons crackle with *balefire*, and Lotte declared, "I claim the next warrior to challenge My Hero and Goddess as mine. I will stick my Yellow Spear in an eye and Red Javelin up their arse, all the way to their heart!"

With that, every one of Boduoc's former Celtic warriors sank to a knee. In return, Breanna demanded of her cousin, *"Swear them!"*

Then she turned to the commander and blithely said, "I guess you're in charge now. Your entire tribe is at risk. Act wisely."

After a moment, he knelt. "We are yours."

Breanna shook her head. "Rise, Carovetos. I promise you that you will hold your land as long as the Dobunni are loyal to the Celts. Root out the bad apples, clean your roundhouses, and we will help you. Until then, we will support other loyal Celtic tribes. Prove you are worthy! Now, present those whom Corovius claimed to be traitors. My Heart will hear their truth."

Two warriors uttered their guilt under *Ćroí Dàn's* gaze, and the third turned out to be a spy for Carovetos, who only appeared to sympathize with Rome. Breanna and her band returned to their mounts as he dealt with the two traitors. As the golden rope snapped in front of Izzy, she took it and let herself be whisked with the rest of them as they traveled back to Caer Didi.

When they arrived, Lotte protested, "Gah! Izzy, you got the first direct kill! So unfair!"

Izzy shrugged. "No, Lotte. Observance won me that action. My grandfather taught me to watch, listen, read facial tells, reason possible outcomes, and then be ready to use my Elements as I act. It's called observing, thinking, and acting at the right time."

Eoin said, "This is not a competition, you two."

Izzy shrugged, and Lotte grunted out a huff.

Breanna turned to Izzy. "Well done, Isobel. That was also a measured response. Lotte, you need to become more than just a warrior. You cannot rely on rage. Focus instead on your cunning. Think about them like hunting skills. Hear me in this. Seek your glory with wisdom. Izzy trained under a *Laoch Druí,* and he proclaimed her as one. Leverage her. She is your sister now—learn from her."

Lotte scowled. "It is a hard way."

"It is my way," Breanna countered. "Follow it."

"Aye, I will endeavor to improve, Bre," Lotte offered.

Breanna nodded and turned to her mate. "Eoin, it was a trying day. Let's retire."

⬥ Breanna ⬥

"Granddaughter," Corbmac said. "A moment, if you will?"

Looking out over Cael Didi and onto the settlement, Breanna answered, "Of course. What's on your mind, Grandpa?"

"I was thinking we should catch up on the state of things," he said. "The armors are building out ballistae rapidly, and the range testing with the forfeit merchant ship is going well. Goibniu is using that information to adjust his new range finders. Toal, strangely, takes to the mathematics that Goibniu outlines for trajectories to reach various ranges. He's a natural. Our ballista build is going well."

"This is positive," Breanna commented. "Are there troubles?"

"Hmm, no, and yes," he said.

"But?" she asked.

"We need to go home. My *fians* are longing for their land."

"We'll be home soon," Breanna added. "Until then, you need to lean on the resources of our band." Then she called across the yard, "Bláth, please, to my side."

"Aye, Bre," she said.

"Corbmac says the *fians* are missing home. Let's have a small Céilí to embrace our new expanded world."

With that announcement, the mood lightened.

The following day, they found Myrddin at a hillfort where the Severn Estuary met the Sea of Erin. The Seer reported that the Silures Tribe was organizing to help all stand up to Rome. They appeared to have contacted the Demeta to gauge that tribe's interest in joining forces if needed.

Breanna then took her band southeast to the Durotriges Tribal area, which had several hillforts on the Severn that would require ballistae to guard the Estuary. Next came the Belgae at their hillfort of Maí Dín and the Atrebates at a hillfort known as Dín Albion. At the latter visit, they discovered the tribe had close ties to their mainland cousins and had been recruiting warriors to send across the channel to fight them. It would likely make them a target of Rome, especially if they defeated the Atrebates on the mainland.

At each stop, they spread the notion that the Celtic Guardians watched over their land and that the leaders were uniting under the banner of the Great Council of Celtic Tribes, led by Vellaunnus. Concern about the Chief of the Catuvellauni Tribe's goal to expand this territory had to be continuously quelled.

The Regini was a small tribe surrounded by the Atrebates to the west, the Cantii to the east, and the Catuvellauni to the north. Their fishing fleet was impressive, and Breanna and Eoin discussed how they could use the boats to deliver *balefire* against the Roman fleets, attacking them from the flanks with the smaller Scorpions mounted at the bow. Next came the Cantíaci, who would take the brunt of the initial contact with General Julius Caesar's invasions launched from the captured Morini port of Bontona the following cycle.

After that came the Trinovantes, with their massive port of Camulodunum, and last was the Iceni, who would bend their knees to Rome first. In the current timeline, a descendant, Queen Boudica, would rise against Roman rule some hundred cycles later, but she would be crushed. Each tribe held promise, but only if Breanna and her Warriors of Destiny could keep them focused on Rome.

Along their travels, Myrddin slipped away to gather insights that the larger band was unaware of, such as vulnerabilities within the underclass, abuses by commanders and their guards, a lack of training for warriors, and a failure to counter various tribal expansionist efforts aimed at seizing other territories. Ultimately, the Celts of Pretannia faced problems that Breanna had not anticipated. On the positive side, word was spreading that the Celtic Guardians were helping all tribes prepare, not just a chosen few.

With Julius Caesar's first landing looming, she knew she needed to leverage time to anticipate his landing in the coming months better than Ecne's date history books had provided. Either way, they needed a break after several weeks of constant travel across the south of Pretannia, and thus, she swept her band back to Caer Didi.

At breakfast one morning, Breanna asked her closest warriors and Druids from this side of the Sea of Erin, "How is your Latin?"

Izzy answered, "Fluent—I have to be in my land."

"Reasonable," Livie said. "We have had so much Roman influence. I can answer for my father, as he taught me that language."

Lotte added, "Enough, but I have a Gaelic accent."

Taliesin stated, "Same, though all languages evolve. As you've seen during our time here, Latin is fluid like Gaelic or Cumbric."

"You're planning a spy mission, yes?" Ecne asked.

Breanna sighed. "Indeed. Izzy is my choice to lead this mission, as she is the strongest in controlling the Aether Element, and I will need to link her to *Croí Dàn*. Lotte, you'll be her second. Sinéidin and you, as Tuatha, are already linked to our Heart, so you do not need to join this mission to observe what Izzy sees. I want to add Myrddin as well."

"What warriors will you send with them?" Sinéidin asked.

"Izzy and Lotte will be enough, with Livie, Taliesin, and Bláth filling in if needed, along with Myrddin," Breanna declared. "I suppose I should ensure he has a small *balefire*-enabled blade and shields. Or maybe in his staff or an amulet."

Livie groaned but nodded, and Breanna knew she was against that idea, as she still did not truly trust her father.

"We should plan on a monthly schedule across the channel to spy on our general," Breanna added. "I need to discuss retrieval options with Goibniu regarding my golden rope."

With that, she sought Toal and Cilla. "Tell me about the ballistae build-out, crossbows, and progress with the southeastern tribes now that the southwest is well in hand."

Cilla deferred to Toal, who answered, "Well, the latest tribes we've met with have much better woodwrights than those here at Caer Didi or even at Caer Went. We'll now have a more rapid ballistae build-out as they ramp up. The crossbows were more complex, so Goibniu designed a simple model for the Celts to build. Your uncle created plans for a lighter-weight ballista, which the Romans called Scorpions. The men can start assembling those soon."

"That's welcome news," Breanna stated. "And what of your Archers? How is their training coming along?"

Toal nudged Cilla, who squeaked, "Um, while Toal's been busy with Goibniu, I've taken over. It's going okay, but we don't have Toal's ability to give ranges mentally as we practice our formations."

Breanna pondered this. "Cilla, would you accept replicas of Toal's sigils?"

The young archer squeaked again, "You could do that?

"Aye. Toal, roll up your sleeves."

Breanna informed Goibniu, *"Uncle, I have a problem."*

"My niece," he answered. *"With what?"*

"Time and space. I must send some of my Warriors of Destiny to spy on Julius Caesar this summer. I can link Izzy to my Heart to communicate over a distance, but how can she use my golden rope or a piece of it to bring them back to Pretannia? Or must I be there?"

"Bre," Goibniu answered, *"as Badb Catha informed you, the Aether Element is key to everything where life is involved, as life lives in time."*

"So I need them to bear an Aether sigil to connect them to me?"

"Aye, you do, my baby goddess. Then you can find them in the when and where of time. You must take them where they need to be, but then you can summon them back to you."

"Can you help me with the first one? With Izzy?"

Goibniu sighed. "Of course, my Bre."

Later, Izzy sat before Breanna, who was saying, "You now know the process of me casting a sigil. In this case, it will tie our lives together. I do not suggest this lightly, but I cannot risk you without doing this. Our planned spy mission is risky. Don't think I'm questioning your ability to succeed. I—I just can't lose you."

Izzy smiled at the heartfelt admission. "I understand, and you won't. My spy bones know this is needed. Know that I believe in you."

Breanna pulled Izzy into a close hug. "As I do you."

A moment later, *Croí Dàn* commanded, *"Bee. Open your mind, seize the void, and let Aether flow through you."*

Goibniu added, *"Isobel, we must create an Aether Life Sigil representing your signature and blend in the special Life Element Sigil that Badb Catha shared with Breanna. It will allow her to summon you from any place or time to her side, along with anyone touching you. You'll also be able to reach each other's thoughts through Mo Chroí. We must etch it into your skin with woad. It will hurt more than the Language Sigil, as the Dark Goddesses used some of the Fire Element in casting it. Are you ready?"*

Izzy shrugged. *"I am Laoch Druí trained. Make it mine."*

A moment later, she hissed as the sigil burned into her biceps.

Goibniu said, *"Isobel, you and Breanna are linked."*

"Thank you, Goibniu. I think I have this now. I can replicate it."

"Of course, my baby goddess."

And she did just that with Lotte, Livie, and Taliesin. She would later determine whether to do the same for Myrddin.

❧ Artur ❧

In the spring morning sunshine, with Lan in tow, Artur approached Breanna and Eoin at their breakfast table in Caer Didi. "May we join you both?

"Of course. How can I help you?" Breanna answered.

Artur and his Protector set their bowls down, with the former saying, "You've been, well, busy. I want to discuss our next steps regarding the Celtic tribes and the threat posed by Rome's invasion in the next cycle. While I'm sure we can blacken Julius's eyes, stopping that campaign is key. Ecne claimed he would be bringing five legions."

Breanna nodded. "You are correct, and Vellaunus needs help and support. Many, well, distrust his conversion, but I believe he's committed. Anyway, what are you proposing?"

"Given we already know Julius only lands this cycle yet does not invade, we need to plan for that happening," he answered.

"How do we best do that?" she asked. "They must be stopped."

Artur was surprised by the question's equality.

Breanna suggested, "Chief Vellaunus needs new advisors. I suggested you and Lan be his key ones. You two should plan the defenses ahead of next cycle's invasion."

"Just us two?" Lan asked.

"Of course!" Breanna answered with a frown. "We now have new Celtic armorers being trained by our armorers. Warriors are training new warriors. You two need to manage that effort. At the same time, there is rot from within Pretannia, which the Romans bought and exploited. Lotte and Izzy just returned from a mission. Settlements along the Albion coast were dirty with the Roman sympathizers. Clean that up soon with my Warriors of Destiny. Lotte and Izzy are good leaders whom you can leverage.

"In the long term, there are significant sites to build out with hidden ballistae along the coast by the next cycle. All the while, you train any warriors you recruit as you develop these defenses. As new armorers are trained, more of our devices can be deployed to match Rome's forces. The less they rely on *balefire*, the better. That needs to be our advantage in key battles."

Artur nodded. "Thank you. I understand it more clearly now."

Eoin interjected, "After we fight off Caesar toward the end of this summer, we need to return to Erin and deal with political issues."

"Yet call on us any time," Breanna added.

"And Myrddin?"

Breanna replied, "He will return from Gesoriacon shortly. I'll send him to you."

"I assume you'll get us there. To advise Vellaunnus?"

"Aye, and we have a new way to summon you," Breanna answered. "This sigil will hurt a bit to impart, as the Fire Element is involved. Eoin, gather the men. I'll cast the sigil on all, including you. Badb Catha advised that I master her Aether sigil for 'someone dear to me,' which could only mean you. In this, you have no choice."

Within the two spans, Artur watched Breanna imprint her Summons Sigil on each of them. Artur turned to Breanna and offered, "When we first met, I think you know I was uncertain we could work together. Your experience and the support from your Tuatha gods have surprised me. I'm glad to hold this land in joint guardianship with you. You make the impossible seem, well, possible."

"Thank you for that." Then she put a hand on his and Lan's mounts and flashed them away to Chief Vellaunnus' sizeable hillfort.

⟶⟶◈ Breanna ◈⟵⟵

On the day Izzy was set to lead her team to Gesoriacon, Breanna stood imperiously over the band of Celtic traders her Heart had formerly sworn to her, where the new Dobunni trade leader had sided with the Romans once more.

Eoin demanded, "How do you plead as a collaborator with Rome?"

"And to what end do you seek?" Chief Carovetos asked.

"We only seek to trade with them," the man protested. "We did not provide any defensive information about ourselves."

Breanna smiled. "Unfortunately for you, I can find in you in time where you supplied just that."

"That's not proof!" the Dobunni trader exclaimed.

Breanna replied, "Very well. *Croí Dàn*, please share with all, including the accused, using my time-shifting ability to see any moment, especially where he and his men sought to betray his people and their oath *Croí Dàn* had sworn them to us."

Croí Dàn cast the vision in their minds, and the Celts who wanted to stand up to Rome gasped. Breanna asked, "Is sharing information about our efforts to deploy ballistae to defend our ports not an important piece of information? What say you all?"

All joined in, "Guilty!"

Breanna nodded and commanded, "*Croí Dàn* will execute the sentence, per their oath."

"By breaking your oath," the Heart of Destiny said, *"I command your hearts to stop."*

The hearts of the accused did just that as the leader and his ten men collapsed—now dead to the world.

Breanna added, "Let the word spread. Those who do not support our joint efforts to help the Celtic Tribes of Pretanni counter Rome will risk death! Your Celtic Guardians walk among you. The Great Council of Celtic Tribes will rule this island, not Rome."

Internally, Breanna groaned at the cost of lost Celtic lives. While she didn't end them, they died because of her tie with *Cŕoí Dàn*. While she was once removed from the action, it was not enough. It was like an anchor weighing her down.

Izzy

Breanna deposited her crew on the outskirts of Gesoriacon late in the day. After surveying the port of Bonona below them, Myrddin suggested they part ways to divide their efforts to infiltrate the Roman command structure. Izzy eyed the Seer skeptically, but her leader conveyed that Lieve's father had had a *conversion* experience. That was likely one where Breanna confronted the recalcitrant Seer's obstinate manner.

Putting that out of her mind, Izzy marched through the gates as if she owned them. They pass through the treba first, where the Celts lived, and then into the magos. With katanas in hand, she cleared the way along a crowded rath that led through a market to a series of taverns, with Lotte gesturing about with her spears crackling with fire, growling at anyone who took an interest in them. Their three more traditional Druids followed them, and their staffs also showed *balefire*, though somewhat subdued. People moved aside quickly.

Whispers and hisses followed them down the narrow road: *Warrior Druids*—m*agic wielders*—*strike you dead with a look*— and *dirty Celts*.

Those words made her grin. Izzy turned toward the door when the tavern she had a *feeling* about came into view— the Boar's Head; she had targeted the place because it was Legionnaire-friendly.

A big, rough-looking guard stepped before Izzy. "This place is not for you. Your kind is not welcome."

"Says who?"

"Me!"

"You want to take me on?" she asked. "A brute against a Warrior Druid? Please, grow some brains instead of thinking with your gonads."

The guard swiped a massive arm at her, which she quickly ducked. Then, with a push of her Air Element, she punched him through the door with enough force that she heard ribs crack.

Izzy stepped over the wheezing guard. "Does anyone have a problem with my fellow Warrior Druids having a drink in this establishment?"

"I do," a Legionnaire said as he rose.

"Excellent! You challenge me under Roman Law!" Izzy exclaimed. "Which Element do you want to fight me with? Air, Earth, Water, or Fire? Any of those will be messy here in the tavern. Who owns this place? What do you want?"

"No mess!" the keeper said.

"Well, okay, keeper," Izzy sighed. "No Element will be used offensively. Only hand-to-hand weapons, but there will be blood. Agreed? Then, when he's dead and bleeding from his severed neck, that's on you, right?"

"It's on me to clean up," he agreed.

"And drinks for me and my band on this warrior's coin?"

"If you win."

The Legionnaire scoffed. "You against me? I'll crush you."

Izzy chuckled. "You can try."

The soldier drew his sword and lunged, but Izzy was no longer in that place. She landed on his shoulders, her katanas crossed behind his neck, asking, "Keeper, do I take his head?"

He answered, "That's on you."

Izzy countered, "Nay, it's on him. He is the aggressor under Roman law. He invoked the challenge. Everyone, what do you say? Do I take his head?"

The crowd chanted, "Head, head, head!"

The Legionnaire started, "You bi—"

Then his head rolled to the floor, and Izzy kicked herself away from the spray of blood to land gracefully next to her fellow Druids.

Lotte said, "You must show us your *Laoch Druí* ways more often. That was brilliant. Not a drop of blood on you."

Izzy shrugged. "I've been practicing that move, if you recall, but I agree it was a pretty moment. Now, keeper, use the unfortunate man's coin to deliver a round of drinks: three meads, one ale, and a meal for each of us. You can keep the difference for the mess."

She turned to the table where the Legionnaire had sat and demanded his fellows, "I think your table is forfeit as well. Care to challenge me for it?"

"No, Warrior Druid," one said, "The table is yours."

Izzy let her blades briefly blaze with *balefire* to clean them, sheathed each, then sat with a thump. Bláth chuckled.

Livie asked, "Did you know they would be in awe of you?"

She lifted her shoulder again. "I'm fortunate to have a true *Laoch Druí* train me. His attention to detail is, well, consummate. I call on the memory of his lessons daily, as he is my master in Elements and blade dancing. It's the little things you watch for."

Lotte sighed. "I wish I had that. My father was a capable warrior, but not a true Warrior Druid."

"Will you claim your trophy, our protector?" Bláth asked.

"Nay, too messy, and it's not something we do in Galicia, unlike Erin's Gaels," Izzy informed them. "Anyway, we need to find warriors in Pretannia for my grandfather to train in the coming cycle. But you all know that. Och, here comes a Centurion, as I expected he would."

The Legionnaire officer said, "Well met, Warrior Druid. I have met some of your kind before, though few as skilled as you."

Izzy gestured to the remaining open chair and kicked it out so he could sit. "And I am familiar with your leader's rampage from Rome to here, as my fellow Celtic tribes have experienced his might. As to my skills, they are a trifle."

"Not a trifle, given a large man lies dead at your small hands this night," he stated. "Which begs the question, why are you here?"

The keeper arrived with drinks, bowls of stew, and a basket of bread as two scullions dragged the dead man away. She answered, "To buy you a drink. Keeper, bring this officer an ale."

"Seriously," he asked.

"Deadly," Izzy confirmed, letting a little *balefire* seep from her blades. "You haven't seen a tenth of the havoc I could wreak."

"Are you challenging me?" he asked.

She laughed. "No. It would be a waste of time, as you'd be dead, and I'd not understand you any more than I do now."

"Understand what?" he prompted with a cocked eye.

Izzy took a hunk of bread, dunked it in the fish stew, and chewed lazily as if in no hurry. After savoring her mead, she finally countered, "Only smart Celts who take advantage of how Rome engages our kind across the channel will prosper. We plan to be very cautious amid rumors of impending invasions. To make us prosperous."

"Engage?"

Continuing to eat deliberately, Izzy finally clarified, "It is seldom that Rome chooses to incorporate rather than obliterate."

"Then you're spies," he accused.

"How so, if I've declared our intentions for leverage?"

He sighed. "You know our language well."

"I do," Izzy confirmed. "I have been well educated in your ways and laws. While my blades danced brilliantly tonight with that unfortunate brute, I prefer dancing to music. Perhaps we can do that another time. Can you suggest an inn for us?"

"That request surprises me. I'll know where to find you."

"Why should we hide?" she asked. "Do you fear Warrior Druids who seek whatever leverage we can out of the coming war?"

"We should fear your kind, as one of your kind carved a warning on the foreheads of Celtic traitors two cycles back in eastern Gaul. While arrogance and superstition hold us back, I know what I saw," he claimed.

"And you think that I might be that Warrior Druid?" she demanded. "That's a stretch, as best."

The Legionnaire officer huffed. "You know the Atrebates Tribe across the channel has been supporting their cousins, sending men to fight us just east of this port."

"I have heard that," Izzy commented as if it were nothing, "but that's been the case since Rome drove deep into these northern Celtic lands. However, I can see how that might irritate your General Caesar. Now, I think we were discussing an inn?"

The Centurion narrowed his eyes. "For tonight, you can seek the Lion's Head. I'm confident we will cross paths again."

Little did he know, she thought. Then, Izzy touched his arm and said seductively, "I hope so. Tell me your name."

He hesitated. "Marcus."

As she ran her fingers up his arm, she added, "I am Isobel."

At that, he smiled. "Well met."

Later, as the four lay in their room, she said, "I set the hook."

"How so?" Taliesin asked.

She answered, "Our friendly Legionnaire officer, Marcus, suggested the Lion's Head. This inn is the Tiger's Tail. He will be looking for us there and not here. Now, we can be ghosts. Cloak ourselves in our Elements, mainly Air to bend sound, a little water for mists, fire to warp light, and Earth to hush our movements."

Livie said, "But we don't all hold those Elements."

"Together, we do. My grandfather taught me how to blend my Elements with his, which he holds all four of. We've never managed to command Aether as Breanna can now, but we have the other four. We will practice tonight so we can be ready in the morning."

With that, Lotte used Water and Fire, Livie her Earth and Water, Bláth her Air, and Izzy her Air and Earth. Taliesin looked on, stunned by what they could do together. Livie coaxed him to try his affinity for Earth to muffle sound; succeeding, he smiled broadly.

When they chose beds, Izzy ended up with Lotte, Livie with Taliesin, and Bláth took a cot they had arranged for. The night was cool because it was still June in the eastern Atlantic Isles as each pair snuggled up for mutual body heat, and the Bard enfolded herself tightly in her travel blanket.

In the morning, they found their way to the villa Caesar had commandeered for his command post, wrapped in Elements to hide themselves. The Romans had set up a tent in the courtyard behind where the general's office sat. Izzy was not surprised to see *her* Centurion in the mix. Using her new sigil, she asked, *"Mo Chroí? Can you pass a conversation on to Breanna?"*

"Of course," was the answer. *"I can also see through your eyes."*

Izzy shivered a bit at that thought. As she watched, Julius Caesar stood with his generals and senior advisors and asked, "What is the state of the fleet, Titus?"

She knew he was asking for a response from General Titus Labienus, as Ecne had provided a detailed briefing on his staff. "To get two legions across the channel, we need ninety to a hundred transport ships and roughly twenty warships to protect them. Our first choice is a natural low point where the Albion Cliffs split, creating a beach for our landing; the locals call it Dubras. Then, possibly, a landing site known as Walmer. It is similar to the first one, as it has a natural shallow point. After that, the Isle of Thanet would be the next choice, as it is where the cliffs end in the northeast."

"Quintus, what about establishing a base there?"

"It will depend on the landing site, Dominus."

Julius grunted, and Izzy thought he was unhappy with the answer. "Tribune Gaius, tell me of your plans for the reconnaissance incursion before we launch the crossing?"

"If we have no opposition at Dubris, that's where I prefer to land, as we can reportedly cut inland swiftly," Gaius responded. "Yet, to provide helpful information, we will need an extraction point."

"Walmer would be my choice," Titus said.

Julius asked, "When?"

"Two weeks," Gaius answered. "Three scouting days should be enough to see if any locals will support us. I'll need three riders for an escort."

"Pick any Centurions you like. Marcus will help you," Julius stated. Then he turned. "Titus, when can you be ready?"

"We are receiving about ten transport ships per week."

"Then three months. So be it." The general grimaced.

With that, the meeting was over. Izzy could see *her* Centurion, Marcus, looking about the room suspiciously, yet their control of the Elements was masterful. It was time to go back across the channel. She touched her still-tender sigil on her biceps, saying,

"Mo Chroí, it is time to come home. How do we inform Myrddin that he is on his own?"

Croí Dàn replied, *"Leave that to me."*

A moment later, Breanna invoked her Summons Sigil.

Breanna

"So we have two weeks to intercept this Tribune spy named Gaius, who will land at Dubras with his band?" Breanna asked. "And his ship picks him up at Walmer a few days later?"

"Yes, that is their plan," Izzy confirmed. "Do we let his ship drop anchor and get ashore for a bit and see who he meets with, or make it a ghost ship before anyone makes landfall? All hands lost at sea."

Lotte gnawed on her lower lip. "I think we should track this Gaius and see if any Roman conspirators among the Celts approach him and his reconnaissance band. Either way, we make them ghosts—and let rumors spread that it was at the hands of the Guardian's Hounds that dealt out death. I expect General Caesar will send another spy, maybe not so senior, within a month. I hope my sister's father can provide that bit of information."

Livie shrugged. "I will not count on him, but we can see what he's learned."

Breanna sighed over the two sisters' similar perceptions of Myrddin. Yet she knew the course she must take. "Lotte, the next mission is yours. It's yours to plan, although I may make adjustments if I *foresee* something important. Sound reasoning is paramount."

"You trust me after—"

"Stop, Lotte! You are sworn as a Warrior of Destiny. Meet this challenge. Embrace it. Live it. Command it."

Livie touched her sister's arm. "You got this."

Lotte said brightly, "Then I accept!"

"Excellent," Breanna exclaimed. "Tell me of your plan later."

Eoin stepped in. "The Fish Head Tavern calls us!"

Later, as they snuggled in their bed, Breanna said, "It's not that I don't trust them, as Izzy was masterful. I feel a need to protect them. Especially when she was wounded the last time, yet I know I can't. Or know how to let go truly."

"It's okay, my love, as you can undo horrible things with time."

Breanna kissed Eoin for the thought, yet she was still troubled, as Badb Catha warned her not to create any alternate timelines to save one of her Warriors of Destiny who might die. It gnawed at her. How to save any one of them? Yet, she had sworn her protection!

Lotte

Two weeks later, after Breanna had deposited them on the coast, it was dusk when Lotte spotted a lone Roman merchant ship approaching the natural landing spot between the White Cliffs of Dubras to their northeast and southwest. She said, *"Mo Chroí, see what I see. Should Rome use this site to land, we must be ready to battle! We need ballistae here!"*

"Noted, Lotte. Trust in me."

As a typical transport ship, the Romans dropped their forward ramp at a low tide to spill four mounted men onto the beach. There was barely enough light to make out their faces. Izzy pointed out Centurion Marcus and Tribune Gaius, easily identified by his unique helmet plume. The two others were unknown. The small band quickly rode inland through the cut the small rivulet had made over eons to wear down this section between the Dubras Cliffs. With appropriate space, Lotte's band followed them inland, with her and her Elemental sister masking the noise of their horses.

Bradaigh rode at her right, and Braoin flanked Izzy. Fergal insisted that he join in this mission. They rode in the shadows, woven by their Elements. Izzy, the most advanced *Laoch Druí* among them, had taken to working with the men, teaching them how to determine which Element they could control. Their Fire and Earth Elements were dominant, but not enough to sustain their pursuit. That was on Izzy and Livie, who had been learning about Aether from Breanna. Lotte knew she needed to do more to be a true *Laoch Druí* like Izzy.

When the four Romans rode to a nearby Ringfort with an agricultural settlement surrounded by low walls, Lotte knew the Romans would be well received. She took note and passed it on to *Mo Chroí* and Izzy.

Izzy, also tied to Breanna's Heart, squeezed Lotte's bicep and nodded. They established a camp on a typical chilly summer night near the strait while Celts welcomed the Romans within the fort's walls.

The pattern repeated over two days as the Romans visited ringfort and settlement after ringfort and settlement, heading northeast and never far from the coast. On the third day, they came upon another break in the Albiu Cliffs, known as Walmer, as the tide was going out.

Lotte commanded darkly, "They must pay."

Izzy suggested, "Sister-mine, they will, but how can we best deliver a message about Warrior Druids in Pretannia? Kill the spies, the ship, or both. We had this debate. Letting the vessel return to spread tales of the Celt Guardian's magic might be better. This band from Rome could die, and the ship takes damage, yet only enough to limp back to Bonona Bay."

Lotte acknowledged, "Wise advice. So spare only the crew?"

Izzy smiled. "Least among the officers is Marcus, the Roman Centurion I met there. He knows about Warrior Druids. He doesn't know he has been compromised. I will play his strings when I next go to Gesoriacon."

"Then let's kill a few Romans."

Bradaigh said, "It's long overdue!"

They drew their *balefire*-enhanced weapons and cut down three of the four Romans. The last one, Marcus, abandoned his mount and bolted for the transport ship, slogging through the tide. As the transport ramp raised behind him, Lotte's spears spat streaks of *balefire* that ripped off its top half. Other shots took out sails while the rowing crew applied their muscles to the oars.

As the ship pulled away from the shore, Lotte said, "Those look like mighty fine mounts that they abandoned. Shall we seize the spoils?"

"Good thinking," Bradaigh agreed. "Let's be about it."

After rounding up the four skittish mounts, Lotte ordered, *"Mo Chroí, have Breanna bring us back."*

 **Izzy**

A few days later, Izzy sat in The Boar's Head Tavern with Taliesin and Livie; Lotte was assigned to Artur to address the issue of traitorous Celts along Albiu Cliffs. This time, no one challenged them as they took a table.

Izzy commanded, "Mead and ale for now."

The keeper personally took their order. "Your reputation as a Warrior Druid precedes you. I hope for a cleaner evening and no more challenges."

Izzy smiled warmly. "As do I."

A while later, the Centurion she knew as Marcus stepped into the tavern and strode to their table with purpose. "You lied to me!"

Izzy beamed up at him, reaching out to touch him. "How so?"

"You did not go to the Lion's Head as I suggested."

Izzy wrinkled her nose. "It smelled poorly, so we decided to sleep beneath the stars and the moon. As creatures of nature, it gives us more energy to wield our not-insignificant powers. Yet, here you are, looking pale."

"Aye," he hissed. "I faced Warrior Druids across the channel and barely escaped with my life. My comrades are dead. It was you!"

Izzy sighed dramatically. "Oh, please, how could I be there and here? But I have heard something. It may not be true. Sit."

As he dropped heavily, she touched his crossed arms.

"What?" Marcus asked, annoyed.

"Just a rumor, but it said the Celtic Guardians are back."

"Who's back?"

"Guardians of the Celts. They are Ancient Druids, blessed by Pretannia's Celtic gods, something not seen in a thousand cycles. They must be responsible for the attack. If the myths are true."

"How could that be possible?" he asked skeptically.

Izzy scrunched up an eyebrow. "How? I don't know. I'm only a Warrior Druid who guards Seers and Seeresses, sometimes Healers, Bards, and Lawgivers. Should the Celtic Guardians have returned with their *Laoch Draíochta*, Warriors of Magic, their abilities would far exceed mine. Either way, how can I help you?"

"I don't know," Marcus said, raking a hand through his hair. "Their power was horrifying. Along with some of the ship's crew, only I survived in my reconnaissance band, and I shouldn't have. Someone spared me. I failed, and I know it."

Izzy whispered, "I have heard the Guardians and their Druidic Warriors are specially trained and chosen. They select only the best from across Pretannia. They are sometimes called Hounds or Warriors of Destiny—fierce and powerful in their magical abilities, and the lead Guardian is supposedly a goddess."

"How would you know this?" Marcus questioned.

"Only rumors," Izzy answered, shrugging. "It's all we have."

"You would support this goddess?" he asked.

"If she had the power to repel Rome, yes."

"Then I should declare you spies," he exclaimed.

"Marcus!" Izzy spat. "You survived facing them. Feel lucky."

He sighed. "Sorry, I don't know what to believe."

"Well, based on your experience, these Celtic Guardians and the Warriors of Destiny are real," Izzy concluded as she laid a hand over his. "You need to be careful. I'd rather not see you die like the others who faced them and lost their lives."

"Why?"

"You are a handsome man."

He furrowed his brow. "Hmmm."

Izzy added, "Yet we must go. This settlement's contamination of the land is poisonous to us as Druids. We need to live in a pure land. It is why we skipped the Lion's Head Inn, as I said. Be wise and stay safe. If you're in trouble, think of me and say my name—I may hear your call."

As Breanna's Heart cast *truth*, he nodded as they rose and left.

Izzy added, *"Ćroí Dàn, find Myrddin, as it is his time to return with us. Summon him now. I've sown my seeds. Let's leave this sinkhole."*

Moments later, the Seer emerged from the mists. "Why did you have your Heart call me?"

"She could only do that if you were sworn to her," Izzy rejoined. "Yet, we have a new way to travel that your goddess must give you, and Artur and Lan need you at their side. Take my hand."

Breanna and Eoin met Izzy's small team as they returned to Caer Didi. The former briefly folded Izzy into her welcoming arms, saying, "Well done, my friend. That last meeting you brilliantly arranged was most enlightening!"

Then Breanna turned to Myrddin and told him, "I have another mission for you, but first, you must accept a new sigil. It will allow you to report in with my Heart, and if you face trouble, I can pull you to me. While I burn that into you, tell me what you learned about Julius Caesar's plans. Then, we have only three months to prepare before Rome invades."

⟶⚭ Breanna ⚭⟵

At the end of the last month of the summer season, on the southeast White Cliffs of Dubras that overlooked the strait between the Island of Pretannia, a collection of Celtic tribes lay hidden but ready to defend their lands. Breanna reached out to Nimuë, hoping she could confirm Ecne's claim that this would be the day Julius Caesar brought his fleet to the shores of Dubras. A moment later, the Sea God's daughter told her what their creatures sensed. Many vessels had been launched, making their way toward her. Standing firm, she waited for the armada to come into view.

Finally, Breanna took in the twenty-plus large Roman galleys called biremes and triremes. They escorted nearly a hundred merchant transport ships, all ready to unleash hundreds of legionnaires per vessel onto Pretannia's shores. Another twenty-plus smaller ships carried supplies and engineers to support the invasion. The night before was stormy, but the next day it turned into a sunny summer afternoon.

After rallying the Celts under Breanna's and Artur's Guardian titles, she and Eoin led their Warriors of Destiny against Julius Caesar's first invasion, backed by those Celt Tribes who had joined the great compact so far. Most were southeastern tribes, but the word had spread far and wide. Other tribes to the north would unite with them by the following season.

With Rome's armada, Caesar would need to break through their hidden defenses, comprised of the local Celtic army they had raised and trained over the past three months. Eoin had deployed the Celts across the beach, hidden by sand berms, where the white cliffs allowed such a landing because an ancient river cut them in two, with Breanna's band clustered in the center. Most of the high white cliffs dropped straight into the sea, yet here was a beach where Roman legionnaires could breach that natural barrier. With the Celts behind illusions cast by Izzy and Braoin, her new fellow Air Elemental apprentice, the beach looked deserted, and the ballistae positioned on top of the cliffs appeared to be just large clumps of grass.

As the Romans came, they were arrayed in lines, with two galleys before twenty transport ships and two galleys trailing them, each stacked roughly five rows deep. Breanna's two Elemental Water Druids, the half-sisters Lotte and Livie, stood on the beach, manipulating the tides to deny Rome ships from any easy landing by controlling the currents.

Standing beside them was Izzy, who ensured the winds kept the low-slung galleys and bulky transports from using their sails to reach the shoreline. Despite those efforts, the ships drew closer and closer under the muscles of their rowers.

"Breanna, summon our Druids to the beach with you!" Eoin called. As Artur and Lan flanked him, Livie, Lotte, Izzy, and

Braoin appeared beside Breanna, and he dropped his arm, calling out, "Fire!"

While the hidden ballistae lit and launched the large fire spears, Corbmac's *fians* pumped crossbow bolts tipped with *balefire* into the air. Toal led his archers across the beach with their long bows as they rode behind the Celtic frontline, unleashing their *balefire*-tipped arrows deep into Rome's second line of ships.

Livie let her staff, with its crystal mounted atop it, blaze forth. Then Bláth, Taliesin, and Myrddin followed suit. Bradaigh, Braoin, and Corbmac each positioned themselves with a *fian*, joining the others in releasing *balefire* from their swords' tips, with Lotte and Izzy joining Breanna in doing the same.

As the long-range ballistae spears closed the distance and struck home, and the shorter-range blades unleashed their *balefire* fury, the first line of ships exploded into tinder, and the afternoon sunny sky rained fire, wood, blood, bodies, and bones into the sea around the second line of ships.

With that line now little more than debris, the second line came within range. Eoin commanded the Celts' ballistae and their *fians* to release another wave of bolts and spears, with Toal's band swinging their horses back along the rear of the front line of Celts as their blooded warriors' weapons followed suit, delivering the same level of devastation to that following line of Roman ships.

When the third line of ships closed on the shore, the Roman galleys unleashed a similar wave of fire spears from their ballistae, without magical explosive tips, at their opponents on shore. Breanna recognized that they were nearly identical to the land-based weapons built by the Celts under their direction.

Eoin commanded, "No time for shields. Direct fire on the incoming fire spears!"

As their warriors focus their minds on the *void* to call forth the Tuatha magic supporting them, Breanna felt Izzy and Livie jointly summon their Earth Element. She merged with them to pull sand from the seabed and pile up a large berm before their fellow Warriors of Destiny and Celtic allies.

Several of the fire spears the Romans launched impacted the new mound of sand, yet three massive flaming bolts cleared the new barricade. Instead of using *balefire*, Lotte thrust out her Tuatha magical weapons, letting her Druidic Element Fire surge through Red Javelin and Yellow Spear. Her wild scream matched her rage as she blasted a projectile into pieces. That left two to strike at Eoin and his combined warriors. With no chance of stopping both, Izzy pushed off with her Air Element, katanas in hand, and sliced *balefire* into a fire spear from above it, and the remaining pieces spiraled into the sand.

Given the size of the fire spears launched by the Roman ships, Breanna held her breath, seeking the *Cycle of Time*, ready to pull her Warriors of Destiny out of harm's way. While Izzy masterfully deflected one, the other struck as Eoin blazed *balefire* from the Sword of Light, but it was not in time as the remnants crashed into him and his line. Breanna gasped as the impact blast sent him flying back, and he hit the sand hard with a grunt, somehow keeping his hands on the hilt of the Sword of Light and his buckler.

Breanna gasped, demanding, "Izzy, Livie, to Eoin!"

The two healers were soon at his side. Drawing upon their Elements, they worked to attend to him, and his fellow wounded *fian* warriors; the latter fared better with their larger shields.

At the same time, the Romans had not counted on the Earth Druids pulling the seabed from beneath their ships as the water rushed to suck those galleys and transports down, drowning all aboard. That caused the third line of ships to sink.

When the fourth and fifth line captains appeared ready to break off their landing, Breanna linked with her blooded to command, *"We need to rain balefire before they can break off! Lotte and I must continue the battle from the heights of the cliff. Only our ancient Tuatha weapons have the balefire reach where we need it to strike!"*

As the following line of ships drew closer, the Regini Tribe's fishing fleet, armed with the smaller scorpions, unleashed their fire bolts. That distraction allowed the two Elemental Druids to finish healing Eoin so he could return to the battle. They then focused on the other warriors hit by the fire spear's remnants.

Breanna's concern over Eoin's wounds gnawed at her. Hating that she had a greater battle to focus on, she touched the *Cycle of Time* to move herself to the top of the bluff. Then she used her Summons Sigil to pull Eoin and Lotte up to her side as her Blades of Destiny raged into the Roman fleet, destroying ships and men. Breanna turned to Eoin, seeing his bloody tunic on the left side, and glared at him. "Are you okay?"

He grunted. "I'll survive."

Breanna nodded, not liking the look on his pained face as she glanced again at the red stain seeping through his tunic above his kilt and the blood dripping down his leg. Yet she said, "Then aim for their hulls at the waterline!"

And then she unleashed *Lann Dàn* once more, with Eoin joining her by raising *Claimh Solais* and *Gáe Assal*, and Lotte pouring herself into her spears *Gáe Ruadh* and *Gáe Buide.*

Six points of *balefire* arched out from the trio, at times crossing over each other as they reached their targets, and galleys disappeared in a brilliant flash, followed by transport and support ships whose hulls tore apart seconds later. As Roman legionnaires spilled into the sea, their Celtic allies below rushed to the shoreline, releasing wave after wave of arrows to ensure no survivors reached their shores. Two Roman legions, nearly ten thousand men, died under their combined fire.

Three lone ships at the tail end of the fifth line turned out to sea and beyond the reach of nearly all, heading back to Gaul. Yet Eoin was not done and gave *Gáe Assal* a mighty heave. "Seek!"

Lugh's magical spear raged with *balefire* that struck the closest ships, ensuring that all of the fifth-line ships still in range exploded. Eoin's spear streaked across the waves to effortlessly pierce the hull of the trailing galley. It burst out of the far side, splitting it in two. The gleaming projectile sought the second ship, blasting into its gunwales at the waterline as it had with the previous ship. As the last vessel was out of range, *Gáe Assal* raced back to slap into Eoin's outstretched palm, and all signs of *balefire* abruptly ceased from the Warriors of Destiny.

With that done, he sank to a knee with a groan, his sword and spear falling from his hands. Breanna cried, "Eoin, you stubborn man! You're still hurt!"

He could only huff as she whisked him down next to Izzy and Livie, demanding of them, "The fool man fought while injured. Heal him, now!"

Looking around, she noted that Izzy and Livie had assured their *fians* were being tended to, with Bláth and Taliesin assisting them. She sighed, relieved that none of their warriors were as seriously wounded as Eoin had been. After a moment, unable to wait, she demanded, "How bad is it?"

"Gah, he undid our previous work," Izzy growled. "He took shards of that fire spear in his side and broke some ribs. We removed the wood bit, but the binding was too fresh when he proclaimed he needed to return to the battle. Give me a moment to reassess the damage."

Breanna nodded, remembering she had left Lotte on the bluff and summoned her. While expecting the standoffish warrior to protest, she did not and knelt next to Izzy and their *Cosantóir*. "I brought your weapons," she said, her eyes glistening. "Tell me you'll be okay. Promise me! We need you."

"Aye, and thank you," Eoin whispered. "Izzy and Livie will make me whole."

Lotte sighed. "Good, but I have to agree with your mate. While brave, you are a stupid man. Yet, you stood strong against Rome!"

Breanna suppressed a groan over Lotte's statement—she should be the one next to him in this moment! Yet she had to command her band. "We need better physical shields for my blooded warriors. This outcome cannot be possible again!"

"We should anticipate Rome will throw more at us next time," Eoin countered weakly. "There will be casualties."

Ecne appeared with Sinéidin, and the former settled next to Eoin's head to stay out of Livie's way, advising, "Lotte was right, as that was foolish of you. For more serious injuries during the Fomorian war, we relied on Dian Cécht and Airmid, who once maintained healing springs in Erin. They saw after our fallen warriors. Babd already commanded that they create and keep one ready near Dun Uisneach for our Warriors of Destiny."

"That would be a good backup plan," Breanna concurred, still concerned about her mate.

Bradaigh added, "While our *Cosantóir* was wounded, we did strike a decisive blow against the Roman general. I'm looking forward to doing that again next cycle."

Lotte smiled darkly. "Aye, me too. I like killin' Romans! Yet, I'd prefer something more personal, something hand-to-hand. Nothing like seeing the light in a man's life go out when you've dealt the final blow in a one-on-one battle!"

Livie scolded, "Lotte! That's enough of your savage side!"

"Aye, Lotte, I'd also prefer you keep those thoughts tamed," Breanna suggested tightly. "Many men lost their lives today—fortunately, none on our side. Most of them would not care an ounce about the Celtic and Gaelic lives they would have taken. Yet we wielded a terrible power. Each of you, treat it with respect and wisdom, especially given that there will be even more who will die in the coming cycle."

Then Breanna suggested, "Artur, you must mingle with our Celtic leaders and draw as much support as you can from them with this humiliating defeat that they helped mete out to Julius Caesar."

Artur nodded and signaled for Lanslod to follow him. Verica, the King of the Atrebates, had committed several warbands to aid the Cantii tribe. With Breanna using Artur as a Guardian and Myrddin as an ambassador to convince various tribes to work together, these efforts culminated in this victory. All who supported Chief Vellaunnus in his efforts to hold off Rome cheered. Breanna knew many had not thought it would be possible to hold against the might of Rome. Yet, they had been victorious.

Julius

As their three remaining ships turned back toward what he called Portus Itius, a stunned Julius Caesar demanded, "What in the world were those weapons?"

Then, the other two ships that had escaped destruction, which bore the commanders of his land forces, exploded from within when those strange weapons struck them. With that, the sea took them, his key allies, to the bottom of the strait they had just sailed across.

"Blast! I've lost nearly a hundred ships, two full legions, and our support troops! Most of my senior leaders are gone!" Julius raged. "What remains of the Senate will eat me alive, not to mention other generals, especially Pompey! In the coming season, I had planned to draw on more legions. Five, at least—two of which are now dead! And where and when did these Celts obtain such weapons as ballistae and those exploding fire bolts?"

A Centurion stepped forward, saying, "Dominus, I am Marcus. I was on the earlier summer reconnaissance mission, where the Celts used those same weapons to attack us, and Tribune Gaius was lost. You know the following two excursions failed to deliver results, with all hands lost. We have heard rumors about newly resurfaced Celtic Guardians and their Warrior Druids, who have powers we do not understand. It all seems so—incredible. Yet, with what we witnessed, it's more than real."

Julius demanded, "Are you serious? Magic is not real!"

"Deadly, Dominus," Marcus said. "I was on that beach when that same directed lightning struck my charges down. No one believed me."

"Do we have any counter to their strange streaking fire? Those were not like our fire lances."

"There's not enough information to say what it was," Marcus answered. "It is clear from the rumors that their Warrior Druids likely did wield their magic against us."

"It must be something else besides fanciful notions of magic," Caesar argued. "Yet, beyond this horrendous magical fire, someone has taught them to build ballistae similar to ours. We need scouts."

"They somehow seem to know we are coming."

"Figure it out!" Caesar demanded. "In the meantime, now that we completely control the Santones, I need to commission more ships!"

"Veneti ships would have been helpful to have right about now."

Caesar glared at his commander for bringing up that sore subject. "Marcus, if you can solve the mystery as to where they vanished to with their fellow Namnetes Celts, I'll give you a promotion."

⟶✦⟶⚛ **Breanna** ⚛⟵✦⟵

Izzy released the Aether life threads she knew as Marcus, saying, "Bre, now you know Caesar will not be able to muster five legions, as we destroyed two he planned on taking with him in his campaign this coming cycle. It will weaken him politically, and he'll likely not receive replacements from Rome. Yet, he will be motivated by the challenge. As you can see, the seeds I planted have taken root."

Ecne added, "In history, the general initially saw the Celts on the Cliffs of Albiu, above Dubras, and moved his landing north, so well done on the hidden execution. We also now have a new target for a possible sneak attack before spring—the Santones shipyards Caesar mentioned. His Centurion's other comment about the missing Veneti ships is curious, though, as history says Caesar's general defeated them last summer. We need to look into where they went."

Livie said distantly, "And when."

Surrounded by her team, Breanna nodded. "That would be a good mission to hamper Roman rule via the seas. Until the next battle season, we must return to Erin for a while. Given this development, I would like to establish a warrior rotation plan to maintain close contact across our teams. As word of our Celtic Guardians' extraordinary win over Rome spreads, that effort should grow easier."

"Indeed," Eoin agreed. "We also need to continue to build our defenses. Toal, you and Cilla must be here most often, along with your archers-turned-armorers and some of Corbmac's men who've done the same. Get our woodwrights involved as well.

You two must oversee building as many ballistae as possible before next summer, especially on the coast and at the mouth of the River Tamesas."

Breanna added, "Izzy, I understand you want to return to Galicia occasionally, but we need a spy network to spread your rumors, especially around Gesoriacon. Yet, you must also recruit warriors to train with your grandfather as *Laoch Druí*. I hope that will get you home often enough. Braoin will be your second, as he needs help with his Elements.

"Lotte, you must support Izzy in these efforts. You'll take the point on any skirmishes with spies or traitors that either she or Artur deem essential to deal with. Bradaigh will be your second, which goes the same for him with the Elemental practice.

"Fergal, you have a mate to look after. Yet, Sinéidin may be needed if we encounter language challenges, such as helping us understand the Gauls on the mainland or the Celts here.

"Bláth, Livie, and Taleisin—you must explore coming threats and challenges through the *sight* and *Cycle* both here in Pretannia and from within Erin. As Badb Catha informed me, changing the timeline over so many past centuries across such a vast area is like altering the path of a mighty river with big nudges—this victory was not that. Our triumph was a slight nudge. That said, when we return, the leadership of our land will be in flux. Be ready for anything!

"That's all, my friends and family. We did more than good!"

Breanna knew that was true. Yet, a mighty river of time stood before them! How to nudge it their way was the question.

EPILOGUE

—⊰ Breanna ⊱—

Having turned away Julius Caesar's first landing of Pretannia, their Warriors of Destiny flashed back to the fall of the cycle they'd left in the fifth century Erin, assembling on the golden plain below Dun Tara.

Eoin stood arm in arm with Breanna, who started to say to her sworn, "Well done, my—"

Yet that was all they heard as thunder shook them all and lightning lit the sky. Then, the white-haired Asgardian God of War and his massive hammer, Mjolnir, smashed into the ground right next to Breanna. He claimed, "Pretannia was fated for our Norvegr warriors to conquer in a few centuries! Now, the Celts will have the backbone to hold off Rome. For that, your land is forfeit!"

Having experienced the Asgardian pantheon firsthand, Breanna spat, "Thor! I already kicked your Norvegr-spawned pieces of shite out of Erin in another timeline, and they will not be able to repeat that trick with Erin's Veil in place!"

She quickly slapped a hand onto his forearm, and she, Eoin, and the Norvegr God disappeared into the space between the realms. A moment later, two of the three appeared on the cliffs above Dubras, back in time and above where Caesar's Roman fleet lay in ruins just offshore. Yet Eoin was missing.

"What did you do with him?"

Thor looked down at the ships, crowing with his mighty hammer held high. "Got you now, you bi—"

Breanna did not hesitate as *balefire* from each *Lann Dàn* blade flared, even though they were sheathed in her harness, and the red-hot fire from them cleaved the head of Mjolnir from its haft. When it dropped with a thud at her feet, she reached out to touch the strange metal block and disappeared with that part of his weapon.

Before she returned, she reached out to Eoin through the Life Element Power Sigil she had cast on his arm, one tied to her new Summons Sigil. Breanna exclaimed, *"Got you!"*

A moment later, without the sundered hammerhead, Eoin appeared next to her, holding the Sword of Light in his hand, its tip pointed at the heart of the Novegr God of Thunder, just inches away. *Balefire* turned the blade a yellowish red as it crackled and hissed, inches from his skin.

Thor demanded, "What did you do with my Mjolnir?"

Breanna answered with a wicked smile, "The Tuatha Goddess of War, The Mórrigan, gifted our weapons with her *balefire* in the physical world. Since you brought your magical Warhammer to my realm, it was my privilege to cleave its head from your little stick! It's likely the size of your manhood. I will hold your magical hammerhead hostage while you scuttle back to Odin.

As the Tuatha Goddess of Time, I have secured it in a where and when that you'll never find."

"What gives you—"

"Shut it and listen!" Breanna commanded tightly. "You came here thinking the Tuatha were weak. My brother gods and sister goddesses will defend our Gaels and cousin Celts through our Warriors of Destiny. The Tuatha-aligned pantheons are behind us, supplying us with magically enhanced weapons! Weapons that just destroyed more than a hundred Roman ships and ten thousand of their men."

Taking a deep breath, Breanna added more calmly, "Once our respective fathers make a truce that you and your kind will not be able to interfere with me and my kind, you'll get your hammerhead back. And do not trouble my lands again with your threats, or I will jam that headless haft you hold up your arrogant arse.

"For now, you can tell your father to contact the Tuatha All-Father, my father, when you want to hold a parlay to regain your hammerhead. Until then, it's mine, as a spoil of war. As per our last meeting, your appearance on my land was just that—an act of war! When last we met, I vowed this. You know, when you tried to end me, unsuccessfully, I may add. Yet Erin and Pretannia are still mine!"

It was then that a large crow settled on Breanna's shoulder, cocking a dark eye on the Asgardian god.

Thor looked at the bird warily, saying, "So you called your Goddess of War."

"No one calls me, laddie," Badb Catha growled. *"I figured you might try something stupid after your last stunt, so I've had my eye on you. Now you've stepped into deep shite. Stepped into my trap!"*

Thor's face fell flat, twisted in pain, and his smile faltered. "I –"

"Shut it," Badb cut him off. "You think you know of the Fates – I am FATE, you boy-shite god! I can make you, and I can unmake you!"

His smile died, yet he tried to turn on his charm, facing both goddesses. "I have underestimated you, my lady. Perhaps we could discuss –"

"What?" Eoin interrupted grimly. "Would that be you turning on your charms to influence my mate? Take on Badb Catha?"

Thor blanched.

Breanna added, "You may have big muscles, but you're still an arrogant arse, with shite for brains."

Thor looked thunderous. Yet Eoin held his eyes with his own, steel on steel, nor did his sword tip waver as he added, "But that will not be today or any day. We've had enough of you and your Norvegrs to last lifetimes. Hear this, Gaels and Celts rule on our islands!"

Breanna put in, "Of which these islands are now mine. Remember that! And remember that our weapons can now unleash *balefire* in both the magical and physical realms."

Thor started, "I will—"

Eoin jabbed the tip of *Claimh Solais* at his chest, losing a bloom of blood and then fire that sealed it. As he hissed, Breanna smiled darkly, "Say nothing if you want the head of your big, magical hammer back. For now, it's mine. Any additional discussions about having it returned will require my father, yours, you, and me. Now, get your arse out of my land!"

Croí Dàn interjected, *"I'd listen to my Hero!"*

Thor appeared momentarily startled by yet another Tuatha goddess—making it three he faced—before protesting, "We're in Albion. This Isle—"

"Belongs to the Gaels and Celts. It makes it mine to protect! Now, take your stick and be gone."

Breanna then reached between realms, ripped open a pathway in space and time, and hurled Thor out of Pretannia as he held his headless haft.

"Where'd you send him?" Eoin asked.

Breanna responded coldly, "Back to Asgard so he can whine to his father about me breaking his pretty magical hammer while attempting to claim Pretannia and Erin for his Norvegrs."

The Mórrigan said, *"Well done, both of you. You ensured that the hothead was dealt with promptly. You handled it brilliantly. You put him in his place. Not to mention blackening Julius Caesar's eye."*

Cróí Dàn offered, *"Thank you, Auntie. It means a lot."*

"Of course, my little Heart!"

With that, the battle crow lifted her wings and was gone.

"Okay then, that was unexpected," Eoin stated. "Now what?"

Breanna nodded firmly. "We get you patched up."

Eoin grimaced again. "I would appreciate that. Afterward?"

"We survive the next cycle's invasion in Pretannia by Caesar, and then we can hopefully turn our eyes toward helping Egypt, as I am not finished with Rome or their general just yet. As you know, we only have twenty-five cycles to save the Egyptians from their coming Empress's foolish notion that she could tempt the Romans into a partnership using her wiles with two different generals."

"Then let's go home," he declared. "We must reassure our Clan of Destiny that we are safe, and let them know we bested the Asgardian God of War!"

"And I have to tell Father to expect a message from Odin about discussing a new truce. Yet, that issue is just noise," she added. "We need a new Great Agreement between our Gaels and the Tuatha pantheon as we straddle both realms. Something that brings us together to fight the coming darkness."

Here ends *Croí Dàn* – Heart of Destiny
Dàn Cycle Three

The *Dàn Cycle* continues in:

Laoch Dàn – Warriors of Destiny
Dàn Cycle Four

And in:

Daoine Dàn – *Immortals* of Destiny
Dàn Cycle Five

Turn the page to check out the Warriors of Destiny preview!

ACKNOWLEDGMENTS

I want to thank Marty, Chris, Cindy, and Kimberly for their contributions to developing the original storyline many cycles ago, as well as all of my early readers who provided valuable input on what was a rough draft at the time. Marty, Chris, and Cindy are still with me, giving feedback on the various editions of Dàn Cycle One, Two, and Three, which Dàn Cycle Four and Five will follow.

I again turned to my trusty editor for her input on Heart of Destiny. Again, I am delighted to thank Holly Atkinson for another job well done. As the owner of Evil Eye Editing, Holly is brutally honest while also letting me shine as an author. Connect with Holly and her team at www.evileyeediting.com!

A big thank you goes to Nadiia Kolpak, a talented illustrative artist from Ukraine, a beautiful, bold, and brave country. She designed my book covers, the website artwork, and the print and eBook layouts. I found Nadiia on the Upwork website – a great creative artist.

As the Tuatha Gods spread all of my musical talents to other, more worthy humans, I want to recognize Claire Odlum and Muse Cilla for evolving our jointly created lyrics and compositions of the songs in the *Dàn Cycle* Novels so far (which you'll find on my website www.destinycycle.com and via various Bards of Destiny YouTube links).

Toledo Vintiñi joined my Bards of Destiny as our new composer. He is creating soundtracks for each book, starting with Blades of Destiny and Stone of Destiny, which are now available to stream on most music services.

GUIDE TO THE GAELIC LANGUAGE

While this novel is set in fifth-century Ireland, I primarily use modern Gaelic for specific words rather than early or old Irish versions. Yet, even with this, there are Irish and Scottish Gaelic variations to consider. Because certain vowels and consonants in Gaelic have no equivalent in English, it can be a complex language to read. A Gaelic-English dictionary (or an online source) helps to translate between the two languages.

Below is a summary of some differences that can assist with the pronunciation of these words. I have included phonations in parentheses to aid in sounding out names on the Central Characters & Places and Glossary pages. For those less inclined to make such an effort, sound out the word as you like. How it sounds to you will not insult the Tuatha Gods! I can't say the same for native Gaelic speakers, though.

Vowels & Vowel Combinations: Individual Gaelic vowel sounds are as follows: *a* is typically pronounced *ah*, as in father; *á* or *à* takes on a longer sound, as in Dàn taking on the sound dawn (note: the author chose Scottish Gaelic spelling of Destiny over the Irish Gaelic spelling, as cinniúint is too lengthy); *he* takes on the sound *i*, as in high; when words end in *e*, it is always sounded out, as in fairie; *i* rarely takes on the sound *eye* and instead is usually an *ee* or *ih* sound, as in feel.

Some vowel combinations take on different sounds from English to Gaelic; *aoi* takes on a long *e*, as in peel; *ao* takes on *ay*, as in pay; *au* takes on the sound *ow*, as in pow. Accents, such as ` and ´ lengthen the sound of a letter.

Consonants: As with vowels, a few Gaelic consonants also take on different sounds from English; *c* always takes on a *k* sound, as in Celtic being pronounced Keltic; *ch* and *kh* are guttural, as in ache; *g* sounds are hard; *h* is not strictly a letter, but rather it's a function to aspirate or lengthen a consonant, and thus *lh* would take on the sound full.

I hope you have some fun with Gaelic!

CENTRAL CHARACTERS & PLACES & TERMS

Aife (Ee-fa) – Mate of Dun Arrogh Chief Cairbre, a Princess of the Blood from Dál nAraidi, and Eoin's mother.

Aos Dána (Ays Dawn-ah) – Led by All-Father, wise ones of the Celts known as Druids collectively and Druí individually; comprised of multiple sects, each wielding Tuatha powers such as the *sight* and *void*, with others controlling one or more of the five Elements.

Ard-Rí (Ard-ree) – The High King of Ireland, the Chieftain to whom all Clan Chiefs swear allegiance.

Bards – History keepers, storytellers, and master musicians of the *Aos Dána*.

Bean-Sidhe (Banshee) – *Sidhe* women who are young and beautiful and wail or keen over the dead or those soon to be so; often referred to as harbingers of death; another name for similar fairies is *Sìthiche* (Shee-uh-khe), who can be both benevolent and malevolent; note the Irish and Scottish Gaels spell the word for fairies differently, with it being *Sidhe* and *Sìth*, respectively.

Badb Catha (Biv Kah-ha) – Goddess of Death and Knowledge, commonly called Goddess of War, and The Mórrigan, often taking the form of a battle crow on the earthly plane.

Beatha (Bay-uh) – A Fire Elemental Druid Seeress, called a Fáidh, at Dun Arrogh, one of the *Aos Dána*.

Bláth (Blaw) – An Air Elemental Druid and Master Bard of Dun Uisneach; Bards were a sect of Druids known as Filídh in Gaelic.

Bradaigh (Brad-ee) – One-time bastard son of Hakon Skadi; now Gaelic Warrior of Destiny who joins Breanna's Band.

Braoin (Breen) – One-time bastard son of Hakon Skadi; now Gaelic Warrior of Destiny who joins Breanna's Band.

Breanna Ban Morna (Bree-an-na Bawn Mor-na) – Initially a Red Branch warrior from Dun Arrogh who is of Clan Dálaigh (Daw-lee) and the daughter of Morna and Nevan, with her actual father being Hakon Skadi. The Heart of Destiny chooses her to be Erin's Hero, and in wielding the *Triple Dàn* magic, she becomes a Time-Walker.

Breitheamh (Breh-huv) – Judicial sect of the *Aos Dána* that acts as judges, lawmakers, interpreters, and negotiators.

Cairbre (Car-bree) – Chief of Dun Arrogh, mated with Aife and Eoin's father.

Celts (Kelts) – People who once occupied a significant part of Europe and the northern Isles; those from southwest France and northeast Spain, specifically those from Galicia, were considered the ancestors of the Gaelic.

Cilla Ban Calla – Daughter of Calla, Dun Arrogh's cook; Warrior of Destiny Archer under Toal.

Claimh Solais (Kly-vuh Soh-lish) – One of the Four Treasures or *Jewels* brought to Erin by Dagda and Danu and wielded initially by the Sun God, Lugh; it was gifted to Nuada of the Silver Hand, one-time King of the Tuatha; once unsheathed, no enemy could resist the Sword of Light or escape from its path.

Corbmac (Korb-mak) – Commander of the *fians* in the south part of Mide; *fian-ceannard* (fee-un kyan-ard) in Gaelic.

Ċroí Dàn (Kree Dawn) – Created by the Mother Goddess, Danu, and known as the Heart of Destiny, *Ċroí Dàn* is a heart-shaped ruby pendant that endows heroes of the land to rise above their mortal beings, become true defenders of Erin, and rally clan warriors to their cause.

Cycle of Time – The Stone of Destiny's magical bridge through time, allowing those with the *sight* to see the many possible timelines of Erin and the world. Also, the Druidic annual cycle of Winter Solstice, Imbolc, Spring Equinox, Beltane, Summer Solstice, Lammas, Autumn Equinox, and Samhain.

Cuilcagh Mountains (Kwil-cah) – Northwest of Dun Arrogh.

Dagda (Dahg-duh) – All-Father of the Tuatha pantheon, Dagda is the God of Life, Death, and Fertility over the land and its people; he is also the first Druid and a master of all things magical, often considered wise, witty, and wily. Dagda typically resides on the Tuatha island of Murias.

Dál Riata (Dawl Ree-uh-tuh) – An area claimed by Gaelic Clans that became known as Scotti territory in ancient times of the many Celtic tribes of Albion; it once comprised the northeastern part of Ulaida in Erin and the northwestern part of what is now Scotland, then known as Argyll; Dál Fiatach and Dál nAraidi remained under the rule of Ulaida.

Danu (Dah-noo) – Mother, Earth, and Moon Goddess of Erin, also known as the Triple Goddess and the Silver Huntress, when she takes her wolf form; she is co-creator with the Dagda of the entirety of the *Tuatha Dé Danann* pantheon.

Druid (Drew-id) – *Aos Dána* are the masters of law, music, storytelling, foreseeing, and healing. Under the guidance of Dagda, most wield Tuatha magic, such as the *sight*, *void*, and *Cycle of*

Time. Some are known to be Elementals, who can also manipulate the elements of Air, Earth, Water, Fire, and Life.

Dun (Doon) – Earth mounds and pickets that usually surround
a settlement of several clans for defensive purposes; duns or
ringforts typically consisted of the main hall and several small
conical-shaped huts serving as living quarters.

Dun Arrogh (Doon A-ruhg) – A moderate-sized ringfort where
Clans Mórdha and Dálaigh splinters settled.

Dun Uisneach (Doon Ish-nach) – A substantial Gaelic ringfort
located in southwest Mide along the High King's Road, also
known as *Slíghe Mor* (Slee-geh More). Chief Faolán and Chieftess Falyn oversee the formidable fortress.

Dun Tara – The seat of the High Kings of ancient Ireland, located
in eastern Mide.

Ecne (Ehn-yuh) – the Tuatha God of Wisdom, History, and Cultures; Grandson to Brigid; father of Sinéidin.

Eigyr Ferch Amlawdd (Eye-geer Verkh Am-louth) – Cymru Seeress, mother to Livie, and mate of Cymru Seer Myrddin Wyllt;
also mother to Lotte by a Dál Riata Warrior Druid father.

Eoin Mac Cairbre (Owen Mak Kar-breh) – *Before-time* Chief of
Dun Arrogh Clan Mórdha, cousin of Fergal, and a Prince
of the Blood via Aife, his mother's Ulaida Dál nAraidi Clan.
Eventually, Erin's Protector, *Taoiseach*, and the Warriors of
Destiny co-leader.

Erin (Eh-rin) - Four primary provinces or Kingdoms comprised
what the Gaelic called old Ireland. Connachta (Kon-akh-ta) is
in the northwest; Mummu (Moo-moo), later called Munster,
is in the southwest; Ulaida (Ul-ay-duh) is in the northeast;
and Laigin (Lay-gin) is in the southeast. Royal Mide (Roy-uhl
My-de) was carved out of the latter two provinces, which held
the High Kings in Tara. Unfortunately, this last Kingdom did
not survive as a province on its own after the heroic period of

the fifth century passed; High Kings would not reemerge for another four to five centuries.

Falias (Fah-lee-us) - One of four fairie islands where the Tuatha resided with Danu and Lugh; often called *Tír na nÓg* (Teer-na-a nug) by the Gaels.

Fáidh (Faw-ee) – The prophetic sect of the *Aos Dána,* typically called Seers or ovates.

Falyn (Fa-lyn) – Chieftess of Dun Uisneach and mate to Faolán; her children are Dáithí (Daw-hee), Oisín (Uh-sheen), and Teagan (Tea-gan).

Faolán (Fae-o-lawn) – Chief of Dun Uisneach and mate to Falyn.

Fergal Mac Conall (Fur-gul Mak Koh-nawl) – Dun Arrogh Red Branch warrior of Clan Conall, a subordinate clan to Clan Mórdha (Mur-dha) and cousin of Eoin Mac Cairbre. Eventually, a Warrior of Destiny and Sinéidin's mate.

fíanna (fee-un-nuh) – Initially, freeborn Fir Bolg warriors – and after a time, interbred Gaels – who once made up the army when the High Kings in Tara ruled in Royal Mide; the *fíanna* were made up of *fíans* (fi-anns), or bands of nine, who eventually served local Chieftains and kings when the first reign of the High Kings ended.

Filídh (Fee-lee) The Bardic sect of the *Aos Dána*, keepers of the histories, storytellers, and master musicians of the *Aos Dána,* commonly known as Bards.

Fir Bolg (Feer Bulg) – The original people of Erin who were subjugated first by Fomorians and then by the Tuatha.

Fomorians (Foh-mawr-ee-uhn) – A race that settled in Erin after the fall of Atlantis and was subsequently defeated by the Tuatha.

Fragarach (Frea-gar-thach) – A sword, also called Answerer, brought from the otherworld by Lugh, the Celtic God of the Sun; known to be able to pierce any armor, and later gifted to the Celtic God of the Sea, Manannán Mac Lir.

Gaelic (Gay luhk)– A people who came to Erin after the Tuatha, arriving from a part of the Celtic empire known as Galicia, also called Gaels.

Erin | Éire (ay-rah) – The Emerald Island, also known as Ireland.

Goibniu (Gohv-nyoo) – A Master Smith and god to the Tuatha pantheon, who created most of their magical weapons with help from Badb Catha and his brothers, Credne and Luchta.

Isobel (Is-o-bel) – An Air and Earth Elemental Druí and Sword-swoman from Galicia (Ga-lee-thee-ah), who is a Warrior of Destiny and Healer; also known by the names Izzy and Bee.

Kyras (K-eye-rass) – Dun Arrogh Smith of Clan Dálaigh, brother of Nevan, mate to Lissa, Toal's Father, and Breanna's uncle.

Lann Dàn (Lanna Dawn) – Blades of Destiny, created by Badb Catha, the Goddess of War; they were a pair of long dia-mond-bladed weapons with oak hafts imbued with the power to battle invaders wielding magic.

Laoch (Lay-ukh) – The nearly forgotten name for the Warrior Druid Sect, once referred to as Laoch Draíochta (Dree-ukh-tah), or Warriors of Magic.

Lia Dàn (Lee-ah Dawn) – Stone of Destiny, a round crystal brought to Erin by the Mother Goddess Danu. It enables those holding it to see both the past and possible future timelines via the *Cycle of Time*.

Lissa – Mate of Kyras, Toal's mother, Master Dyer, Weaver, and a member of Clan Dálaigh.

Livie – Water and Earth Elemental Druí and Seeress from Cymru, and a Warrior of Destiny; half-sister to Lotte.

Lotte – Fire and Water Elemental Druí and Spearwoman from Dál Riata (Dawl Ree-uh-tuh), and a Warrior of Destiny; half-sister to Livie and daughter of Eigyr.

Lugh (Loo) – Sun God and wielder of Tuatha's magical *Jewels* and other items of the *Tuatha Dé Danann*, sometimes seen as a great white stag in his animal or familiar form known as Cernunnos.

Maorgairme (May-or-gair-mee) – An amulet ring created by the Dark Goddess to aid the bearer with fickle magic, and can also summon the Tuatha Gods if there is a great need.

Mórrigan (Mohr-ree-gan) – Goddess of War, Fate, and Knowledge, also known as Badb Catha or the Dark Goddess; takes her battle crow form in the mortal realm.

Morna Ban Cahir (Mor-na Bawyn Kah-hee) – Mate to Nevan, mother of Orla, Ronat, and Breanna of Clan Dálaigh.

Myrddin Wyllt (Mutth-in Uhlt) – Cymru Druí Seer, mate of Eigyr Ferch Amlawdd, and Father to Livie.

Nevan – Warrior mate to Morna, brother of Kyras, father of Breanna, and member of Clan Dálaigh; died before Breanna was born in the after-time created by the casting of the *Triple Dàns*.

Niall Noígíallach (Nye-al Nee-Gal-ach) – High King in fifth-century Ireland, also known as the *Ard-Rí*; the ancestor of the Uí Néill dynasties, which governed significant parts of the Emerald Isle for many centuries; his son, Lóegaire Mac Néill, would have followed him as the next High King; son of Caireen and mated to Rignach.

Ogham (Oh-am) – Typically only used by the *Aos Dána*, it is the written language of the Gaels and Celts.

Ollamh (O-lam) – Healer sect of the *Aos Dána*.

Sinéidin (Shin-ay-deen) – Tuatha Goddess of Languages, Daughter of the Tuatha God Ecne, and mate to Fergal.

Red Branch – A band of warriors in old Ulaida led by Rory the Red; in Gaelic, they were called *Craeb Ruad* (krayb roo-ad); it was a name resurrected by Eoin Mac Cairbre of Clan Mórdha when he organized the young warriors in Dun Arrogh to fight the Dreadlord in the *before-time*.

River Shannon – Divides the Kingdoms of Connachta, Mummu, Laigin, and Mide.

Sidhe (shee) – What the Gaelic people call fairie or Tuatha mounds and living places; also spelled as *Sìth* (shee) in the northeast part of Ireland and the western coast of Scotland, in the region once known as Dál Riata.

Sight – A common name for the vision state of the *Aos Dána* used to touch the *Cycle of Time* to see a past or possible future.

Tir na nÓg (Teer-Na-Nug) – Alternate name for the Tuatha realm of Falais (Fall-eece); Findias (Fin-dee-us); Gorias (Gore-us); and Murias (Mord-us).

Toal Mac Kyras (Toe-al Mak Ky-rass) – Dun Arrogh Red Branch warrior of Clan Dálaigh, cousin of Breanna; newly a Warrior of Destiny and leader of the archery unit.

Tuatha Dé Danann (Too-ah-ha Day Dah-nahn) – Magical beings who came to Erin after the fall of Atlantis, some known as *Sidhe or Sìth*, often mistaken as faerie or fae, which originated as a new concept introduced in the sixteenth century. In Destiny Cycle, the author uses the mortal reference of *fairies* to depict the Tuatha.

Tuatha Dé Danann Islands – Falais (Fall-eece); Findias (Fin-dee-us); Gorias (Gore-us); and Murias (Mord-us).

Urghabháil an neamhní (ur-guh-vawl un nyow-nee) – Means to "seize the *void*." This state allows some of the warrior class who have reached mastery level to access the magic of the Faerie realm, similar to the *sight* typically used by other Tuatha *Aos Dána* sects to access Erin's *Cycle of Time* through *Lia Dàn*, the Stone of Destiny.

Ulicia (You-lee-see-ah) – An Earth Elemental Druí and Healer, known as an Ollamh in Gaelic, and one of the *Aos Dána* assigned to Dun Arrogh.

MYTHOLOGY & LEGENDS

The *Dàn Cycle* series, you now know, revolves around Gaelic and Celtic mythology, especially that of the Irish. Their myths, legends, and lore have been interpreted in many ways over the centuries. For authors in such a genre, we pick which threads to present among those posited by many historians. For those who follow Fae fantasy themes (which I also love), those myths emerged over a thousand cycles after the Tuatha legends were written. Thus, I used as close to a semi-historical setting as possible to build this world, so there are no faeries, only fairies, in this fairyland.

As for the characters, I based some on historical figures and others on fictitious characters. The same goes for titles like Erin's Hero. As to the use of names for gods, they are all of myth and legend.

Speaking of capitalizing words referencing gods and goddesses, I use the following conventions: Tuatha gods, Asgardian gods, or any general god. As with proper names, it is: Tuatha God All-Father, or just All-Father, Sun God (with or without a name like Lugh), Mother Goddess, Dark Goddess, Goddess of War, One God, Goddess of Language, God of History, etc.

Additionally, Gaelic words for Druids and their English counterparts are capitalized, thus Bard (*Filídh*), Healer (*Ollamh*), Seer/Seeress (*Fáidh*), Lawgiver (*Breitheamh*), and Warrior (*Laoch*). Similarly, the Druidic Elements powers are Air (*Aer*), Water (*Uisce*), Earth (*Talamh*), Fire (*Tine*), and Aether (*Eitear*).

About Gael Druids & Sigils

I n the *Dàn Cycle* series, the first Druid was the Tuatha God All-Father. In the days when the Gaels first came to Erin from the coastal region of the Spanish region once known as Galicia, Dagda created five sects. He passed his magic to them once the *Tuatha Dé Danann* and the Gaels forged the Great Agreement, where they both would halt their battles in exchange for the Gaels paying homage to the Tuatha Gods. In turn, the Tuatha ceded the land of Erin to the Gaels, with some Tuatha remaining in the underhalls of Erin that Danu, All-Father, Badb, and Lugh had created.

Others chose to retreat to their magical island realms. Dagda's Druids were the skilled guides who ensured the Gaels remembered the myths and legends of the Tuatha and continued their worship of the adopted gods.

Dagda's five Druidic Sects are Lawgivers, Healers, Seers, Bards, and Warriors, where he passed specific knowledge to each sect, along with how to seize the *void* and the *sight* when they needed to connect the realm of Erin with the Tuatha realms. Using the high council of each Druidic sect, All-Father also passed on the secrets of manipulating the five Elements: Air, Water, Earth, Fire, and Aether (the energy of life). Details on each of these sects can be found below. The singular form of Druid is *Druí*.

Fáidh: Seers used their sight to touch the Cycle of Time, seeking to understand possible future timelines and listen to the voices of their *Tuatha de Danann* gods. Seers and Seeresses often would have an affinity for the Water and Aether Elements and wore green and red robes.

Filídh: As history keepers, storytellers, and master musicians, a Bard used the *void* to retrieve the mass of words that comprised the entirety of the Gaelic people's experience; none could recall that much knowledge without it. They wore yellow and green robes and were often Air Elementals, allowing them to cast their voices with ease.

Ollamh: Healers could seize the *void* to draw on the deep understanding of healing and pull power from the Tuatha realm to mend the sick and wounded. They wore green and red robes, typically commanding Aether and Earth or Water Elements to heal.

Laoch: Warriors focused on ensuring their Gaels had the expertise to protect their people. The most proficient of these warriors bore the title *Laoch Draíochta*, a Warrior of Magic. They could seize the *void* in battle and typically wield one of two Elements, such as Earth and Water or Air and Fire. Their strategy and battlecraft skills earned them the title of Battle Masters, with the most senior ones commanding all of the physical Elements.

Sigils of Power: Using the Druidic (rune-based) language of Ogham, Druids create sigils as amplifiers of intent and typically incorporate one or more of the five Elements. They would etch them in wood, metal, or stone. Applying woad on one's skin (called woading) was also used by a Druid to leverage such sigils. The sigil below represents the five Elements.

About James

I grew up on a small lake in the upper Midwest of the USA and explored the nature surrounding me, with miles of trails, rivers, and creeks branching out from my family home on that lake. I could travel across my lake, slip into a tributary creek or river, and go up or down them for hours with my small boat and its little outboard motor. My trusted dog sometimes joined me, standing at the prow like a warrior sentinel. Other times, he would rather sleep in the comfort of his home, leaving me to roam alone.

He was often fickle like that, sometimes deciding he needed a "Canadian Walkabout" in the neighborhoods around the lake and getting into trouble. Our family has a long line of Quebecers, and the women in our line used a euphemism to describe their men who would roam the land in search of *adventure*. Anyway, I remember the little rascal fondly.

Like many at the time of my youth, I experimented with some forbidden things, things that quickly grew old. Esoteric matters caught my attention for a time, and I found a young lady with similar thoughts on the cycle of life. As I pursued college and tried my hand at fine arts, I found that my right hand wasn't so good at the fine part. With that same lady, we married, and I fell into the technology sector to make a living. Then, I switched my major from Fine Arts to English - Creative Writing.

After a failed first attempt at writing a set of great fantasy novels, work, raising a family, and life took over my time. Writing faded as a priority. Yet it resurfaced years later as a Gaelic adventure set in Celtic Ireland, which literally started as a dream. We traveled across the pond to see that land so I could better envision a story based there. And its people captured my heart and imagination.

That was when I wrote the first edition of Stone of Destiny and self-published my tale. It was frankly not very good. As we moved from the Upper Midwest to the Great Northwest for an opportunity to keep working in the tech sector, the Irish still held my heart. After twenty-some years, I took up the notion of rewriting that first effort, and I realized not only was the prose not good, but the story was rushed. Thus, Destiny Cycle was born, and one book became three! Blades, Stone, and Heart of Destiny. Now, I'm working on Book Four, Warriors of Destiny, and have mapped out Book Five, Immortals of Destiny.

After getting the first two novels in the cycle copyedited, I launched them as the First Edition. Then, with more feedback, I found a fantastic pair of developmental and copy editors, Holly Atkinsen and Sigrid Harris, at Evil Eye Editing. That was when Blades of Destiny Revised Edition III, Stone of Destiny of Destiny Revised Edition II, and recently released Heart of Destiny truly came to life.

In the process of this rewriting and expanding the storyline, the Gaels seeped deep into my psyche. Being a quarter Scottish of Clan Ferguson, the Gaels became my people; their history, legends, and mythologies became mine; the Celts of Europe, where the Gaels originated, became mine; the druids and their gods became mine; and the injustices inflicted on my people became a vision.

What if the Gaels of Ireland could change the history of the world by changing the Isle of Erin's timeline? And Britain's, starting with Rome's first-century BC invasion?

It would take a Hero and the *Tuatha Dé Danann* who backed her to make that happen.

Welcome to *Dàn Cycle* (aka The Destiny Cycle)! I hope you enjoy reading this adventure as much as I did writing it.

It is where Gaels Rule! www.destinycycle.com

Join my (no spam) fan club for exclusive content at www.destinycycle.com/about-james

For those interested in a sneak peek of Warriors of Destiny, turn the page!

LAOCH DÀN - WARRIORS OF DESTINY: PREVIEW

HOME AND ABROAD

Breanna

As she flashed into the Dun Uisneach ring fort's yard with her Warriors of Destiny, Breanna Ban Morna glanced around warily. Then she sighed in relief that their victory over Julius Caesar in the past had not changed the land of Erin in her time, yet. Perhaps it was because the new timeline had not yet played out, but she would take that boon for now. Being a Time-Walker was still something she was getting used to.

The warriors left behind welcomed Corbmac and his four *fians* warmly, with arm clasps and slaps on the back aplenty; the tradesfolk followed suit. Falyn's children, Dáithí, Oisín, and Teagan, swarmed around Breanna's inner circle, with the latter proclaiming, "Auntie Bre, I've been practicing the forms you taught me!"

Dáithí, not to be outdone, exclaimed, "As have I, Uncle Eoin!"

Oisín groused sullenly, "I have no one teaching me."

"Now, lad, that was my oversight," Eoin admitted. "I should have arranged a tutor for you. Will you forgive me for this lapse?"

The boy hesitated, his low lip trembling, and then nodded.

"Thank you for that, my laddie," Eoin said seriously before he tousled his hair. "As you're young and lithe, I will match you with two of our best Warriors of Destiny. First, Braoin, as he is also quick like you. And Izzy, our most talented Elemental, who can suss out which of them you might be able to command."

Braoin and Izzy nodded thoughtfully at Eoin's declaration.

Oisín beamed at the pair. "I want two blades, like Teagan demanded, but not like Braoin's—his are too plain. Nor long blades. They must be the same as Izzy's. What are they?"

Izzy smiled, drawing her two curved blades from over her shoulders, steel ringing softly as each cleared her sheathes, and slowly danced with them, swirling smoothly through a few of her forms like water poured into a glassy pool. Then she knelt before the lad. "They are called katanas, which come from my grandfather's lands in the Far East. I bested your Auntie once with these blades, but only because I used my Elements—Air and Earth—before she had mastered hers. Now, she has all of them! Yet if you work hard, you, too, can be a Warrior of Destiny. What do you say, young Oisín? Will you have Braoin and me as your tutors? Of course, with wooden blades to start."

"I accept the challenge!" the young lad proclaimed.

Croí Dàn interjected, *"I love these children!"*

"Aye, agreed," Breanna said, casting warmth to *Mo Chroí.*

Faolán demanded, "Enough badgering, my children! Now, be off to your classes. We have important matters to discuss with Erin's Hero and her *Cosantóir*. And Eoin, why do you look so pale?"

Breanna said sternly, "It was a near thing, but we're working to ensure it doesn't happen again! Are we not, my mate!?"

Eoin could only nod with a grimace.

Falyn queried, "I suspect you need a good meal. All else can wait. Keegan, prepare the hall for a welcome home to all!"

While Falyn and Keegan set about the preparations, Breanna heard Ecne in mind-speak request that Dagda's brother, Dian, and the latter's daughter join them. After the pair flashed in beside them, Ecne informed them, "We underestimated Rome's weapons. Eoin was gravely injured. If you recall, Badb Catha commanded you both to recreate our healing pools while we were at Dun Gaillimhe. It's time to make that happen now."

While Dain nodded, Airmid said, "We will try. No promises."

Breanna rejoined sharply, "Do you need Badb's help?"

"That will not be necessary," Dian said firmly. "Yet, for now, we can make Eoin whole again."

Breanna sighed. "Thank you. Badb Catha warned me that once we created an alternate timeline, there is no going back, because any such meddling could shape it in ways that could create multiple timelines, what she calls fractures. Only through the Fates can changes occur to prevent new lines from forming, particularly around deaths that take hold in a new timeline. I have now created one that I must work inside of. According to our Dark Goddess, I have little time to save one of my Warriors of Destiny before such an action fractures the line I have set in motion.

"Thus, there are only moments to sweep someone grievously wounded or newly dead into one of your healing pools. My challenge is to select who dies or doesn't when things go awry while battling Rome or anyone else."

Dian pondered her words for a moment before turning to his daughter. "Airmid, I know we have challenges from our past – that I admit I created – which we are still dealing with regarding your brother's death at my hands. For that, I'm sorry. In this case, these Gaels would not need our springs as we used them in times past. During the war with the Fomorians, it was a gruesome parade of the walking dead. With Breanna and her band, I expect they should only need it occasionally. Not brutally. Recharging it will be less taxing. Can you join me in this?"

After a moment, Airmid nodded reluctantly but said nothing more as Dian motioned for Eoin to join them. As the Healers led him out through the gates, Breanna trailed after them with Izzy and Livie in tow. Breanna hoped all of them could learn something from her fellow gods about healing any future severe wounds.

As they entered the forest that surrounded the Hill of Uisneach, she was not surprised to find that they sought a gnarled old black oak, just as Ulicia and Beatha had done with her not so long ago.

Having Eoin sit with his back to its large trunk, Dian turned to Breanna. "Wake this tree."

She shook her head, saying, "Nay, not I, as this Warrior of Destiny is better suited for your request. Izzy, wake the ancient one. Then, we'll all bond our Aether Elements with the life essence of the tree, and request its help."

Breanna noted Izzy's narrowed eyes as she watched her lay a hand on the tree, clearly reaching out to the elder's spirit as her grandfather had taught her, calling to it as she had with the old tree in Pretannia. Breanna felt her new sister reaching into the natural realm, commanding, *"Awaken, ancient one. We need your strength."*

The tree spirit rumbled. *"Fierce Little One has called upon us, as she did across Erin's sea. You are known to us, as our mutual roots run deep under the sea. And we know you, Dian and Airmid, as we supported your healing springs in times past. It is good to see the Tuatha and Gaels working together at this time. It's long overdue."*

The two Tuatha Healers flinched at the subtle rebuke from an ancient one of their former land. Yet each put a hand on Eoin's head and the oak. With that, Breanna touched the tree and took Livie's hand, who took Izzy's free one. Hand in hand, she felt each reach out to the other, binding their individual Aether Elements into one.

With that, aided by the ancient oak, a rush of healing power flowed into Eoin. Breanna, bound to all, could only watch in wonder as the two Tuatha Healers wove that energy through Eoin's veins, arteries, organs, muscles, and bones, mending all that the fragments of Roman fire spear had damaged. And each of them acquired a valuable technique their previous training had overlooked. She would see that Brigid helped her address that before their next battle.

With a nod indicating they had finished, Dian and Armid flashed away to Falias. Breanna saw that Izzy looked at her with a raised eyebrow, saying gruffly, "You planned this – this tree summons!"

Breanna turned her eye to the Galician warrior and said quietly, "No, Izzy, I did not. Yet I have foreseen the greatness of your destiny, and I must ensure that you can fulfill that vision for our lands and our future, one in which we can all remain strong. At this moment, you, Livie, and I just became much better Healers. Something we can now repeat."

Izzy looked deep into Breanna's eyes, but then just huffed.

Livie turned to the pair. "You're correct, Bre – that experience did make us better Healers. Yet, Izzy, I need you to teach me how to wake a tree if needed; their power runs so deep it's beyond comprehension, and I may need it when you're not at my side."

Izzy nodded in resignation. "Hopefully, if you must do so, you'll not be given a name like *Fierce Little One*."

Livie just smiled, adding, "And you, Breanna, can help me be a better Seeress. Take me into your past; share your experiences with me as you transitioned from mortal to goddess, for I believe some of us may face that moment in the future. I sense that lived experience has left you scarred, though I've only seen flashes of it."

Breanna sighed. "It was deeply personal. The chaos of battle. The deaths of those close to me. The crushing despair of losing Eoin. And before that, seeing a demon blade in Toal's chest. Then, drifting in time. The awakening. The reclaiming of my land. I'm not sure I'm ready to relive all of that."

Livie pulled her leader into a hug. "Soon, sister-mine, soon. Think of it as the healing you deserve, like Eoin needed from Dian and Armid. Trust me, for I am yours and you are mine."

Croí Dàn interjected quietly, *"She's right, you know."*

Breanna had no words to counter that and nodded in agreement.

Livie suggested, "Let's get Eoin into a bed for a few hours of rest. Izzy, can you make him lighter with your Air Element? Carrying such a lug of muscle and bone will strain all of our backs."

Looking down at their peacefully sleeping Protector, Izzy answered, "Aye, that I can do! Observe and learn."

Breanna watched the lithe Galician warrior dance with her Element and was relieved to see Izzy easily lift Eoin on a bed of Air. Using such magic felt new to her, yet not, as she tried to follow the Elemental warrior's weave. Latching onto it, she added her own strength in Air to spread the effort between them. While they had been traveling together in time for many months, in this timeline, it had only been as many weeks.

Later, in the main hall, as Falyn orchestrated their subdued welcome-home celebration, Breanna and Eoin sat with their band, drinking mead and ale.

Bláth stood, saying in a reverent tone, "Tonight is not the time for a proper celebration, yet it is one of wonder. A marvel at how so few brave Gaelic warriors, backed by our Tuatha Gods, albeit with Celtic supporters, could decimate two Roman legions at sea, denying them the shore in Pretannia. It was both terrifying and a marvel to behold, with Bre and Eoin leading us to victory."

While there were some cheers, Breanna rose to quiet them, saying, "It was not a battle without cost, as Eoin almost lost his life to a Roman fire spear. We will work on improving defenses, but know I am proud of you all, my Warriors of Destiny. It was an epic defeat for Rome's greatest general at that time. For now, we are home and hale. While we have more battles before us, take stock in the simple fact that home and hearth are worth protecting. We have many years ahead of us to change the mighty flow of the river of time. But know, with you all at our side, we will ensure Gaels are never to be ruled by any king!"

Her Warriors of Destiny thumped dirks on their tables, chanting a somewhat subdued, "Bre! Bre! Bre!"

Gesturing for everyone to eat and drink, Breanna dropped onto her bench. She smiled at seeing her mate begin to inhale a large amount of meat and tubers from his trencher. Since Dian and Airmid had attended to him, his color was back to normal. Knowing Eoin was now fully healed, she grumbled, "Do not ever do that kind of bravery shite again."

Eoin shrugged stoically. "It was necessary. I needed to target Caesar's invasion command structure on those last two ships.

Only *Gael Assal* could do that, given the required reach with them fleeing."

Breanna bristled. "As you say, we have time."

"Sorry, love, you made it clear once you set the timeline, we needed to be all in."

"Gah!" she growled. "Don't use that on me!"

When Lotte looked over at her, Breanna saw a narrowed expression, knowing the exclamation was one uniquely the Fire Druid's own, but while its use had rubbed off on others, it was something that was truly hers; Breanna could only shrug sheepishly.

Eoin put his strong arm around her waist and pulled her close, off the bench and onto his lap. "Never tempt the Fates."

"I'm coming to dislike the mysterious Fates. Yet, we only have one Fate, and ours is named Badb Catha!"

"Aye," Eoin agreed. "Given this, we need to be smarter about using *balefire* and shields, with some using the former and others deploying the latter. We must alternate casting and shields so that no single power is locked out. Some must shield those who are casting. As commander, that's on me. I should have thought about it. No doubt my wounds were Badb Catha's punishment for that oversight."

"I don't have to like it," she countered with a kiss on his cheek, and shifted herself back to the bench, resuming her examination of the food on her trencher. As always, Falyn's staff excelled; yet, she was pensive about any next steps. Maybe she just needed sleep.

As if reading her thoughts, Eoin suggested, "Let me have a word with Ecne before we retire for the night. I'll bring along a little something to tide you over until morning, and we'll have breakfast in bed. While there's much to do to get the Council of Erin set up, and we have provincial Chiefs and Kings to cajole, it can wait. Slumbering in a comfortable bed will renew us both."

A short while later, in their little abode, Eoin set a cup of mead and a trencher with soda bread, cheese, and some smoked boar down next to Breanna, asking, "Shall we bathe soon?"

"Not yet. I must know how our shipyard plans are progressing."

"Ecne assured me plans are in hand, but it's soon to be winter," he chided. "We're now back here at nearly the same time as when we left. Whatever you have in mind, the building team needs four to six months to construct the shipyard and the ring fort to protect it near the settlement of Átha Cliath, even if it has no ships yet.

"It's where River Poddle meets the Liffey, inland enough to be protected from the Sea of Erin's storms. Given that we need it ready this coming spring, you'll need to use the *Cycle of Time* to take the builders to that place during our previous spring. That will give them time to make headway on the projects. We should consider offering Énnae Cennsalach a role overseeing it, given his and his son Eochaid's experience with seafaring. Maybe offer to help him build a shipyard in the southeast at Dun Fearna."

"That's a good idea. It would keep those two in our fold."

Eoin asked, "Now, can we bathe and then sleep?"

"Only if you hold me during the latter."

In the morning, a page awaited them as they requested breakfast in their hut. Breanna was pleased to see the cook remembered her preferences. Gooey sicín eggs with fresh soda bread, fried sliced boar, and sliced poached apples. As she finished devouring her meal, Breanna stated, "We need to talk with my father about Thor's attack."

"Surely, Badb Catha would already have told him what happened with that arrogant boy-god," Eoin countered.

Breanna just nodded. "Then let's see what the morning has in store for us and get in a round of sparring. I want to make sure Dian and Armid have truly healed my mate. Once he proved himself in a blade dance, the small crowd that had gathered to watch applauded their match. She knew Eoin was not at his peak, but said nothing.

Breanna cast her gaze around the yard, sensing an ancient mind's attention on her being. Then she recognized who it was. *Caoránac* – the Great Wyrm of Erin, who felt like a primeval and feral creature. Breanna, recalling how Danu and Dagda had pulled her from the *before-time* and into this new timeline, had felt that touch before.

The welcome of her land was profound, and that *Caoránac* had been there as well. The creature who had once given her a nudge, one that meant nothing at that instant, had done so again. Only this time was more insistent. Yet Breanna ignored the beast for now; she knew such a denial would not last.

After cleaning up with a quick bath, Breanna and Eoin sat in her adopted uncle's private room. Then Breanna summoned her father. Would he think her pretentious? She honestly didn't care. It was he who had manipulated her into this role.

When Dagda flashed in beside her, he bent to enfold her in a hug, but she held out a hand to stop him. "You have no such privilege at this moment, Father."

He looked wounded as she stared him down – well, up – but she cared not because of the risk he put Eoin in. He tipped his head, asking, "Daughter, how may I help?"

She stated, "No games. Those nearly got Eoin killed. It is the one thing that will turn me against you. I expected more from my father. Yet you did not support Eoin or me as we recruited the Celts of Pretannia and then fought the Romans. We jointly destroyed the seventh and tenth legions and took all but one of Caesar's ships off the board, leaving only his afloat."

Dagda sighed. "Daughter, my mate, who, as you know, is on again and off again like the wind changes direction, has forbidden any interference on my part with your new timeline."

Breanna curled her lip, spitting, "That's shite! You know it is, as do I. Advice is not interference."

"No, it's not," Dagda said softly. "You know, one of Badb's roles is similar to the Titans' Themis, managing the Fates. We all have our roles and must be careful not to step over those lines."

Croí Dàn commented drily, *"I've watched you all for eons, always the good little goddess my mother cast in a gem. You all have continually been too careful. And because of that, we drew back from our Gaels. It's like the Tuatha had forsaken them."*

Again, Dagda winced, this time at the jab from Danu's daughter.

Breanna smiled at her Heart's rebuke. "Father, my Heart is correct, we are at a precipice. You all need to learn how to evolve your roles to make a genuine connection with our Gaels! We will not survive if we do not change! Goibniu, Ecne, and Sinéidin each contributed to our efforts. Advice is not interference, and that's mostly what they provided. If you recall, this was your idea. I expect you to be part of its execution, and I care not if that angers your mate!"

Dagda nodded, but said nothing.

After a moment, Breanna changed the subject and added flatly, "Speaking of which, I assume Badb – I'm not sure if I should call her Mother or what – told you that Thor broke the truce you arranged with Odin. And that I sheared his magical hammerhead from its pretty handle and hid the damn thing in both the wherever and whenever. Badb was there, supporting us. Not you. Expect Odin to reach out for another *parlay*, but this time, make it on our terms. Thor and his Norvegr ilk will not have Pretannia or Erin."

Dagda let a small grin slip, adding, "That's my spicy daughter and her Heart. You two fit well together. I'll do better and let you know when we hear from the Asgardians, which, I expect, will be soon."

Then her father turned to Eoin, asking, "I understand Dian and Armid healed you, and they've agreed to create a Healing Spring nearby as Badb commanded. I will assist them in that effort, but I could use a few of your Druids as assistants. Who do you have in mind?"

Eoin answered, "Izzy and Livie would be best suited."

With that, Breanna stalked out of the room, with Eoin in her wake, offering no apologies to her father.

 **Izzy**

Having just finished her sparring matches with Braoin and Bradaigh – the two-on-one blade dance made it more of a challenge, but not by much – Izzy looked at Breanna's and Eoin's expectant expressions as they approached her with Ecne and Lotte at their sides. She sighed. "So, there's another mission already?"

"Aye, there is," Breanna answered. "For my Chief Spy."

"As I've heard Corbmac say, that's mighty thick butter you've spread on my bread," Izzy countered dryly.

Breanna offered with a coy smile. "Aye, my grandfather does like that saying, but it's lovely butter. Right? I even threw in a promotion!"

Izzy rolled her eyes at her leader; she had come to admire her, but her passion to defeat Rome was, well, very focused. "Hmmm. I thought we'd have time for a visit home. It's been many months."

Breanna corrected, "For us, but not for your family."

Eoin sighed. "Bre, please. Izzy, we also expected to see our home, as we have not been back to Dun Arrogh since the start of this march through time. Yet it will be a short mission, one for reconnaissance and to formulate a plan to remove a key piece from the chessboard that Julius Caesar is counting on in the next battle season. Rebuilding the seventh and tenth Legions will be impossible in one season, but he can draw in the second, ninth, and fourteenth legions if he can gather enough ships for the crossing. So we need to make sure he does not."

Izzy frowned and shook her head doubtfully.

"How about a gift?" Breanna asked brightly. "Unfortunately, it will hurt to accept it."

"I am *Laoch Druí* trained," she rejoined darkly. "What is this gift?"

Croí Dàn exclaimed excitedly, *"Fire!"*

Izzy was surprised. "You're gifting me an Element?"

Breanna sighed. "It's part of the mission Eoin and I envisioned."

"It's the shipyard Caesar and Marus spoke of," Izzy stated.

"Aye," Eoin agreed. "But it's not just the Santones shipyard, but two, with the other being in northwestern Gaul."

Lotte put in sullenly, "I command Fire. I can lead."

Breanna turned to her most difficult recruit. "Yet you don't command Earth and Air. Support this mission, and maybe I'll grant you access to another Element. If you have it in you."

"Gah!" Lotte growled. "I should know better than to barter with you. But, as you say, it might be worth it."

Izzy placed a hand on Lotte's shoulder. "Sister-mine, we are in this together. Breanna, why do we need to have multiple Fire Druids?"

"That's the best question you've asked yet," Eoin stated. "Livie helped our smith find the plans, but we need you to create multiple Elemental sparks to set off the *balefire* bombs Gobiniu is making for us."

"Bombs?" Lotte asked.

"Something from the future," Breanna answered.

Eoin added, "They need a spark of Elemental Fire to, what's the word Gobiniu used, ah, detonate them. Hopefully, all at once. Thus, both of you are needed to wield Fire, in addition to Bre and me."

"So we just blow up the ships and the yard?" Lotte asked.

Breanna gave her wicked smile, "Not the ships, just the shipyard. The ships, well, those we will steal into time."

Eoin piled on with, "And maybe recruit the Celtic Veneti Tribe shipwrights to join our cause in Pretannia. Strike a blow to Rome."

Ecne put in, "Yet we need to confirm a hunch. We heard Caesar mention using the Santones on the southwest coast of Gaul to rebuild his fleet. He had already managed to get the Santones and Pictones to capitulate in fifty-eight and help him with shipbuilding, so that is not surprising. Yet he also suggested the Veneti had gone missing."

"Where could they have gone?" Breanna asked.

Ecne answered, "Caesar recorded how he conquered the Veneti in the summer of fifty-six, along with the surrounding northwest Gaulish tribes. The Battle of Morbihan took place in Quiberon Bay, not far from the River Loire, where your King Niall just lost his life.

"The Veneti were known for building sturdy ships at Portus Vidana, on the River Auray, ships capable of withstanding the rough weather in the Great Western Sea. We encountered Roman galleys and transports specifically designed for the Inner Sea. Next time, we might encounter these sturdier ships if Rome somehow took them. They'll be much harder to sink."

Breanna inquired, "How do we confirm this?"

Izzy cocked her head, her eyes glazing for a moment. "We find out if Marcus is at this Portus Vidana. Caesar will dispatch him to get the ships he needs, wherever that will be."

"Should we do this now?" Lotte asked.

Breanna rejoined, "Is there a better time? Let's find your Marcus, Izzy."

"He's not mine!" she growled.

Eoin ignored that protest and suggested, "Pick a point in time, say four weeks after our battle with Caesar."

Breanna nodded and held out her hand for the others to take, adding, "Let's make this quick if we can. Izzy, you take the lead when we arrive."

With that, Izzy felt the shift when her leader took hold of the *Cycle of Time*, with Dun Uisneach fading and replaced by a wooded area that lay above a deserted ring fort, settlement, and shipyard. She noted that no life forces were nearby and that no ships remained anchored in the bay. Then she called on the Aether Sigil that Breanna had gifted her, seeking the life force of the Centurion known as Marcus; Izzy found nothing and no one else to lock onto either.

"He's not here," she whispered. "In fact, no one is."

"But the Vindana shipyard, *treba*, *magos* all appear intact," Ecne protested. "It is like the Battle of Morbihan never happened."

Eoin stated, "Then they did go missing."

"The Veneti just can't have disappeared," Breanna declared. Let's check the Sartones shipyard. To see if the ships are there."

Izzy placed her hand atop Breanna's, with the others doing the same. They appeared in a narrow limestone cleft with a view of the docks, and she cast for Marcus once more. Izzy instantly locked onto him.

"He's here," she whispered. "We should not linger. He might feel my touch on his essence."

Eoin replied, "Good enough. We'll return for a proper survey."

Breanna held out her hand for the others to take. They appeared where they had left Dun Uisneach yard a moment later. She looked at Breanna, who said, "Well done, Izzy. At least we didn't see Veneti ships in that yard. We need to talk with Badb Catha."

Eoin added, "Indeed. And we still need a plan for the Santones shipyard. Stealing those ships might be more of a challenge, but we need a mission to see what it will take."

Izzy looked back and forth between her leaders. Sighing again, she demanded, "Then I can go home?"

Breanna offered brightly, "Aye, with us."

Izzy narrowed her eyes again. "Us?"

"We have fledgling Druid Warriors of Destiny who need training, including the one who is yours," Breanna added. "And each needs to become, well, more than what they are. Your father can help with that."

Izzy groused, "Braoin is not mine."

"And Bradaigh is not mine," Lotte added firmly.

Breanna shrugged, offering, "We will see. Still, their Elements are still weak, and you both must help with improvements on that front across our entire band."

Izzy locked eyes with Breanna, holding them for a moment, and then nodded. She saw that her leader turned a stern gaze on Lotte, daring her new sister warrior to challenge her; Lotte bowed her head. Izzy noted Braoin and Bradaigh shifted uncomfortably at her and Fire's Druid's joint proclamation about any relationship status.

"So, back to the gift," Eoin said as he snapped his fingers, and a flame erupted from his fingertips. "Breanna gifted it to me, and

I'll admit the casting of the Fire Element Sigil was unpleasant at best. Yet having your decision would be better sooner rather than later."

Izzy sighed and turned to Breanna. "Fine, bring it."

Lotte demanded, "I want Air so Izzy can teach me to cloak!"

Breanna countered, "Earn it!"

Lottie exclaimed, "Gah!"

Laoch Dàn – **Warriors of Destiny is expected to be released in 2026!**

Available at Amazon, Apple, Barnes & Noble, Google, IngramSpark, & Others

Formats: eBook, Paperback, and Audiobook (early 2027)

And do not miss **"Bards of Destiny"** on Spotify, Apple, YouTube Music, and other streamers for paired music!

Sign up for my Fan Club:
www.destinycycle.com/about-james to get updates!

www.ingramcontent.com/pod-product-compliance
Lightning Source LLC
Chambersburg PA
CBHW050611110726
47899CB00001B/59